Prai

"This book was amazing; it had many elements of surprise, intrigue and political unrest in a futuristic world. I highly recommend this book for anyone who loves a sizzling story."

—Susan Holly, *Just Erotic Romance Reviews*

"If you are looking for a fabulous futuristic love story with a touch of political intrigue, *For the Love of Rigah* is for you. Be forewarned though! Once you pick this book up you will not be able to put it down until you have read it in its entirety!"

—Gina, *Love Romances*

For the Heart of Daria

"From the first page to the last, *For the Heart of Daria* will leave readers with warm, gratifying feelings as Daria and Gray unite futuristic Earth to make it a better place."

—Patti Fischer, *Romance Reviews Today*

"Doreen DeSalvo dishes up a sexy journey through the stars that is sure to enrapture romance readers everywhere. If you like your romances electrifyingly hot and out of this world, I recommend you go and buy your very own copy of *For the Heart of Daria* and lose yourself in an erotically stellar read."

—Lady Novelistic, *Romance Junkies*

Loose Id

ISBN 10: 1-59632-127-X
ISBN 13: 978-1-59632-127-4
THE PRENDARIAN CHRONICLES
Copyright © 2005 by Loose Id, LLC
Cover Art by April Martinez
Edited by: Maryam Salim

Publisher acknowledges the author and copyright holder of the individual works, as follows:

FOR THE LOVE OF RIGAH
Copyright © November 2003 by Doreen DeSalvo

FOR THE HEART OF DARIA
Copyright © August 2004 by Doreen DeSalvo

All rights reserved. Except for use of brief quotations in any review or critical article, the reproduction or utilization of this work in whole or in part in any form by any electronic, mechanical or other means, now known or hereafter invented, including xerography, photocopying and recording, or in any information storage or retrieval is forbidden without the prior written permission of Loose Id LLC, 1802 N Carson Street, Suite 212-2924, Carson City NV 89701-1215. www.loose-id.com

This book is an original publication of Loose Id. *For the Love of Rigah* was previously published as a single title in e-book format only by Ellora's Cave. *For the Heart of Daria* was previously published in e-book format only by Loose Id. Each is a work of fiction. Any similarity to actual persons, events or existing locations is entirely coincidental.

Printed in the U.S.A. by
Lightning Source, Inc.
1246 Heil Quaker Blvd
La Vergne TN 37086
www.lightningsource.com

Dedication

For Sam, who told me I could quit writing if I really wanted to...

And for Allie, who wouldn't let me.

THE PRENDARIAN CHRONICLES

Doreen DeSalvo

LooseId
www.loose-id.com

Contents

For the Love of Rigah
1

For the Heart of Daria
147

FOR THE LOVE OF RIGAH

Chapter One

Rigah stood and gazed out the window of the conveyance. The sun had finally broken night, but the view held nothing but long, endless fields of *quaanti* grain, glowing pink and ripe, swaying in the gentle breeze.

She drummed her fingers on the communication console in an impatient rhythm. If only she could have traveled by hovercraft. A hovercraft could race over the open ground, without the side-to-side swaying of this ungainly conveyance. The large vehicle lumbered along like a methodical beast, a crawling armored machine on this narrow, provincial road. At this pace, she would not reach her household before nightfall.

A screech rent the silence, and the conveyance jolted with unsteady force. She nearly lost her footing as the vehicle shuddered to a halt. What now?

She walked through the connecting chamber to the front of the conveyance, unlocked the loading doors, and descended the steep ramp. A cloud of dust hung over the road, and a mass of twisted metal was wedged underneath the front wheels of the conveyance. Damn the gods. Some kind of farm equipment, no doubt left lying in the road by an idiot slave. At least the machine appeared to be empty. A human could not have survived the heavy crush of her conveyance.

She put one foot on an edge of the metal wreckage and pushed down hard. No movement. The ruined metal was wedged tight. It would take many men to pry the wreckage free, and she had left her entire contingent of soldiers in the Western Quarter to quell the slave uprising. Only two servants accompanied her this day.

She would send a servant for assistance. All would be eager to assist the Leader Elect. But even if a hundred men suddenly sprang from the *quaanti* fields, she would not reach home before nightfall. The gods truly frowned upon her. She kicked the metal wreck.

"You'll have to kick it harder than that to move it," a masculine voice said.

Who dared speak to her so insolently? She spun to face the rude man. He stood twenty paces away in the field, cutting the long stalks of grain with easy sweeps of a threshing blade, clearing a path as he moved closer. An Earther. Handsome, for a slave, with dark hair pushed back from his high forehead. The heavy threshing blade swung gracefully in his powerful grasp.

He reached the edge of the field and stopped with the blade above his shoulder, at the end of a long sweep. He stared at her as if he had never seen a woman before, his gaze moving rudely over her form.

His clothes were as rough as his manners. He wore no tunic, only a loose-fitting shirt and trousers. Broad shoulders. A chest so wide, a woman could comfortably lie upon him. His waist was narrow, but his loose trousers showed nothing of him below the waist.

Her gaze swept up again, and she found him looking back at her face. Never had an Earther dared to meet her gaze so boldly.

Such unusual eyes. Amber brown. She'd seen many Earthers since her people had conquered their world, but she had never seen such stunning eyes.

The color was rare, but she recognized the look in them.

Hunger.

He swung his threshing blade down, resting it on the ground at his feet. "At least no one was on the baler."

What manner of slave was he, to speak directly to a member of her race? Perhaps he'd been sheltered from her people here in the wilderness. Yet he spoke Prendarian well, with only the barest hint of an accent to betray his Earth origins.

He crossed in front of her and studied the wreckage. How dare he turn his back to her?

But she would not reprimand him. A field slave could not be expected to know how to behave in the presence of the Leader Elect. And he looked too delicious, rumpled and slightly damp with a light sweat despite the cool breeze. A handsome man could be forgiven much.

He crouched down and began prying at the twisted metal with his threshing blade. His shirt pulled tight across his broad shoulders. She moved to his side and studied his profile. A strong nose, straight but not delicate. His lips were full and sensuous. Exotic. As were the best of his fellow Earthers.

Tempting.

She had never lain with an Earther. She chose her consorts from the elite of her own race—men who inevitably wheedled her for political favors. No wonder it had been months since she had bothered to take a man.

Perhaps her mother was right. Perhaps a low-ranked man, a concubine, was more suited to serving the Leader Elect. A man who would pleasure her exclusively. A man who would request nothing from her.

A man like this Earther.

Ah. Her journey had been tiresome indeed, to make her stand here in idle musings.

Her derelict conveyance operator approached, head lowered in shame. She would deal with his neglect later. Six weeks of scrubbing in the kitchens would teach him to be attentive. "Eldin," she called to him. "Move the conveyance back." Perhaps the wreckage would free itself.

He bowed without speaking and drew away.

The Earther stood. "No," he shouted to Eldin.

He thought to give orders to her servants? Eldin ignored him and went inside the conveyance.

"Stop him," the Earther said.

Who was this slave, to challenge her orders? "Do not speak," she commanded. He clenched his hands into fists, but said nothing.

The conveyance moved back, dragging the wreckage with it. The crumpled metal dug hard into the road, ripping huge trenches in the dirt and tearing up rocks as it moved.

The conveyance ground to a halt. A thick haze of dust drifted along the road. For at least twenty paces, huge holes had been torn into the surface. The conveyance would not be able to pass, and the wreckage was still caught underneath it.

A dozen men appeared from the fields, no doubt drawn by the noise. Slaves, all of them. "Repair this road," she ordered.

They stood mutely, heads hanging, afraid to look at her. Proper slaves. Proper and incompetent.

The handsome Earther sighed. "Rick, bring shovels and a leveler. Everyone else start gathering rocks. Hurry, before the owner sees this mess."

The men scattered, obeying the man's orders without comment or question. He was a slave, as all Earthers were. Did he hold a formal station that commanded such authority? "Who are you?"

"Jason."

That could not be his station. "Jay-sun. That is your name?"

He nodded once, curtly.

The strange name suited him, strong and distinctive. He walked to the conveyance and studied the wreckage, without bowing in farewell or asking for her permission to leave.

Assuredly, he knew nothing of correct behavior. He must be newly arrived on her world. "How long have you been on Prendara?"

"Nine hundred and thirteen days."

Surely bitter about his captivity, to keep count of the days. "Why do you assist me willingly, while the other men are reluctant?"

"They're afraid," he replied. "Afraid to make matters worse." He glared at her. "I'm hoping that if we fix the damage, we won't be left hungry after we're flogged."

What a trespass, to flog such a proud man for problems not of his making. She saw her attendant hovering near the doors of the conveyance, waiting patiently for orders. "Darnal," she called.

The woman moved quickly to her side, head bowed politely.

"Find the owner of this plantation. Compensate him for this equipment. Be sure to tell him that the accident was not the fault of his slaves."

Darnal bowed. "As you will," she said softly.

"His house stands east of here," Jason said.

Darnal looked at him, her mouth open in surprise, then quickly moved away. The Earther's boldness surprised even her serene attendant.

Rigah caught his gaze upon her. "Now the owner will not punish you."

He snorted. "Of course he will. The hours we spend fixing this road should have been spent threshing. We'll be woken before dawn for a week to catch up the time."

She'd known many handsome men. None had ever spoken so plainly to her. It was rude, yes. Also a novelty.

And another novelty, having an Earther look directly into her eyes. Those golden eyes blazed with anger now. But she could easily imagine seeing those eyes look up at her with passion. Seeing them glow, heavy-lidded with warmth, after passion was satisfied.

He turned back to the wreck and started prying at it with his blade. "We may have more work to do, but at least we won't be tortured when we're finished." He glanced up at her. "I suppose it's the least you can do, considering this mess is your fault."

She gasped. "I could have you killed for speaking to me with such insolence."

He raised an eyebrow. Such an expressive face. Did all Earthers give their emotions free rein over their facial expressions? She had not done so for many, many years. Emotion was unsuited to her station, as her mother often reminded her. "You would have me killed for speaking the truth?" he asked.

She would not. She was a powerful woman. Second in power only to her mother. She need not kill a man for insulting her. Yet her position stood in jeopardy if she did not return to her household in good speed. "Can you pry the wreckage free?"

He looked surprised by the change in topic. "Yes, I think so." He studied the wreckage, then shoved his threshing blade into a tight crevice. He stood on the wooden handle. A small piece of twisted metal broke free. He tossed it to the side of the road.

Behind him, the men filled holes in the road with loose rocks, shoveling dirt in and smoothing the surface. It would take them an age. The gods only knew how her sister would take advantage of this delay. No doubt Shalawn would use the time to ingratiate herself into Rigah's household.

The landscape here was arid, sparse. *quaanti* fields stretched out in every direction, the road a narrow path through the swaying sheaves of grain. Only a distant range of mountains, far to the north, lent any interest to the horizon. Her compound nestled against those blue-gray foothills, where streams from the high ground ran wild through dense, lush forests. The only place on the planet where precious water ran above ground.

Movement at the edge of the field caught her eye. A small face peered out from between the stalks of grain.

"Show yourself," she commanded.

A small boy, perhaps eight years aged, cautiously emerged from the field.

"Billy," Jason said. "I told you to stay out of sight."

The boy scuffed the ground with one foot, sneaking curious glances at Rigah. At least he did not stare. "Can I help?"

"Not right now," the man replied.

Enough. These slaves behaved as though she, the Leader Elect, had no command of them. "Help repair the road," she told the boy.

The boy looked at Jason. "Can I?"

Jason glanced at her, frowning. "He's a child. He can't do a man's share of work."

"So your habitual practice is to do the work of two men yourself, to spare him," she guessed.

His scowl deepened. "That is no concern of yours."

Would he ever learn his place? "Billy," she said. The boy nodded, but kept his head bowed. The child knew how to behave, even though this man did not. "Gather small rocks to repair the damage of the road."

Jason opened his mouth, as if to argue. Would he dare? "Stay out of the way of the other men," he told the boy.

The boy nodded again, then scurried off.

Jason returned to the wreckage. How carefully he studied the mess, moving from one side to the other, peering underneath, rocking different pieces to discover where they were caught. So methodical. If he were not a slave, she might suspect him of being an engineer. He wedged the end of his blade into a crevice and leaned against the handle. A large piece of metal snapped out of the tangle. With the force of the release, he lost his footing and stumbled against the conveyance.

He hissed and grabbed his forearm with one hand as he straightened.

"You are injured."

"It's nothing." Blood leaked from between his fingers, staining his sleeve.

"Speak truth," she commanded.

"It's just a scratch," he said through clenched teeth. He bent and picked up his threshing blade, still holding his forearm in a tight grip.

She stepped closer. "Show me."

He lifted his hand and pushed up his sleeve. Blood ran from a long cut on his forearm. "You use the incorrect word. This is not a scratch. This is a wound."

She looked around. Darnal had not returned. She would have to tend his wound herself. Or order Eldin to do so.

There he was, filling a hole in the road, the boy standing beside him. "Eldin!"

Eldin rushed up to her, head bowed.

"Pry the remainder of this wreckage from underneath the conveyance." She turned to Jason. "Come with me."

He gave her a wary look, but did not step toward her.

He had not the sense of a small child. "Your wound was made by farm equipment, filthy with dirt. If allowed to fester, then..." She made a chopping gesture across her own arm.

He said nothing, but his eyes widened in understanding. She took a step toward the conveyance, and he dropped his blade and quietly followed her.

She led him into the small back chamber that served as her sleeping quarters when she traveled by conveyance. Sparse, but she needed only the pallet and the cleansing station.

She took him to the cleansing station. "Remove your shirt."

He peeled the shirt off in one swift movement. By the gods, his chest was magnificent. Broad and golden, with only a smattering of hair. Her hand itched to touch him.

And why resist? His wound must be tended.

"Your hand," she ordered, reaching out for him. He put his hand in hers. So hot. Her own hand jerked. She'd heard that Earthers had a higher body temperature, but had never felt one's flesh.

He frowned. "If touching me offends you, just give me a dressing. I'll do it myself."

"No." She gripped his hand more firmly.

She drew his arm over the cleansing station. His hands were large. Large enough to easily cover her breasts as she rode him. Oh, it had been too long since she had taken a man, to cause her such visions.

She held his arm steady until the sonic shower had removed the blood and dirt from his wound. The cut was deep and long, almost the length of his forearm. She found a film bandage in the cabinet and smoothed it over the injury. Even through the shielding film, his heat radiated against her hand. She willed her fingers to release his arm.

He flexed his hand, twisted his forearm against the resisting bandage. "I've never seen a bandage like this."

No doubt slaves were given few necessities. "It will dissolve as your wound heals."

He said nothing, merely stared into her eyes.

"Do you intend disrespect?" she asked.

"I don't understand."

"You look into my eyes. Not even servants of my own race behave so."

His head bowed, eyes lowered properly. A smile graced his lips. "It seems more disrespectful to stare at your breasts."

No man had ever spoken to her like this. She should be angry. But the heat that suffused her was not anger. Not at all.

His smile was purely carnal when he lifted his gaze to her face. He wanted her. And no man should be punished for wanting a woman. Not when the woman wanted him in return.

She stepped closer. Her hand lifted as though drawn to him, and she pressed her palm over his heart. By the gods, his flesh was hot.

He drew back slightly, but not enough to dislodge her hand. "Don't," he said huskily.

"Why not?"

"Because I haven't even seen a woman in months."

She moved closer, until her body brushed lightly against his groin. Yes, his member was hardened. "And now that you see one, your reaction is natural."

He closed his eyes, but said nothing. Probably thanking the gods for his good fortune this day.

As was she. There was something about this Earther. Perhaps the startling amber of his eyes, or the fall of deep black hair against his shoulders, or the heat of his chest. No, it was simply this blatant pride of his, as though he was her equal. As though being a slave did not make him less of a man.

Such a man deserved a respite from field labor. Just as she deserved a respite from the labors of government. Her position would not fall if she spent a few moments in pleasure.

She brushed against him again, and felt his hardness move. Her privates tingled, warm with arousal. Yes. She would take him. They were both in need.

"You shall pleasure me." The words sounded harsh, sharpened by her need.

He raised one eyebrow. "How graciously you command me."

Yet he was not unwilling. She ignored his comment and drew him into her arms. His scent was musky and warm, like the forest on a still, damp day. He was so tall that she had to tilt her head back to see into his eyes. She reached up to kiss him, closing her eyes in anticipation.

She felt his lips on her neck instead. Oh, he definitely had a mind of his own, this Earther. She trembled as he nipped and suckled on her flesh. She leaned back, giving him better purchase. He knew exactly how to arouse her—when to suckle, when to lick, when to surprise her by giving her a gentle bite. His face was shaved, yet she felt the slight abrasion of stubble on his chin as he tasted her, a sensual contrast to his soft, wet lips.

But she wanted to taste him as well. She pulled his head up just enough to meet his lips with her own. He controlled the kiss, slanting his mouth against hers at his own will. She met his motions eagerly. His tongue parried with hers, his teeth caught at her lips. What a thrill, to have a man so hungry for her. Usually men were more submissive, more cautious, in awe of her station.

Not this man. His hands took her hips and dragged her up against him. His sex stood proud against her belly. One of his legs parted her thighs, and she rode him, trying to ease the ache of her own need.

His hands fumbled with the closures on her shirt, then ripped the fabric open. He stilled suddenly, gasping for breath, and she met his wary gaze. What was the destruction of a uniform next to this incredible passion? "It's all right," she assured him. She pulled open the tattered shirt herself, baring her breasts.

But when she tried to draw his head down to her chest, he resisted. Instead, she felt his hands close over her breasts, his thumbs stroking her nipples into stiff peaks, gently pinching.

When he finally lowered his head to her, she felt his hot breath against her for long, torturous moments. Then he licked her nipple, but before she could truly relish the wetness, the warmth, he withdrew and breathed on her wet flesh. Then he licked again. She moaned at the deliberate teasing. Finally, he suckled on her, and his hands found her ass and urged her higher, harder against his thigh. She clutched his head to her chest.

"That's it," he muttered thickly against her. She felt the vibrations of his voice rumbling in her breast, making her shiver. "I'm going to make you climax so hard, they'll hear you three fields away."

She gasped at his bold words. Such blatant need.

"You don't believe me?" he asked. "Wait and see." He moved his leg back, away from between her thighs. His hand cupped her sex. "Wait until you feel my tongue here."

His mouth found her breast again and he nipped gently at her nipple. The shock of feeling his sharp teeth against her sensitive flesh made her buck against him.

He rubbed her more firmly through her pants and murmured something against her breast. Something in a foreign tongue, something she had no hope of understanding.

"What?"

He sighed and lifted his head. "I said, I'm very good at...at..." He struggled for words. "...at eating a woman. It's my favorite thing in the world." He shrugged. "In two worlds, I suppose."

Enough talk. She pulled him closer and rubbed the wet peaks of her breasts against his chest. Oh, he felt so warm. The light pelt of hair on his chest abraded her nipples, sending arousal straight to her core. She reached for the fastenings of his pants, unhooked them quickly and let the loose material fall to his ankles. Her hand grasped his root, milking him. His heat was even more incredible in his sex. How hot would he feel deep inside her?

After no more than a moment, he pulled her hand away and dragged her to the pallet, pushing her onto her back. Only the gods knew why she let him, when she should be the one pressing him down. Then he stood above her, proud as a warrior, letting her look at him. His broad chest moved with each harsh breath. His root stood out from his body, hard and tall. He kicked off his shoes and the pants around his ankles, somehow managing to look graceful in the act.

He studied her, running one hand over his chest, then the other. One palm stroked his root, and he smiled down at her as though he was the Leader Elect, and she the slave.

"Like what you see?" he asked.

He would pay for teasing her like this. With one hand, she stroked her own breast, felt the hard nub of her nipple with a fingertip. "Do you?"

His eyes flared. "Yes."

She licked her fingertip, letting him see her tongue, and stroked the wetness over a nipple.

He came down on top of her, full length. His heat covered her like a thermo blanket. "You didn't bring me here to watch you touch yourself, did you?"

Before she could answer, he bit her neck, letting her feel the sharp edges of his teeth. He moved against her, rubbing his chest against her breasts, his root against her thigh. She pushed up against him until she could move her legs apart and feel his hardness pressing against her nest. Even through the cloth of her pants, his heat made her tingle.

His lips moved to her ear, licking and nibbling. His breath came harsh. "If I tear your pants off, will you beat me?"

He must be beaten regularly in the fields, although she'd seen no marks on his body. Owners must be careful when punishing valuable slaves. But what a trespass, to risk marring such beauty. "I would not," she answered.

He lifted himself away, leaving her cold, and fumbled with the fastenings of her pants. No tearing this time. Cool air met her skin as he pulled them off, taking her loose shoes with them. He grasped her knee and lifted it, opening her sex to his gaze. His head dipped. She closed her eyes, eager to feel the first brush of his mouth.

She felt his breath instead, hot puffs of air against her yearning flesh. He lay beside her, and his hand met her sex, fingers stroking, exploring, probing. She clutched at his arm, trying to push his hand away, to roll him to his back so she could mount him. He resisted, so she stopped. She would not show herself desperate to be astride him, to have him inside her body. Even though his hand—his wicked hand—made her crave the deeper penetration of his root.

He suckled on her breast, drawing a moan from her throat as his fingers tormented her. Her hands curled into fists, her teeth clenched. She would not beg to ride him. She would not.

His hand left her suddenly. At last. She sat up, ready to cover him, but he pushed her back and knelt between her thighs. His head lowered, his hands grasped her hips, and she felt his mouth, felt the warm pulse of his tongue against her nest. He licked at her bud, then suckled on it. Gently…too gently. Her hands found his head, guiding him, showing him the pressure she needed.

But he resisted, the arrogant man. He lapped at her, exciting her, but not enough…not enough. He flicked the hard tip of his tongue across her bud, then moved down and drove it deep inside her, wriggling, teasing, pressing fervently against the walls of her nest. His nose nudged her bud with each dip of his tongue. No one had ever eaten her so passionately. He suckled again, lightly, teasingly.

"Harder," she commanded.

He shook his head.

Cursed man. She grabbed his head, forcing him, but he strained against her hands. She let go, swearing, and clawed at the pallet with her fingers. And still he nuzzled and licked and teased, until she was pounding the pallet with her fists, swearing with frustration, ready to fight him, hold him down and force herself upon him.

"Please," she moaned. "By the gods, please."

And he gave in at last, kissed her throbbing bud in a long, long pull. She cried out as her orgasm wrenched through her, every cell in her body convulsing with pleasure so intense, so sharp, so heightened by his teasing, that she was left drained, trembling, and curiously eager to thank him. To thank him and hold his hot, hot body against hers.

He rose above her, his mouth glistening wet as he lay on top of her. His root was still hard, she felt it against her belly, and his eyes glinted with the fever of need.

"That's one," he said.

Chapter Two

By the gods, he was arrogant. But she couldn't be angry, considering the bliss he'd just given her. "You will cry out soon enough," she promised. "You'll cry out my name."

He smiled down at her. "Impossible."

Now she was angry. "You dare to challenge me?"

His smile faded into a bitter frown. "A mere slave would never dare to challenge you. But it's impossible for me to call out a name I don't know."

She, who had never been speechless in her life, suddenly could form no rebuttal. Did he really not know her station? "I am Rigah."

She saw no recognition in his eyes. Gods above, he honestly did not know of her.

"Rigah. I'll remember that."

He rolled off of her and lay beside her on his side. His hand idly stroked up her arm, cupped her neck. She felt his fingers weave through her hair. He seemed in no urgency.

"Don't you wish to climax?" she asked.

He didn't answer for a moment. "It's been three years since I had sex," he said at last. "Do you know what that does to a man?"

Three years? By the gods, she could imagine what it would do to her. She nodded.

"You probably think it makes him greedy, ready to take the first woman he sees and rush to climax as quickly as he can. But it doesn't."

He propped his head up on his hand and looked down into her face. "It makes him want to touch, and kiss, and pleasure a woman. It makes him want to look at her, look at her body everywhere, and know that he can touch anything he wants to."

He moved his free hand to the side of her face, and his thumb lightly stroked the corner of her mouth. "It makes him want to touch her in little ways. Like this."

He pressed his hot root against her thigh, his eyes staring into hers. "It makes him enjoy how badly he wants her, because he knows he'll be deep inside her soon enough."

Earther sentimentality. She'd never understood it. But she understood his need, the need to climax at his own pace. She turned her head a little and kissed his thumb, then lifted his hand and placed it on her breast. "Touch me now," she said. "Touch me however you like."

He did, stroking her lightly, his golden brown eyes watching as his hand moved on her flesh.

She kissed him softly with open lips, her tongue leisurely meeting his. No frantic tugging now—her fevered need already satisfied, she would let passion build slowly. He kissed down her neck to her breasts, suckling gently. She pressed up into the wet heat of his mouth, felt his tongue lave her, the barest touch against her straining nipple.

Even when he reached between her legs, his fingers were light and exploring, spreading easy trails of fire where before they had sparked an inferno. Such clever hands. He rubbed gently, then flicked her bud with a fingertip. The sharp pressure stole her breath. He pressed inside her with one finger, so hot, reaching so deep, she felt the tip of his finger against the entrance to her womb.

His root would reach deeper. Would feel hotter.

She squirmed against his hand. Her hips moved in a slow rhythm, the rhythm of mating. And he moved with her, rubbing his hard member against her thigh as his hand explored her sex.

"You feel just like an Earth woman," he murmured.

Of course she did—she was human, after all. Merely a different race of human. A better race of human.

He took that hot hand away from her and held his fingers to his lips, inhaling audibly. He closed his eyes. "You smell just like an Earth woman."

He spread the wetness from his fingers across her nipple, then dipped his head and suckled deeply.

"You taste just like an Earth woman," he muttered against her breast. He reached between her thighs again, pressed deep inside her with two long, strong fingers. She gasped. By the gods, her nest ached. She had never spent this long in sex play. She had always mounted a man long before she felt such craving.

Suddenly he rose above her, his knees spreading her thighs. Surprised, she let him cover her, let him guide his root to her nest. He pressed into her with a long, slow push, sighing above her. And she let him ride her, let him set the pace, let him take her knee and lift it outward so that she opened even wider beneath him. And it felt good, unbelievably good, to have a man ride her, to feel his body moving on hers, to feel the strong muscles of his biceps working as he pumped. His chest was hot above her, pressing down on her tender breasts. She felt protected in the shelter of his body. She felt needed.

His thrusts quickened and his breath rushed past her ear, tickling her sensitive nerves. "Climax for me," he urged. "Climax for me again."

As if that were not her right. And the novelty of having a man above her, riding her, driving his hardness into her...oh, she would climax easily. Each gasping breath in her ear, each thrust of his hot root, brought her closer. Closer. He nipped her earlobe, then licked. Such a hot tongue, so hot...so wet... She cried out as she reached her climax, her fingers clutching on his arms.

"Yes," he murmured as she convulsed around his root. "So tight..."

She squeezed her inner muscles around him to hasten his pleasure. He climaxed with a groan, trembling above her as he pressed deep, deep inside her. Then he collapsed, taking a fraction of his weight on his forearms.

She stroked his hair lightly. Again, she felt that compulsion to thank him. She would resist. Sanity would return soon enough, the sanity that would make her feel shame for letting an Earther slave ride her at his will.

She wouldn't thank him, but she would acknowledge him by name. Would he even understand that she never did such a thing? She had never even known the name of a slave before. "Jason," she said softly.

He nuzzled her ear. "That's two," he murmured.

He sounded half-asleep, hardly ready for another riding. She smiled at his conceit. He pulled out of her nest and lay beside her on his back, one forearm across his eyes, leaving her chilled by the loss of his incredible heat. After only a moment, his breathing deepened and slowed into the even rhythm of sleep. Typically male, to sleep straightaway after the bout.

Rigah rose from the pallet, found her blankets, and covered them both, lying on her side to study him. He was truly blessed by the gods, with strong features, an elegant nose and a full, luscious mouth. And the things he could do with that mouth…

What a trespass, that such a sensual man should be wasted in the fields.

* * *

Jason looked up at a blue sky dotted with puffy white cumulus clouds. Earth. He was lying on the grass in Golden Gate Park, warmed by the sun, with a light breeze stirring the leaves of the oak trees overhead. Billy laughed in the distance. He heard a dog bark playfully. Then his sister laughed; his crazy, wonderful sister. God, he missed her. If he opened his eyes, would he see her?

No. It was only a dream.

He hovered between sleep and wakefulness, grateful that he'd had a pleasant dream for once. He usually dreamed of the war. Of his capture. Of his last day on Earth. September 21, 2010. He still remembered the date. He had no idea what date it was now. The days on Prendara were longer. So long they seemed endless.

A paneled wall met his sleepy gaze. This wasn't his bunk. The last thing he remembered was...ah, yes. Rigah.

He rolled over and looked around, but she wasn't in the room. The scent of sex still hung in the air, and he could smell her musk on his lips. Maybe she'd come back soon. After that long stretch of celibacy, he could use another couple of hours in the hay with her. Hell, he could use another couple of days. And he wouldn't mind proving—again—that Earth men were dynamite in the sack. Proving it to her and the men she'd marched him past out on the road, like he was some naïve little peasant girl and she was a lordly pasha. God, she was arrogant, even by the standards of this crazy planet.

He heard a scraping noise and turned his head to see her enter the room. With that curly blonde hair and those dove gray eyes, she could have stepped out of a Boticelli painting. Her posture was perfectly erect, and she moved with a graceful stride. She looked so proud and regal, he'd never have guessed that she'd been on her back, hot and sweaty and moaning, just a short while ago.

But he knew. And so did anyone within a mile, after the way she'd screamed. Twice. He held back his smirk. If the past was any indication, the memory of this woman would have to last him a long, long time.

She set down a small bundle she'd been carrying and walked to the side of the low mattress. From outside, he heard the faint sounds of the men repairing the road. But the look in her eyes told him she had other work in mind for him.

"The road will not be passable for another span," she said.

He hadn't caught on to their system of telling time, but a span sounded like long enough for a good fuck. And he was more than ready for it.

Even after all the years on this planet, he still thought in English at times. Times like this, when he didn't know enough Prendarian words to express his thoughts. Thoughts like how much he wanted to screw her again. That he could still taste her sweet pussy. That he'd give anything to have her suck him off.

Yeah, right. She didn't look like the type to want a man's cock in that elegant, bossy mouth. But just thinking about it made his balls ache.

She had a new shirt on, a form-fitting deep blue uniform just like the one he'd ripped off of her earlier. He wanted to rip this one off, too.

She ran her fingers down the front, undoing the fastenings. She must have read his mind. That cool, confident look in her eyes pissed him off. She wouldn't look that cool when he fucked her to another screaming climax. He'd never had a screamer before. Those throaty cries had made his ears ring. He'd felt like the best lover on this god-forsaken planet.

She stripped off her shirt and dropped it to the floor, then started on her pants. She kicked them away and stood naked, looking down at him.

He let himself enjoy the view. She was strong and tall, but there was nothing mannish about her. Her bush was dark blonde and full, and her belly curved sweetly like a woman's should. Her breasts were generous, crowned with thick, pink nipples. He remembered exactly how they felt against his tongue. He'd always liked soft, voluptuous women . . . and she was one of the prettiest he'd ever seen.

He swept the blanket off his body, and her gaze zeroed in on his hardening cock. She joined him on the bed, lying on her side, and leaned over to kiss him. Her mouth moved over his with assurance, meeting his tongue stroke for stroke, nipping at his lips with her teeth. She was all but lying on top of him, rubbing her chest against his, stroking him with the hard nubs of her nipples.

Her hand drifted down his side, over his hip, to brush lightly against his cock. Too lightly. Was she going to tease him? Two could play at that game.

He reached between her legs, and she parted them for him. He stroked her gently, not giving her the hard pressure he knew she liked. God, she was wet. All this moisture, just from kissing him.

He pushed her onto her back and slid a finger deep inside her body. She gasped. Her outer body temperature might be a couple of degrees cooler than the average Earth woman's, but here, deep inside her body, she was hot like lava. His cock burned to be inside her.

And she was still stroking him in that light, teasing way. He wrapped his hand around hers, showing her how he liked to be pumped. Miracle of miracles, she followed his rhythm. He'd reward her.

He pushed a second finger in to join the first, finger-fucking her slowly, deeply, until she cried out. Then he drew wet circles over her clit, lavishing her own moisture on the distended little bud.

She let go of his cock and clutched at her own breasts, whipping her fingers back and forth across hard nipples. God, he loved to see a woman pleasure herself. He watched for a moment, then grasped one of her wrists in his free hand and pulled it away so he could suck hard on that luscious nipple. She moaned and moved her hips in tandem with his probing fingers. He wanted her to move just like this when he was buried inside her.

Enough foreplay. He lifted himself on top of her, kneeling between her thighs, and she grabbed his hips, pulling him down, as eager as he was. He sank into her with one long push, his cock so deep inside that he felt the blunt edge of her cervix. He pounded into her madly, frantically, and she clawed at his ass, urging him to thrust harder, faster.

He'd never last. She felt too fucking good. He bit her neck to punish her, and she moaned in his ear. To hell with her. He'd eat her later to get her off. God, he couldn't wait to eat her. He moved faster, harder. Any second…any second…

She froze for an instant, then shuddered wildly, muffling her orgasmic scream against his neck. That was all it took to push him over the edge. He came hard, so hard, his whole body clenched with the agony, the pleasure. One last groan and he collapsed on top of her.

They panted together for long moments. But it felt too intimate, resting on her like this, his face in the crook of her neck. As though they were lovers, instead of just two horny strangers. He rolled off. Maybe she wouldn't say anything. Maybe she'd think he'd been worried about crushing her.

They lay in silence, not touching, for several still moments.

A low tone sounded. She got up and walked to a small panel set in the wall. Must be some kind of communication device. But she didn't speak, she merely pressed a lighted button.

The vehicle moved forward with a small lurch. And it didn't stop.

What the hell? "Where are we going?" he demanded.

She raised her eyebrows. And said nothing.

"Tell me."

"We are going to my household."

Oh, no. He leapt to his feet and rushed to the window. The fields moved past at a blur. "When will I be back?"

She looked puzzled. "I do not intend to return you."

"No." He went to her and grasped her elbows. "I have to stay here. I can't leave."

She shook off his hands. "Calm yourself. Why do you wish to return to the fields? Your life will be much easier with me."

He struggled for a logical reason, something she'd believe. Something that would at least get him out of this damned vehicle. "My things. I have possessions."

She pointed to the bundle she'd dropped just inside the doorway. "They are there."

She'd touched his things? Sifted through his meager possessions? He couldn't worry about that now. "You have to let me out. Please." He almost choked on the word. He'd never asked his captors for a damned thing. Now he was begging, and he didn't even care.

"Why do you resist? You cannot possibly prefer a life in the fields to a life in my household."

"In your bed, you mean."

She shrugged. "You prefer to be a field slave, not my consort. Is that what you would have me believe?"

Consort. A genteel synonym for whore. "Yes."

"Impossible. And the choice is not yours."

What else could he use to convince her? Nothing but the truth. "The boy…" He broke off, his throat tight. To think that he might never see Billy again…

"The boy? What of him?"

"He…he means a lot to me." Feeble, but telling her the whole truth would give her too much power over him. She had enough as it was. And he couldn't remember the Prendarian word for *nephew.*

"You should know better than to become attached to others. As a slave, you could be sold at any moment."

As he'd just been, obviously. Satisfying her so well, proving he was such a hot stud, had backfired big time. "Bring him with us. He's just a boy, he can't cost much."

"I have no use for a boy in my household."

"He's a hard worker. He'll be very useful to you. He won't be any trouble at all."

"I do not keep Earthers as domestic servants."

She seemed to truly not understand. "I love him," he admitted. "At least let me say goodbye to him."

"Love," she scoffed. "You Earthers and your excess of sentiment."

No one could be so callous. "He's my flesh and blood," he said. "You would feel the same."

She sighed, as though she had to force herself to be patient with him. "I have affection for those of my relations who are kind and intelligent. I do not aggrandize my feelings for them by professing to love them." She waved a hand dismissively. "That which you call love is merely possessiveness."

She actually meant it. She couldn't care less if he saw Billy again. "I pleased you, Rigah," he said. Maybe reminding her of their intimacy, using her name, would get through to her. "Do me this favor. Don't take me."

"I want to take you," she said, as though she'd never been denied anything she wanted.

All she wanted him for was sex. "I won't satisfy you again," he threatened. "I'll be the worst lover you've ever had."

She smiled, damn her, a smile of real amusement. "I doubt you can prevent your member from hardening."

"You can bet I'll try."

She stepped closer to him, glaring into his face, lightly brushing against him. "It is my place to satisfy myself with your body. You have little control in the matter."

She might be right about that. But he didn't have to go willingly. "I control my mouth, though. And I know how fond you are of oral pleasures."

Her eyes narrowed. "You will satisfy me in any way I wish you to, on penalty of death."

"I would prefer death to being your whore."

"Fine," she said, her voice level. "Since your own life means little to you, you will satisfy me or I'll find the boy and kill him instead."

Oh, God. She couldn't mean it. Could she?

"And if you please me well," she continued, "I may be moved to grant you special privileges. Privileges like visiting this boy whom you profess to love." She gave the last word a heavy dose of sarcasm.

He turned away, teeth clenched. No way would he let her see his frustration, his raw anger. He couldn't take another lecture on foolish attachments. He'd go crazy and do something stupid, she'd kill him, and then he'd be no good to Billy at all.

He stared out the window. Poor Billy. Did he realize yet that he was all alone, without a protector? The next time he woke from a nightmare, the next time he took a beating, the next time he cried himself sick over his mother's death, Jason wouldn't be there to comfort him. And how long would it be before one of the sex-starved men broke down and tried to abuse him? The keeper used threats and beatings to keep everyone in line, and it seemed to work, but that wasn't a guarantee.

He'd promised to always take care of him, to never let them be separated. A promise he couldn't keep. Even if he managed to escape from Rigah, she'd know right where he was going and follow him straight to Billy. And now she knew the perfect way to keep him in line. Just threaten to kill his sole surviving relative, the only person in the universe that he gave a damn about, and he'd be on his knees, begging to please her.

His hands clenched into fists. He could kill this woman.

Maybe, God willing, he'd get the chance.

Chapter Three

Rigah made good use of the rest of the trip, exercising in the main chamber of the conveyance. Physical exertion always helped to calm her mind, to relax her body after a challenge. She had spent much time in exercise in the past months. From all sides, she was challenged. Her faithless sister sought to take her station. And her mother...her mother was blind, blind to all Rigah had accomplished. Impossible to satisfy. She sought nothing but the weakness, the sensitivity, the signs of emotional instability. The days of Rigah's youth, the days of being ruled by emotions, were long behind her. Could her mother not see how ruthlessly she'd squashed her feelings? How governed by intellect she had become?

She would see now. Rigah had brought down the rebellion with no hesitation, no qualms of the spirit. And if she had felt a brief moment of sympathy for the Earther slaves, it was merely a natural pity for the condition the foolish emotions of their own race had brought them to. There was no shame in that feeling.

And there was no shame in the anger she had shown Jason. As her consort, as a slave, it was his place to obey her without question. No doubt the man had been beaten often in the fields—he was incautious with his insolence. He had raised her anger to a point she'd not often reached. A point where she'd lost her honor and threatened the life of a child.

Not that she relished taking him from the boy. Was the child his son? Jason hadn't specified, yet his feelings were strong enough to be those of a parent. If he'd smiled at her, cajoled her, sweetly pleaded with her, she would have relented. One small child would hardly be noticed in a household as large as her own. But to dare to order her, to threaten not to satisfy her...such disrespect would not be borne.

She had to break him of this outrageous arrogance. Such behavior was not permitted from trusted servants of her own race, and was most definitely unsuited to the station of a slave. If he challenged the wrong person, it would mean his death.

Perhaps it was just as well. As matters now stood, he didn't know that a smile on his handsome face, a tender word in his deep voice, would likely cause her to grant him most any favor. No doubt he'd please her well in the coming months, and she would relent and grant him the boy—with no loss of her authority.

A short tone sounded from the control console. They were home. She set down the weight she had been hefting and wiped her sweaty face with a damp cloth. Then she walked back to the sleeping den.

Jason stood by the window, his back to her, as if he could see anything under the murky, faint light of the smallest moon. As if he hadn't moved since she'd left him hours ago. He wore his rough clothing now, so he must have moved at some time.

"We have arrived," she said.

He didn't stir, didn't acknowledge her.

"Follow me." She turned and left, not waiting to see if he obeyed. If he didn't, she would be forced to punish him.

A small group of attendants waited for her as she left the conveyance. Merko came forward. "*Senhab* Rigah. Praises on a successful trip."

She smiled at her old friend. Since childhood, he had been destined to be her Primary. She could not ask for a more trustworthy advisor. "I gather you have heard the news. There will be no further slave uprisings in the Western Quarter."

Merko didn't respond. He stared over her head, mouth agape.

Rigah turned and saw Jason in the doorway, his pathetic bundle in one hand. "Merko, this is Jason." She did not explain further. That would come in private, when Merko would no doubt voice his concerns over the wisdom of taking an Earther for consort.

She led the way into the courtyard. "He needs some decent clothes," she informed Merko. "And he will occupy the chamber adjacent to my quarters."

"I will see it done," Merko replied. She could hear the curiosity in his tone, but he knew better than to question her in front of others.

"I would have the evening meal soon," she continued.

"It is in readiness."

How nice to be home, where everything was efficient. She had long since tired of the inconveniences of travel. "Give me a moment to wash, then have the meal brought to the dining chamber."

"As you wish, *Senhab*."

She walked through the main entrance, paused, and turned. Jason's eyes were downcast, carefully averted from her. Still brooding over the boy, no doubt. Foolish man. The sooner he smiled and pleased her, the sooner she could relent.

She would force him to be civil. "Jason will dine with me this evening. Show him to his quarters, then see that he finds the dining chamber."

She walked away, leaving Merko to deal with the moody Earther for the present. Tonight, he would begin his new duties. Tonight, she would show him the natural order of things.

* * *

Rigah's household, as she called it, was more like a village. It would take him days to find his way around this huge compound. There were at least five separate buildings, and the one he'd been brought into seemed palatial. It looked approximately six stories tall, and the ceilings in the entryway were at least twenty feet high.

The man Rigah had spoken with outside led him up a winding ramp. Clearly these people had never invented staircases. Rooms and corridors seemed to branch off in every direction. The walls were some kind of white substance, but not brick—the surface was all smooth. He reached out, touched it. The material felt cool against his fingers.

He should probably start trying to find out all he could about this place. Information was power. "I'm sorry, but I don't know your name."

"I am called Merko."

"Merko, will you tell me...what is your position?"

"I am Primary to *Senhab* Rigah."

"Primary?"

"I am her advisor. Her counsel." Merko stopped, and turned to face him. "And I am the man who will see you suffer a slow, painful death if you harm her in any way."

Charming. That made twice in one day his life had been threatened. "I do not intend to harm her." He couldn't, not as long as she held Billy over his head.

"That is wise." Merko continued up the ramp and Jason followed.

Might as well try to make conversation. If Merko was as close to Rigah as he seemed, he could give up some useful information on how to manipulate her. "You don't approve of Rigah buying me."

"It is not my place to approve or disapprove. I will say, I do not trust you."

At least he was honest about it. "Will you tell her to get rid of me?" He'd tried to keep the hopefulness out of his tone, but hadn't succeeded.

Merko snorted, a sort of abrupt laugh. "If I wished my service to *Senhab* Rigah to be brief, I would dare to tell her such a thing."

"But you said you're her advisor."

Merko turned left, and the corridor they'd been in opened into a wide space with doors on all sides, kind of like a hallway. The doors had odd-shaped vertical handles, not knobs. They looked almost Medieval, but classy. Rich.

"I advise *Senhab* Rigah in political matters," Merko said. "Not in her personal affairs."

Something in his voice made Jason doubt it was as clean-cut as all that. Politics always involved the personal. "Why do you call her *Senhab?*"

"It is a term of respect befitting her station."

"Her station?"

Merko led him to a wide door and waved him inside. "Do you know nothing? *Senhab* Rigah is the eldest daughter of the Premier Leader. She is Leader Elect."

Well, that explained her arrogance. Holed up in the *quaanti* fields like he'd been, he hadn't heard much about the politics on this planet, but he knew that the Premier Leader was the one running the whole show. It sounded like Rigah was next in line to take over. She must be the most famous person on this world, since they didn't have any actors or other celebrities.

He'd fucked a famous celebrity. Someday he might laugh about that.

The room was huge and furnished with a table, a couple of chairs, a strange type of dresser that had shelves instead of drawers, and a bed big enough for three. No decorative touches, no art, nothing beyond the necessities. The plantation barracks had been almost this Spartan. Strangely, there were five walls, not evenly spaced. The lack of geometric harmony would probably drive him crazy. A tall window looked out over some kind of forested wilderness area, barely visible in the moonlight. He set his bundle down on the bed.

"I will leave you now." Merko pointed to a small alcove in the corner. "You may wash there. The dining chamber is downstairs, to the left of the entryway."

He nodded as if he remembered the route. He'd be lucky to find his way downstairs again, but he wouldn't mind having some time alone.

"You have a few moments only. *Senhab* Rigah will be annoyed if you are late for the meal."

And God forbid anything annoy *Senhab* Rigah. He nodded, and Merko left.

He turned to the cheap cloth sack on the bed. His possessions were pathetic and few, but they were all he owned. He'd been too upset about Billy to check them out before, but now he untied the drawstring and looked inside.

Damn it. The baseball was Billy's. He'd left it lying on Jason's bunk this morning, so Rigah must have taken it as his. He set it carefully on the top shelf. Someday, maybe he could return it.

His slender volume of Hamlet was still intact, although the cover was half torn off. A thin stretchy band, this planet's equivalent of rubber, held it together. He opened the book, carefully flipping through it until he found the faded, wrinkled snapshot of his parents he'd stashed there. He caught a line of text at random.

I could be bound in a nutshell and count myself a king of infinite space, were it not that I have bad dreams.

He closed the book and carefully re-banded it. Shakespeare wasn't exactly his style, but he couldn't be picky. It wasn't like he could run down to the local Barnes and Noble and pick up a Tom Clancy. Besides, he'd played Laertes in high school.

High school—a lifetime ago and half a galaxy away. Earther sentiment, as Rigah had called it, kept him hanging onto the book. And it was a secure place to stash his tattered photo. Few people on this planet would open a book written in English.

There wasn't much else to sort through. A deck of playing cards in a small, worn cardboard box, the edges soft and frayed from frequent use. A postcard of San Francisco, the last city he'd lived in on Earth. The last place he'd been a free man. Was the Golden Gate Bridge still standing? He'd never know.

All together, his worldly possessions took up a quarter of the top shelf.

He'd owned a condo in San Francisco. A condo and a BMW and a collection of DVDs that he'd been stupidly proud of. And he'd lost it all in the Third World War. Stupid war. All for big business, all for oil.

And after the Earth's infrastructure had been smashed by corporate greed, the aliens had come, and there'd been no way to organize against them. He'd been living in an abandoned warehouse on the wharf with Billy when they'd been rounded up. The lucky ones had been kept on Earth, slaving to rebuild everything they'd torn down. The unlucky ones had been brought to the alien home world.

He'd never been a lucky man.

He looked out the window for a minute. There were no bars and it opened wide, but there was a steep drop to the ground, at least fifty feet. Not that he could escape anyway, not now that Rigah knew about Billy.

How ironic. This single room of his was larger than the hut he'd shared with twenty men back on the plantation, and it didn't have bars on the window. But it was even more of a prison. He had no companionship here. No Billy to take care of. No hope of escape.

No hope at all.

* * *

This goddamned building was a crazy maze of random corridors and doors. He followed every ramp that led further downward, but hit a dead end.

"Are you lost?" a female voice said from behind him.

He turned. The woman was shorter than Rigah, but her face was strikingly similar. She had the same curly, cropped blonde hair, the same gray eyes, the same high forehead. But Rigah moved with graceful precision, while this woman walked with a hip-rolling sway, like a young, alien version of Madonna. Her clothes looked richer than any he'd seen on this planet, some kind of shimmery blue material wrapped around her in a loose sheath. Far more exotic than Rigah's practical uniform.

"Who are you?" she asked. She stood an arm's length away, looking him over. Thoroughly. Were all of the women on this planet sex maniacs?

"My name is Jason," he said.

"An Earther."

"Yes."

"You're new. Are you Rigah's?"

She didn't use the respectful *Senhab*. Must be a relative. "Yes," he answered. "I arrived today. Could you..." Maybe he wasn't allowed to ask her a favor.

"No doubt you're looking for my sister. Follow me."

She led him through the maze of ramps and corridors, never pausing. At the main entrance, she stopped outside a wide door. "Go in."

Why wasn't she leading him? He cautiously pushed open the door and walked in. The room was sparsely furnished, just like the bedroom Merko had taken him to. Rigah sat at an oblong table, eating. The food smelled great, spicy and warm, better than anything he'd had since coming to this god-forsaken planet. His mouth watered.

She looked up. "You are late."

Would apologizing make this better or worse? He said nothing.

"Do you deliberately seek to anger me?" she asked.

The door opened behind him. "I delayed him," her sister said. She drawled it out suggestively, making it sound like they'd just had a quickie against a wall. What was she trying to do, get him flogged? "Don't punish Jason for my faults."

Rigah didn't look pleased to see her sister. "Good evening, Shalawn," she said brusquely.

Shalawn brushed against his side as she walked to the table, but she stayed standing.

"Sit," Rigah said to him, as if he was a disobedient dog.

He walked to the table, carefully stepping around Shalawn, and took a seat across from Rigah.

She turned back to her plate. "Shalawn, do you stay for this meal?"

She paused, no doubt deliberately. "The gracious offer is tempting. But no."

"You wished to speak with me?" Rigah sounded impatient. Clearly there wasn't a great deal of Earther sentiment between these two.

"No," she answered baldly. "I wanted to be sure of your safe return." Was that a trace of sarcasm in her voice? "I'll visit you later. And you also, Jason." Shalawn left without another word.

"Eat," Rigah ordered him.

He lifted the lid of the bowl closest to him. Some kind of stew, pungent with spices. He spooned a little onto his plate, then took a cautious taste. Good. Really good.

Rigah pointed to a metal coffer. "There is grain here."

He obediently added the grain to his plate. Even better.

She ate in silence, seemingly unperturbed by it. Maybe she ate alone every night. Should he try to explain that nothing had happened between him and her sister? No, that might make him look guilty.

"Merko will take your clothes for measuring tonight," she said.

She obviously didn't need his approval, but it seemed rude not to acknowledge her proclamation. "All right."

They ate in silence for a short while. "Merko calls you *Senhab* Rigah," he said at last.

"It is a title of respect," she explained.

That hadn't been his point. "Would you like me to call you *Senhab* Rigah?" Not that he wanted to, but if it would make her think he was a respectful little slave, he'd do it.

She thought for a second. "That seems unnecessary."

Unnecessary. Yes, their positions were clear. She owned him—she could have him killed if she wanted. No title could give her more authority than that.

He didn't break the silence again. He concentrated on his food instead, digging through three servings. When he was finished, he noticed that she was done already. She'd been watching him.

"You enjoyed the meal." She didn't make it a question.

"Yes." He wasn't going to thank her for saving him from the slop he'd been given at the plantation. He'd rather eat that gruel with Billy than eat a seven-course meal in her palace. Besides, he wasn't quite sure how to say *thank you* in Prendarian. He'd never had any reason to thank anyone for anything.

She pushed her chair back from the table. "If you require something, tap the console in your room and you will be attended to." She rose from the table. Her gaze swept over his chest. "I will visit you shortly."

So tonight she wanted him to pleasure her. He'd be a good little slave and do it. He'd do exactly what she ordered him to do.

And no more.

Chapter Four

He played solitaire whenever he was nervous or bored. Tonight he was a little of both, sitting here in his bare room, waiting for Rigah to show up.

A soft knock came from the door. Right on cue, but why was she knocking? She owned the place. She owned him. "Come in."

The door opened and Rigah entered. She wore a silky, deep purple shirt that fell to mid-thigh and fastened up the middle, and she was barefoot. She looked like she was ready for bed.

She looked stunning.

Her legs were awesome, long and strong, well curved. Generous thighs…the kind of thighs that cushioned a man's hips when he was buried between them. He shouldn't stare. He shouldn't let her know she was getting to him already.

Her gaze swept his bare chest, and she smiled. "I see Merko took your clothing."

"Yes." At least he'd given him a loose pair of pants to preserve some semblance of his modesty.

She moved to the side of the table where he sat. "Unusual cards."

"An Earth game. I was bored." He would not stand up, not until she asked him to.

"You are not restricted to your chamber, Jason," she said. "You may explore the house, the property, if you wish."

He didn't want to sound too eager. "I am permitted to leave this building?" There. He'd managed to sound docile.

"Yes. But be warned, there are guards and alarms at the perimeter of the grounds. Do not venture too far from the buildings."

He nodded. At least he could go out, scout the lay of the land. Get a little exercise.

"Come here," she said softly, as if it wasn't an order. He got up and stood in front of her. She put her arms around him and kissed him. God, she tasted sweet. Her breath was minty, her lips mobile, moving over his with gentle assuredness. It took all of his willpower to stay passive.

"Kiss me back," she whispered.

He had to obey. Didn't he? So he kissed her back gently, molding his lips to hers but letting her run the show. Her tongue stole into his mouth, teasing, and then she pulled away and planted sexy little bites on his neck. She was right—nothing could have stopped him from getting hard. Not with her nipping at his neck, rubbing her breasts against his chest through the silky material of that shirt.

He kept his hands still on her hips. She hadn't told him to move them. And no matter how much he wanted to run them up under her shirt and find out what she had on underneath it, he wasn't going to. Not until she asked.

She kissed and licked her way over his collarbone, down his chest, until she reached a flat nipple. She kissed it, then suckled, nice and hard, letting him feel her teeth. He gasped. Just the way he liked it. How had she known? Her belly pressed against his cock, and he gritted his teeth to resist the temptation to grind against her.

She let go and cocked her head toward the bed. "Let's lie down."

She didn't have to ask twice. He lay on his side, but she gently pushed him onto his back. She leaned over him for a tongue-filled kiss, then backed off and ran her hands over his chest. "Your chest is magnificent," she murmured, planting sucking kisses and little bites all over his pecs. No one had ever worshiped his chest like this. It was damned erotic, lying back passively while she stroked him, kissed him. But he wouldn't let her know he enjoyed it. He wouldn't give her that satisfaction. He forced himself to lay still, to keep his hands at his sides.

She lifted his hand to her breast, as if she'd read his mind. "Touch me," she said. Thank God she'd asked. He stroked and squeezed and teased her breast, lingering over the hard nipple. Her shirt was driving him crazy. He wanted to strip her, to taste her, but that had to be at her command. He wouldn't do anything she didn't command him. The sooner she got bored with him, the sooner she'd let him go.

"What clever hands." She sighed. With one fingertip, she traced his bellybutton, then moved lower to the waistband of his pants. "Take these off."

Another timely order. He was more than ready. His cock felt hard enough to break granite. He stripped off the pants and threw them to the floor. She took off her shirt at the same time.

Naked. She'd been naked underneath it. Her body was every bit as beautiful as he remembered, from her full, swaying breasts to her strong, sexy legs.

In a blur of motion, she lifted herself, pressed him onto his back again, and sat astride his thighs, leaning forward to rest her hands on the bed at either side of his rib cage. She studied him, her head tilted to one side, as if looking for the best place to take a bite.

She touched his cock with one hand. He tried to lift his hips, tried to press harder into her hand, but she was sitting on his thighs and he couldn't move an inch. She smiled, clearly enjoying being the one in charge. "Soon," she said, taking her hand away.

She shifted up onto her knees, crouching above him, and leaned forward to kiss him. A long, wet, passionate kiss. She rubbed her breasts against his chest, driving him crazy with the feel of those hard nipples. She slid forward a little more, then a little more, moving up his body inch by inch until he felt the brush of a nipple against his cheek. Nothing, not his pride, not her arrogance, could stop him from sucking that luscious nipple into his mouth. She made a soft, mewling little noise as he drew on her, pulling back only to present the other breast to his lips.

To hell with it. If he waited another minute for another order, she'd have him begging. He reached between her legs, giving her the hard strokes he knew she liked, keeping up the suction on her nipple. She cried out.

"You're so wet," he mumbled, his lips against the side of her breast. "You want more, don't you? You want me in your—in your—" He didn't know her word for it, and she sure as hell wouldn't know his.

"My nest," she answered. "Yes, I want you in my nest."

She pulled his hand away and sank down onto his shaft, taking him inside her. Her cunt gripped him like a slick fist. She didn't pause, didn't miss a beat, fucking him with a slow, steady rhythm.

He'd had women on top of him before, but it had never been like this. This wild. She bent over him, kneeling, moving in a feral rhythm, her breasts brushing lightly against his chest, as if this was the most natural sexual position in the world. On this world, maybe it was.

And she moaned, God, she moaned, soft little groans and gasping cries, eager, shameless noises of need that took him right over the edge. He had to think of something else, anything else, but the hot slap of her breasts against his chest…the sharp tang of her teeth nipping at his neck…the sliding, pumping heat of her cunt.

Too late. He couldn't stop.

She clamped down on his cock, shuddering, and he let go, grabbing her hips and thrusting up into her, exploding deep, deep inside her.

She collapsed onto his chest, panting. One of her hands found his cheek, stroked into his hair. He resisted the urge to hold her, like he would have held any other lover. They weren't lovers. He was a toy for her amusement; she was his master. Nothing more.

His heart rate slowed. She moved to his side, laying a possessive hand on his chest. Her hand seemed startlingly pale against his darker, tanned skin. He'd never seen skin so fair. It seemed to be common among her race, this skin that was whiter than white, almost translucent, but hers had a light peach tint that gave her a little color.

He stole a quick peek at her face. Her eyes were closed. She truly was a beautiful woman. No doubt a lot of men would consider themselves lucky to fuck her. And considering her appetite for it, no doubt a lot of men had.

She smiled a little, looking thoroughly satisfied. No wonder—she'd gotten exactly what she'd wanted. He'd been a good little harem boy, done everything she'd ordered him to do. He'd even managed to wait for her to come first. Barely.

He yawned.

"Are you tired?"

He nodded. He wasn't really, but if she left soon, he could go explore the house a bit.

She got up and pulled the blankets over him, then dimmed the lights and climbed back into bed, curling up against his side.

"Are you going to sleep here?" he asked, surprised.

"Should I not?"

Oh, boy. She sounded annoyed. He'd better tread carefully. "I assumed your own bed would be more comfortable."

"No. It is the same as this."

Made sense, especially if she planned to spend a lot of time in this one. How many other men had been kept in this room before him? Must be a high-turnover job. Maybe he'd be back in the fields soon.

"You speak my language well," she commented.

No kidding. "We were forbidden from speaking in alien languages at the plantation."

"Say something in your native language."

"Yes, master," he said in English. "How high would you like me to jump, master? Your wish is my command."

She raised her head and looked at him curiously. "What did you say?"

He couldn't think of a reasonable lie. He just stared at her, fumbling.

"Don't tell me," she said. "No doubt your words showed insolence."

"You know me too well."

She laughed, she actually laughed. And he couldn't help smiling himself.

He closed his eyes and relaxed. He might be a whore, he might not know where Billy was, he might have no more than a handful of pathetic possessions. But at least for tonight, he had a full stomach and a comfortable bed.

* * *

She lay quietly beside him as he fell asleep. His mouth opened slightly as his breathing slowed and deepened. She wasn't tired, but she hadn't wanted to leave him so soon.

He'd pleased her well, exactly as she had planned. He had been submissive and let her lead him. But oddly, she was not content. He'd been satisfied, he'd enjoyed the pleasuring, but he hadn't been truly eager for her. She wanted him to feel the passion, the hunger, that he'd shown her in the conveyance.

Ridiculous. Why was she discontented? She had power, property and a handsome man, exclusively hers. Yet she wanted more.

He must be angry over the boy. She could not relent on that issue. She could not appear weak in his eyes. But she could grant him other favors. She'd have Merko order a lavish new wardrobe for him, in fabrics and colors that would look magnificent against his tawny skin, contrast nicely with his dark hair and golden brown eyes.

Fabrics as exotic as he was himself.

That should improve his mood.

* * *

Jason looked in the mirror and grimaced. Unbelievable. Did she really expect him to wear these?

The pants were black, the fabric some stretchy material that clung to his ass and groin, molding to reveal every nook and cranny of his package. They loosened up a little below his thighs, but at the top…he looked like Baryshnikov.

Maybe the shirt was long enough to cover him. It was bright blue, made from the same silky material Rigah had worn last night. He grabbed it from the shelf, pulled it over his head, and went back to the mirror.

It covered his groin—barely—but the neckline dipped into a low V in front, showing most of his chest, including a couple of the hickeys Rigah had left on him last night. And to really ice the cake, the thing was sleeveless.

And this was all he had to wear.

Rigah came in, smiling delightedly. "You look wonderful!"

She meant it. Obviously this was her idea of the ultimate wardrobe for a sex slave.

"More clothes will be brought this evening," she went on. "This was all that could be done by morning."

Great. More clothes, no doubt all of them as clinging and low-cut as these. She could spend a small fortune outfitting her personal whore, but she couldn't spend the pittance it would cost her to rescue Billy from the fields. "I hope some of the others are less revealing."

"Don't you like these?"

She looked puzzled. If he didn't know better, he'd think her feelings were hurt. "I'm used to being more...covered."

Her deep blue uniform covered everything but her head and her hands. Maybe these spandex-inspired clothes were *his* uniform.

She stepped in front of him, brushing against him lightly. Her hands ran up his arms, squeezed his biceps. "Your body is glorious. You have no reason to conceal it."

Clearly personal modesty wasn't reason enough.

She stroked his bare chest with one hand. The plunging neckline made it easy for her. No wonder she liked this shirt. She watched her hand move over him.

His gaze followed that pale, pale hand. He had so many hickeys, it looked like he'd been branded. "You like seeing your marks on me, don't you?"

"Assuredly." She looked up into his eyes. "And there will be the marks of no other on you, Jason. The scent of no other."

Was she kidding? At the rate she was going, he wouldn't have the energy to eat, let alone satisfy another woman. Even so, he recognized the warning in her words. "Of course not."

She tilted her head back invitingly, pointed at the small bruise under her ear. "You have marked me, as well," she said huskily.

"Should I beg your forgiveness?"

"No," she answered, as if he'd been serious. "You should mark me again. Now."

He knew an order when he heard one. He kissed her neck, sucking lightly. Her hands took his ass and gently squeezed. "I very much like this clothing," she whispered.

"Perhaps you could wear something similar," he said against her neck. "This shirt would look intriguing on you."

She giggled. "But it would not cover my breasts."

"Exactly." He wrapped an arm around her waist lightly. His teeth caught at her earlobe. "Think of the convenience," he whispered. "I could reach right inside and touch your bare flesh." With his free hand, he gently squeezed her breast through the fabric of her shirt.

She wriggled up against him. Incredible. Just having her against him, just tasting her neck, feeling her up outside her clothing, made his cock stir to life. God damn her for making him horny. At this rate, she'd never get bored with him.

"I must work soon," she said. Yet she ran her hands down the front of her shirt, opening the small fasteners. Then she grabbed his hand and put it on her bare breast. She was one insatiable woman. Her nipple pebbled to hardness in his palm.

She backed up, pulling him with her, until they bumped into the table. She jumped up to sit on the edge, parting her knees and pulling him against her.

"You want me," she said.

No sense in denying it. The proof was rubbing against her belly. Must be the long stretch of celibacy he'd endured. "Yes." He bit her neck, just hard enough to get a squeal out of her, to punish her for making him admit it.

She grabbed his ass and pulled him tight against her pussy—against her *nest,* as she called it. He swore he could feel the heat of her all the way through the pants of her uniform. She rubbed up against him, notching her cunt against his cock, driving him crazy.

He'd never be able to wait for her to order him to please her. Maybe he could screw her fast. Fast and hard. Maybe he could come first and leave her unsatisfied. That would piss her off, maybe enough that she'd let him go.

He reached for the fastenings of her pants. The small hooks were hard to grab, but he managed. As he pulled her pants down, she lifted her hips to help, then scooted to the edge of the table. She couldn't possibly be ready. Could she?

Not that he cared. He grabbed the waistband of his spandex-like pants and tugged them down to his knees. His cock sprang free.

He didn't even have to bend his knees—the table put her at the perfect height. With one hand, she guided him into her cunt. She threw her head back and closed her eyes, jogging her ass to meet his thrusts. He kept his eyes open, watching her. Watching a woman while he fucked her always got him hot. He watched her throat move as she gasped, watched her breasts bounce with each thrust.

Watched her reach between her legs and rub her clit.

God damn it, she was getting herself off. He could pull her hand away, but she'd probably kill him for doing it. Maybe he could still beat her to the finish line. He thrust harder. Faster.

Too late. She fell back on the table and screamed as her climax hit. He pounded into her, hating her, craving her, gripping her ass so tight, he hoped his fingers left bruises. And finally he came, pouring into her in a great wrenching spasm of anger.

She'd gotten exactly what she wanted. Again.

"God damn you," he said in English.

He didn't want to touch her anymore, didn't want the pretense that they had any affection for each other. He pulled out and put his hands on the table, leaning his weight against it as he caught his breath. Not a millimeter of his skin touched hers.

When he finally looked down at her, she smiled languidly. Damn her.

He stood and turned away. "I need to bathe."

"I will join you."

Great. The last thing he wanted. He stripped off his clingy clothes and went into the small bathing alcove without waiting for her.

He flipped the switch that activated the sonic shower. He still didn't know how it worked. Some kind of electron shower that dissolved sweat and dirt. All he had to do was run his hands over his body as the electrons made his skin tingle.

Water was scarce on Prendara. He hadn't seen an ocean, a lake or a river. Or even a puddle. It seemed that all of the water was underground, running in subterranean rivers. And when it drained off, the ground collapsed above it, creating huge craters that pockmarked the planet's surface. The last time there'd been a collapse at the plantation, two men had been killed.

He missed the Pacific Ocean. He missed San Francisco Bay. The Sacramento River. Bathing in water.

But at least this sonic shower would get him away from Rigah faster than a traditional shower would. A quick shake of his head and a finger combing of his hair and he was finished. It took less than a minute.

Then he was out, leaving her to bathe alone. He didn't want to put those clinging clothes back on, but what choice did he have? Parading around naked? He reached for the Baryshnikov pants and tugged them on.

She came in as he dropped the shirt over his head. Her smile showed that she had no clue how angry he was. He turned away as she got dressed.

She came up to him and gave him a soft kiss on the lips. He didn't dare pull away, but he didn't respond either. He felt her hand on his ass, squeezing. At least one of them enjoyed these pants. She rubbed against him like a cat. A cat in heat.

"You'll have to wait a while," he said, as dryly as he dared. Nothing could make his cock rise this soon, no matter what she did.

"There are ways of pleasuring that don't require a hard root," she answered.

Root. So that was her word for cock.

Before he could answer, she touched his mouth with the tip of her forefinger. "You are familiar with some of those ways."

Damn, damn, damn. If she kept getting satisfied, she'd never let him go. What could he say to piss her off? Something mild. He wanted her annoyed, not angry. If she got too angry, she might harm Billy. It didn't seem to be in her nature to hurt a child, but he couldn't risk it.

"I thought you had work to do," he said. Lame. Totally lame.

"It can wait a few moments longer," she answered. She tilted her head back and drew his lips to her neck. "Bite me," she said.

He'd make her order him through this and do his best to leave her frustrated. Maybe, if she had to resort to her own hand again, she'd get tired of him. He bit her neck, gently, and she gasped and thrust her breasts against him. Even through the thick fabric of her uniform, he could feel her pointed nipples.

"Rigah!" barked an annoyed voice.

He lifted his head and Rigah whirled to face the door. Shalawn stood there with an older woman in a uniform, the woman who must have spoken. The woman looked extremely irritated. Shalawn, on the other hand, smirked with delight.

Rigah pulled away from him slowly, as though she had nothing to be ashamed of. As though she got caught making out with men every day of the week. Hell, maybe she did.

"Greetings, Mother," she said.

Chapter Five

Rigah led the way to the strategy chamber, walking at her normal pace. She felt no hurry to reach it, to face her mother's questions and Shalawn's sneering. Nor would she drag her feet. Was she a mere girl, to be humiliated for having a man? No. She was Leader Elect, at least for the present.

In the chamber, she sat behind the tall desk. Let her sister see her in command. Her mother sat opposite the desk and Shalawn lounged against the back of her mother's chair. The two of them faced Rigah together. Much as they always had.

"He's a fine man," Shalawn said. How typical of her to mention a topic best left unspoken. "So strong, yet he knows how to lie back and let a woman take him."

She almost smiled. Her sister had described many men, but not Jason. No man had ever dared to ride her before. The mere thought of his dominance caused a rush of heat. "I know you did not have him."

Shalawn raised one corner of her mouth in a little smirk. "So he claimed, I have no doubt. He lied to spare himself your jealous rage."

Never, in the whole of her life, had she been in a jealous rage. Always Shalawn would use the phrase that made Rigah look the worst. The most unbalanced. Yet her statement must be challenged. "We were separated for only a moment last evening," she lied. "Had you taken him, you would have relished the experience for quite a while longer."

"Stop," her mother commanded. Her face was red with the flush of anger. "Must I view my own daughters squabbling over an…over an Earther?" She spat out the last word in disgust.

Rigah bowed her head low in apology. Mother's physician had warned her that anger placed a great strain on her heart. When she raised her gaze, she saw her mother take Shalawn's hand in a tender gesture. "Leave us, please," her mother said quietly.

Please. Her mother never said please to anyone but Shalawn.

Shalawn left. No doubt she would listen at the door. Perhaps Merko would be near to prevent her. Though he had said nothing, Rigah knew he was sharp to her sister's ambitions.

"I am pleased to see you, Mother," she said softly. Too softly to be heard through the door.

Her mother raised a hand to stop her. She rarely had the time, or the patience, for pleasantries. "You have recently returned from the Western Quarter."

She nodded. "The uprising is over. Order is restored." And she had done the work. She, not Shalawn.

"A slave uprising," her mother said. "And now you have an Earther slave in your household, in the sleeping chamber next to your own."

She frowned. Was she expected to deny her needs? Certainly her mother had never done so. But she was well aware that her mother held different standards for her eldest daughter than for herself. "It is my right to have a consort. Or several consorts, if I wish."

Her mother's eyes narrowed, no doubt with annoyance. "I question not your rights, but your wisdom."

As she always did. Why spend a moment congratulating her daughter on squelching a dangerous rebellion when she could be censuring her sexual activities instead? "My wisdom is not at fault. I wanted him. I took him. There is nothing more to discuss."

"What do you truly know of him?" her mother asked. "Do you doubt he is a rebel? A spy?"

Jason? No. "He was working in the *quaanti* fields far from the Western Quarter," she explained. "He did not wish to come with me. A rebel would have been more eager."

"A clever strategy."

"Perhaps." Perhaps he had known her route. Perhaps he had been at the edge of the field on purpose. Perhaps his resistance to coming with her had been a pretense. No. No, he had sincerely cared about the boy.

"And though he may not be a rebel, he may yet harm you."

Merko had made the same argument. She replied now as she had to him. "He is well-treated. He will have no cause to harm me."

Her mother shook her head fiercely, as if she couldn't believe her own daughter's silly words. "You claim to know his mind? Do not delude your own."

How typical of her mother to denigrate her judgment. "He is intelligent," she argued. "If he harms me, his life will be brief. This he knows." Merko had promised to threaten him daily, as well. She had assured him there was no cause.

Her mother waved a hand angrily, dismissively. "I see your mind is fixed. But recall, Earthers are like caged animals. They cannot hold a rational mind." Her voice trembled, as it sometimes did when she was angry.

"Yes, Mother." Pointless to debate her mother's prejudice. She would argue no further, would strain her mother's heart no more. If she capitulated, the discussion would end.

"I know your spirit, Rigah," Mother said, her voice thin. "You wish to confirm the best in people, not seek the truth of them. You were ever one to attach yourself to others."

Mother had always warned her of sentimental attachments. Sentiment was for foolish Earthers, driven by greed and lust to decimate their home world. Sentiment was for those of a lower rank, for those who need not be objective. For those who could attach themselves to others without fear of losing their position.

As Leader Elect, there was no possibility for true attachment. No one could understand what it meant to be of her station. And when—if—she became Premier Leader, she must be even more cautious. More untrusting. More alone. It hardly seemed possible.

"An attachment to an Earther," her mother continued, "would be most unwise."

"Attachment? Mother, I assure you—he is an amusement only, easily discarded."

Her mother's brow rose skeptically.

And she wondered herself just how easily she could discard a man as stunning, as sensual, as Jason.

* * *

Jason turned the corner, but the main entrance wasn't there. He must have missed a turn.

Lost again. At this rate, he'd starve before he found the dining room. He'd skipped breakfast, not wanting to show up bare-chested. The revealing clothes he had on now weren't much of an improvement, but he was too hungry to care.

He backtracked and tried the previous left turn. This corridor led up; up so far he must be above his room. What the hell, might as well explore a little.

The corridor opened onto a huge atrium. Trees dappled the sunlight, their leaves rustling in a light breeze. Plants and trees grew in seeming abandon, but he spotted a few cleared grassy areas with benches and tables. Insects and birds chirped in happy chaos. Walls lined the perimeter of the garden, but he spotted a door and a few windows. The upper floor of the building must surround this rooftop garden. A path seemed to lead around the perimeter of the planted area.

He stepped onto the path. With the trees on one side and a wall to the other, it was hard to believe he was on the top floor of the building. Must be a nice view from these rooms. He peered into a window, but saw only a blank green slate. The glass they had here was some kind of one-way material—he couldn't see in, but anyone inside would see him.

He passed a heavy door, right before a corner. He turned left to continue around the path.

Shalawn crouched about twenty feet ahead, obviously listening at the next door. Whoa. Time to beat a hasty retreat. He took a step backwards.

She must have heard him, because she turned toward him quickly. But she smiled and laid her forefinger across her lips. She didn't look annoyed to see him. He crept up to her, careful not to make any noise.

"They're talking about you," she whispered.

This should be interesting. He leaned close to the door, but the voices were faint and muffled.

"Attachment?" Rigah said clearly, her voice raised, incredulous. "He is an amusement only, easily discarded."

Yes, they were talking about him all right. It wasn't exactly news to hear that Rigah could discard him with a wave of one imperious hand. But to hear her say it so callously, so bluntly, as if he wasn't even human…

"Entertaining, but not important," she said next. God. He shouldn't be so surprised. This was the woman who'd heartlessly taken him, against his will, from his only family. The woman who'd threatened the life of an innocent young boy just to make sure Jason would screw her on demand.

More muffled words came from behind the door. Words like "treasury" and "collection. " A new topic. He'd heard enough. He turned and walked away.

At the entrance to the atrium, he saw Shalawn following him.

"Where do you go?" she asked.

"To eat." If he could find the way.

"Follow me."

It must be obvious that he was lost. Well, following her would get him fed more quickly than wandering around on his own, overhearing conversations he didn't want to hear.

He paid attention to the route. The faster he learned his way around this labyrinth, the better.

The dining room was deserted, but there were a few covered serving bowls on the table. She sat down and watched as he took some food. Some kind of scrambled eggs, it looked like, with meat mixed in it. He lifted the lid of the other dish. More grain on the side. He added a little to his plate, sat across from her, and dug in.

He paused with a forkful halfway to his mouth. "You aren't eating?"

"No."

Well, she could watch him eat if she wanted to. He was too hungry to worry about whether or not it was polite to eat in front of her. But every time he glanced over, she was staring at him. Or rather, at his chest. He wouldn't bother trying to pull closed the open gap in the front of his shirt. That would make him look like some kind of nervous virgin.

He hoped she wasn't going to make a pass at him. Rigah had let him know he was her exclusive property, but rejecting her sister would be tricky. If he pissed her off, she could make up some story, something that would get Rigah to kill him. To *discard* him, as she'd said. He knew the word for the euphemism it was.

Shalawn leaned forward, resting her elbows on the table. "What are your feelings for my sister?"

Feelings? She had to be kidding. And he could hardly be honest with her, even though there seemed to be no love lost between her and Rigah. "I have none," he answered. None but loathing and anger and lust. He had to find a way to control the lust. It gave Rigah too much power over him.

Shalawn looked speculative. "You appeared quite angry when we were listening outside the strategy chamber."

So that's where they'd been. Sounded like a glorified title for Rigah's office. He couldn't think of a good answer, so he said nothing. Let her do the talking. Maybe she'd let something useful slip.

"My sister must enjoy you a great deal," she went on, as though there hadn't been an uncomfortable silence. "She dresses you lavishly."

He should be grateful for these clothes? Clothes that told everyone who saw him exactly what he did for his keep? "She appreciates these clothes more than I do."

Her gaze raked his chest yet again. She smiled, really more of a leer. "I cannot fault her for that. I appreciate them a great deal myself."

Uh-oh. That was definitely a come on.

She looked back up at his face. "Maybe we can help each other, Earth man."

No way could he trust this woman. But he needed some kind of ally. And at least she seemed to be off the topic of his clothes. "What do you mean?"

She smiled coyly, twining her hair around one forefinger. "I know what you desire, Jason. I can see you receive it."

Was she really coming on to him? Their language was still strange to him. Maybe he was reading too much into her words.

Then again, she hadn't taken her eyes off of his chest since they'd sat down. "I don't..." He stopped, struggling to find words that didn't sound rude. "Your sister has forbidden me from other women." There. Crisis averted.

She laughed. "You mistake my words."

"Forgive me, I thought—"

"You thought I desired that attractive body of yours." She looked at his chest again, and sighed theatrically. "And I do, most assuredly. But I will deny myself that pleasure. There are more profitable things that I wish to take from my sister. Things that will profit you, as well."

At least he wouldn't have to worry about getting it up for two horny women. "I have no use for profit. As a slave, I cannot spend money."

"There are more kinds of profit than money," she said. "Think about what you truly desire, Jason. I can gift it to you."

Billy. Freedom. Neither was hers to give.

The door opened and Merko came in. He glared at Jason but said nothing. He just stood there, right inside the door, arms folded in front of him, watching.

Jason turned back to his food. He was hungry. Let them both watch him.

Shalawn stood up. "We will speak later," she whispered. She walked to the door and left.

He took a quick glance at Merko. Still glaring.

Great. Now Rigah's advisor thought he was plotting against her—or cheating on her. Either way, his ass was probably toast.

* * *

Rigah left the dining chamber and walked to the upper story. Jason's door was closed. He hadn't appeared for the evening meal. Merko had seen Jason with Shalawn, eating the noon meal several hours after noon.

Merko had voiced grave concerns about her Earther consort. Concerns that Rigah had begun to share. Her mother was wise, for all her criticism. She knew more of Earthers than Rigah did. Perhaps there was cause for unease.

Perhaps there was not.

She went into her chamber and washed, then scrubbed her teeth. It was still early, barely a span past sunset. Yet she changed into a loose, short gown, one with a low neckline in front, suitable only for sleeping in the summer months. Or for sex.

She had given her mother the truth. The only way to ensure that Jason did not harm her was to see him content. And nothing kept a man content like sex. Especially a man who had been deprived for so many years. Granting him this would be no great burden for her.

She crossed the antechamber to his door and knocked softly.

"Come in."

She opened the door and entered, closing it behind her. He sat at the table once more, playing with his Earth cards. He didn't look up. Insolent again. She would not grow angry.

Instead, she moved to stand behind him. With her bare hands, she stroked his warm, smooth shoulders. "Good evening, Jason," she said softly. Bending, she lightly kissed the top of his head.

"Good evening." His voice sounded flat, uninterested.

She ran her fingers through his hair. So soft. She had noticed the texture the first time she had felt it, had eagerly tangled her fingers in the silky strands when he'd been licking at her nest in the conveyance. She grew moist at the memory. She wanted the same tonight. Then she would ride him, ride him as she had last evening, and look into his heavy-lidded amber eyes as she climaxed.

But he seemed strangely uninterested in pleasuring. He had yet to look at her, and he continued with his game, slowly turning cards over, occasionally moving them from one pile to another. If she was possessed of his Earther sentiment, she might accept his wishes and leave him in peace tonight. But she was not an Earther. She had been craving him all day, since their brief morning encounter. Since first viewing him in these tight pants, in this alluring shirt-vest that showed his magnificent chest. Since seeing the small pleasure marks she'd left on him.

She would seduce him. Slowly. She bent her head, letting her breath tease his ear before she nipped at the lobe. No response. Stubborn man. She would show him great patience tonight, until he was hot and eager for her.

She straightened. A few piles of clothing were neatly folded on the shelves. "You received more clothing."

"Yes," he said. Nothing more.

She took one of the folded items and held it up. The shirt had long sleeves and the back was low enough to cover his firm ass. A pity. But the color was wonderful, a rich gold that would complement his amber eyes. "This should be more comfortable for you."

He looked up then. When he saw the garment, surprise shone on his face. "I didn't think you wanted to see me covered."

She smiled. "I do not. But since concealing your body is your preference, I will indulge you."

"I am thankful to you." His mouth twisted, as if he hated to say the words. And he hadn't said the phrase correctly, not quite as a member of her race would, but she would not correct him.

She folded the shirt and replaced it on the shelf. He had turned back to his cards, no doubt feigning interest in the game. She moved to stand behind him again. With one hand she stroked down his neck, over the bare chest revealed by the vest. His skin felt hot. The fine hair on his chest, warm and silky, tickled her fingers. "Perhaps you will continue to wear this shirt in the privacy of your chamber. For me alone."

He shrugged. "If you want me to."

Why did he resist? She knew he wanted pleasuring. His breath had quickened and his heart beat rapidly under her hand. She bent down and found his neck with her lips, her tongue. "Join me in your bed," she whispered.

"As you wish." The words seemed oddly polite, from him. He stood slowly and her hand slid off of his chest as he rose.

Before he could reach the bed, she stopped him with a hand on his arm. She reached up and kissed him, twining her arms around his neck. His lips were soft, but still. As though he was unwilling.

"Kiss me back," she whispered, so it would not seem a command.

His lips moved, giving her a bare minimum of suction. Oh, she could slap his arrogant face. She pulled away. "Do not be insolent."

He looked angry, yet she had done nothing to anger him. "What would you have me do?" he asked.

Stubborn, stubborn man. As if he did not know. As if he had never been hungry for her body. "I would have you kiss me with passion," she said. "You will fondle my breasts. You will delve into my nest with your fingers and then you will eat between my legs as though you are starving for me." She broke off. She had never spoken such crude words, never commanded a man in such a blunt way. By the gods, he provoked her.

His eyes glinted with fury of his own, yet he closed them and lowered his mouth to hers. He kissed her, truly kissed her, his lips almost bruising hers. She pulled lightly on his hair, warning him, and he softened the pressure of his mouth. She teased his lips with her tongue and he responded, twining his own tongue with hers.

She reached for his taut backside, pulling him against her. His stiffening root pulsed against her belly. Yes. Yes, he wanted her. She rubbed against him and he grew harder. His mouth left hers, gasping for air, and she moved her lips to his neck, suckling and biting, gently teasing warmth to the surface of his skin. His hands came up between them, squeezing her breasts, gently pinching at her hard nipples. She moaned.

"This is what you ordered, is it not?" he asked.

She tugged at his hair, pulling his head back so she could see into his eyes. "Do not feign disinterest," she said. She pressed her palm against his hard root, stroking, and he closed his eyes. His jaw clenched, as if he was holding back a moan. Why did he resist?

She would force the sound from his throat. She took the waistband of his pants in both hands and pulled them to his knees, then grabbed his throbbing root in her fist and pumped him, hard.

He gasped. "Stop."

No. Not until he gifted her with the moan he was suppressing.

"Stop," he said again, louder. "Or I'll climax in your hand."

That would be a trespass indeed. She stopped and fondled him lightly, testing the hot weight of his stones. A groan left his mouth. At last. He took her wrist and pulled her hand away.

She would have him naked now. He did not resist, nor did he help her pull off his vest. But he did bend down to free his legs from the clinging pants. She stood back and looked at him, at his ridged muscles, the sparse hair on his sculpted chest, the arrogant thrust of his root. She reached up, curving her hand around his neck, and kissed him, kissed him with her tongue, relishing the heat of his naked body through the light fabric of her short gown.

Yet he remained unresponsive, despite his obvious need. Could she command him to feel the hunger, the wanting, that he had felt in the conveyance? That he had felt this morning? Perhaps she could command the illusion of such.

"Lift me," she said softly. "Lay me on the bed."

His eyes opened in surprise, but he bent and lifted her against his chest, one arm under her knees, one across her back. She was not a small woman, yet he carried her easily, his muscles strengthened from the labor of the fields.

He laid her on the bed and stood over her. She held her arms out to him, and he lowered himself into her embrace. His strength, his heat, his musky scent, all set her nerves tingling.

She kissed his neck, bit gently where his pulse throbbed. She could order his death, could still his pulse forever. This he knew. Yet he risked her anger, refusing to temper his pride. And to speak truth, his domineering ways excited her. She had never felt more like a woman than she did in his arms.

She tilted her head back, exposing her neck, and drew his mouth to her. He suckled, then nipped. Oh, that felt good. He wished to mark her. He hungered for her.

His hands pulled up her gown, uncovering her chest, and he stroked her breasts, rubbing her nipples in his hot palms. She pulled his head to one breast and he drew on it while his fingers pinched at the other. She arched her back, pressing herself closer, closer.

Her legs shifted restlessly, until his thigh came between them, pushing against her aching nest. After only a moment he pulled his leg away and his fingers spread through her damp folds, rubbing her wetness, stroking over her bud, until she felt nothing but a throbbing, tingling ache deep inside. With his mouth suckling at her breast and his fingers playing in her nest, she trembled on the edge of climax.

No. Not like this, not without feeling his root deep within her. "Stop."

He stopped, but did not remove his hand from her body. He lifted his mouth from her breast and looked into her eyes. "What do you want me to do?"

An echo of his earlier words. A request for orders. How could she tell him that she wanted him to cease asking for commands? That she wanted him to press her down into the bed, to pound his root into her nest, to take her with the tender ferocity of a man who had been denied pleasuring for three years?

"Ride me," she said. Heat bloomed in her cheeks at the words. Words she had never, in her darkest dreams, imagined she might voice.

He lifted his body over hers, spreading her thighs with his knees, lowering himself onto her. He took the crumpled gown from around her neck, eased it over her head, and threw it to the floor. His lips came to rest against her ear. "You wanted me to eat you," he murmured.

So cruel, to tease her when she squirmed with need, when she had admitted to wanting him above her. "Later," she said.

"As you desire."

He thrust into her then, hard. Her body tensed, clenched around him, welcoming him. He didn't pause, didn't miss a thrust. His rhythm was fast and fierce. Ah, he needed her. Truly needed her.

She could not order him to moan, yet she wished to. He kept silent, but his body spoke to hers, crashing into her again and again. He thrust wildly, yet his forearms cradled her head. She reached for his ass, urging him on, but he grabbed her wrists and pulled her arms over her head, holding them down tight. Restraining her. She pulled against him, but he held her fast.

And she relented. Gods help her, she relished his mastery. She could not fight him. He would do whatever he wished to her.

She wrapped her legs around his, holding onto him with her calves as he pumped with abandon. He needed her. Much as he had that day in the conveyance.

That day in the conveyance. The thought brought her to the pinnacle. She tensed for a moment and then came apart, climaxing long and hard, straining up against him, shuddering and trembling under his heat. After long moments of wrenching spasms, she collapsed into stillness.

He was soft within her; his full weight lay motionless upon her. She hadn't felt his climax. An odd regret came over her. Very odd. Almost as though she had been denied part of her pleasuring.

Chapter Six

He quickly rolled off of her and turned away, lying on his side with his back to her. She felt cold without his warm body against hers.

"Jason?"

"You'll have to give me some time to recover," he answered. "I can't perform again so quickly."

As if he hadn't really wanted her. His body did not lie. But she would not force the issue. Not tonight.

She pulled the blankets over them, then rolled against him, pressing her front against his broad back. He stiffened for an instant, but didn't draw away. He dared not, not unless he wanted to feel her wrath. He was hers, and if she wanted him for pleasuring or for warmth, he could not refuse.

She draped an arm over his waist. He didn't move, didn't acknowledge her by even a hitch in his breathing. Still brooding.

Would nothing satisfy this man? After the pleasure they had just shared, he should be content.

Perhaps he was content, only too stubborn to admit it. Rather than accept his station, he seemed determined to resent it. He would waste energy challenging her, infuriating her, the one who had rescued him from the fields.

Or perhaps her mother and Merko were correct. Perhaps his discontent posed a threat to her safety. She had seen no outward sign of it, but her mother was right—one could not predict the mind of an Earther. One could not predict the mind of any human. Especially one kept in captivity for so long.

Last evening, he had complained of boredom. Perhaps other things would appease him. He enjoyed his Earther cards, though they looked to be worn through. She would have them duplicated. She would speak to Merko about it in the morning. And he had a book of some sort, one in his native language. She would grant him access to the library. If he couldn't read her language, she would see that he learned.

Little enough things. Perhaps they would make this difficult man content. If they did not, she would have to admit the truth of her mother's concerns.

She would have to remove Jason from her household.

* * *

After a solitary breakfast, Jason spent the morning wandering the corridors. He didn't open any of the closed doors, didn't want to make anyone suspicious, but after an hour he could find the atrium, the dining chamber, and his room without getting lost.

Merko turned up several times during his wanderings, just watching and glaring. Keeping an eye on the slave, no doubt. Rigah didn't seem to have any other slaves in the house, just him. Didn't that make him feel special.

Everyone else in the house seemed to be a servant or a politician. The servants wore loose, but neat, clothes. The politician types wore dark blue uniforms like Rigah's, but none of them had the turquoise stripes across the shoulders. That must be a kind of insignia that indicated her rank. Neither the servants nor the politicians deigned to speak to him, or even look at him. He happily returned the favor.

A corridor next to the dining chamber led down and off to the side. He followed it for at least a hundred feet. Faint light shone at the far end of the corridor and he felt a steady, strong draft. When he emerged, he was outside.

The plants and trees surrounding the building were mostly shades of green and brown, just like on Earth, but nothing could mute the alien weirdness of the pale pink sky with its puffy blue and white clouds.

He'd like to know more about Prendara's geology, but he wouldn't ask Rigah. This cursed planet might be his home for the rest of his life, but he would never let her know he was interested in it. Or in her. No Stockholm syndrome for him. These were the people who'd enslaved him, and he'd never forget it.

There was a carpet of low-growing, fine-bladed plants covering the open area, almost like grass, and a large expanse of bushes and trees a couple dozen feet ahead. At a guess, the forest stretched out for dozens of acres.

He turned and looked back at the house. This must be the forested area he could see from his room. At least he knew another way outside now. A way that didn't take him through the heavily populated courtyard of the main building.

Best to keep his discovery secret. He turned to go back, but a glimmer of sunlight low, near the ground, caught his gaze. Water? Could it really be water? Or was something else behind those low-growing shrubs causing the shimmer?

He walked toward the shrubs and found a small opening. And there it was—water, bubbling up from the ground. Just a trickle, not even a stream, seeping from a small fissure and flowing just a few feet before it was absorbed back into the soil.

Water.

He knelt near the small puddle and reached out a cupped hand. The seeping water didn't rise more than a couple of inches from the ground, but he managed to get a few tablespoons of the cool liquid in his palm. He closed his eyes and rubbed it over his face, relishing the simple wetness.

Unbelievable.

It wasn't the Pacific, but it was better than nothing.

He'd come back here. But for now, he'd better head inside before anyone saw him and got suspicious.

He headed back through the corridor and met a glaring Merko at the other end. Uh-oh. He smiled nonchalantly at the man.

"Do you seek a particular place?" Merko asked.

What could he say? Just looking around? Lame. "I was hoping to find an exercise area." Whew. Good cover.

"Follow me," Merko said.

He paid attention. There, that was the dining chamber. Now right, past the kitchens. Merko opened a narrow door and led him into a huge room with high ceilings and windows on three sides. Odd equipment was scattered around the room. He recognized some weights and a few contraptions that looked vaguely like treadmills.

"Can I use all of this stuff?"

"Yes," Merko answered. "It is a public chamber." He left without closing the door.

At least this would kill some time. And help keep him strong. He walked over to a setup that looked vaguely like a bench-press and tested the weights. Just about right. He'd start slow. He stripped off his shirt and lay down, positioning the weights over his chest, and did a few reps. One, and two, and three…

After just a few minutes a light film of sweat had formed on his brow. He felt better. More like himself. He'd needed this, needed to burn off some steam, some frustration.

He couldn't let things go on like this. Being used for sex—it was more degrading than the beatings he'd taken in the fields, beatings for minor infractions. He'd taken more than one beating to spare Billy, including the time his baseball had broken a window. Now the poor kid must be taking his own punishments, or learning fast how to keep out of trouble. That didn't seem likely—he was too spirited. Just like Jason and his sister had been when they were Billy's age.

God, he still couldn't believe Rigah had taken him away. Maybe he should ask her again, plead with her to bring Billy here. He'd have to swallow his pride, but Billy was worth it. He could find more to do around her compound, find some way to work off the cost.

The cost of a human life.

Who was he kidding? There was no way she'd do him a favor. Not after the way he'd been acting. Morose and moody, reluctant to screw her, pretending she didn't have the hottest body on this god-forsaken planet. Pretending disinterest when she gave him free access to that delectable body. Acting sullen after she'd driven him to a mind-blowing orgasm.

So she only wanted him for sex. Oh, big hardship there. It beat the hell out of hard labor on the plantation. If he was smart, he'd go out of his way to show her a good time, use all the tricks he knew and make up a few more besides. But he wasn't smart. He was too damned angry to be smart.

He saw movement out of the corner of one eye and dropped the weight onto the crossbar. Shalawn. Exactly the person he wanted to find him sweaty and bare-chested. Not.

She leaned on a nearby pole while he sat up and pulled on his shirt. "You need not dress for my presence," she said.

Great, just what he needed.

She'd closed the door. Maybe he could get her out before Merko caught him alone with her for the second day in a row. "We probably only have a minute before Merko comes to check on me."

She looked worried. "Has he been watching you closely?"

"I'm not sure."

"You must be cautious. Merko is sharp of mind."

He shrugged. "I have nothing to be cautious about."

She tilted her head a little to the side, as though she was assessing him. "Do you desire to leave my sister's household?"

Sounded like a loaded question. "I wish to live in freedom. As any slave would."

"Would you risk your life for freedom?"

"Yes." Although he wasn't willing to risk Billy's life.

"I can see that you live in freedom."

Who was she kidding? "An Earther can't be free on your world."

She looked surprised. "Have you not learned? There are small encampments of freed Earthers scattered throughout the remote provinces."

"There are?"

"Assuredly."

"How were these people set free?"

"Some have grown feeble and are sent to the encampments as pensioners. Sometimes a slave's owner comes to disapprove of slavery and frees the worker in restitution."

He'd never heard of this, not in all his years on this planet.

"A few of my people have joined them," she continued. "People who oppose slavery. Rebels."

"And you would have Rigah free me to live in one of these camps." Not likely. Not the Rigah he knew.

"Rigah? Free you? No." She leaned closer. "I would see you escape and find a rebel encampment."

So she was offering him freedom after all. But he didn't know the catch. "And in return? What do I do for you?"

She smiled a little cat-like smile and held out one hand. In it, she held a small, black box about the size of a cassette tape. "Take this."

He reached out and she dropped the box into his hand. It weighed more than he'd expected, and there was a row of buttons on the top. "What is it?"

She seemed shocked by his question. After a quick glance at the closed door, she leaned closer. "A disrupter," she whispered.

A disrupter. He'd never seen one. They hadn't used them on the plantation. From all accounts they were outrageously expensive, and besides, technology was kept under government control on Prendara.

She reached for it impatiently. "Here, give it to me."

He did.

"You aim it like this." She held it out toward a treadmill. "This button activates the charge." She pointed to a small red button, the only red button on the thing. "Your thumb fires by pressing this white button."

He nodded.

She handed it back to him. "Keep it well concealed," she said. "You will leave the household by the western gate. The guards there will expect you and allow you to pass."

He didn't trust her. Not by a long shot. "Why would you help me?"

She smiled again, that coy little smile that unnerved him. "You are to help me, as well."

"Help you? How?"

"Must I speak plain?"

He nodded.

She glanced at the door again, then back into his eyes. "You will fire the disrupter at my sister's heart," she said.

Kill Rigah? Could he do it? It was a chance to get free, but what kind of freedom would he have without Billy? Then again, if Rigah were dead, there wouldn't be anyone to follow him to

Billy. She wouldn't have bothered to mention a small slave child to anyone. Not even Merko.

"Decide now, Earther. Either live in freedom or be my sister's tame little whore." She paused. "Until she tires of you and gives you to another owner."

Give him to another? God, he'd never thought of that. She might not let him go at all—she might just hand him over to someone else. Someone who'd take him even farther from Billy.

He slid the disrupter into his pocket. "I'll do it."

* * *

He walked to the window, turned, and headed back toward the shelves. Pacing. He was pacing like a caged animal.

The disrupter was hidden under the pallet on his bed. There weren't that many other hiding places, and he didn't want to risk leaving it in another room.

Could he really do this? It was the only way to get free, to make something out of his life. He could go grab Billy from the plantation and they could live with other Earthers. Maybe even speak English again.

But he didn't trust Shalawn, not one bit. All she cared about was getting rid of Rigah. If he died trying to escape, the only person who knew about her plot would be permanently silenced. She could easily arrange it so the guards at the west entrance shot him on sight.

But it was the only way. Even if he convinced Rigah to bring Billy here, they'd still be slaves. And when Rigah got bored with him, they'd end up doing hard labor again. If not worse. She'd *discard* them.

He'd killed people during the war—people who'd been trying to kill him. He'd never killed anyone in cold blood. He could do it. He had no choice. He just had to psyche himself up for it.

Rigah would be here any minute. He reached under the pallet, and his hand froze when he touched the cold metal of the weapon.

Wait a minute. Maybe he should play the game according to his own rules. He was already Rigah's puppet—he didn't have to be Shalawn's, too. Maybe he should play it smart for once in his sorry life.

First things first. He had to convince Rigah to bring Billy here. If Billy was here, Jason could escape without going to the plantation to get him. And if he wasn't going to the plantation, Rigah wouldn't be able to find him. He wouldn't have to kill her before he escaped. He could use the disrupter to get past the guards. But if she got in his way, the disrupter would help him get past her.

A knock came from the door. Rigah. During supper she'd told him to expect her, as if she didn't come to him every night. But tonight she was in for a treat. Tonight he'd do his damnedest to please her. He'd make her scream until she tore the paint off of the walls. Pleasing her well might convince her to bring Billy here.

He stood up quickly. "Come in."

She smiled at him as she walked in. Lord, she looked sexy. Her nightgown was baby blue. It barely hit her thighs and it shimmered as she walked to the table. Her hands were full. She dropped the stuff on the table.

He stood next to her, looking down at a large, flat device with a screen on it and a small box. "What are these?"

She sat down and motioned for him to sit next to her. Then she picked up the device. "This is a reading panel." She pressed a green button and it flickered on. "Can you read?"

He nodded. Not well, but he could.

"Touch here to scan the index." She showed him a simple alphabetic menu. "You have access to all of the literature in the central library. Also to proclamations and reports of current events, if political matters are of interest to you."

Wow. He could study this planet without ever asking her a thing. Without ever telling her that he'd been a geologist on Earth. "Why are you giving me this?"

She lifted one shoulder in a delicate shrug. "I thought you would enjoy it."

God. She was being nice to him. That did it. He couldn't kill her. He'd get her to bring Billy here, then he'd escape.

What was the right expression? Even after three years, her language was still strange to him. "My thanks to you," he said. He knew he'd said it wrong. He'd look it up in the library later. On this fancy reading panel.

She picked up the small box and handed it to him. It felt warm, like wood. The lid was hinged. Inside, he saw a bright picture. The King of Hearts. He tilted the box and a whole deck of cards fell into his palm. Brand new. "Where did you get these?"

"I had your Earth cards duplicated."

This was the woman who'd made him a whore? "I don't know what to say. Thanks to you, again."

She leaned back in her chair and studied his face. He looked away, shuffling the cards just for something to do. They were almost the perfect thickness. When he glanced up, she was still staring at him. "Why, Rigah?"

She tilted her head slightly, as if seriously considering her answer. "I would see you content, Jason."

Content, not happy. Did she know there was a difference? "And it's easy to give me material things." Oops. That sounded shitty. He didn't want to piss her off.

She frowned a little. "What would you have instead?"

He glanced down at the cards. Would it be too obvious to mention Billy? He should take her to bed first, bring it up in the afterglow. After he'd given her three or four orgasms. "Dignity," he answered. "Freedom." Neither of which she would give him.

She was silent for a moment. "The boy," she said suddenly, startling him. "He is your son?"

Would it be better or worse to say yes? She might feel bad about splitting up a father and son. But that would make her more likely to threaten Billy, too. Hell, he'd just tell her the truth. "He's my sister's child."

"I see."

Did she really see? How could she, when she didn't even love her own sister? She didn't even think love existed. "He's all I have."

"You have your life."

True. Life as a slave. "Sometimes that doesn't seem like much."

"It is all that any of us truly has."

He frowned. "You can't honestly believe that. You're a wealthy woman. You have power."

"Material goods, power..." She waved a hand dismissively. "All of this can be taken away. There have been dozens of bloody revolutions in the history of this world."

"As with any world," he replied. "But you are among the privileged few. You are second in power only to your mother." And Shalawn was third in line. The sister who wanted her dead. No wonder they didn't love each other.

"My succession is not guaranteed," she said, as if she'd read his mind. "I am Leader Elect by the grace of my mother." Her gaze shifted from his face to the table. "My mother is not in best health. She has been contemplating which of her daughters will lead after her death."

Shalawn as leader. Now there would be a government rife with pettiness and corruption. If their mother had any sense, Shalawn's only chance of taking over was to get rid of Rigah. "I can't imagine anyone thinking that Shalawn would make a better Leader than you."

She smiled, a small little smile. "You are a loyal man."

You bet. So loyal he had a disrupter hidden under his bed, just waiting for a chance to aim it at her heart. So loyal he was about to use sex to manipulate her. But she still didn't understand this basic difference between them. The difference between slavery and freedom. "Even if you lose your position, you will have a great deal more than I do."

"I will have my life," she answered. "As you have yours."

"That's hardly the same as being a slave."

She looked as if she didn't understand him. Did she really not see his point? "A slave's life is not his own," he said softly. "You control my life, Rigah. You could sell me to another, at any moment. You could command my death in an instant. Just as you command my body."

She reached out and brushed her fingers through his hair. Here it came, the move to the bed. She'd have his shirt off in a minute. For once, he wouldn't resent it. He'd give her the best night of her life. A night that would make her forget every other man she'd ever had. He leaned closer.

She stood up. "I will not command anything of you tonight, Jason. Sleep in peace."

She was gone before he could say a word.

Great. She was bored with him already.

Chapter Seven

Rigah didn't show up in the dining chamber for breakfast. Jason roamed the corridors, even ventured outside, looked briefly in the other buildings, but no Rigah. If he didn't know better, he'd think she was avoiding him. But he wasn't important enough to her for that.

He'd really blown it last night. Made her feel sorry for him. Way to turn a woman on. She'd probably found another man for the night. No. No, he'd seen no evidence that she treated anyone else with the same possessiveness that she showed toward him. He was the one she owned, the one she dressed up like a model in the International Male catalog.

And as soon as he found her, he was going to take her into a dark corner of this labyrinth and kiss her senseless. Maybe she'd drag him off to bed in the middle of the day. He could get an early start on his campaign to please her until her eyes crossed. Until she agreed to bring Billy here.

It was early for the midday meal, but he headed to the dining chamber anyway. If Rigah showed up early, he didn't want to miss her.

He pushed open the door and went in. Only Merko was there. It figured. He sat at the table, across and a few chairs down from Merko, and dished out a little food for himself, even though he wasn't hungry. Some kind of stew today, with the ubiquitous grain on the side. He'd never noticed, but the bowls had some kind of elaborate wiring around the outside, wiring so fine it looked like decoration. Must be what kept the food warm.

He forced himself to wait a minute. Then two. Then he spoke. "Merko?"

The other man looked up, seeming annoyed as usual. He didn't say a thing, just sat there staring expectantly.

"I was wondering if I could talk to *Senhab* Rigah for a minute."

"No," Merko answered, turning back to his food.

What a helpful guy. Jason really didn't want to wait until tonight to start his seduction program. "Is she busy today? Maybe you could tell her that I'd like to see her."

"No. She is not here."

"When will..." He stopped. Best to be polite. "Can you please tell me when she will return?"

"She did not specify. Perhaps tomorrow."

Oh, well. At least he had another night to himself. He could finish the book he'd started reading. Somehow the thought didn't sound appealing. He'd much rather be working on getting Billy here.

She'd left without telling him. Not that he really expected her to share her schedule with him, but this just underscored how badly he'd botched things. She was already bored with him. And no wonder—he hadn't been the sex toy of her dreams lately. Nowhere near it. Maybe she'd pick up some other lucky bastard by the side of the road and give him a thrill. He scowled.

His jaw ached. Damn, he was grinding his teeth. And his hands were clenched. Almost as if he was...no. No, he was not jealous. No way. No how. He didn't care if she fucked the entire male population of this planet. As insatiable as she was, she probably already had.

Well, she'd be back soon enough, and he'd show her that he could still rock her world, that he hadn't even scratched the surface of how many ways he could excite her. *Look, master, I've learned some new tricks.* Hey, getting Billy was worth sacrificing his pride.

* * *

Rigah took the hovercraft. It was fast and sleek, not sluggish like the conveyance. Of course, the conveyance could hold more people, could carry a whole battalion to protect her. But she had no need of a battalion this day, only Darnal, her favorite attendant. Darnal was a loyal woman. She would not gossip about the Leader Elect's private business, and for that Rigah was grateful. None need know what transpired here today. She would tell Merko later, when it was too late for him to convince her she was being unwise.

It was full night when they arrived. She found the owner's lodge easily enough and led Darnal inside. The owner was a thick, sweaty man and his breathing wheezed through his mouth.

He looked up at her entrance, then prostrated himself on the floor in an antiquated gesture. "*Senhab* Rigah," he said. "How might I serve you?"

No doubt he expected another broad reward for his service. She had paid a hefty price for Jason. "Rise," she said.

He lifted his bulk from the floor and stood before her, keeping his gaze to the ground. Very respectful.

"You have another Earther slave that I wish to acquire for my household," she said.

"Of course." He all but leered. "There are many fine, strong men for you to choose among."

What a crude, coarse man. "The Earther I seek is a small boy child, perhaps eight years aged. He is called Billy."

"As you wish," he said. "I will return with the child in a moment."

He likely thought she wanted the boy for some perversion. She had seen the curiosity in his eyes, the titillation. Vulgar man. What a trespass, that such a man had beaten Jason, had tried to humble his arrogant spirit.

Perhaps his arrogance would be tempered when he saw the boy. Perhaps he would be content. She had granted him this small favor—a favor, not a material thing—and he would feel tremendous gratitude toward her. She would visit his chamber, and he would be eager to please her, to show his appreciation. She would not sleep alone tomorrow. Nor for many nights after.

The owner returned, dragging a child by the collar of his filthy shirt. She reached down and took the boy's chin in her hand. He looked half asleep, yet he glared at her with angry eyes. By the gods, she could not recall if this was the same child she had first seen with Jason. "Do you remember me?" she asked.

He said nothing. He jerked his head, pulling his chin out of her hand.

The owner's meaty fist swung, clouting the side of the boy's face. He stumbled, but steadied himself without dropping his balance. No doubt he was used to such treatment. A fall might be met with a vicious kick, as she had learned in combat training.

She caught the man's fist before he could swing again. "I will not take the boy if you damage him," she said.

He bowed his head. "Forgive me."

This time, she would not touch the moody child. "Do you remember me?" she asked again.

He ignored her.

"Answer me," she commanded.

The child stepped back, ducking his chin even closer to his chest. He cowered against the wall, quivering.

"*Senhab*," Darnal said softly behind her. "If you will allow me?"

Perhaps he would speak more easily to a servant. She waved Darnal forward.

Darnal dropped to her knees before the child, low enough that she could look up into his downcast face. Inconceivable. Never had Rigah seen anyone kneel before a slave, let alone a slave child. Yet Darnal made the action seem natural. Almost tender.

"My name is Darnal." She spoke softly, gentle as a whisper. "How are you called?"

He mumbled an answer that Rigah could not hear.

"How many years aged are you?"

"Nine," the boy whispered.

"My son is the same," Darnal said. Inconsequential words, meaningless, yet the boy responded to her. "Do you recall the woman who stands above us?"

He nodded, but did not look up.

He recognized her. He must be the nephew Jason so valued. Rigah turned to the owner. "You may settle your payment with my attendant. Reasonable payment," she warned.

She motioned for the child to follow her. "Come with me."

He drew back, glancing nervously from the owner to her. Never had a child been frightened of her. She frowned. He scooted to Darnal where she knelt on the floor, pressing up against her side.

Darnal put one arm across his back. "Follow my mistress. She will not harm you."

He looked up at Darnal. "Will you come with me?"

She smiled at him. "In a moment. Go now."

Rigah walked outside with the boy following like a pale shadow. Only a thin tuaari light broke the darkness. She could barely see the outline of the hovercraft in the distance. She reached down for his hand to lead him, but he pulled away.

Were all Earthers so full of anger? Even the small ones? She sighed. Had she received beatings at the hands of that imbecilic owner, she would be angry as well. No wonder the slaves in the Western Quarter had rioted. And they had not been the first.

"Your name is Billy, is it not?"

He nodded.

He would answer her with his voice. "Is it?"

"Yes."

How fiercely he spoke. "Why are you angry?"

He looked up at her then, small eyes narrowed, lips scowling. "You took my Uncle Jay away."

He drew back suddenly, ducking his head as if she would strike him. Beaten regularly, dragged out of his bed, missing his only relation...he must be terrified, and anger was his defense. She knew little of children, but she knew this technique.

She bent over until her eyes were level with his, but he looked away. "Do not be frightened."

"I'm not."

Clearly lying. She moved to stand in front of him, but he turned away again. "My name is Rigah."

He shrugged, his thin little back twisting even farther away from her. "I want to stay with Darnal."

Ordering him would have little effect, as she had seen. Perhaps she could tempt him. "You would like to see your uncle, would you not?"

He looked at her then, through wary eyes. Eyes so like Jason's, she should have recognized him at once. "Yes."

"I will take you to him."

"Really?" He sounded suspicious.

"Yes." She carefully laid her hand on the child's back. He didn't move away. "Your uncle speaks of you constantly." Untrue, but it would help the child trust her. And no doubt Jason thought of him often enough, though he did not speak of the boy. At least not to her.

"Is he all right?"

As if she would mistreat him. "Assuredly. We best leave now, to see him all the sooner."

She led him toward the waiting hovercraft. Halfway to the craft lot, she stopped. She would not take him away as thoughtlessly as she had Jason. "Is there anyone you wish to see? To bid farewell?"

He shook his head.

"Do you have any possessions?"

He nodded.

"Very well. You may gather them."

He scampered off toward the huts, leaving her to follow. It would be a small delay and would calm the child. She could wait a few minutes longer before viewing Jason's gratitude. Before enjoying his willing body.

* * *

Jason couldn't concentrate on the book. Every other minute he had to look up a word. At least he'd figured out how to use the electronic dictionary. And his vocabulary was growing, not that he'd have much use for it in a colony of Earthers.

The sun was about to set and Rigah still hadn't returned. He'd taken the reading panel to the dining chamber so he'd be near the main entrance. He wanted to hear her arrival. She'd been gone for two whole days.

Voices came from beyond the doorway. Had she brought someone home with her? A new playmate? Maybe he could still get another chance to screw her before she discarded him.

Maybe he'd tear her new guy apart with his bare hands.

He stood up. Before he could take a step, a small figure ran into the room. "Uncle Jay!"

God, it couldn't be. Billy hurtled himself against Jason's legs and held on tight.

"Billy!" He stooped down and lifted his nephew into his arms, cuddling him like a baby. "How did you get here?"

"Rigah and Darnal brought me," Billy said, his voice muffled against Jason's shoulder. "I got to ride in a hovercraft!"

He held the small body tighter, swung him around in slow circles. "Did you get dizzy?"

Billy laughed. "No. But I am now."

He set the boy on his feet and crouched down next to him. An ugly bruise marked one cheekbone. He knew better than to ask about it. Asking always made him want to kill something. "Look at you. You've grown taller."

"Nuh-uh." He punched Jason lightly on the shoulder. "I missed you, Uncle Jay."

He kissed the top of Billy's head. "I missed you, too, sport. Have you been all right?"

"Yeah. I only got hit once. I lost my baseball, though."

Thank God nothing worse had happened to him. "I have it."

Billy's face lit up like he'd just gotten a new bike for Christmas. "You do?"

"Yes. Let's go play catch."

He took Billy's small hand and led him to his room, half listening to his chatter about the weird house.

Unbelievable. Rigah had brought his nephew here, even though he hadn't exactly been a sex stud lately. He'd never understand women. Especially this woman. She claimed to have no sentiment, no emotions, but only a woman with feelings would give him a gift like this.

And now he could escape. After he gave Rigah a night to remember. A night to make sure she regretted losing him.

Chapter Eight

Rigah took a leisurely shower. After a long evening of policy discussions and debates, she relished the time alone. Although she was eager to see Jason, she would not rush to his chamber. No doubt he would be with the boy most of the night. And she did not wish to appear desperately eager to collect her reward for bringing Billy to him.

The warm air of the sonic shower felt luxurious against her skin. As hot as Jason's flesh. Perhaps she would hurry to his chamber after all.

She went into her sleeping chamber and took a clean nightgown from the cabinet. A knock sounded. Probably Merko, with another policy comment that he had neglected to mention earlier. She slipped the gown over her head, then called out, "Enter."

Jason stood in the doorway, looking impossibly fine in a golden-brown shirt that reflected in his eyes. What a beautiful sight.

"I hope I'm not disturbing you?" His deep voice lifted into a question at the end.

Disturbing her? Indeed he was, but not in the manner he spoke of. "Not at all. Enter."

She waved him toward the conversation nook, a group of chairs and a couch near the large corner windows. He sat on the small couch. She took a seat next to him, facing him with one leg tucked under her.

"I didn't see you at supper," he said.

Had he missed her? How very like an Earther. "I dined in the strategy chamber. When I travel, much work must be done upon my return."

He smiled and reached out to take her hand. His skin always felt so hot against hers. "Thank you for traveling on my account, Rigah."

She returned the smile. He was so handsome it was easy to smile at him. Especially when he spoke sweetly. He'd voiced few sweet words to her. "You are most welcome. Is the child comfortable?"

He nodded. "He's sleeping already." He raised an eyebrow. "His chamber is one level below this. Even though there's an empty chamber right next to mine."

She felt a tinge of heat in her cheeks. "I thought it wise to have him sleep a small distance away."

"Very wise." He slid a little closer and his hand released hers and moved to the back of her neck, stroking gently under her hair. So very gently. "There may be a lot of noise on this level soon."

His teasing caused her heat to rise. "Assuredly," she said.

"We wouldn't want him to hear…us." His eyes gleamed.

She knew his thought—that it was she who would be heard, she who always cried out in passion. "You are often loud," she said. Let him contradict her.

His lips compressed, as if he stifled a grin. What a lush, mobile mouth. Soon, very soon, she would kiss him.

"One of my many faults," he replied.

So now he sought compliments? She would resist. "Indeed it is."

He smiled outright. "I have another fault." His tone was soft, beguiling.

"Of what fault do you speak?"

He leaned closer, so close his chest almost touched her breasts. His head came alongside hers, his hair brushing against her cheek. His breath, hot and moist, rushed over her ear. "I complain a lot," he whispered, as if confiding a dark secret. Then he sat back, withdrawing his heat, though his hand still cupped her neck.

No man had ever teased her in this warm, seductive manner. "Would you complain of something now?"

He nodded. "My bed was cold last night."

She inched closer and laid her hands on his forearms. "You feel warm enough now."

His thumb stroked gently across her jaw, just under her ear. "I feel warm when I touch you." He moved his hand across her collarbone, over her shoulder and down her arm in a long, smooth caress. She shivered and closed her eyes. She could not allow him to see her need. Without even a kiss, with only a simple caress, heat flowed within her. She wanted him.

But she would not order him tonight. Tonight she would grant him another favor. Tonight she would let him lead her, guide her, take her. At his own pace.

And then, if they had strength remaining, she would repay the favor in kind.

He lifted her hand and she felt his lips on her palm, felt his hot breath rush over her skin. "You bathed tonight," he said softly. The vibrations from his deep voice made her hand tingle.

She opened her eyes, met his gaze. "Yes."

"I plan to make you dirty again. Very dirty."

"Dirty?"

He nodded. "Sweaty." His tongue snaked out, licked warm wetness against her knuckle. "And wet."

He pulled a finger into his mouth and sucked on it. The heat, the wetness, made her draw a sharp breath. He smiled wickedly when he finished. "You'll need to bathe again in the morning."

She would tease him as well. She leaned over and kissed his forearm, then dotted his skin with her tongue. "As will you."

"We can bathe together," he suggested. "You could wash my...back."

She could not resist. She moved closer to him until she could reach his firm ass with one hand. She squeezed gently. "You have a very comely back."

He grinned. "You noticed."

"I am ever observant."

She moved her hand to his thigh and he covered it with his own. Close, so close, to his root. Was he straining at his pants, as she was flowing? She lowered her gaze to view, but his forearm was in the way.

"Looking for something?" His eyes danced with amusement.

"No," she lied.

His humor faded. He reached up and tucked a strand of her hair behind one ear, then cupped the side of her neck in his warm hand. "You're very beautiful, Rigah."

Many had said so before him, but none with such wonderment. Or such patent honesty. "Thank you."

"Thank you for letting me touch you." He stroked down her arm, then back up to her neck. "Thank you for taking me from the fields. Thank you for bringing my nephew here."

Ah. So it was the favors he appreciated. She need only appeal to his sentiment to keep him agreeable. "You are content, then?"

"Content? No."

What? He could not mean it. She opened her mouth to speak, but he laid a finger across her lips, stopping her.

"I'll be content when you're lying next to me, drowsy and satisfied." He brought her hand to his mouth and his tongue dabbed her palm. Her fingers twitched. "When I've bathed every measure of your skin with my tongue. When your scent is on my fingers." He rubbed her fingertips across his lips, teasing her with damp warmth. "When your scent is on my lips."

He cradled her face in his hands, holding her still as he moved closer. She closed her eyes, waiting, waiting.

He kissed her. So soft, so warm. Passionate, yet tender. Seductive.

He deepened the kiss slowly, gradually, until their tongues were at play in each other's mouths. His arms came around her, lifting her, settling her in his lap. She broke the kiss, gasping for air, and felt his lips move over her neck, tasting and teasing. Such carnal lips. His hands, hot as a torch, branded her as they wandered over her back, her neck, her breast. She pressed against him, melting under his touch.

She found the bottom of his shirt and her hands slid underneath it to graze his hot, hot skin. She pulled away to tug it off. Ah, his chest glowed in the warm light. She smoothed her hands over his glorious flesh, let his sparse hair tickle her palms.

His lips quirked up. "You look hungry."

Teasing again. "Assuredly." She leaned forward to suckle on a flat nipple. His groan rewarded her.

His hand slid up her thigh, under her gown, stopping before he reached her nest. Would he tease her to insanity? She raised her head and looked at him, to plead, but when their eyes met his hand found her sex, stroking, spreading her wet silk over her bud. She closed her eyes against the fire, and his hand stilled. Only when she looked at him did he begin again. Cruel man.

Looking into his eyes, so deep and golden, while his fingers played beneath her gown, between her legs…the intimacy stole her breath. He could see every need, every desire, written in her eyes. Just as she viewed the passion in his. He pressed inside her with one finger, then two, stretching her open. Her hips jerked a little, wanting to get closer, closer.

His hand left her, and she almost begged him to touch her again. But with his gaze still locked on her eyes, he brought his fingers to his mouth. His tongue came out and licked along one finger, then the other. Ah, that tongue. She longed to have more of it.

She took off her nightgown. Naked, she straddled his waist, sitting astride him with her sex open and vulnerable. He bent his head and captured a nipple in his mouth, suckling, biting gently, surrounding her with the heat of his strong arms.

He would tease her to death.

"I would have you now," she whispered.

He shook his head. "I would have you first."

He lifted her by the waist, slid out from under her, and knelt between her knees. His head dipped and she felt the brush of his warm mouth over her nest. Hot fingers gently opened her; his stealthy tongue darted knowingly, confidently. And before she could stop him, before she could even draw breath to speak, a startling climax burst over her, leaving her trembling and dazed.

He sat beside her and pulled her into his arms. Her head fell against his shoulder, and she laid her hand on his stomach. The muscles under her hand tensed, then relaxed. He must be wanting, yet he kissed the top of her head as though satiated. Unselfish man. Always rushing her pleasure, never his own.

She felt for his root, fondling him through the cloth of his pants. So hard. So hot. So full of need.

She, who had knelt before no one in her entire life, knelt at his feet. Her hands tugged at the waistband of his pants and he obediently lifted his hips from the couch so she could slide the garment off.

She hesitated, touching his root with a nervous hand. She had never done this before. Would he know her ignorant? But she wanted this, wanted to give him this pleasure. She bent her head and carefully took his root into her mouth, then suckled upon it.

He gasped and his hands cupped her face, holding her gently, feeling her mouth move upon him as she mimicked the rhythm of joining. She had never imagined the joy of this. The pleasure of feeling his pleasure. Every twitch of his muscles, every soft sound of need, was a gift to her. And by pleasing him, her own passion rekindled.

Soon, too soon, he pushed her away from him. "Bed," he said hoarsely. "Now."

He stood and lifted her, then settled her on the bed and came down beside her. She reached out for him. "Cover me, Jason."

"No." He pulled on her hip, turning her so that they lay face to face, pressed against each other. His eyes, heavy-lidded, mesmerizing, were a mere hand's width from her own. "We are equals in this."

Did he believe so? His voice was dark with need, as was her being. She would not argue with his statement. A challenge would delay their joining.

With one hand, he took her knee and pulled it over him, wrapping her leg over his thigh. His hips shifted, lifting, seeking. At last he found the mark and sank deep within her. Such fullness, such pressure. She drew a sharp breath and closed her eyes.

He kept his hand on her hip, pulling her toward him for each thrust, showing her his rhythm. He didn't moan, but his breathing was harsh and needful. She wrapped her arm around his waist, holding him, feeling him move within her. Feeling his desire...his desire for her.

"Rigah," he said, gasping. "Can you climax like this?"

She shook her head. "No matter. I will feel yours." And she meant it, by the gods. She would have his climax, would take his pleasure.

"I will feel yours. Again." He slid a hand between them. With his thumb, he found her bud, circled lightly against it. Too lightly.

"Say my name," he commanded.

A simple enough request. "Jason," she murmured.

His eyes glittered. He pressed that taunting thumb against her more firmly, stroked her bud more rapidly. "Now scream it."

She gasped, closing her eyes against the coiling passion. That insistent stroking, the hard pumping of his root... In mere moments, she trembled and shook with the force of a draining climax, pressing her lips against his shoulder to muffle her cry. And before she finished, he thrust deep inside her one last time, shuddering as he met his own release.

They panted together for long moments, still joined. His hand cupped the back of her head and she heard the rapid thump of his heartbeat against her ear.

"Thank you," she whispered. What demon had possessed her to say those words? His station was to please her. No thanks were necessary.

He kissed the top of her head and pulled her closer. "Thank *you*. Even though you didn't scream my name."

She smiled, still languid from sated passion. "It would not be prudent to satisfy your every whim."

A deep rumbling came from his chest. Laughter. He'd laughed. The sound had been rusty, as though he was out of practice. And it was infinitely precious. She hid her face against his chest.

His hand softly stroked her back. He held her ardently. He had never done so before. Not after his passion was spent. She blinked a few times. Her eyes felt suspiciously moist. Why did she feel this mix of tenderness and passion? This attachment?

Attachment? Oh, no. No, by the gods.

Yet truth would be truth, plain to see. She was well and surely attached to him.

Chapter Nine

The smell of mint woke Jason. He opened his gritty eyes and saw Rigah sitting up in bed, drinking from a steaming bowl.

She smiled down at him. "Good morning."

"Good morning." He stretched and yawned. His eyes were scratchy from lack of sleep, his body achy from the wild sex of the night before.

He'd never felt better. Wild sex was definitely the ticket.

He reached a hand out toward her bowl. "Will you share that tea?"

She pulled it further away. "That would be unwise. This is a female contraceptive."

He snatched his hand back.

She laughed, probably at the horrified look on his face. "I will signal for plain tea."

"Don't bother." It was too early to wake up, anyway. He laid a hand on her thigh and closed his eyes again.

"Poor Jason," she said. "I have drained your strength."

Rigah, teasing him? Would wonders never cease. He opened his eyes. "You're lucky you're holding that hot tea."

One eyebrow lifted in her most supercilious expression. She set the bowl down on the bedside table. "And if I was not?"

"If you were not..." He reached out stealthily under the covers and tickled her side.

She shrieked with laughter and slapped his hand away. "Stop!"

He stopped and stroked softly along her stomach. "As you wish."

She grabbed his hand through the covers, holding him still. "So agreeable. Should I trust you?"

No, she shouldn't. But he couldn't tell her that. Not even teasingly. He forced a smile. "As always."

She smiled back, then picked up the bowl and took another sip of tea. After she set down the bowl, she turned to him with a look he'd come to recognize. God, the woman was insatiable. And he was willing, but his flesh was weak. After a night like that, he'd need some help getting started.

Maybe she'd be willing to provide that help. "Rigah..." He broke off, unsure of the words to use. Unsure of her reaction.

Her fingers wandered across his chest. "Hmm?"

"Would you tell me something?"

Her brows furrowed. "What do you wish to know?"

He'd go for the gold. Might as well start with his number one fantasy. "Have you ever lain with a woman?"

"Of course."

Of course? "Are such pairings common on Prendara?"

She shrugged. "They are neither common nor uncommon. Young people are encouraged to experiment before they select a mate. To learn their true preferences. I was no different."

He stroked her breasts idly. "Would you tell me about it?"

"Why?"

How could she be so experienced, yet know so little about the workings of a man's sexual mind? "Because imagining you with another woman excites me."

"As you wish." She slid lower on the bed, until they were face to face. "She was an advisor to my mother."

Rigah and an older woman? He'd never have guessed. "How did she approach you?"

Her eyes widened in surprise. "I approached her, of course. She would not have presumed to touch me otherwise."

Now that he could believe. "Tell me more."

She smiled, a thoughtful little smile. "Hetna preferred women to men. This was well known. I merely told her that I was curious. That I wished to affirm my true inclination. She was eager to assist me."

Who wouldn't be? Rigah had to be the sexiest woman on this entire planet. And no doubt this Hetna had received additional privileges after she had sex with the boss's daughter.

"She had hoped for many years that I would approach her," Rigah continued. "We spent several spans in bed together."

His cock stirred at the thought of Rigah with another woman. Of a woman's soft hands on her lush breasts. "What did you do?"

"We pleasured each other."

She sounded so prosaic that he almost laughed. Clearly, he'd have to prod her for the details. "Will you tell me more?"

"As you wish. She could see that I was nervous."

Nervous? Rigah? She must have been young. Young and uncertain.

"So she began very slowly," she went on. "Very cautiously. She touched my neck first." She ran her fingers over the side of her neck, as if remembering. "It was many minutes before she kissed me. And half a span before we disrobed." Her eyes met his. "Does this truly excite you?"

He took her hand and put it on his semi-hard cock. "Yes."

She smiled and stroked his cock. "What else would excite you?"

He swallowed. "Seeing you touch yourself while you tell me more."

She let go of his cock. With both hands, she fondled her breasts. "She stroked my body slowly. Carefully. As if she was afraid of my reaction." Her smile turned languid. "She grazed my breasts for a long time. I was wet and eager before she moved lower." She licked her finger and rubbed it across one nipple, as she had that first day in the conveyance. His gaze fixed on that wet fingertip, that hard nipple.

"When she finally reached my nest, I was gushing." Her hands ran over her chest, her shoulders, back down to her stomach.

"Then what?" His voice came out hoarse.

"She ate at my nest for greater than a span." She sighed. "I have never climaxed so often in such a short time."

Wow. "But you decided you preferred men?"

She nodded. "I prefer the strength of a man." She moved her hand from her breast and stroked his chest. "I prefer the breadth of a man's chest to the softness of a woman's. And when it came time to pleasure her in turn, I found little enjoyment in the act."

"How did you…" What word had she used? He was so hot, his brain wasn't functioning at full capacity. "How did you pleasure her?"

"I used my fingers upon her." She kicked off the blankets, reached between her legs and moved her hand slowly. Her gaze met his, hot and yearning. She wanted him as much as he wanted her. "And I ate at her nest," she added.

His imagination went wild, picturing those angelic blonde curls of hers between another woman's legs. He was stiff as a board now.

He shifted so that he was above her, leaning over her, his mouth hovering an inch above one of her breasts. "Did she suckle at your breasts?"

"Yes."

He drew her nipple deep into his mouth and sucked hard, using lips and tongue and teeth. She grabbed his head with one hand, holding him there, while her other hand found his cock and pumped with a tight fist.

He'd go off like a rocket if she kept that up. He pulled away, forcing her to relinquish his cock, and moved down the bed until his head was above her thighs. "Did she eat at your nest like this?"

"No."

"No?"

She pushed him to his back, then straddled his chest, kneeling across his neck. Slowly, she inched up toward his face.

He slid down until her pussy was right over his mouth and started licking for all he was worth.

She moaned, cried out, and shunted her hips over his face, showing him exactly what she needed. Her juice drenched his chin. God, he'd love to have her suck his cock at the same time. Would she do it? Only one way to find out.

He slid out from under her, then turned around so her head was level with his thighs. He pulled her to her side, facing him head to feet in a sixty-nine. Maybe she'd get the idea.

He pressed his mouth to her cunt again, sucking at her clit, holding her ass still so she couldn't move away. Her hand cupped his balls; her hair tickled his legs. And then he felt the moist heat of her breath on his thighs, the wet wonder of her mouth sucking his cock. Miracle of miracles.

He sucked faster, harder, the way he knew she liked it. He imagined her in this position with another woman. Imagined her breasts brushing another woman's stomach, just like they were brushing his...her mouth suckling a clit, just like she was sucking his cock. He imagined her moaning like this, sending these same vibrations of ecstasy through another woman's cunt. God, he was going to come any minute.

Suddenly Rigah jerked and spasmed, crying out around his cock, and the sexy sound, the shaking of her breasts against him, were more than he could bear. He gave a strangled cry of his own, lifting his hips to force his cock deeper as he came, and came, and came, shooting his passion into the heat of her mouth.

He collapsed into the bed, every muscle in his body turning to pudding.

God, what had he just done? Too late to worry about it now. Even if she punished him for coming in her mouth, it had been worth it. But when she released him, he felt her tongue lapping at his limp cock, licking him clean. So softly, so gently, he could almost imagine she cared for him. He could almost imagine she loved him.

But she didn't believe in love.

And he did.

No. Hell, no. He didn't love her. Not even close.

He was just grateful to her. Grateful that she'd brought Billy to him. Grateful that she'd sucked his cock. After all those long celibate years, he'd feel this way about any woman who gave him a blowjob.

When she finally lifted herself away from him, she avoided his gaze, turning to sit on the side of the bed, reaching out for her bowl, draining the last of her tea. Was that a blush on her cheeks? He'd tease any other woman about it. But not this woman.

He pulled the tangled blankets over his body and turned on his side, yawning. She'd worn him out. Again.

She still had her back to him.

"I'm glad you prefer men," he said. Truer words had never been spoken.

She faced him then, and her smile was his reward. "I am glad of that, as well."

"Whatever happened to Hetna?"

She blushed a little. "She is Chief Arbiter of a ward in the Northeastern Province."

What the hell? He must have looked puzzled, because she added, "My mother promoted her."

He laughed. "No wonder, after she pleasured you so well."

She gave him a look of mock disdain. "She was promoted for her political astuteness. Nothing more."

"Oh, certainly. Very *astute* of her to give the Leader Elect such a rousing experience."

She smiled wide. "You were roused by that experience as well."

He laughed again. Too bad he didn't know how to say *touché* in Prendarian. "Indeed," he said instead.

She bent down and kissed him, a soft, passionless kiss. A strange kiss. Strange for her, at any rate. He hadn't known she was capable of this basic affection, this need to simply touch.

When she moved back, she looked regretful. "The sun broke night many spans ago. I must work. You may rest here as long as you wish." She rose from the bed and went into the bathing area.

He closed his eyes. He'd wait until she left before getting up. If she thought he was sleeping, she wouldn't check on him too soon.

He needed privacy today. He had to figure out what to do about Shalawn. How to find a rebel encampment. How to escape from the grounds.

The one thing he didn't have to worry about was how to get back in Rigah's good graces. After last night and this morning, there was no way she was bored with him.

And all that wondrous sex had bought him some time. Time to make a plan.

* * *

Rigah forced herself to read the communication for the third time, making sure the text was complete before she signed. Her brain functioned poorly this day. And no wonder, with the small amount of sleep she'd had. Her body felt tender. As tender as her feelings.

She must protect herself from this attachment. No foolish sentiments would alter her decisions, affect her judgment. Her emotions would be governed, as always. Perhaps she would go to him more often, enjoy the fullness of her attachment by reveling in his touch. Perhaps this attachment would resolve itself by more frequent contact. Perhaps she would go to him now, with daylight still upon them. His lips would soothe her tender flesh.

Merko came in, rushing to her desk. "*Senhab.*" He bowed his head. "A most urgent matter has arisen. It involves the Earther slave."

"Jason?"

He gave a curt nod.

"Is he injured?"

"No." Merko sounded puzzled. Her concern must seem strange.

"What is the matter?"

Merko shifted his balance from foot to foot, as he did when he was deeply troubled. "He had a weapon hidden in his chamber."

"A weapon?"

He looked at her gravely. "A disrupter."

A lethal weapon. Even loyal servants of her race would be imprisoned for holding such a weapon in her household. By the gods, how could Jason obtain such a thing? How could he conceal it? "Where was the disrupter found?"

"Under the pallet of his bed."

The bed she had lain upon, with his body hot and yearning against hers. He could have killed her in the aftermath of passion. Killed her as she slept. He may yet plan to do so. She swallowed. "Who found it?"

"A servant. He was changing the bed coverings."

"It may not have been Jason's."

Merko's mouth dropped open for an instant. "Forgive me, *Senhab*. But who would put such a dangerous weapon in the chamber of an Earther?"

No one would. Merko spoke wisdom. As he had from the beginning. The servant would have no reason to lie. Her staff was loyal, had been in service to her family for generations. Foolishly, she had granted Jason the same trust.

His brooding, his teasing, his tenderness—all had been lies. Lies designed to relax her defenses. Devious, clever man. And she had fallen neatly into his plans, had granted him endless favors. Favors she would never have imagined. She had brought the boy to him. She had given him the freedom to roam her household, the freedom to take her body in whatever manner he wished. She had taken his root into her mouth. She had even taken his pleasure into her belly. She nearly gagged at the memory.

He had thanked her so tenderly for her favors, his voice deep with warmth. But in truth, he thanked her by planning betrayal. By planning murder.

"*Senhab?*"

She had forgotten Merko. He stood before her, worried, waiting for orders. "Where is the disrupter now?"

He reached into a pocket, brought forth the weapon, and laid it on the desk. She felt no desire to examine it closely. From where she sat, she could see the gels held a full charge. A deadly charge.

"Have the energy gels drained," she said. "Then return it quickly to his hiding place, before he discovers the absence."

"You would not have me confine him?"

"No," she answered. "I will deal with him myself. You need not be present."

"*Senhab*, I must protest. The Earther is a danger to you."

Always Merko would advise excessive caution. "You have searched his chamber?"

"Assuredly." He almost sounded affronted. "I have searched the household in whole. There are no other weapons outside the armaments building, and nothing is missing from it."

"Then he will not be a danger to me," she said.

"Allow me to confine him, so you may speak to him in absolute safety."

"His chamber will be safe enough. He will have no weapons. I shall guard against attack." She wanted him defenseless. Defenseless and alone with her. Oh, how she would savor his punishment.

"*Senhab,* please do not speak with him alone. The risk to your person—"

She raised a hand, and he stopped. "He will not harm me. I will confine him myself."

Merko grabbed the disrupter and clenched it in one hand. "You are Leader Elect. My duty is to protect you."

"Your duty is to obey me!" She stopped abruptly. Never had she raised her voice to Merko.

He bowed his head, but said nothing.

Merko was her loyal Primary. Her loyal friend. He did not deserve her anger. "You are correct," she said softly. "Your duty is to protect me. As you have always done."

He raised his head. "Though you will ever make my duty a challenge." His tone was resigned. The tone he used when he recognized her resolve. With a final bow, he left.

And now she would deal with the Earth man. How long before he planned to use the weapon? No matter. She dared not wait to see his attempt. She would strike while her anger was hot.

Yes, she would make him pay for his deception. And she would enjoy collecting his payment.

* * *

Jason set down the reading panel and rubbed his tired eyes. He hadn't had enough sleep last night, and he'd been reading for most of the day. He got up and put the panel on a shelf. Rigah would probably show up soon. After last night, she must be eager to see him. He didn't want her to catch him reading old news.

He sat back down at the table and laid out a game of solitaire with the new cards she'd given him. Might as well kill some time without straining his eyes too much.

At least Billy had been easy to entertain today. They'd spent hours in the library, with Billy studying the alphabet while Jason read old news reports. He'd searched for any reports of Earther encampments and transferred every matching article to his reading panel. So far, none of the dozens he'd read had given a location. But there were hundreds more on his panel to scour. There had to be clues somewhere. As soon as he found the location of a camp, he could start planning their escape.

The door opened and Rigah came in. She hadn't knocked, and she wore her uniform. She smiled, but her smile looked strained. Or maybe it was the uniform. She usually wore a sexy little nightgown when she came to see him this late.

She walked up behind him and laid her hands on his shoulders.

He looked up at her and the side of his head brushed her breast. "Good evening." He moved his head from side to side, letting his ear rub against her nipple.

She tugged on his shirt. "Stand up."

Sure. Why not? He stood up and turned to face her. Before he could get his arms around her, she pulled his shirt over his head and dropped it to the ground.

Two could play at this game. He reached for the fastenings of her shirt, but she brushed his hands away. She tugged on the waistband of his loose pants and they pooled around his ankles.

"On the bed," she said. Not quite an order, not with that curious little smile on her lips. He'd go along with it.

He stepped out of his pants and lay on his back on the bed. She walked over and sat down near his head, taking one hand in hers. Before he knew what hit him, she had some kind of band strapped to his wrist and he couldn't move his hand in any direction.

She had both of his hands tied down before he thought to fight back. He struggled, but his hands were locked down to the bed, his arms stretched out to each side.

"Do not resist," she said, still in that calm tone.

He relaxed. If this was some kinky bondage fantasy of hers, he was willing to participate. More than willing.

She gave his ankles the same treatment, then stood above him. Spread-eagled, naked—definitely a bondage fantasy. She dropped out of sight suddenly. She wasn't going to leave him like this, was she? He bit his lip. "Rigah?"

She came into view then, standing next to the bed. He heard something drop onto the bed, but couldn't see it. Her hands moved down the front of her shirt, opening it. "I have given you endless favors, have I not?"

From her way of thinking, she probably had. And he was grateful to her, especially for bringing Billy here. "Yes."

"I allow you to take my body in any fashion you desire," she continued. Her shirt hit the floor and she started on her pants. "Now *I* will take *you*." Her smile faded and her eyes grew cold. "I will take you as a master takes a slave."

This was no game. She looked furious. He swallowed.

She jumped on the bed like a tiger, naked, and straddled him. She bent over and brushed her breasts against his chest. Her nails ran over his biceps, over his pecs, scratching lightly, spreading lightning. His stupid cock stirred to life.

He closed his eyes. "Rigah, stop. Don't do this."

She looked at him. "Why should I not?"

"Because this isn't who you are."

Her eyes narrowed. "And who are you, Jason? Are you the man who spoke tender words to me in my bed? Or are you the man who would kill me with this?" She reached behind her, then whipped her hand around. She held a disrupter, pointed straight at his chest.

Oh, God. No wonder she was angry. "I wouldn't have killed you."

"Oh, of course I shall believe you."

She pressed the cold metal of the disrupter to his chest, but he felt her other hand cup his balls, stroke his cock. Damn it. His body had a mind of its own. His brain registered terror, but his sorry dick was hard as a rock. Hard as a rock and sweating with fear.

"Just as I believe you don't enjoy my hands on you," she said.

He had to talk her out of this. "You can force my body to respond. But if you take me against my will—"

He broke off as her hand swung up. She pressed the disrupter against his lips. "You have no will. You are a slave. You are *my* slave."

She tossed the disrupter onto the bed. "I will kill you later," she said casually, as if his life was of no consequence. "For now, I have better uses for your body."

Her head ducked low and he felt her nip at his chest. Marking him with hickeys again. A shudder ran through him. "Let me explain about the disrupter."

She raised her head and glared down at him. "Do not speak again. I will not be manipulated by your words."

"I know that you aren't this heartless. This brutal."

She raised an eyebrow. "Brutal? Brutal would be if I did not allow you to climax." She bent again and suckled on his neck. "Rest assured, I probably will. You deserve one last climax before you die." She bit down on the sensitive skin of his neck. A firm bite. A warning.

So this was the price for betraying her. Rape and execution. He kept his mouth shut, his teeth clenched, his eyes tightly closed. She crawled over him, touching, tasting, rubbing her nipples against his skin. She licked his ear and his muscles tensed, but he forced himself not to turn his head away. She kissed his jaw lightly, then moved on to his chest.

Thank God, she hadn't kissed his lips. He wanted to remember their last kiss, the soft kiss she'd given him in her bed that morning. The most affectionate kiss they had ever shared.

He'd die thinking of that kiss.

Her hand took his cock then, holding it steady as she pressed her body down onto him. She leaned forward, resting her hands on his chest, and rode him fiercely, gasping with each thrust. She felt so damned good. God, he was one twisted bastard. He couldn't move an inch, he was going to die, and he didn't care. As long as she didn't stop, didn't stop until he'd come deep, deep inside her.

Her hand cupped his face and he felt wetness spread over his cheek.

Oh, God. He was crying.

She froze. He didn't open his eyes, didn't want to see her enjoying the look of anguish on his face. He felt her fumbling with his wrist; suddenly one hand was free. Then the other.

He wrapped his arms around her. "Don't stop," he said. God help him, he meant it. He didn't care what kind of pervert this made him, he only knew that he had to come, had to come now, had to have this orgasm if it was the last thing he did. And it would be, if she killed him soon.

She gave a small gasp, then started moving again. His hands found her hips, urging her on, faster, faster, and his pelvis rose to meet her, over and over again, until she cried out and collapsed onto his chest. Almost there. Almost there. Another hard thrust and he hit it, clutching her hips tight, holding her still as he poured all of his frustrations and fear into her.

As soon as his hands fell from her hips she climbed off of him and freed his feet, then tossed a blanket over his shivering body. She lay beside him, both of them breathing heavily, probably from a combination of emotion and exertion.

He swallowed. "Will you kill me now?"

She covered herself with half of the blanket before she answered. "The disrupter is near to your hand. You can easily reach it yourself."

Was she inviting him to kill her? He deliberately rolled toward her, away from the disrupter. Her expression seemed oddly vulnerable, even a little frightened. But it wasn't fear of death clouding those gray eyes. She looked...*hurt*. Emotionally hurt. Where was the proud, arrogant Rigah now? The Rigah who claimed to have no feelings? This vulnerable Rigah, stripped of all her arrogance, looked like she might cry in a moment.

Guilt and an unfamiliar emotion—tenderness?—made his chest ache. He'd do anything to wipe that sorrowful look off her face. Anything.

He reached out and touched her cheek gently, stroking her soft skin with trembling fingers. "I couldn't kill you. I never could have killed you."

She looked back at him, her gaze steady. "Then why do you have this weapon?"

Would she believe that her own sister was the treacherous one, not him? He had to make her believe it. He had to stop Shalawn. Once she realized that he wasn't going to do her dirty work, she'd try to find another patsy. Rigah would be in real danger.

The door burst open, slamming hard against the wall and shaking the shelves. Merko stood there, a look of stark surprise on his face. He must have expected to find Jason dead on the floor, not lying naked in bed with the sainted *Senhab*.

Rigah sat up. "What is the matter?"

Merko bowed his head. "Forgive the intrusion, *Senhab*. I bring tragic news." He lifted his head and looked at her. "Your mother...her heart..."

Rigah drew in a sharp breath, a little gasp. Jason reached out and grasped her hand. How long would it take the man to say it?

Merko took a deep breath. "Your mother has died."

Chapter Ten

"Rigah?" a soft voice called.

She looked up. Billy stood a distance away, barely inside the atrium's borders. His hands were shoved into his pockets, his shoulders up around his neck in a defensive pose. Would he always look so frightened of her?

The household had awakened with the news. She had come here to hide from the furor, from those eager to press their concerns and their own grief upon her. Yet the child had found her. She gave him a feeble smile.

He stepped closer. "Uncle Jay told me about your mom." He scuffed one foot on the ground, looking downward. "I'm really sorry."

He feared her, yet he would share sympathy with her. The child had a generous nature. "Thank you."

He walked to her bench, pulled himself up, and sat next to her. "My mom's dead, too."

She nodded. She could force no voice through her tightened throat.

"It's not so bad," he said. She could hear the lie in his words. "At least we still have my uncle."

She closed her eyes against the pain. Oh, how she envied this small child. He might be a slave, but he could live assured of his uncle's caring. His uncle's love. She was the Leader Elect, possibly the Premier Leader. A woman born into generations of wealth, power, and prestige. And she had no one who cared for her the way Jason cared for this child.

"He tells me stories about my mom," he went on. "Stories from when they were my age. Stories from when I was a baby." He sighed. "I don't remember her that well."

"How aged were you when she died?" Her voice sounded raw, chafed, though it barely rose above a whisper.

"Four."

No wonder he remembered little of her. No doubt his mother had died at the hands of Rigah's own people. During the war, or perhaps in slavery. And yet this child would sit at her side and offer comfort. Comfort for the death of her mother, the Premier Leader who had commissioned the war that caused his own mother's death. The Premier Leader who had enslaved him and his beloved uncle.

"At least you're old enough to remember your mom," he said. "And you must have pictures and stuff like that."

Countless pictures. Pictures and holo-projections and a library of official proclamations issued in her mother's name. A legacy of power and diplomacy. Memories of training sessions, of lectures, of advice and instructions. But precious few tender memories.

She could not speak. If she spoke, her voice would break.

His little hand awkwardly patted her own. "You'll feel better after you cry. I always do."

She laid her free hand over his and squeezed gently. She could not cry. Regardless of her own need, she would not shed tears. Tears would have offended her mother.

Motion at the entry caught her gaze. Merko stood there, hesitating. She took a deep breath, collecting her emotions.

"Enter," she said.

Billy squeezed her hand and stood up. "Goodbye," he whispered.

She nodded at the child, and he turned and scurried out.

Merko came to her. "*Senhab,* forgive me. Do I intrude?"

She shook her head. "You have news?"

He held out a small reading panel. "Your mother's final proclamation."

She took the panel from him, stroking it with her forefinger. Now that revelation was here, she did not want the knowledge. As long as she sat in ignorance, she could pretend that her mother had favored her. That her mother had loved her.

Merko bowed. "I will leave you in privacy, *Senhab.*" He left calmly, slowly, as if the fate of their world did not rest on the proclamation in her hand.

No sense in delay. She pressed the power switch. An access screen appeared and she touched her thumb to the light for verification. In an instant, a holo-projection of her mother appeared above the panel.

"My daughter," her mother's image said. "You receive this proclamation upon my death. Do not grieve, for my death is a new beginning for our people.

"Rigah, you have served as Leader Elect for many years. Often have I disagreed with your decisions, questioned your judgment. You are ruled by emotion, daughter, yet you deny this truth. I fear your sentiment will make you weak. Shalawn would be more even in her judgments, but her ambition may lead her to excess. Each of my daughters holds a different strength. Yet only one of you may rule."

Rigah held her breath, waiting.

"In the absence of strong conviction, I rely on tradition to make my choice. Rigah, I pass the station of Premier Leader to you, my eldest daughter."

Typical of her mother. Even in passing her station, she could find no good to say of Rigah. The random chance of birth order had granted her this station, not her capabilities.

The image bowed. "May I be first to honor you, Premier Leader. And may I ask you, in honor of my memory, to find a place for your sister. Accept her counsel. Ask for her guidance, so that your sentiments will be tempered by logic."

As if Shalawn had ever been logical.

"Yet I am certain you will issue proclamations that I would never condone." Her mother smiled. "Such is the way of succession. I trust that you will do your best."

Her mother raised a fist to her breast in the ancient warrior's gesture. "Be strong. Be wise. And I will ever be proud of you."

The image bowed again, then faded.

* * *

She'd done a disappearing act. Jason looked in every room in the lower levels of the building, including her bedroom. No Rigah. Just hours ago, the house had been milling with people, everyone rushing and talking and worrying. But now the entire household was asleep again, so there was no one he could ask about her.

And he had to find her. He had to explain about the disrupter. About Shalawn. She needed to know just how treacherous her little sister could be.

He walked around the perimeter of the atrium, shivering in the cold night air. Atriums were nice in good weather, but in the middle of the night it was freezing. Mist dripped from the leaves, an eerie, irregular soundtrack to his search.

The strategy chamber was deserted, as was the library. He didn't know what the other rooms were called, but Rigah wasn't in them.

The last door was locked. He knocked. "Rigah?"

Nothing. He pressed an ear to the door, but it was thick and no sound came from the room. If Rigah was in there, she wasn't answering.

He'd check her bedroom one more time. This close to dawn, she must be exhausted. If she wasn't in her chamber, he'd come back to this locked door and pound on it until she let him in.

He took the shortcut through the center of the garden.

And there she was, sitting on a stone bench, clothed only in her uniform despite the cold breeze.

Her face looked pale, drawn. Closed. As if she had no emotions. He knew better. She was strong, arrogant, but she had feelings. She just hid them well.

She didn't move as he approached. "Rigah? Are you all right?"

She said nothing, moved not a fraction, as if she hadn't heard him. As if she was numb with grief. He sat next to her. God, she was cold. He could feel it through the fabric of her sleeve. "You're freezing, Rigah. Come inside and rest."

"No." She didn't sound angry. Just empty. Vulnerable.

And he couldn't resist the vulnerable Rigah. The vulnerable Rigah who made him want to hold her and protect her. The vulnerable Rigah who turned him into a sentimental fool. A sentimental fool who dared to imagine that she needed him. Worse—that he needed her.

He kissed her forehead softly. "I'm sorry about your mother." Feeble, but what else could he say?

"Thank you." Still no emotion.

"I know how it feels to lose someone you love." He didn't give a damn if she hated that word. "Do you want to talk about her?"

"She was strong. Stern. I was ever a disappointment to her."

And now she'd never have a chance to say everything they'd left unsaid. He knew the feeling. "She must have been very proud of you. She probably just had trouble showing it."

"She respected me. But she—she loved Shalawn."

Now wasn't the time to tell her that Shalawn wanted her dead. She was far too fragile. She'd already lost her mother—he couldn't take her sister away, too. Not this soon. "I'm sure your mother loved you both. Any mother would."

"Earther sentiment," she said, though her voice had no sting. She pointed to a scraggly tree in front of her. "You view this mingha tree?"

"Yes."

"My mother planted this tree on the day of my birth. To honor my first moments as Leader Elect."

Was that really all she had been to her mother? Someone to carry her title? Idiot that he was, he couldn't think of anything to say to comfort her. He put an arm around her and held her shivering body against his side.

"Now I am Leader Elect no more."

Inconceivable. How could her mother have picked Shalawn over Rigah? She must have been a piss-poor judge of character. "I'm sorry."

She shook her head. "You misunderstand me. I am no longer Leader Elect. I am Premier Leader."

Congratulations didn't seem appropriate. Not when her promotion came at the cost of her mother's life. "You need rest. It's almost dawn."

"I cannot sleep."

He stroked her back. "Then just come and lie down with me."

She drew away from him slightly. "I cannot rise to passion now."

What did she think he was? A cold-hearted sex maniac? "I don't mean for passion. I mean for comfort."

She looked at him with surprise on her face. Had she never been held for comfort? He drew her into his arms, her head onto his shoulder, and patted her back gently. "Let me comfort you tonight, Rigah."

She nodded against his shoulder. "As you wish." Her voice still sounded calm. Too calm.

"Let it out," he said.

She shook her head. But her arms came around him, clinging to him with the force of the grief she wouldn't express.

* * *

Jason opened his eyes to pitch black darkness. He felt Rigah curled up next to him, sleeping peacefully at last.

Why was he awake? He was exhausted. The sun wasn't up yet. It must have only been a few minutes since he and Rigah had lain down in her bed.

A soft noise came from near the door, a shuffling footstep. Then light flooded the room, blinding him.

He sat up, blinking against the glare, waiting for his pupils to adjust.

Through the flare of the sudden light, he saw Shalawn standing inside the door. "Good morning," she said.

Damn it. He should have warned Rigah last night. He should have told Merko. Now they were defenseless, facing her crazy sister.

Rigah stirred next to him, then sat up. "Shalawn? You have learned about Mother?"

She nodded. "Assuredly. You may say I was the first to learn."

That sounded like a confession to him. He put an arm around Rigah. She was going to need more comforting any second now.

She drew closer to him. "What are you saying?"

She obviously had no idea how treacherous her sister was.

"Such a variety of poisons are available now," Shalawn said casually. "Some quite effectively mimic heart failure."

Rigah gasped. "You killed Mother?"

Shalawn shrugged. "There is no one to say I did. Her heart was weak."

Rigah put a hand over her heart. "Mother loved you."

Shalawn glared at her, sneering. "Yet she granted you her station. And clearly you are far too trusting to be Premier Leader. You never discovered that this Earther, this slave you let run tame in your household, planned to kill you in your sleep?"

Would Rigah believe her? If only he could give her some kind of signal. Maybe the two of them could rush her sister together.

Shalawn looked at him and shook her head, as though deeply disappointed in him. "I guessed that your courage would dissolve between my sister's thighs."

She pulled out a disrupter and pointed it at Rigah. "I must always attend to my own concerns."

Rigah was on the far side of the bed from Shalawn. Maybe he could push her to the floor and somehow get that disrupter. And if he couldn't, she could only shoot one of them at a time. He could give Rigah a fighting chance.

"You will be caught," Rigah said. Her voice was strong, confident. The voice of a born leader. "You will not leave this household a free woman."

"You are wrong," Shalawn said. "As you have been wrong about so many things." She waved the disrupter toward him. "Your Earther whore will kill you. I will be the brave hero who executes your murderer. And I will be Premier Leader as well."

"None will believe it," Rigah said. Confident again, as though she had no fear of dying here and now. Brave woman.

Her sister smiled. "All will believe it," she answered. "There are already rumors about your fetish for aliens. About how dangerous it can be to have an Earther in the household."

Rumors spread by Shalawn, no doubt.

She raised the weapon. No. He couldn't just lay here and let her kill Rigah.

He pushed Rigah over with all his might. He heard her hit the floor as he flung himself toward Shalawn.

He never even made it off the bed. A bolt of pure lightning hit his chest; every muscle in his body screamed. The scent of burning flesh gagged him. And then blackness descended.

Chapter Eleven

Rigah heard the hiss of the disrupter. Could she reach Shalawn before her second charge? She stayed low, diving toward her sister's feet. Her shoulder crashed into Shalawn's knees. Shalawn fell down upon her, kicking.

A foot connected with Rigah's stomach. She bent over reflexively, clenching her teeth against the pain.

Pain later. Fight now.

She reached out blindly and caught hold of Shalawn's hair. With all her might, she drew back a fist and smashed her sister's nose. Blood spurted, warm and slick on her hand. She slammed her fist hard into the side of Shalawn's head, aiming above the ear, where the skull was tender.

Shalawn lay still. Rigah raised herself from the floor. Her sister's face was covered with blood, her eyes closed. She was unconscious.

Jason. She looked around frantically. There he was, on the bed, breathing harshly. She stumbled to her feet and slapped her hand on the control panel. "Merko!" she yelled. "Bring a physician!"

She rushed to the bed, kneeling over his body. A terrible hole was burnt straight through his shirt, just below his heart. His flesh was singed. His chest rose and fell with each labored breath. Thank the gods, he was breathing. But his limbs twitched erratically. A dangerous sign.

"*Senhab* Rigah?" Merko's sleepy voice came from the control panel.

"Bring a physician!" she shouted at the panel.

She turned back to Jason and cradled his face in her hands. "Jason? Can you hear me?"

His eyelids fluttered, his lips twisted, but no voice left him.

"Do not speak," she commanded. "The physician will be here soon."

"Billy," he said, his voice rough. Only half of his mouth moved. "Will you…"

No. He would not speak so. "You will care for him yourself," she insisted. "You will recover."

"Don't…think so," he whispered.

With each word, he seemed to grow paler. Where was the physician? "Conserve your strength," she ordered.

"You won't…" he whispered, then stopped. "Won't have to discard me now," he finished.

Foolish man. "I could never discard you." She bent and pressed a light kiss to his forehead. He felt cold, so cold. Where was the heat she'd come to relish?

His breath grew more labored, wheezing from his mouth as if his lungs were failing. A drop of liquid landed on his cheek.

She must be crying. Yes, she was sobbing. By the gods, he meant so much to her. Why had she hidden it for so long? Now it was too late.

"I love you," she said, her voice breaking.

Half of his mouth moved, a grotesque imitation of his usual smile. "Now...now you tell me." His breath rushed out in a final sigh. His chest did not rise again.

"Do not die," she pleaded.

"*Senhab!* Are you injured?"

Merko. She turned and saw the physician kneeling by her faithless sister. "Leave her!" she commanded. "Attend to this man at once."

The physician leaned over Jason. She reluctantly let go of his face, but touched his hand instead. Merko gently drew her away. "*Senhab,* the physician must have space."

He pressed a small cloth into her hand. A handkerchief. She dried her face, but could not still her tears.

Merko wrapped a strong arm around her, watching with her as the physician cut away Jason's shirt. A full hand's width of his beautiful flesh was blackened. The physician shook his head.

She pressed a fist against her mouth. He must live. By the gods, he must live.

* * *

Jason awoke with a start. The room was dimly lit. A jolt of electricity caused a muscle twinge somewhere near his heart, and his left side was pinned down. No, his left side was numb. Dead. His arm, his leg—God, were they missing? He tried to reach his left arm with his right hand, but the blankets were too tight. He struggled against them.

Rigah's face came into view, leaning over him. "You are awake."

"I can't feel my arm. My leg." Only half of his mouth seemed to be working, making his words come out slurred.

She laid a hand on his right arm. At least he could feel that. "Your limbs are fine. The nerves are damaged. Healing will take time."

Memory came to him then. Shalawn, the disrupter, shoving Rigah to the floor. "Were you hurt?"

"No. You shielded me and took the blast yourself."

"Shalawn?"

"In confinement, thanks to your courage." She stroked his forehead. "Are you in pain?"

He'd laugh if he didn't hurt so badly. He felt like he'd been run over with her conveyance and plugged into a power plant. "You've obviously never taken one of those blasts."

"I would have, had you not saved me." She straightened. "The physician did what he could to relieve your pain, but I will summon him again." Her eyes looked troubled, as if she felt guilty.

"Don't bother. It's not too bad," he lied. "Where's Billy?"

"Asleep. You have been unconscious for a full day's length. The sun will soon break night."

That explained why she was wearing a nightgown.

"I will summon him." She took a step back.

"No." He wanted to reach out a hand to her, but couldn't. "Let him sleep."

She didn't quite look into his eyes.

"Why are you awake?" he asked.

She shrugged. "I have been working."

So she hadn't been concerned about him? Who was she trying to kid? "Working?"

"Yes. I have already issued my first proclamation as Premier Leader."

That was fast. But why was she telling him this? "Congratulations," he said dryly.

She didn't respond to his sarcasm. "I have declared slavery illegal," she said. "Your people are free."

Unbelievable. Rigah, the Great Emancipator. "Without money, freedom will do them little good."

"Those who were slaves are free and equal citizens. They can now earn profit. The unified treasury will subsidize their wages for some years, until the economies that depended upon slave labor have adapted."

"Economies like the plantations."

"Yes. And the mines. A few others." She smiled, a little sadly it seemed. "My mother assured me that I was destined to issue proclamations she would never have condoned. No doubt this is the first of many such ones."

Had she done it for him? Was he some pitiful Oliver Twist character to her? "Why are you doing this?"

It took her a moment to answer. "Many say slavery is necessary to the economy," she said. "Yet it costs much to subdue the natural tendency of human beings to rebel against confinement. These rebellions have strained our treasury. And the issue is not merely one of economy."

She seemed to struggle with her thoughts. "To keep intelligent beings in slavery is unjust. We should not hold others in contempt for their origins. It damages my people as well as yours." She smiled faintly. "This was all stated in my proclamation. Perhaps you should simply read it."

Maybe, when he could lift his arm. "What about me?"

"You are free as well." She looked up, away from his face. "Free to leave. With Billy, of course."

Free to leave. Was he free to stay? Had she forgiven him for having that damned disrupter? For plotting with that idiot sister of hers? For nearly getting both of them killed?

She looked down at him again. "I will give you money. And property. In thanks for saving my life."

Thank God he'd been there to save her. "You don't owe me anything."

She shook her head. "I owe you more than I can grant you." Her voice sounded a little rough. She coughed. "When you wish to leave, I will send attendants with you. But the physician advises that you rest here for a few weeks. You may not heal completely for several months."

Based on the dead weight that used to be his arm and leg, it would take at least that long for him to have any feeling in them. But did she care if he left? Only one way to find out. "Come here."

She moved closer to the side of the bed. "What do you need?"

"Sit by me."

She sat down on the edge of the bed and looked at his pillow instead of his face. If only he could reach out and touch her. But she was on his left side, his bad side, and he couldn't reach her with his right hand.

"Rigah." She looked into his eyes. "I remember, you know."

She drew back a little. Would she pretend to have forgotten? "I remember what you said," he added.

"I was upset to see you injured. That is all."

She sounded like she'd rehearsed that line. "So upset that you were overcome by Earther sentiment."

She turned her head, but not before he saw tears shimmer in her eyes. God, how he wanted to touch her.

"Rigah." She still wouldn't face him. "I feel those Earther sentiments for you, too."

She looked at him then, with an expression of such patent disbelief on her face that he almost laughed. "Truly?"

"Truly." He patted the bed with his right hand. "Lie down next to me."

"You are too injured."

"Please."

She walked around the bed and carefully climbed in, laying on his right side without touching him. He wrapped his good arm under her neck and urged her closer. She pillowed her head on his shoulder and draped her forearm across his stomach. He could only feel the part of her arm that was on his right side. Bizarre.

At least Rigah hadn't been hit with that damned disrupter. He'd take a dozen more blasts to save her from just one. "I love you," he said.

He felt her lips curl into a smile against his shoulder. "I am pleased. Though it seems strange to hear those words."

He couldn't resist the urge to prod her. "And even stranger to say them?"

She nodded. "Yet I know they are truth. I do…" She took a deep breath. "I do love you, Jason."

The wonder in her voice, the sweet hesitancy, almost brought tears to his eyes. He could turn his head just enough to kiss her forehead. "You'll get used to saying that with practice."

"Assuredly. And to hearing it, as well."

"We'll practice often," he promised.

"My mother believed that tender feelings would make me weak. A poor leader."

She'd asked the right man for reassurance. "The best leaders on Earth were those who cared for their subjects," he said. "You have the courage to make unpopular decisions, and your feelings will tell you which decisions are best for your people."

She kissed his shoulder. "I hope you are correct."

"I am. Just look at your first proclamation. You freed my people for the good of all, even though many will disagree."

She nodded. "Many have disagreed. But the economy will hold, and they will be silenced."

She said it with so much conviction, he didn't doubt her for a second. "You'll be the best leader this planet has ever seen," he said. And he meant it.

They lay in silence for a moment before she lifted her head and looked down at him. "There is something I wish to ask of you."

She sounded strangely timid. Why didn't she just ask? "All right."

She took a deep breath. "Will you mate with me?"

Leave it to his Rigah to put things in the baldest possible terms. He smiled. "Of course. I'd love to have children with you."

She didn't smile back. Her fingers toyed with the edge of the blanket, as if she was nervous. "Traditionally, there is a partnering ceremony first."

That sounded like marriage. And surprisingly, marriage to Rigah sounded just fine. Better than fine. But there was one thing he needed to tell her.

"Among my people, partners are considered exclusive." He didn't know if there was a Prendarian word for *monogamy*. "They are not free to lie with others," he added, to make his point crystal clear.

She frowned, her brow furrowing with worry. "You would desire other women?"

She hadn't understood him at all. And even though he could have kissed her for the jealousy in her voice, he didn't like seeing insecurity in those gorgeous eyes. "Of course not," he said. "But you...would you be satisfied with one man?"

She cupped his face with her hand. He'd never have imagined that she could look at him with such tenderness. "So long as that man is you."

"Then we'll have this partnering ceremony. Whenever you want."

She smiled at last. "As soon as you have recovered." She kissed him gently, then snuggled up against him again.

"Will your people object?" he asked. "Will they mind if you have an Earther for a partner?"

"Do you jest? You are a hero to my people, Jason. You risked your life to save mine." She gave a husky little laugh. "Even Merko would kneel at your feet to thank you."

That was hard to believe. And fun to picture.

She curled her hand around his neck. "We will become a fine example. I have said that I wish to see our people integrate."

Our people. He liked the sound of that.

Freedom. Family. Love. Everything he'd ever wanted, all here in this woman's arms.

He squeezed her with his good arm. "Thank you, Rigah."

"For what?"

"For bringing me home."

FOR THE HEART OF DARIA

Chapter One

San Francisco, 2038

"May this night bring you untold pleasure, *Sarjah.*"

It took Gray a moment to realize the title of respect was directed at him. The Prendarian word sounded strange tacked onto the end of an English sentence.

The young man in front of him nearly bounced with excitement. Had Gray ever been that eager for sex? "I thank you, Ensign. But I plan a quiet night alone this evening."

"Oh." Flustered and clearly finding no words, the Ensign bowed his head respectfully. "Enjoy your evening, *Sarjah.*"

With one last puzzled look, the Ensign kept going.

William Gray—"Billy" to his family, "Gray" to his friends, and "*Sarjah*" to everyone else—leaned against the doorway of his quarters, feigning tiredness as he watched the crew rush down the bleak pre-fab corridor and out into the humid Earth night. After six months in space, everyone wanted to disembark and lose themselves in the most raucous pleasures San Francisco had to offer.

Everyone except Gray.

He probably looked strange, standing in the doorway of his quarters watching them hurry by in small rowdy groups, but he didn't care. Let them think he wanted to spend the evening alone...that he was too tired for a wild night. He'd had enough wildness on Prendara. This was his first night back on the planet of his birth, and he didn't want to spend it with uncouth space sailors looking for casual pleasures. Or worse, with political cronies droning bits of their personal agendas in his ears.

No, he wanted solitude. So he nodded at the crew as they filed past the open door of his quarters, doing his best to look tired. If they thought he was sleeping, they wouldn't dare to bother him before morning.

Anshar, quite possibly the sexiest ship captain in the entire fleet, strode down the hall with a provocative look in her eyes and a seductive swing to her hips. She wore her uniform, perhaps to guarantee that she received the proper respect in the riotous dockside bars of San Francisco. Or maybe she just wanted everyone to know that she held a station deserving of those green shoulder stripes.

The form-fitting navy blue uniform did nothing to disguise her voluptuous figure. She'd let him know she was available for pleasure during the long voyage, no doubt believing that lying with him would help her add more stripes to her shoulders. He couldn't really blame her. Most women wanted him more for the political favors he could bestow than for his own self.

Even so, he'd joined her a few times early on—but lately he hadn't accepted her invitations. Only the gods knew why. She was strong but curvy, pale-skinned and fair like most

Prendarians, but he hadn't been more than mildly interested in sharing her bed. And now, the sight of her generous hips coming toward him didn't even cause a stir in his trousers.

She stopped at his doorway and laid a slim, pale hand on his arm. "Waiting for me?"

He hated her easy self-confidence, the way she assumed that everyone was waiting for her, thinking about her, or wanting to bed her. She'd even spoken in Prendarian, deliberately defying his order that the crew speak English. There was enough resentment against Prendarians on this planet as it was—no need to make it worse by speaking in what the Earthers considered an alien language.

He smothered a fake yawn with one hand, dislodging her fingers from his arm in the process. "I'm tired tonight," he said in English. "I plan to stay on board and rest."

She raised her eyebrows. "Are you ill? I can summon the physician."

As if he couldn't take care of himself. At least she'd answered him in English. She knew better than to test his resolve on diplomatic issues. "No, let the physician disembark. The entire crew has earned a rest."

"I doubt any of us will rest tonight. Any of us except you."

She brushed up against him, letting her breast touch the side of his arm. He resisted the urge to pull away.

"Are you certain I cannot change your mind?" she murmured. "I know places in San Francisco that will make everything you've done on Prendara appear tame."

No doubt she did. Like all Prendarians, Anshar had an active sex drive. A sex drive he usually appreciated. But not tonight. "I'm certain."

"There are people on Earth who pleasure for money." She gave a throaty chuckle. "They'll do things you can't imagine. All for a few credits."

He had no interest in exploiting prostitutes. "I can easily forego that pleasure."

"They are required to license their persons. You need not fear disease."

"I need sleep." He took a step back into his quarters. "Enjoy your entertainment."

Her chin went up, a haughty gesture. "As you will." She turned and strode down the hall.

He watched the sway of her ass as she walked away. By the gods, what was wrong with him? One of the sexiest, most voracious women on the ship offered him a night of lust, and he said no like some kind of monk from distant history.

Maybe he was simply bored. Bored with sex.

The back of a security envoy blocked his view of Anshar's ass, so he looked the other way down the dimly-lit corridor. Only a few stragglers left. Soon he'd be alone, with only a sparse security crew to oversee the ship.

He retreated into his quarters and let the door slide closed behind him. He'd give the crew a couple of ticks to clear the ship, then a few more to get off the space dock. Then he'd head out and see the city for himself. See how much he remembered.

Assuming he remembered anything at all.

He'd only been six years old the last time he'd been on Earth. Here in this very city. He barely remembered the rat-infested warehouse he'd lived in with Uncle Jason, even though they'd camped there for a year after the Third World War had ended. Until the aliens had rounded them up and taken them to Prendara.

Strange how life turned out. Ironically, their enslavement had led to freedom. Freedom for them and all Earthers. And all because Uncle Jason had fallen in love with his Prendarian owner. The Premier Leader, of all people. It was almost enough to make Gray believe in fate.

He lay on the bed, arms folded behind his head, and stared up at the soothing sky-pink ceiling. The Earth sky was blue, he vaguely remembered. The only pink sky he knew of was on Prendara. It had taken him years to adjust to the alien color.

The first time he'd been pleasured, so long ago, he'd been outdoors, flat on his back, looking up at that pale pink sky while an eager Prendarian girl four years older rode him to ecstasy. They hadn't even disrobed completely. Not for that first coupling, at least.

He smiled fondly at the memory. That moment had started him on a long journey of happy couplings.

Was he really bored with sex? Gods, he might as well be dead.

He couldn't be bored with sex. Maybe it was simply Anshar. No, that wasn't it. She was more attractive than most women, and as well-versed in the arts of pleasure as anyone.

Maybe that was the problem. Maybe he was bored with quick, easy sex. Sex with nothing but passion and, if he was lucky, friendship behind it. All too often, women pursued him—or gave in to his pursuit—for political favors. He enjoyed them, usually he even liked them, but now the encounters left him feeling…cold. Empty.

He wanted more. His aunt and uncle had fallen head first into love, showing him how much sweeter passion could be when combined with genuine warmth of feeling. He wanted that warmth for himself.

He wanted it all.

He sighed. Might as well try to juggle the moons. Love was as rare as water.

Well, as rare as water on Prendara.

San Francisco was surrounded by water. He couldn't wait to see it. Just a few more ticks, then he'd head out and tour the city. Tomorrow he'd be too busy, meeting with all the factions he was here to unite.

Maybe that's why he hadn't been interested in Anshar. He'd spent most of the six month voyage to Earth studying, preparing, learning everything he could about every random Earth faction. He'd been too busy for sex.

The mission was far more important than sex. More important than anything he'd ever done.

More important than anything he ever would do.

* * *

Damn. She'd missed the target.

Daria pushed her hair back with one hand and grabbed for her talkie with the other. Nothing but static. She slid the selector tab back and forth, but in the weak light of a fog-shrouded moon, the settings were damned near invisible. The built-in light on this unit had broken years ago.

Great. She'd have to move closer to a *tuaari* light. Getting out of the shadows would be nice, but she couldn't afford to be spotted.

Maybe no one would see her. The space dock seemed deserted now, with nothing but cawing night birds and the occasional lap-lap of waves against the outer barrier breaking the silence.

Where the hell was the target? This was the only way out of the docking chamber from the pier his ship was on. She'd watched a dizzying stream of crew members disembark, all of them making coarse jokes and laughing wildly, looking forward to spreading fear and credits through the city in their pursuit of pleasure.

So many of them Earthers. Earthers who worked with Prendarians, ate with Prendarians, *slept* with Prendarians.

Traitors.

Collaborators.

She'd hugged the shadows, hiding from them, not wanting to be picked out by one of those horny bastards. They'd passed her by without a glance, not even seeing her. She only wanted one man to see her dressed like this. The man who hadn't appeared. The target.

She knew he hadn't walked past her. After studying holo-projections of him for weeks, she could probably spot him from over a hundred yards away. The target was tall and lean, just a little muscular, with straight dark brown hair, light brown eyes, and a striking nose, even though it was a bit too large for handsomeness. No way could she have missed him, not even in this fog.

He must have stayed on the ship.

Now she needed new orders, but she wouldn't find anyone on her talkie without some light. She took a deep breath. The nearest *tuaari* light was about fifty yards away, a shimmering halo in the mist. The dock was deserted...or seemingly deserted. In the gloomy fog, she could barely see ten feet away. Why did the damned Prendarians have to prefer low lighting? Decent people didn't shroud themselves in the dark.

But there was nothing out there in the dark that wouldn't be there in the light. No reason to be afraid. Besides, the team was counting on her. She could do this. She *had* to do this.

One step at a time.

She walked slowly, making sure her ridiculous shoes made no noise on the wooden dock. High heels. As anachronistic and outdated as the wooden pseudo-pier she stepped across.

The aliens had gone retro when building the space dock, using real wood from real trees to mask the huge pre-fab shell. The whole port was modeled after the old wooden sea docks in San Francisco's distant past, with wooden piers serving as walkways and vertical log pillars lining the pre-fab walls. God knew why they bothered with the wooden façade, considering all the high-tech materials they had at their disposal. Maybe the Prendarians had a nostalgic streak. Or maybe they simply wanted to show their dominion over even the trees in the forest.

She kept her gaze on her talkie as she approached the light. Only when she was directly in the brightest spot could she see the tabbed slider. Great. She was lit up like a deer in a gas-car's headlights. Any Enforcer who saw her in these clothes would check her ID for a prostitute's license. A license she didn't have. She had to hurry.

She lined up the tab with the small mark she'd made on the lycene case. This was Tank's frequency, all right.

"Tank?"

Nothing but static. Where was he?

She slid the selector tab again. Trisha should be online somewhere. Trisha, Don, Tank...they were the only other people on the mission, as far as she knew. Names were always kept as private as possible. You never knew when the Enforcers might bust you.

"You on here, kid?"

Tank's voice. Faint. He must be nearly out of range. Why wasn't he nearby, waiting for her to call him to pick up the package?

She lifted the talkie so fast it hit her in the chin. "Yes."

"Where you at?" She could barely hear him, but he sounded winded.

"I'm at the take out spot," she replied. "Where are you?"

"I can't tell you. But I'm mobile."

Mobile. A code word for *escaping*. Oh, no. Her heart sank.

"They're on to us. Got everyone in the clink—"

More static. With a trembling finger, she nudged the tab until Tank's signal came back in. "...Just you and me. Looks like you're the only one they didn't ID. You're on your own, kid."

Damn, damn, damn. "I can't do it alone." Her voice echoed in the huge, nearly empty docking chamber.

"You have to." His voice sounded annoyed and stern, that gruff, pseudo-menacing tone that always made her smile. But not this time. "You can do it, kid. I know you can."

Shit. Was that a footstep off in the distance? She slid the volume down just a bit and held the talkie to her mouth so the mic would catch a whisper.

"Tank...he'll be too heavy. I'm not strong enough to execute the plan alone."

"Then come up with a new plan."

Alone? Hell, this was her first big mission. He'd always kept her in the background before; kept her safe. And now he wanted her to take over? "I can't. Not without you." *Not without someone, anyone, to help me.*

"You know how to do this, kid. We ran through contingencies. Just take it one step at a time. First you screw him. You're dressed for it, and he'll be horny as hell after half a year in space. Then improvise."

"Improvise? I know you're not big on ironing out the details, Tank. But—"

"But nothing! You have to stop him. You have to. He's here to take away any hope we have of governing ourselves. If he succeeds, we'll never be free."

She'd heard it all before. Even so, Tank was right. If the target succeeded, they'd never get rid of the aliens. She couldn't let that happen.

"But he didn't get off the ship."

"So go in after him." Even through the static, he managed to sound exasperated. "You can screw him on the ship, you know."

"And after that? I can't kidnap him without help."

"You'll figure it out when you get there, kid. One step at a time, remember? Screw his brains out. Get him to trust you. Once you're hooked into him, you'll think of some way—"

Static cut him off. "Tank? Tank?"

Oh God, was he gone?

The signal peeled in with a screech. "It's all up to you, kid. And I know you can do it."

If only she had half his confidence in her. She took a deep breath. "I'll do it. No matter what it takes. I swear it."

"That's my girl. Do it for Don and Trisha."

"No, I'll do it for all of you. For all of us." Good, she'd kept her voice strong. She didn't want Tank to worry.

"Kid?"

"Yes?"

"Dar—hell, I can't say your name on this thing. Might be traced. Kid, you're like a daughter to me. You know?"

And he'd been the father she'd never had. Her throat closed. "I know," she whispered.

"All right then. It's all been said. And I need to lose this talkie before they pick us up." His voice was breaking up badly, chopped by static. "I'll see ya, kid."

But he wouldn't. He'd never see her again. Static filled the air. Hot tears blurred her vision, and she could barely hear over her pounding heart.

Tank on the run. Everyone ID'd except for her. Don and Trisha in prison.

Alone. Oh God, she was alone. Alone and clueless.

Now everything depended on her. A rank amateur, the one Tank had always kept out of the thick of things. Damn him, he should have known something like this might happen. He never thought ahead. He never—

Her throat burned. No point in blaming Tank. He'd only been protecting her. And he'd done a good job of it all these years, ever since she'd been a filthy, hungry teenager and he'd taken her off the streets. A sob escaped her. Damn it. Crying wouldn't help any of them now. There'd be time for grieving later.

Her fingers shook as she scrubbed wetness from her cheeks. A deep breath helped steady her. Time to get moving.

She tucked the talkie into the small pocket hidden in the back of her skirt. She'd incinerate it later. Without a team, the talkie was no good to her. But she couldn't risk leaving it on an open dock. Not with her prints and bio-signature on it.

First she had to find the target. Find him, screw him, convince him to let her stick around. Oh, she'd stick to him like glue. Then she'd worry about how to finish the mission.

He must still be on that ship. She'd go up to the docking bay and find a way on board. Over a hundred crew members had gone past her, so finding the target shouldn't be hard. When she found him, she'd jump in his bed. After six months in space, he'd be primed for sex. That's what she'd give him. That was the original plan. Part of it, at any rate. No reason to change it. Best to follow Tank's plan, as much as she could. Tank's plans were always the best.

She turned to head deeper into the docking bay—and found two men standing just a few feet away. Her hand flew to her throat. Damn. The leering smirks on their faces meant trouble.

"What have we here?" the taller one asked.

As if he couldn't tell. Best to get rid of them quickly. She raised her chin, trying to look cocky. "Five hundred credits. Each." An exorbitant price. Maybe they wouldn't notice the blush she felt in her cheeks. "And triple that if you want to tag team me."

The men exchanged surprised glances, then laughed. "Five hundred creds? Oh, that's sweet. This dockside whore thinks she's in the Avenues."

The short one looked nasty, with harsh lines in his face and a glitter in his eyes she'd come to recognize. Hard and cold. The look of a man all too familiar with crime.

He edged around her, and she turned slightly to keep them both in sight.

"Maybe we should find out what you got worth that tall a price," he said, his voice slurred. Drugs, maybe. Damn.

Survival instincts kicked in, honed during years of living in seedy warehouses. *Stall, then run.* "Credits first."

"No," the tall one said.

She gave him a haughty stare, trying to look tough. If she could get him to back up just a step, she'd be past him before he could think to touch her. She shifted to the right, ready to run.

A hand grabbed her ass and squeezed. Her hips swung forward involuntarily. She tried to turn, but the short one had an arm around her waist, his breath hot and damp against her neck.

"Nice ass," he grunted. A wet tongue laved her neck. Her flesh crawled, and she jerked her head away.

He pulled her up against his wiry body. His stiff cock rubbed her hip. Oh, God.

"How much to ream your ass?" Then he laughed. "Not that you're gonna get any creds for it."

She tried to yank his arm down, but he resisted, giving her ribs an aching squeeze. Her nails dug into his forearm.

"Stop it, bitch." He wrapped his other arm around her with bruising force.

The tall one came closer, and she tried to kick him, but only managed a light blow against his thigh. He grinned and blew her a kiss. "Oh, a wild one. Sweet."

Hell yes, she was a wild one. She wasn't going under them without a fight. But maybe she should play along until the one holding her—the one with the meanest eyes she'd ever seen—loosened his hold. Then she'd strike out with more force than he expected.

But she couldn't make it too obvious. She let go of his arm and pretended to go just a little weak, leaning the weight of her body away from him.

He hauled her back against him and shoved a hand between her thighs. She struggled, trying to pull free, trying to kick his shins. He laughed, clearly enjoying her movements. His cock ground hard against her ass. Her stomach clenched.

"Be nice," he warned. "Be nice and beg us, and maybe…just maybe…we won't kill you when we're done."

They were going to kill her. Rape her and kill her. How could she stop them? How, how? She couldn't think of a damned thing. She could barely breathe, the way he was squeezing her ribs.

The tall one reached out and grabbed her breast.

She screamed.

* * *

Gray waited twice as long as he thought necessary. The last thing he needed was to have someone see him leave; they'd try to force him to take a security envoy along. Everyone wanted to make sure the nephew of the Premier Leader was kept safe. But tonight, for just one night, he wanted to see the city alone, as a civilian.

With a disrupter in his pocket, he'd be safe enough. He left his quarters with the door locked. If anyone stopped by, they wouldn't dare to disturb him. Then he made his way down the corridor toward the loading ramp.

The blast doors were wide open. So much for security. He walked down the steep ramp to the space dock. The strangest space dock he'd ever seen. Wood everywhere, a bizarre homage to the seafaring San Francisco of decades past.

After he'd taken only a few steps down the wooden pier, a woman screamed.

He ran toward the sound without hesitation. Would he even see her in this dim light? Between the dark and the fog, he could barely see his own feet. He stumbled, then kept barreling forward.

There she was—a scantily-dressed, dark-haired woman struggling with two men. Men with hands on her breasts, between her legs, even though she fought them. *By the gods.*

At least they were under a *tuaari* light. He'd get a good shot off. He found the disrupter in his pocket, drew it out, and aimed before he'd come to a complete stop.

"Let her go."

The men froze, then reached into their loose, open tunics. *Coats.* They were called *coats* in English. *Sanwar,* as if the word mattered. While the men fumbled, he fired reflexively, sweeping his arm to catch both of them.

Which meant the woman was caught as well. She collapsed to the ground with her attackers in a heap.

Gray stepped closer and knelt by her side. Her flimsy shirt had been torn half-off, her legs were bare...in truth, she wore very little, considering the cool weather. Ah. A prostitute.

Her breathing was erratic but deep, her limbs twitching, but not too badly. She'd recover.

The men were both shaking with the odd, seizure-like muscle spasms of a full blast. Good. They'd be unconscious for many hours, and when they woke up, every muscle in their bodies would be screaming. They deserved worse.

And this unfortunate woman deserved the best care he could offer. He lifted her in his arms and headed back to the ship.

He had to walk slowly, between the dim light, the fog, and the burden he carried. She looked frail, but she wasn't a lightweight. Her eyelashes were dark against her pale cheeks, her chin just a little pointed. Not a beautiful woman, not by any measure, but she had a winsome face. A surprisingly innocent face, for a woman who obviously sold her body.

He frowned. They'd never had a need for prostitution on Prendara. There must be a better way for women like this to earn their credits.

The blast doors were still wide open. His boots clomped up the ramp, but no one came to investigate. There were probably only a handful of security guards left on the whole ship. What was the English expression? He'd known it years ago...had even heard his uncle use it on occasion. Ah, yes. A *skeleton crew*.

Back at his quarters, he slapped his hand on the access panel, saw the light turn white to signal recognition of his bio-signature. "Open."

The door slid open and the lights came on automatically. The woman gave a small whimper; no doubt her eyes were sore from the blast. "Dim lights by fifty percent." The lights dimmed.

He laid the woman on his bed, then went to the communication console. "Security."

No response.

"Security," he said again, louder.

"Yes, *Sarjah?*"

"There are two men on the dock approximately five measures from the ship. Take them into confinement."

"Yes, *Sarjah.* Shall we subdue them?"

What was the English word? He'd remembered it out on the dock. "Unconscious," he blurted. "They're already unconscious."

He glanced at the woman on his bed. She was stirring, but not with the jerky movements he'd seen after a severe disrupter blast. She'd be awake soon. His sweeping shot must have barely caught her. "Has the physician left the ship?"

"Yes, *Sarjah.* Are you injured?"

"No." And the woman wasn't seriously injured, either. Still… "Have him contact me when he returns."

Probably not until morning. Gray closed the connection and returned to the bed, staring down at the woman he'd rescued. Her skin was interesting, a combination of peach and beige that he'd rarely seen on Prendara, even among Earthers. Creamy skin. In the dry, sunny atmosphere of Prendara, that peachy skin would be dark with a tan. Only the native Prendarians stayed pale; their race had adapted, evolved, until their skin was naturally shielded from the harsh sun of their home planet.

The woman's mouth twisted as if in pain, and she struggled to sit up.

He sat next to her and laid a hand on her arm. She jerked away from him. "Alone," she mumbled. And then a horrified look crossed her face, no doubt because she couldn't speak. Or maybe because she couldn't open her eyes.

"You're safe now," he said. "Safe," he repeated, in case her hearing was affected by the blast.

Her expression relaxed, but she curled up on her side until she was a tight little ball. She still shivered.

Poor thing. He reached out to brush her long black hair off of her face, but stopped. Maybe she wouldn't want him to touch her. Her legs were trembling fiercely now, from either the blast or the cold. The docking chamber had been freezing, and her legs were bare.

Completely bare. His gaze wandered from the spiky shoes she wore up to her extremely short skirt. By the gods, her legs had no hair on them. What would all that creamy, bare flesh feel like?

No. He shouldn't be fantasizing about a woman who'd been attacked for sex. There wasn't even a word in Prendarian for what those men had tried to do to her.

He pulled one side of the thermo blanket over her, hiding those tantalizing legs. She sighed and burrowed down until her shoulders were covered. Maybe she really was cold.

Perhaps a gentle touch would calm her. No reason to resist. He reached out and brushed that long ebony hair back from her forehead.

She opened her eyes and gave a start when she saw him. But the expression in her eyes wasn't fear. She almost looked like…no, she couldn't recognize him. He'd never seen her before. Those huge, velvety brown eyes of hers wouldn't be easy to forget. They dominated her angular little face.

"I won't hurt you," he said softly. "Try to relax."

Her hand curled into a fist under her chin. "Thank…" Her brows drew together in a frown, and her eyes glistened with tears. She must be frightened by her helplessness, especially after those criminals had attacked her.

But she didn't seem to mind his presence, so he stroked her hair soothingly. "You won't be able to speak normally for a few minutes," he said, keeping his voice soft. "When you've recovered, you can make your claim to the Enforcers."

"No!" She struggled to sit up, but the tangled blanket and weakness from the disrupter blast kept her down.

"Relax. You're safe."

"No…" Her mouth twisted, but no more words came out. "No…no enf."

"No Enforcers?"

Her head jerked in an abrupt nod.

He frowned. The Enforcers must be contacted. They were responsible for gathering evidence against criminals like the two men who'd attacked her.

Her eyes were luminous, gazing at him steadily. She took a deep, shuddering breath. "Please," she said slowly, as if the word cost her strength. "No Enforcers."

She was recovering quickly. Already she could speak, even if her speech was slurred. But why didn't she want to give evidence to the Enforcers? Perhaps she knew those two criminals.

No. Even if she knew them, she surely wouldn't want to protect them from prosecution. Maybe she was afraid for herself.

Ah. Maybe she was an *unlicensed* prostitute. The Enforcers would trace her identity. They'd search her credentials, find no license, and confine her. No wonder she didn't want to talk to them. As an unlicensed prostitute, she'd be locked up like her attackers.

He'd never broken the law himself. Never even bent it. But he couldn't stand to see her look so agitated. And after all she'd been through, he wasn't going to cause her any more anguish.

"As you will," he said. "The Enforcers will collect the men who…" He didn't know the English word for what they'd tried to do to her. "The men who attacked you," he finished. "But you won't have to talk to the Enforcers if you don't want to."

She put her hand over his. Her skin felt warm. Prendarian women were cold, their body temperatures a couple of degrees below his. With so few Earth women on Prendara, he'd rarely felt warm flesh against his own.

"Thank you," she said.

He covered her warm, slender hand with his own. "You're welcome."

She smiled a little. "Who are you?"

"Gray." He didn't want her to know any more, didn't want her to know he was the privileged nephew of the Premier Leader. He wanted to be himself, for once.

"I'm Daria."

He'd never heard the name before, but it suited her. What was the polite response in English? Oh, yes. "It's nice to meet you."

Her smile widened. "So formal," she said, almost teasingly. "After all we've been through, I feel like we're old friends."

If she could smile like that after what had happened to her, she was clearly a resilient woman. Her speech sounded almost normal now, barely slurred. Her lips were full, her mouth too big for her narrow chin. What would it be like to kiss a woman whose mouth felt warm against his?

Gods, what kind of lunatic was he? After enduring that attack, she'd probably want to keep her distance from all men for at least a year. Including him. He pulled his hand away from hers and shifted his weight off the bed, then stood up.

Her smile faded. She reached out and grasped his hand. "Don't leave me."

He sat down again. "You need to rest."

"No, I need…"

Her face flushed with rosy color. Fascinating. Prendarian women, for all their paleness, rarely blushed.

"What do you need, Daria?" The strange name sounded lyrical.

She looked away from him. "I need some water. I'm thirsty."

Hardly a request worth blushing over. He kept a tension bottle next to the bed. He reached down, found it, and handed it to her.

She fumbled with the toggle. "I can't open it."

Strange that her fingers were still weak, considering how well she could speak. Disrupter blasts could have strange effects. He opened the toggle and handed the bottle back to her.

She rocked back and forth, struggling to sit up. Big brown eyes pleaded up at him. "Will you help me, please?"

He'd have to get a lot closer to support her. He gathered her in his arms, blanket and all, then sat on the bed with his back against the wall and her body cradled across his lap. He propped her head up on his shoulder. She fell back against him, resting limply in his arms.

He took the tension bottle in one hand, brought his arm around her, and lifted it to her mouth. "Can you nod when you're finished?"

"Yes."

She took a small sip, sucking water from the bottle. Then another. When she tipped her head back her hair brushed his cheek, smelling like some kind of exotic flower. Why had he assumed prostitutes would wear harsh perfume? This sweet-scented woman was nothing like he imagined a prostitute to be.

Lost in her fragrance, he almost missed her nod. He closed the toggle and dropped the bottle back onto the floor. He should leave her now.

Her hand came up and rested on his chest. "Thank you."

That gently stroking hand became the focus of every nerve ending in his body. If he didn't get her off his lap soon, he'd disgrace himself with a full arousal.

But another moment would do no harm. "You must be recovered now. Your fingers are wriggling."

Those tormenting fingers stopped. "I guess so." She sounded uncertain. "But I'm still cold."

He pulled the blanket closer, up over her shoulders. "Better?"

She nodded, teasing his chin with silky hair again, and nuzzled her cheek against his shoulder. Her mouth brushed his neck in an accidental kiss. "You feel so nice and warm," she murmured, lips moving against his skin.

Gods, those lips were hot. Unbidden, his root swelled against her hip. *Sanwar.* He didn't know the appropriate word to swear in English.

She shifted away a little, then back against him. Her hips moved, gently nudging his hardness. Though she stayed in his arms, she must have noticed his erection.

"I'm sorry." He loosened his hold on her. "I'm not always the master of myself."

"It's all right," she said, her voice husky. She snuggled even closer, her warm hand curling over his collarbone. "I'm still cold. You're warming me up." When she gave a little laugh, her breath rushed against his neck. "I guess we're both warming up. And I...I don't mind."

But he did. He very much did. Holding her like this, enjoying her body, when all she sought was warmth... This was not principled.

He lifted her and stood, then laid her gently down onto her back, cushioning her head, releasing her slowly. Reluctantly. When he let go of her completely, he very nearly bent his head and kissed her.

He stood up instead. "You need rest. I'll leave you in peace until morning."

"No! Gray, please don't leave me."

How could she look at him with such distress? He had to leave, for his own sanity. And for her own peace. He'd find a different woman—a willing woman—to share his pleasure. Or he'd ease his own needs. "No one will harm you. You're safe here."

"I know." Her voice seemed unhappy, and uneasiness still dimmed her expression.

"Do you need anything before I go?"

That rosy blush flooded her cheeks again. She bit her lower lip between little white teeth. "I need you to stay. I need you to hold me again."

That made no sense. "After what happened to you tonight, I'm surprised you want anyone to touch you." *Especially a man.*

Her blush spread, creeping down her neck, disappearing under the thermo blanket. How far did that rosy color go? He vaguely remembered her breasts as small, but firm. Was she blushing that far?

Sanwar, he had to quit thinking like this.

"Actually, I..." Her blush turned even more fiery, and her gaze dropped from his eyes to his chin. "I think I need to get back on the horse."

He understood the words, but they made no sense. Was she delirious? "Back on what horse?"

She gave a breathless, husky little laugh. The sound made his stomach tighten for some inexplicable reason. "You've never heard that expression?"

He shook his head. "I grew up on Prendara. My English is a bit..." What was the word? Something about metal...an ancient metal...iron. Ah, yes. "Rusty."

"Oh. Well, getting back on the horse..." She swallowed. "After you fall off a horse, they say you should get right back on, or else you'll always be afraid to...to ride."

Afraid to *ride?* Did she mean...did she want to have *sex* with him?

It seemed a gift from the gods. He'd been lusting after her, and now she was offering herself to him.

Offering herself out of fear.

No man of principle would take pleasure from a woman in her situation. And in his position, he was expected to have more principles than most.

Unfortunately.

"You have no cause for fear. Those men are in confinement."

She frowned, and her eyes grew misty. "You're turning me down." Her voice sounded brittle. As if he'd hurt her.

As if she really did want to lie with him.

He sat on the edge of the bed. "You were attacked less than an hour ago. It's difficult to believe that you want a man to touch you at all."

She gave him a sliver of a smile. "It's like I said...I want to get right back on the horse."

She sounded sincere. What did he know about sexual attacks? Nothing. All he knew was that Daria was asking him to lie with her...and he wanted rather desperately to do it. To join her in this bed, *his* bed, and show her more pleasure than she'd ever known from any of the callous men who paid for the use of her body.

Her fingers twined with his, spreading warmth through his hand. "Maybe I need someone to remind me that not all men are animals."

Now that he could believe.

"Maybe I just need *you*," she murmured.

His breath caught. "You don't even know me."

Her fingers tightened on his, as if she'd never let go. "I know that you saved me."

"Anyone would have done the same."

She took a shuddering breath. "Plenty of men would have joined right in. Offered to hold me down. Taken a t-turn."

Praise the gods, he'd been there to save her.

"But not you." Her voice seemed softer now. Tender, like a lover's. "I can tell you're a really nice man."

He almost smiled. A *really nice man* wouldn't be thinking about tearing the blanket off of her and burying his face between those bare, hairless thighs. "Believe me, the world's full of nice men."

Her eyes shuttered, as if a veil hid her feelings. An expression she probably had a lot of practice using. "I don't meet many nice men."

In her occupation, it was no wonder. Lying in his bed, under his thermo blanket, gazing up at him through those long-lashed eyes...she looked so innocent. Innocent and warm. He could kiss those warm lips...run his hands over those long, smooth legs...bury his face—

"Please, Gray," she said softly. "Help me. Help me forget."

Chapter Two

His name did it. Hearing his name in her husky voice. Nothing could stop him from touching her again.

He stroked her cheek with the back of his fingers. Her skin felt as soft as it looked. No, it felt even softer than it looked. And warm. So warm.

"They were going to kill me." She gripped his hand, her eyes huge. "Show me that I'm alive, Gray."

She knew his name, but she knew nothing else about him. Nothing about his influential position, nothing about his powerful aunt. And yet she wanted him.

She wanted *him*. Just him.

And he wanted her. He wanted to pleasure her with tenderness. The tenderness she must rarely see. The tenderness she deserved.

She nuzzled her cheek against his hand. "Please."

Soft and warm…how would the rest of her body feel? He ached to find out. "As you will."

She smiled again, causing his stomach to give a little lurch. She looked so sweet, with that gamine face and those big brown eyes. How could she look so sweet, so untouched, when chains of men used her body every night?

Men would pay dearly for that look of innocence. She must be very popular.

He frowned.

She lifted her hand to her face and brushed her hair back. "I probably look like a mess."

He must have been studying her intently, making her self-conscious. This wasn't the typical scenario of a beautiful woman begging for flattery. He wouldn't pacify her with trite compliments. She wasn't a beauty, and she didn't deserve a lie.

"You look fine," he told her. "Just a little strained. Like you've been through an ordeal. Like you need some..." It took him a moment to find an appropriate word. "Comfort."

Her smile was nothing but flirtatious. "You can comfort me better if you get under this blanket with me."

But she was rolled up in the blanket. She sat up, slipped off her ridiculous shoes, and slid underneath the blanket again. With a quick motion, she spread it across the bed and turned down the free corner, then looked at him expectantly.

He wanted to stay on top of the blanket with her, where he'd have more access to her body, more ways to pleasure her—and himself—but he restrained the words. If she felt more comfortable covered up, he'd oblige.

He pulled off his shirt and dropped it to the floor. When he stood and reached for his pants, he heard her indrawn breath and froze.

She was staring at him with wide eyes.

"What's wrong?"

She shook her head. "Nothing."

At last she seemed a typical female, making him guess her true thoughts. "I can leave my clothes on, if you will it so."

"No, I..." She licked her lips. "I was just surprised. You have a great chest."

Was that the kind of remark she gave to men who paid her? No, she sounded far too confused to be repeating a practiced phrase. Confused but sincere. Perhaps she was surprised to find enjoyment in looking at a man.

Her steady stare almost made him self-conscious. His body was nothing special, merely lean and moderately fit. "Dim lights twenty percent." The lights went down to a soft glow.

He kicked off his boots, took his pants down quickly, then slid into the bed, facing her on his side. She moved, pressing her body against his. So warm and soft. Even through the filmy shirt she wore, her breasts teased his chest. His very ordinary chest.

She sighed, her breath raising nerve endings where it rushed over his shoulder. "Mmm. Nice."

Yes, she felt nice in truth. Nice and warm. Nothing like the other women he'd pleasured.

He stroked her back slowly, letting her get used to his body. Giving her a chance to change her mind.

The torn fabric of her shirt caught on his hand. An unpleasant reminder of the men locked up in confinement.

"I can comfort you better if you take this off." Good. His voice hadn't betrayed his anger.

"All right."

She managed to struggle out of the shirt without leaving the cover of the blanket. Unfortunate. He wanted a look at those pert little breasts. *Soon.*

But he felt them, felt them as she pressed her chest to his, as she rubbed her nipples against his skin.

His hand found her chin, tilting her face up for a kiss. Oh, what silky lips. He licked at them, teased them, until her mouth opened and his tongue could slip inside. She tasted minty, like an exotic spice he'd long forgotten.

Delicious…sweet but spicy.

Cinnamon. Yes, she tasted like cinnamon.

He kept the kiss gentle, kept his tongue soft, kept his hands light so she could pull away if she wanted to. Gods, he hoped she didn't want to. He licked the inside of her mouth with shallow strokes, feeling the sharp edges of her teeth. Heat pooled in his root. His *cock.* That was the English word.

Her tongue came alive, fluttering in his mouth with delicate little thrusts. He cupped her cheek, felt her jaw move as she met the eager motions of his mouth. Her fingers wove through his hair.

Suddenly she broke the kiss, gasping.

Her eyes were wide. What…

Ah. His cock, hard and heavy, was pressed against her thigh. An unconscious act on his part, trying to ease himself.

He stroked her hair gently. "Don't worry. It won't go anywhere without your consent."

Her cheeks blazed with color, and he grinned. She was such a shy little thing. At least with him. Maybe it was just a reaction to what she'd been through tonight.

He had to ask. "Are you certain you want this?"

She nodded. "You're exactly what I want."

Her hand came up to stroke his chest. She touched him lightly, hesitantly, as if she didn't know exactly what to do, and she watched her hand move over his skin as though she was amazed by her daring.

He mirrored the motions of her hand with his own, stroking her breasts ardently. She closed her eyes, turned her face away. Hiding from him.

But not resisting.

He managed to ease the blanket a little lower as he fondled her breasts. They were small but nicely shaped, rounded and firm. And her areolas were huge, the largest he'd ever seen. He traced the velvety texture with his fingers, then strummed her hard nipples. Her breath came faster, and she bit her lip, but kept her eyes closed.

Since her lips were so far away, he kissed her neck instead. She drew in a sharp breath but didn't pull away. No, praise the gods, she lifted her breast more firmly into his hand.

He didn't want to rush this...didn't want to rush *her*...but those hidden legs tempted him beyond all restraint. He stroked slowly down her stomach...over her hip, still covered by her scrap of a skirt...then to her thigh. Oh, yes. Silky hot skin over yielding flesh and firm muscle—more enticing than he'd imagined. He'd never felt anything like this warm, hairless leg.

He couldn't rip the blanket off—not yet—couldn't give himself the visual feast, but he'd had a good, long look earlier. He could imagine these legs, could picture what she'd do with them. First she'd part them for his hungry mouth...and he'd pillow his head on this strong thigh while he ate her tender sex. And when he rode her, she'd wrap these eager legs around his hips. Yes.

Yes, he'd ride her. Prendarian women preferred to take the dominant position themselves, but Daria wasn't a Prendarian woman. He'd ride her...and she'd find pleasure in his rhythm.

But she had to be naked. Now. He tugged her skirt down, and a scrap of an undergarment went with it. She helped, kicking her clothes off somewhere deep under the blanket. She held the blanket up to her waist, hiding those luscious legs from his gaze—but not from his touch. He kept his hand on her thigh.

He found her breasts with his mouth, suckling while he stroked her leg, and she held his head against her, tangling her fingers in his hair, holding him as if she'd never let him go.

He waited for an age...he waited forever...just suckling her breasts, occasionally nipping at her neck, one hand teasing her hip, her thighs, until she was whimpering and squirming and lifting her hips a little. Then he reached between her legs.

She felt wet and hot...unbelievably hot. His fingers slipped easily over all that wet skin, parting her, dipping deep, teasing her bud with light, rapid strokes of his thumb.

He'd torment her until she begged. Then he'd settle in and find her rhythm.

Suddenly she gave a sharp, wordless cry and froze, but before he could speak, before he could even lift his head, she climaxed with long, shuddering spasms, clutching at his back as if he was the only solid thing in the world. Gods, he'd never seen a woman climax so quickly.

Or so deeply.

He lifted his head to see her face. Even with her eyes closed, she looked dazed. Confused. Like she hadn't expected to climax at all.

No doubt she rarely did. Not with men who paid her for their pleasure.

Selfish *rumaariti,* all of them.

His root was achingly hard, pressed against her smooth thigh, but he'd never been more satisfied. He'd given her pleasure. Pleasure that had taken her by surprise.

And now he'd give her even more.

* * *

Daria opened her eyes and found *him*—Gray...the target...God, the man who'd saved her life—gazing at her with a satisfied smile on his face.

She wanted to slap him. To slap that arrogant smile off of his face.

But it wasn't really an arrogant smile. He didn't look triumphant; he didn't look like a man who'd just made an easy conquest. No, his smile seemed...genuine. Tender. Like he was simply happy to have given her pleasure.

And he had.

Even his eyes were lit up with that smile, those stunning golden brown eyes, more compelling in person than in any of the holo-projections she'd studied. Amber eyes. And like amber, his eyes held secrets.

She knew most of them. But he didn't know it. And he didn't know that she had secrets of her own.

His fingers, the fingers that had brought her to a shattering climax, were still nestled between her legs. One finger was even partially inside her, a subtle invasion of her body, staking a claim. She felt unbearably exposed, looking into his smiling eyes while his hand rested on her most private parts. She couldn't think of a single thing to say.

She'd been prepared to fuck him to stay close to him. She'd steeled herself to endure it. To fake pleasure at his touch. To hide her revulsion, her hatred.

She hadn't been prepared to *enjoy* it.

Nothing could have prepared her for the way he'd kissed her. The way he'd touched her.

Why couldn't he have jumped on her like a horny space-sailor, fucked her quickly, and left her mildly disgusted? She'd expected him to treat her like a whore. Why did he have to treat her like a...like a lover?

He'd made a traitor of her body. And she'd gone down without a fight.

When he lifted his hand away, she almost thanked him for letting go. But he brought his fingers to her breast and rubbed wetness over her nipple. Even though she'd just climaxed, his wet fingers made her tingle.

His head dropped to her chest, his mouth closing over that nipple and suckling. Hard and deep. God, her breasts were excruciatingly sensitive. No one had ever played with her like this. Not after she'd climaxed.

She lifted herself against his sucking mouth and felt his chuckle deep inside her breast.

Enough. She needed to satisfy *him.* That was the whole point of sleeping with him. To make him want to keep her...just until she found a way to finish her mission.

She pushed at his shoulder. "I want to touch you."

He rolled off of her and settled on his side, facing her. "As you will."

An odd way to say "OK," but that must be what he meant. She stroked his chest, let her hand wander down to his belly, felt his muscles tense. Leaning closer, she kissed his neck, then gave him a little bite. His breath caught; she felt it against her lips. She kept going, laying down a ring of nips and kisses on his neck. He'd have a few hickeys to hide in the morning.

His fingers wove through her hair, holding her close. She moved her face down to his collarbone, ran her hand down his taut stomach, then back up again. Why did he have to have such a great chest? Tanned and broad, just enough hair to tease her skin with masculine roughness. Not too broad, not too muscled. Just…perfect. She followed the trail of hair down to his navel, dipping into his bellybutton.

She kept her face against his neck as she reached lower and found his cock. God, he was hot. Hot and hard…and longer than she'd expected. Not that she'd known what to expect. Her lips quirked up in a smile. That information hadn't been in the files she'd studied.

She wrapped her hand around him and gave a tentative stroke. Would he like it hard and fast? Soft and slow?

A firm hand caught her wrist before she could do more. "No."

"Why not?"

He rolled her to her back and bent his head to her breasts, licking across a sensitive nipple. "Because you'll make me climax too quickly, *dahsh'kara*."

She didn't know that alien word. And she didn't care to. But she couldn't muster up any outrage at him for speaking in that hateful alien language, not with his mouth on her breasts, planting sucking little kisses on her straining nipples.

She whimpered. God, she shouldn't feel this good. Not with him. Not with a collaborator. "Stop. Let me…" She could barely think. "Let me touch you."

"I'm not done touching *you* yet."

"But I already…" Her face heated. Ridiculous, considering she was naked in bed with him. Even at twenty-seven, she still blushed like a nervous virgin. "I already came."

She felt him smile against her breast, but he didn't lift his head. "Yes, *dahsh'kara,* you certainly did. But only once."

Could he possibly be serious? "Once was…" He nipped at her breast, just hard enough to sting her gently with his teeth. "Oh! Once was fine." *Understatement.* "Once was more than I expected."

He chuckled. "I won't settle for less than three."

"*Three?*" She'd heard rumors about Prendarian women—insatiable sex maniacs, every one of them, or so the legends said. She'd never believed those stories.

"At least three," he murmured. "And you'll find me very determined. Best for you to accept my will."

"What's the most…" No, she didn't want to know. She didn't want to be interested in his past. Or in him.

"The most times I've seen a woman climax?"

Well, since he'd guessed… She nodded.

But he couldn't see her nod. He was still nuzzling at her breasts, flicking the hard tip of his tongue over an even harder nipple.

"Yes," she said on a gasp.

"Five."

"*Five?*" God, he must be a tireless lover...and an arrogant one, for sure. Her mouth hung open. She closed it quickly, even though he hadn't lifted his head.

"Mmm-hmm." She felt him smile again, probably at her astonishment. "Fear not. I'm certain you can exceed that record."

Hell, *two* would be a record for her. But she wasn't averse to faking them. Not if it kept him happy. Not if it kept him wanting her.

She'd planned on faking one anyway. So much for that plan. He'd barely touched her and she'd gone off like a barrage of missiles.

She felt his tongue, so hot, wet and raspy, licking across her breasts, from one to the other and back again.

His hair, softer than she'd imagined, slid through her fingers. With his mouth teasing her like this, she couldn't resist him. And why should she? The more he enjoyed himself, the more likely he'd be to keep her with him.

Yes, this was strictly for the sake of the mission. The fact that she wanted it, that she wanted *him,* that he was working so hard to please her...oh, that was irrelevant. She'd enjoy his wonderful mouth...his wonderful hands...

One of those hands slid over her hip, stroked her bush. She parted her legs shamelessly, and then those curious, knowing fingers were spreading magic over her sensitive clit.

A climax built inside her...inexorable.

Unbelievable.

His hands were wondrous.

He nuzzled his mouth against her neck. "You're very wet, *dahsh'kara.*" His breath rushed over her ear, set her heart racing.

"And I'm very thirsty." He teased her earlobe with the point of his tongue. "I'm going to take a long, long drink."

God, no. Not that. She'd come in his hand, she'd fuck him, she'd do any perversion in the universe to him...but she couldn't let him...she couldn't let him get that close to her. She couldn't let him do anything so *intimate*.

He slid down the bed before she could think of a way to stop him. The blanket went down with his body, off the foot of the bed, slithering to the floor and leaving her exposed. He ran his hands up her legs as he rose to his knees.

His gaze was locked on her thighs, and he couldn't seem to stop stroking her legs. "Beautiful."

Then his hands cupped her ass, lifting her, and his hair brushed her thighs. Her legs fell open to the nudge of his face...as if he owned her, as if she had no will of her own. God, she didn't. His hands came around to her thighs again, his thumbs spread her open—a pause, a heartbeat—oh God, was he *looking* at her? Before she could pull away, his mouth settled on her sex, kissing, licking, sucking...and she couldn't stop him, couldn't fight him, couldn't fight *herself*...couldn't keep herself from whimpering and moaning and clawing at the bed as he drank deep.

"Mmm..." He murmured against her, and the vibrations made her lift her hips, trying to get even closer to that maddening mouth. He settled on her clit, sucking and moaning until she trembled with feverish need.

Then he thrust a scalding hot finger deep inside, and her body jolted with fierce pleasure. She cried out and came, came right against his mouth, with shuddering gasps and endless spasms. She came as though she trusted him with everything she was...with every dream...with every secret. As though she trusted him with all of her heart.

As though he was her lover, not her enemy.

And then she was panting for breath, trembling with aftershocks, staring up at the strange pink ceiling. She felt him smile against her thigh.

Probably an arrogant smile this time.

The smug, conceited smile of a man who'd just made a whore scream his name.

She choked down a sob.

Damn him. God damn him.

* * *

The flavor of her sex lingered in his mouth; her scent consumed his nostrils. Enticing, musky woman scent. Woman *taste*. He'd been far, far too long without it. Until this moment, he hadn't even realized how much he missed that taste. Craved that taste.

His whole body felt hard, aching, strained.

He needed release. Now. Desperately.

He rose above her hot, sweat-sheened body, yearning to settle between her wondrous legs. He wanted to ride her. Hard and deep. For hours.

She lay passive beneath him, her gorgeous thighs wide. Ready for him. Open. He lowered himself slowly.

She jerked a little, a tiny movement. Had she flinched? Didn't she want... At the last moment he shifted, lying beside her instead of on top of her.

He reached out and cupped her cheek. Those soft brown eyes stayed closed.

"Daria."

No response. No movement.

As if he hadn't just satisfied her. Twice. Now, by the gods, she would grant him the same. "Woman, I can't wait another moment to be inside you."

Her eyes were huge then, gleaming. With tears? "Then don't wait."

Acquiescing. Not encouraging.

"You will it?" His voice sounded hard, urgent with his need.

"Yes."

Yet she stayed flat on her back, making no move to mount him as a Prendarian woman would have done. But her hands reached out to him, beckoning him down, down on top of her silky length. Welcoming his weight. And oh, he wanted her too much to restrain himself.

He'd rarely been on top of a woman. And never, never one so warm. So very warm and giving. She smiled a little and sighed as he slid over her. Soft arms circled his back when his hips settled between the heat of her thighs. Irresistible heat.

Craving her fire, he pulled back and thrust inside her, deep inside her. *Sanwar,* she felt hot. He groaned.

He'd never last. Maybe talking would help. But her eyes were closed tight, her head turned to the side.

"Am I too heavy?"

She shook her head, but didn't open her eyes. "No. No, you feel...wonderful."

Her tone seemed strange. A little sad. As if she didn't want to feel good.

He couldn't use her for his own pleasure. Too many men had done so before him.

Far too many men.

When he pulled away, withdrawing, his cock all but howled at the loss of her wet heat. "You don't want this."

Daria clutched him closer, and her eyes opened. "No, please. I do want you."

A lie. Perhaps she was sated; she'd climaxed twice. But by the gods, he wanted her to climax again. Again, with his cock buried in her flesh as she quaked around him. He wanted her to feel the same fire, the same passion, that he felt for her. That she'd felt just moments ago.

He thrust back into her, urgent and deep. She gasped and closed her eyes.

He kept the rhythm slow, slow enough that he didn't climax, gnashing his teeth to hold his need in check. Gods, what a challenge to his control. With her breath tantalizing his ear, her hands pressing him down, her body yielding to his...her knees lifting...her legs enfolding him...

Her legs. Her long, warm, bare legs. Sliding over his.

Ah, damn the gods.

No control now, none. Greedy fingers grabbed his ass, urging him, encouraging him, and his straining body couldn't wait another moment. He slammed into her fast and hard, shaking, swearing. "*Ab'tah...ish ab'tah...sanwar.*"

Passion burst in a wrenching climax, tearing a cry from his throat. *Gods, yes.* He thrust one last time and pulsed deep against her womb, groaning, losing his seed deep inside her heat. Such welcoming heat.

He collapsed on top of her, trembling and suddenly cold. Her arms had left him.

And he'd left her unfulfilled. How could he face her? Yet he must.

But first he'd enjoy this moment. Breathing in the scent here, where her neck joined her shoulder. Relishing her warmth. Feeling her wonderful silky legs wrapped around his own.

His body, tired and sated, relaxed onto the soft cushion of hers. He'd face her soon enough.

At least he'd proven one thing: he wasn't bored with sex.

He smiled, then yawned.

He'd speak in a moment. Apologize, then give her that third climax. But first…first he'd rest.

Just for a moment.

She'd still be here in a moment.

Chapter Three

Every deep breath expanded his chest, pressing her down into the bed. Squished between his solid chest and the mattress, she couldn't breathe until he exhaled. And every exhalation ruffled her hair, tickling her ear.

Had she ever been this close to a sleeping man? No, never.

Daria lay underneath him, trembling, biting her lip.

He'd fallen asleep. On top of her. Still inside her.

God.

If she pushed him off, he'd wake up. And she couldn't talk to him. Not yet. She'd burst into humiliating tears if he even looked at her.

She took a shuddering breath.

He shifted, nuzzling against her neck, and she froze. What if he woke up? She wasn't ready to face him, not by a long shot. But his breathing evened out again. Thank God.

She'd wait a little longer, until he was deeply asleep. Then she'd get out from under him.

By then she might have herself under control.

Control? Hah. Who was she trying to kid? The word didn't exist anymore.

Screwing him had been...unbelievable. She'd almost had that third orgasm. With him on top of her, thrusting so steady and deep, moaning and groaning with desire...making her feel like he truly needed her. And she'd been right there with him, climbing, reaching for that elusive brass ring...until he'd spoken in that damned alien language.

Reminding her of who he was. A collaborator. The target. Nothing more.

Nothing more.

Until that moment, he'd been someone else. Not a lover, not exactly. No, he'd been worse than a lover—he'd been a person. *Gray.* The man who'd rescued her. The man who'd taken a whore into his bed and shown her pleasure. Given her two shattering orgasms.

Given her the illusion of tenderness.

But other than that, there was nothing special about him. She'd just overreacted. After the night she'd had, it was no wonder. She'd earned the right to be so emotional. So vulnerable. Her friends were gone. Her possessions were gone. She couldn't risk going back to the warehouse they'd called home. Odds were the Enforcers had the place staked out. They'd ID her if she showed up.

Homeless. Friendless and homeless.

Well, it wasn't the first time.

Besides, the plan was to get Gray to keep her, and things were off to a good start. He certainly seemed to like fucking her. At the end, he'd been out of control himself, shouting those harsh, needy alien words. The alien words that had hit her like a cold shower.

Until that moment, she'd almost forgotten she was only here to destroy him.

She wouldn't forget again. That crazy, mind-altering passion wouldn't happen again. And even if it did, she'd find a way to compartmentalize. What happened between them in bed would be completely separate from everything else she had to do.

Completely separate.

He rolled off of her suddenly, stretching out on his side, facing away from her. She froze. A sigh, a small cough—then his breathing settled into a regular, even pattern.

The room was cold without him blanketing her. She sat up slowly, keeping her eyes glued to the back of his head. He didn't stir.

Her body felt strange. Achy and languid. He was an excellent lover, no doubt about it. He must have had a lot of practice. Far more than she did. Hell, just about anyone was more experienced than she was.

He must be used to those wild Prendarian women. A woman like her would be a novelty to him.

A woman who admitted she felt accomplished if she came once.

Yeah, he'd liked the shy, nervous act. Though it hadn't been much of an act. Every time she thought of those two druggies groping her... She shuddered.

But she could play up her natural shyness. Play the shy, confused, troubled prostitute. The prostitute who hadn't known much enjoyment when it came to sex.

And why shouldn't she enjoy it now? She'd sacrificed enough for the sake of this mission, and she'd planned on sacrificing her body as well. She'd expected him to be rough and quick; she'd planned on faking every orgasm. She should be happy that he was great in bed. If she liked fucking him, if she *showed* him that she liked fucking him, he'd trust her that much sooner. He'd think they were lovers in truth. It'd help convince him to keep her around for a while.

Until she found a way to stop him.

Her eyes teared up. What the...

God, she actually *wanted* to stay with him. And not just for the sake of the mission. Or the hot sex. She wanted to stay with him because he'd been...he'd been *kind* to her. She pressed a fist to her mouth, choking down a sob.

All this emotion—it was nothing more than stress. The stress of finding out she was alone. The stress of nearly being raped out on that abandoned dock. The stress of having Gray—the target—save her.

He'd saved her. No wonder she wanted to stay with him.

No. No, that wasn't what she wanted. Everything was just catching up with her. Learning about Don and Trisha. Talking to Tank for the last—probably the very last time. Tank, the gruff, burly anarchist who'd taken her in when she'd been fifteen and hungry and he'd caught her trying to steal his wallet.

Enough. She needed to let it all out. Let out all the stress. Start over fresh.

And she needed to incinerate her talkie fast, before Gray found it.

She slid from the bed. Her skirt was buried somewhere under the tangled blanket on the floor. She dug through it until she found the stretchy bit of fabric. Good, the talkie was still tucked in the hidden pocket.

Even in this dim light, she could see goose bumps on Gray's arm. He must be cold. If she covered him, he'd sleep longer. Give her more time to herself.

She desperately needed more time to herself.

That was the only reason she cared about his shivers.

The only reason.

* * *

Gray woke slowly, blinking even though the lights were dimmed. Had he...had he actually *slept?*

Yes, he had.

Oh, no.

He'd ridden Daria to his own satisfaction, then fallen asleep right on top of her. Leaving her pleasure incomplete. What a skillful lover.

He must have been a great *comfort* to her, lying on her like a lumbering, sweating *rumaarit.*

He rolled over to apologize, but found an empty bed. Had Daria left him?

He frowned. He'd find her somehow. Haunt the docks. Have his personal aide make inquiries. Privately hire an Enforcer. Whatever it took.

He got off the bed and stumbled over something hard and spiky. What—

Ah, her ridiculous shoes were lying on the floor. She couldn't have gone far barefoot. Although how anyone could walk at all on these narrow, elevated heels was a mystery to him.

He prowled his quarters naked, looking for her. There wasn't much to search. He'd insisted on quarters as spartan as most of the crew. Only two rooms, a small waste room, and a tiny cleansing station.

He found her sitting on the floor of the small cleansing station, her knees drawn up to her chin, her arms wrapped around her bare legs. She wore her torn scrap of a shirt and her tiny, clinging skirt. Wetness glistened on her cheeks.

She sniffled.

By the gods, no.

Seeing him, she gave a little start and tried to wipe the tears on her tiny sleeve, pretending she was merely yawning.

Plenty of women had tried to sway him with tears. Daria had hidden hers from him. Something tightened in his chest.

"I wanted to wash." Her voice wavered a little. "But I couldn't find the shower."

He couldn't stop the smile. "You're sitting in it."

She looked up, surprised. "There's no showerhead. No faucet."

He reached a hand down to her. "Here. Let me show you."

She took his hand, let him pull her to her feet. She seemed frail, but she wasn't a tiny woman—the top of her head nearly reached his shoulder. Her shyness, her tears, made her seem vulnerable. He cupped that pointed little chin in his hand and gazed down into her face. Her eyes were red from crying, her cheeks blotchy, her eyelids puffy. She looked terribly unhappy…and wretchedly unattractive. Yet he'd never felt more protective of a woman. Those tears were his fault.

"I'm sorry," he said.

Her reddened eyes went wide. "Sorry for what?"

"For giving you cause to cry."

She shook her head, and his hand fell away. "You didn't."

"I should have known." He clenched his hands. "I *did* know you couldn't possibly want a man. But I wanted you, so I ignored my principles."

"You…" She dropped her gaze to his chin. "You really wanted me?"

If she came any closer, or even glanced further down, she'd note the evidence of how badly he wanted her right now. Despite the puffy eyes and unattractive sniffling. It must be those incredibly shapely legs of hers. "You know I did."

A ghost of a smile curved her mouth. "I thought you were just…doing me a favor."

"A favor? Had I granted you a favor, I'd have left you in peace. And you would not be weeping."

She shook her head. "I begged you to get in bed with me. To hold me. I…I wanted you, too."

Yes, she had. Even though she didn't know who he was. She hadn't wanted anything more from him than comfort. Than pleasure. She'd wanted *him.* Only him.

"Daria, stay with me."

That made her eyes come back up. What was he saying? He felt as surprised as she looked.

"What?" she asked, as if she'd read his mind.

"Stay with me. I'm going to be on Earth for at least six months." Longer, if the election went his way. But thinking of that was totally premature. "I want you to stay with me...for a time."

She bit her lip. Clearly thinking of the words to refuse him.

He touched her elbow; she didn't pull away, nor did she meet his gaze. "I'm usually a better bed companion than...well, than I was with you."

She gave a watery laugh. "If you were any better, I wouldn't be able to walk."

"Then you'll stay?"

Her head dipped even lower, hiding more of her face. "I don't know."

"I'll pay you." How much could she be earning? It didn't matter. "Just tell me what you earn in your best night. I'll pay you more."

"You'll pay me for sex," she said tonelessly.

He gripped her upper arms with both hands. "By the gods, would you rather have other men pay you? Strangers? Would you rather be out on the docks, where men can take their pleasure from you by force?"

Her face paled. "You're hurting me."

Her whisper stunned him more than the loudest shout. He released her arms and saw white and red marks from his fingers...just below another bruise, perhaps from those *rumaariti* criminals. "I'm sorry." The words sounded stupid. And inadequate.

As inadequate as his offer. He didn't want to pay her for sex. He wanted to help her. Help her out of the dangerous profession she was in.

"You don't have to pleasure me." *Sanwar,* he sounded desperate. Desperate and deranged. He'd just admitted that he'd wanted her; he wanted her still. Why was he telling her she didn't have to lie with him?

Her chin rose a notch. "I won't take your money for nothing. I'm not a charity case."

He'd never heard the expression, but her meaning was clear. "You can do other work for me. I need..." Inspiration struck. "I need an assistant."

She looked skeptical. "What kind of assistant?"

He had four hands' worth of assistants already. What could she... "My English is terrible. Sometimes I can barely understand you." Far from the truth, but a plausible lie. "I need someone to instruct me."

"You could hire a tutor."

"I need someone who knows colloquial English," he countered. "I'm going to be meeting a lot of different people here. People from other cultures. Other continents. I need someone to help me communicate with them. Someone who can understand their concerns. Someone like you."

She tilted her head a little to one side, obviously considering his offer. Suddenly her cheeks flooded with color. "What if I want to sleep with you?"

Sleeping next to her, unable to touch her, would be akin to torture. Why would she even want that? But he shrugged, feigning indifference. "I'm happy to have you sleep with me. Although you might appreciate the privacy of your own bed."

She smiled. "You really *do* need a tutor. *To sleep together* is just an expression. A euphemism for having sex."

What a ridiculous, paradoxical expression—with her in his bed, they'd have little sleep. "I would enjoy *sleeping* with you," he answered. "If you will it."

"For money?"

He almost said yes. A reflexive answer. But was that a challenge in her voice? A trace of pride in the tilt of her chin? She couldn't possibly *want* to sell her body. Not even to him.

"No," he said. "I'll pay you to help me with my English. But if we *sleep together*, it will be only for the pleasure we give each other."

When she smiled at him, he knew he'd said the correct thing. The rush of happiness he felt took him by surprise.

She nodded. "I accept your offer."

He wanted to kiss her, but she held out her hand. He shook it in the ritual Earther fashion, absurd as it seemed with him naked and his turgid root a scant hand's width from her belly.

"Now will you show me how this crazy alien shower works?"

"There's a skill to it," he replied, closing the door behind them.

She looked up at him expectantly. "What skill?"

With effort, he restrained a smile. "Shower on."

Electrons hummed, swirling on a warm rush of air. Now he couldn't help but grin. "There. That's the only skill required."

She looked astonished. "Where's the water?"

He laughed. "Water? Prendara's an arid world, Daria. Water's precious. We shower with sonic waves. Electrons."

"It tingles."

She spoke as if this was as new to him as it was to her. The wonder in her voice made him feel rather...tender. "I know," was all he could think to say.

"What do I do? Just stand here?"

The confined space, the closeness of her body, the rush of warm air ruffling her hair...somehow this seemed more intimate than being in bed with her. He'd had more sexual encounters than he could ever recall, but he'd never bathed with a woman before.

And he couldn't resist the urge to touch her. He brushed a hand over her head, weaving his fingers through her long black hair. She might not be a beautiful woman, but her hair was quite lovely, straight and thick. "Rub your hands over your skin."

He stroked over her shoulders, then up her neck to her cheeks, cupping her face in his hands. The swollen, blotchy redness—remnants from her tears—was fading, leaving her skin creamy and pink.

Her lips were full, far too lush for her slender face. Strange how he could know that for a fact, yet be unable to resist them. He pressed a gentle kiss to that wide mouth, and electrons hummed between their lips. A sigh brushed his chin before she leaned away—not withdrawing, just looking up at him.

She laid her hands on his forearms, then skimmed her way up to his shoulders, spreading tingling electron waves in her wake. "Like this?"

"Yes."

Her eyes were wide and wondering. "How does it work?"

"When you move your hands, the sonic wave moves with you." His fingers slid down her arms, demonstrating. He knew she felt the rush of warm air and electrons tingling on her flesh. "The electrons dissolve oil and dirt."

"Without soap?"

He stepped closer and stroked her back, embracing her but not holding her. "It's better than soap. It's ecological. And it won't dry your skin." *Your soft, silky skin.*

Her arms came around him, her small hands mirroring the motions of his. She moved closer, closer, until her breasts teased his chest. Her nipples were already hard, scoring his skin with every breath she took.

She turned her face and rested her cheek on his collarbone as she rubbed his back. He tilted his head, pressing his lips to her forehead. Prendarian women were too tall. He'd never noticed until this very moment. Daria seemed the perfect height, small enough to shelter in his arms, but not so small that he felt like a giant oaf.

Gentle fingers sifted through his hair, curved around his neck, and stroked down his arms. Her warm body, her petting hands, sent little tingling pulses over his skin. Was it the sonic wave, or merely her touch? No matter. Whatever the source, she made this shower seem more erotic than any experience he could recall.

The tingling centered in his chest, under the heat of her stroking fingers. He felt as if every hair, every nerve ending, strained toward her hand.

She pulled her head away and watched her hand move on him. As if she'd never touched a man's chest in her life.

Sanwar, he was a fool. She'd probably touched hundreds.

Fortunate that he'd never been a jealous man. Nor was he now. There was no cause to be jealous of men who paid her for pleasure. She'd wanted none of them…not like she wanted *him.* She was here with him willingly. Giving him pleasure willingly.

He lowered his head and caught her mouth in a kiss. She tilted her face up, moving her lips on his. Not just willing—*eager*. Without thought, he pulled her close. Her fingers curled in the hair on his chest, and she murmured against his mouth...something unintelligible.

"I hope that was *more*," he said. "*Or yes.*"

She smiled against his lips, then leaned back to look into his eyes. "Maybe."

The teasing light in her face drew a smile from him. He'd tease her in turn. With his body, not his words. "Lift your arms."

She lifted her elbows, keeping that tantalizing hand on his chest. The skin under her arms felt unbelievably soft. Soft and hairless...exotic silky skin, tender and bare under his hands. Like her legs. His knees grew weak, and he had to lock them to stay upright.

"Are you sure we're getting clean?" Her voice sounded husky, needy. As if she didn't care about bathing at all.

His hands drifted over her collarbones. Gods, how he hated seeing her in this torn shirt. If he'd waited even one more tick before leaving the ship, he might have been too late.

"The shower works best if you're naked."

She blushed, just a hint of delicate color. With a coy little glance, she turned her back to him. The shirt came off over her head and fell to the floor.

He reached around her and cupped her breasts. She gasped. His fingers wandered upward, finding her peaked nipples. His cock, already hard, grew to full length.

"You see?" he murmured against her neck. "Now you're getting clean."

She pressed back against him, and he couldn't resist. He rubbed his cock against her ass, pulling her hips tight to increase the pressure. He wanted to tear off this stretchy little skirt…to bend her over and plunge deep into her heat.

Not yet. Not until she was feverish with need.

One greedy hand wandered from her hip to her sex. His fingers touched her nest, teasing through the thin fabric of her undergarment. Ah, time to begin his tutoring.

"What do you call this sweet place, Daria?"

She stiffened. In embarrassment? "What do *you* call it?"

He nuzzled the space where her neck met her shoulder and dipped his fingers deeper. "In Prendarian, we use the word for *nest.*"

"There are…dozens of words in English."

Why was she reluctant to tell him? Was she so shy? "Which of those words do you prefer?"

Her shoulder lifted in a delicate shrug. "I don't have a preference."

"You agreed to be my tutor." Her neck, so warm under his mouth, demanded a long, slow lick.

She gasped. "You're not helping me bathe."

"I'm not?" His fingers slipped beneath her undergarment and brushed the curls between her legs. "I seem to be washing your body more than my own."

When he delved deeper, slick moisture covered his hand. The sonic shower dissolved it as he rubbed her, but more fluid leaked from her body. She tilted sideways suddenly, resting part of her weight against the wall.

He pressed her closer to the wall, closer to him. Wherever they touched, the electrons pulsed between them. "Tell me," he urged. "Tell me the English words. I want to speak to you in our native language, Daria."

"In *my* native language."

She sounded fierce. She must resent Prendarian words, as many Earthers did. He truly didn't understand. Language was merely language; communication had no race. But he respected her feelings. And with her ass pressed against his cock, her body oozing creamy warmth onto his hand, he would not debate. "As you will."

She turned in his arms, dislodging his hand from her nest, then slipped her hands around his neck and pulled his head down next to hers. Her belly, softly rounded, brushed his stiff cock; her breath whispered in his ear over the soft whirring of the sonic waves. "Pussy," she said. "Cunt. Twat. Snatch. Vulva."

She must be blushing. He tried to lift his head to see, but her hands refused to release him.

Enough. He pulled her skirt down, and her scrap of an undergarment came with it. His hand wriggled between her thighs again. "You said there were dozens."

"I can't remember any more."

He punished her by dipping a finger into her heat, then withdrawing. "Tell me the word you prefer. Or shall I use them all?"

She drew a deep breath. "I can't…can't think with your fingers there."

He grinned. A Prendarian woman would have demanded a climax by now. Her artless ways made him feel very much a man. "Shall I stop?"

Her hands clutched at his arms. "No."

"Then tell me the word. Give me the word for this little nest that weeps upon my hand."

For long moments he felt nothing but the heat of her breath against his neck, the sheen of her intimate fluid rapidly dissolving in the shower. He kept his strokes light, teasing. She'd climax with a fury this time.

"Nest," she answered at last. "I like...your word."

Perhaps she wasn't as opposed to Prendarian as she seemed. Or perhaps she truly objected to the English words.

"And you like my fingers in your nest?"

He felt her swallow. "Yes."

"Does the shower make you tingle?"

She nodded, her face buried against his shoulder.

He found her bud with a finger; stroked it lightly. She leaned on him and whimpered. With his hand focusing the electrons, she must feel torment in her sex.

He touched her bud more firmly, and she gasped. "This sweet little spot—is this your pussy?"

"Clit," she said breathlessly. "Pussy means...the whole thing." Her fingers dug into his biceps. "And in...in your language?"

He kissed the top of her head. "English *is* one of my languages." But he grasped her meaning. "In Prendarian...*bud*. Like a flower...waiting to open."

He'd never understood the analogy before. Now, with Daria squirming against his body, writhing against his hand, it seemed she would literally bloom into climax.

Her breath rushed against his shoulder in shallow pants. Everywhere they touched, electrons whirled against his skin, raising sensitive nerve endings. Especially in his cock.

"Climax for me, Daria." What word had she used earlier? "*Come* for me."

He nuzzled down until he found her mouth and kissed her, filling her with his tongue, licking deep inside even as one finger plunged into her nest.

He thrust his hand in a harsh rhythm, the way his cock would thrust into her. *Soon.* He waited a moment...a moment that felt like an age...then he gave her a second finger, thrusting deep. Ah, she was tight...and hotter than anything he'd ever felt.

With a turn of his wrist, his thumb tickled her bud. Her clit. She cried out, a cry quickly muffled on his shoulder. Her mouth dampened his skin.

He kept the rhythm steady, kept brushing her clit with his thumb. *Patience.*

He knew the signs, knew them well. Her breath came harsh, her body felt tight. *Almost there. Almost.* He pressed his cock against her hip to ease his need, moving in tandem with his fingers, but never relenting in the rhythm of his hand.

She clung to him and gave a sharp, wordless cry. And then he felt her shudder against him, felt her tiny feminine muscles contract around his fingers, felt a spurt of heat, of wetness.

And he cradled her in his free arm, stroking her pussy while the spasms shook her. Sheltering her body until she relaxed against him, limp and drained.

When his lips met her forehead, he felt dampness at her brow. Oh, no. More tears? He leaned back and looked at her.

No, just a sheen of sweat from her exertions. He smiled and took his hand from her nest so he could wrap both arms around her, holding her close.

It took several moments before her breath was calm. Then he felt her fingers skimming down his chest...oh, so slowly...dipping into his navel...reaching for his cock. The shimmering waves from the shower followed her tormenting hand.

When she grasped his root with those warm fingers, the sensation was beyond imagination. Throbbing, tickling, teasing. As if she cupped fiery electrons in her hand and held them against his cock.

He'd burst in an instant. In her hand.

He groaned. "By the gods, I want to fuck you."

She jumped a little, but held his cock fast. "That's one English word you know."

His head was fogged with desire; he could barely think. But he recognized a hint of surprise in her voice. Perhaps...disapproval. "Too vulgar?"

"Not for me." She brushed her lips across his chest, finding a nipple and suckling hard. Exactly the way he liked it. "But we can't lie down in here."

And she was too short for a vertical coupling. He groped at the wall behind him, found the hidden catch, and slid out the short utility seat. When he sat down, her hand released his cock.

He reached out for her with empty arms. Arms that craved her warm, soft body. "Come. Sit astride me."

She moved to stand beside him, then sat on his lap with her legs together, her side against his chest. How did she think to ride him like this?

Before he could open his mouth to speak, she turned to face him and her knee lifted. When that incredible leg passed in front of his face, only to settle around his torso, his mouth went dry. By the gods, just the sight of that stunning leg flashing a mere hand's width from his lips nearly caused him to spill.

His hand followed, found the satiny limb...and almost pulled it back up so he could kiss and nibble at her calf. Later, at his leisure, he'd explore these smooth, exotic legs with his mouth.

But now...ah, now she was sitting astride him, her nest open and oh, so close to his aching cock. And she looked—why, she looked nervous. Blushing, her eyes downcast.

She should look proud. Arrogant. Like a woman who knew that her man truly lusted for her body. Like a woman who knew the power she wielded. Ready to mount him and ride him to pleasure. Couldn't she tell how badly he wanted her?

"Daria." His voice sounded far more serious than he'd intended. Somehow, it seemed vital that she believe him.

"Yes?"

With both hands, he touched her thighs, spread so wide on his lap. Relishing the heat under his palms. "Your legs are beautiful."

She blushed and smiled, just a tiny smile. "Thank you."

He reached up and stroked her hair back from her eyes, over her shoulder. "And your hair..." *And your eyes. And your lush, too-wide mouth...*

"Very beautiful," he said, his voice hoarse.

The color in her cheeks deepened. "I don't need compliments."

"Yes, you do." His fingers were tangled in her hair already, so he brought her head down, then reached up to kiss her. She scooted closer, shifting her weight up his thighs, until the wet heat of her nest pressed against his cock.

She straightened, moving her lips out of reach. He almost complained, but now her breasts were level with his mouth. Those huge, velvety areolas beckoned to him. He sucked one nipple deep, and she cried out.

"Too much?" he murmured.

"No," she whispered. Her hands cradled his head. "I'm just...sensitive."

He smiled against the slope of her breast. "I'll be gentle." *Gentle but persistent.*

"But I thought..." She fell silent.

"What?"

"I thought you wanted to fuck me," she said, all in a rush.

With his cock rubbing against her pussy, that must be obvious. "You'll hear no objections from me."

He grasped her hips, lifting; she reached down, holding his cock steady. They moved in perfect accord. When he settled her onto his lap, his cock sank deep into her heat. And still the shower flowed over them, around them, a rush of warm air and tickling electrons.

She wriggled on his lap, gripping his shoulders for leverage, nudging back and forth. Nudging his cock by tantalizing degrees. He was buried so deep, he swore he felt the edge of her womb.

"I can't move," she said.

He released a shuddering breath. "You're moving quite well."

He pushed at her hips, pulling her back and forth, his cock moving barely a finger's width inside her. Even that slight movement was too much. *Almost* too much.

His mouth went to her breasts, licking, sucking, seeking sustenance. And still she wriggled, pulsing around his cock.

"Can you...like this?" she asked.

Even riding him, *fucking* him, she hesitated to say the words. If he fucked her a hundred times, she'd probably still blush in his arms. He nuzzled his cheek against her breast. "Can I...what?"

Her breath puffed against his forehead, an exasperated sigh. "You know."

So shy. He'd make her say the words. "Tell me."

"Can you come like this?"

Barely a whisper. No doubt her cheeks blazed. Just imagining it made him smile, despite her squirming, teasing thrusts. "Can you?"

She shook her head, and the ends of her hair brushed over his shoulders. "It's your turn."

His turn? Did she not realize how many times a woman could climax? This time he'd bring her with him, by the gods. He dropped one hand between them, found her bud with his thumb, and stroked. Relentlessly.

"Climax for me," he demanded. "Come around my cock."

She whimpered, a restrained moan. Ah, the words stirred her. Excited her. "Ride me, Daria. Fuck me."

She moaned outright. Her breath rasped against his ear; her arms clutched him tight.

His thumb made a tiny circle against her. "Feel the electrons on your clit. My thumb on your clit."

Her breath came quickly. She clutched at him wildly, pushing against him faster. Harder. His back stung from the bite of her fingernails.

But he wanted more. He wanted words from her. "Feel good?"

She whimpered.

His thumb stopped. She cried out.

"Tell me."

"You feel...oh..."

He grabbed her upper arm with his free hand, urging her higher, giving her more friction, deeper thrusts. His hips strained against her. And he gave her his thumb again, gave her the pressure he knew she needed.

Her body fluttered around him.

"Yes, yes." He groaned. "So tight..."

"Don't stop." The words came between gasping breaths. "Oh, please don't stop."

"Never." His thumb, slick with her fluid, slid against her clit.

Her eyes went wide with wonder, then closed. With a little cry, she climaxed—she *came*—gripping and squeezing his cock with rippling contractions, shuddering on his lap. His own need took over, desperate and insistent. He thrust up—hard—driving into her with a fierce rhythm, gripping her hip with his free hand to grind her down against him. And the milking heat of her body took him with her. He shattered in a mindless rush of sensation, letting go of all restraint, letting the rush of his seed fill her, claim her.

She collapsed onto his chest, her head falling to his shoulder, and he held her close, gasping for air.

"*Dahsh'kara*," he murmured.

She shifted a little, but didn't raise her head. "What does that mean?"

He smiled. "I'll tell you soon…after you climax five times in one encounter."

"Hmm. Only two this time," she said, a teasing note in her voice. "You must be slipping."

"Slipping?" He knew the word, knew its meaning, but with him sitting firmly on the shelf, it made no sense.

"You must be…letting your standards relax."

"Ah." He smiled. "Thank you for tutoring me." He thought of the other words she'd taught him. Erotic words. Words that had excited her. Perhaps she thought of them, too. Perhaps she blushed, even now, naked in his arms, sated with pleasure.

Lifting his head to look at her seemed a great effort. He stroked her back instead, then slid his hand up to cup her neck under the veil of her hair. A gentle caress.

She sighed. "Thank you for teaching me how to shower."

He grinned. "Next time, perhaps you'll even get clean."

She laughed. Only a brief burst of amusement, a sound he felt as much as heard. His limp cock, still deep inside her body, vibrated with her laughter…and felt as happy as she sounded.

He'd made this sad, brave, winsome woman laugh.

Somehow that seemed a great achievement.

Chapter Four

Gray lay on the bed and watched, amused, as Daria searched his quarters. She made thorough work of the task, exploring with the tenacity of an archaeologist. She'd already hunted through his drawers, ostensibly to find a garment for herself to sleep in. And she'd commented on his utilitarian clothing before dropping a large, lightweight shirt over her head. Gold suited her, made her dark hair shimmer. And best of all, the shirt was short enough to reveal most of her legs.

After she was dressed, she prowled through the main chamber. Nothing of interest there—a table and chairs, a few of his rations for the week, tiny cooking facilities for when he didn't want to go to the main dining hall. She returned to the sleeping chamber, and now she hunted over the narrow shelves, examining the few souvenirs he'd brought with him.

She looked at the delicately carved, expensive *mistira* figurine, but seemed afraid to touch it. "Do you mind?"

He shook his head. Her curiosity made him smile. After six months spent in these rooms, he knew them all too well. To Daria, they must seem brand new. Interesting.

She gingerly lifted the intricate vial. "What is this?"

"It's called a *mistira*. A good luck token." A gift from the Premier Leader, his gracious Aunt Rigah—a constant reminder of her faith in him. A constant reminder that he could not disappoint her. And he would not. He would succeed, no matter the cost. Even if success meant sacrificing his hopes for the election.

Prefect of Earth.

Gods, how he wanted that title. The election would prove he was more than Rigah's nephew—if he won, it would prove that he was capable in his own right.

"Hmm," Daria said, tilting the *mistira*. "Prendara must be really arid, if a sealed tube of water is considered a good luck charm."

She set the vial down and picked up his baseball carefully, as if it was more delicate than the costly *mistira*. Then she tossed the scuffed ball between her shuffling hands, back and forth, spinning it rapidly as it leapt from palm to palm. His precious baseball—the only item that had gone to Prendara with him when he'd been taken there as a child. But she asked no questions, so he volunteered no information. The ball was returned gently to the shelf.

She seemed fascinated by the hand-held reading panel, pressing her fingers to the screen. Was she searching for something? Her tongue made a small annoyed sound, a kind of *tsk* noise, and she set the panel down.

He had to know. "Something troubles you?"

"Yes," she said, her voice sharp with annoyance. "That word you said earlier...it's not in the dictionary."

"Which word?"

"*Dahsh....Dahsh'kara.*"

Her pronunciation was off; she'd probably spelled it wrong. Certainly the dictionary would include it. The endearment was common, even though he'd never used it in the past.

Why with her? Perhaps because she'd seemed so fragile. She'd needed tenderness. All the tenderness he could muster.

But she disliked Prendarian words. He should find an English endearment for her. What did his uncle sometimes call his aunt in quiet moments? Something similar to Daria's own name. Daria. Dar... Darling?

She reached for the holo-projector he kept on the uppermost shelf. Her shirt—*his* shirt—rode high with the lift of her arms, giving him a perfect view of her legs and the lower portion of her rounded ass.

Even those lovely legs couldn't make his cock rise, sated as he was. No matter. The view was still quite spectacular.

She turned to him with the holo-projector in her hand. "Who are they?"

He had to prop his head up on his hand to see the shimmering three-dimensional image. Four happy young people smiled at him. Praise the gods, she hadn't seen the one of his aunt and uncle. Perhaps she didn't know how to change images on this advanced projector. "My..." What was the English word? No point in struggling. "My uncle's children."

"Your cousins."

Of course. He'd spoken English for the first six years of his life; sometimes he only needed to be reminded of the words. "Thank you."

She closed the holo-projector and put it back. No comment on his cousins? On the fact that they were obviously half Prendarian? She must have noticed, as closely as she'd studied the image.

She came to the bed and sat cross-legged next to him on the pallet. "Tell me what you're doing here, Gray. About the people we'll be meeting."

He didn't want to think about his mission. He'd thought of little else for nearly a year. "They're diplomats. Rather boring diplomats. Like myself."

"Boring like you?" She smiled. "Well, I would never dream of contradicting my boss."

Her teasing manner had him returning the smile, despite his fatigue. "A wise practice."

"When will we meet them? Tomorrow?"

So earnest. He little needed her help, but having her with him would be a joy. "Yes. In the…" The word came to him in a flash. "In the afternoon."

"Are they Prendarians?"

"Some are. Some are of Earth. But we will all speak English."

Her eyebrows rose. "Even the Prendarians?"

No need to tell her they'd speak English at his insistence. He didn't want to appear to be seeking her favor. "Yes."

She shifted on the pallet, stretching her legs out in front of her. What a vision. "What will you talk about? What do you want from them?"

So many questions. He felt too tired to explain. He just wanted to look at her legs, to feel them stretched out alongside his, and to sleep next to her warmth. And he wanted a few more hours of having her see him as a man. Tomorrow she'd see him among jaded, fawning politicians. Tomorrow she'd know him for what he was. *Sanwar,* would she try to coax favors from him? No. No, she seemed too proud.

Proud but shy. She might be intimidated once she knew his station. He'd have to reassure her. Perhaps with sex. His gaze slid up her legs. Mmm. Assuredly, with sex.

But now she looked at him expectantly, waiting for an answer. "Let's speak of it tomorrow."

She opened her mouth, then closed it and shrugged. "As you will."

Her tone mimicked his. He very nearly grinned. "Now you mock me?"

She smiled, then pressed her lips into a thin line. "I would never mock my boss."

Amazing, that she could tease him. Despite the violence on the dock, a disrupter blast, and sex that had left him drained, she looked completely at ease. As if this night had been one among many. And she'd indulged in only one bout of tears. Perhaps she restrained her emotions to spare his.

"Are you hiding what you truly feel?"

She looked startled. Oddly frightened. Then she smiled. Ironically, the smile made her look even more apprehensive. "What do you mean?"

He laid a hand on her knee. "You seem very calm…considering you were attacked so recently."

Her smile faded a bit, then reappeared. "I'm not thinking about it. You've been a good distraction."

Brave words. Was she so used to harsh treatment at the hands of men? How could he ask? "What almost happened to you...it's unheard of on Prendara."

She took a long moment to answer. "Quite the little utopia you have up there."

She sounded odd. Cold. If he knew that word, he might understand why. "Utopia?"

"Paradise."

Ah. "It's not paradise. It's merely...different." *It's a world where a man would never dream of taking pleasure from a woman by force.*

"Obviously." She looked sad suddenly. Her eyes shifted to focus on the wall behind his head.

"Has it happened to you before?"

"Has what happened before?"

Forced to speak plainly, he kept his voice gentle, kept a yoke on his anger. "Have you been attacked for sex before?"

"No." Her voice was equally soft. She reached out and took his hand. Her eyes looked deep into his. He'd never seen such velvety eyes. Like...chocolate. Smooth, hot chocolate. One of the few things he remembered from his early childhood on Earth. "I haven't thanked you."

If he hadn't been there...no, by the gods, the thought was not bearable. "Don't thank me." He squeezed her fingers. "I count it a privilege to have helped you."

Before she could answer, a giant yawn consumed him.

She smiled. "I guess it's bedtime."

He slid under the covers, settling on his side to face her, and Daria joined him. She lay close, though her body did not touch his. He reached out and rested his hand on the curve of her thigh. Her shirt was a barrier. He nudged it upward so his flesh could meet her own. "Lights off."

She put her hand on his. "Can you turn them up just a little? I don't like sleeping in total darkness."

She sounded worried. Timid. Fearful that he'd refuse such a simple request? No—fearful of the darkness. He sensed it in the trembling of her voice. One day he'd learn the secret of her fear. But not tonight. "Lights on ten percent." The room filled with a dim glow. "Enough?"

"Yes. Gray?"

"Hmm?"

"Why does your command center recognize English?"

His pupils had adjusted to the low lighting; her eyes were closed, and she muffled a yawn behind one hand. She must need sleep, after the night she'd been through. "Because I had it programmed for English. Every command center on this ship will recognize any of the remaining Earth languages. And Prendarian, of course."

"Seems like a lot of trouble, programming them so extensively."

He shrugged. "It's practical. I wanted the crew to practice speaking in Earth languages." And they'd had a long voyage, with plenty of time to fill.

"I'm surprised the Prendarians allowed it. They force us to use their alien language whenever they can."

He frowned. "Not all Prendarians are…certain their own culture is best."

"Ethnocentric," she supplied. "The ones I've met are. Not that I've met many. I avoid them like the plague."

She said these harsh words, knowing his own cousins were half Prendarian. Perhaps she hadn't noticed after all. How would she feel to learn that his beloved aunt was not just any Prendarian, but the Premier Leader? With her prejudice, she must hate Rigah, even though they had never met.

By the gods, she should be *grateful* to his aunt—she'd been brave enough to emancipate all Earthers. Including Daria's own parents. But not Daria herself—she looked far too young to have been born into enslavement.

Easy enough to find out. "How old are you?"

Her eyes went wide with shock. Then she suddenly grinned at him. "OK, you need a lesson in Earth culture. It's considered rude—extremely rude—to ask a woman her age."

"Rude? Why? Age is merely a fact."

"Because Earth women like to pretend they're younger than they actually are."

She must jest with him. "That makes little sense. Why pretend youth? With experience comes wisdom."

"I agree with you. Just trust me, don't ask any other women. OK?"

"OK." The word sounded strange; how many years had it been since he'd said something so colloquial? She was helping him sound more natural. And that would help him win the election. But first he must see the constitution ratified. Only then could the election take place.

She took a deep breath, as if confessing a great secret. "I'm twenty-seven."

He'd have guessed younger, with her shy blushes. He took a moment to convert his Prendarian age into shorter Earth years. "I'm thirty-six."

"Any other rude questions you'd like answered?"

Her tone was light. His question was not. "Do your parents still live?"

Her mouth thinned to a harsh line, and sudden coldness filled her eyes. If only he could retract the words.

"No." From the coldness in her eyes, he knew she would say no more.

Maybe telling her a bit of his own history would help her overcome the bitterness of her own. "Neither do mine. My father died before I was born. My mother when I was four. I barely remember her."

"Prendarians?"

"The invasion," he corrected. "I don't know which side caused their deaths. I never will. It matters not. They're gone. That's all that matters."

"It matters." She said nothing else.

Inexplicably, he wanted to share more with her. "My uncle married a Prendarian woman."

She didn't look shocked, or even surprised. She must have realized it when she'd seen the holo-projection of his cousins.

"You knew that already."

She looked shocked then. Shocked and a little…frightened? "No, I didn't know," she said with a little laugh. "But I'm not surprised. And I'm sure he's not alone. I hear those alien women are all sex maniacs."

He smiled at the phrase. He'd have to remember to use it with his uncle. Uncle Jason hadn't forgotten much English. Perhaps he knew that expression already.

"I'm surprised you don't have one yourself," she went on.

He blinked. "A wife?"

"A Prendarian wife." Then her eyes grew wide. "Or do you?"

Was that a jealous frown on her face? He could kiss her. Instead, he merely touched her chin. "No, I don't have a Prendarian wife." Nor did he want one. "Not all men wish for a...sex maniac. Modesty has an appeal all its own, I have recently discovered."

She turned her face away, looked up at the ceiling. "I wasn't begging for a compliment."

"Most women say *thank you* when they receive one."

But she wasn't most women. And what if *she* had a partner? On Earth, partners were not always monogamous. No reason a prostitute would not be partnered. Especially one as sweet as Daria. "Will someone worry if you don't arrive home tonight?"

Her eyelids fluttered down, then up again. As if she hid the truth. "No."

The fortunate man who partnered her would surely worry. "I'll give you privacy if you wish to contact him. Or have a security envoy deliver you home, if you will it." He hoped, with an urgent sense of desperation, that she'd stay the night with him. A desperation he'd never felt before.

"No," she said again. "There's no one for me to go home to."

Perhaps she spoke truth. Perhaps she had no partner. There seemed nothing to say in response. He watched her eyes close, and her breathing slow. But he could not let her rest—he couldn't rest himself—without learning one more thing.

"Daria?"

"Hmm?"

"Before we bathed...when I found you in the cleansing station. Why were you crying?"

Brown eyes met his. She opened her mouth, then immediately closed it. Her brow furrowed; her gaze seemed troubled. He knew the signs of a woman searching for a polite untruth.

He held his forefinger to her lips. "Don't dishonor me with a lie. Better to say nothing."

Her gaze held steady. "I cried because I didn't want to leave you."

And then she blushed. From speaking a lie? Or from admitting truth?

Gods, how he hoped she spoke truth.

* * *

Daria woke to the smell of frying eggs. A pink ceiling met her blinking gaze. Where the hell—oh, right. The ship. Gray's quarters. God only knew why the ceiling was pink, but at least it reflected the dim light evenly.

And at least he hadn't asked her why she wanted the lights on all night. She was prepared to tell him anything that might hook him, but not that. Never that. She'd never even told Tank.

Ancient history. No reason to dwell on it now.

She stretched and yawned. Amazing how well she'd slept, in a strange bed with a strange man. She'd woken once in the night and found him pressed full-length against her back, his arm draped over her hip. He'd felt solid and comforting. She'd fallen right back asleep. As if they'd been sharing a bed for years.

As if she trusted him.

Dangerous thought. Well, at least she knew to watch out for these misguided feelings. To keep a lid on her emotions. And even if—*if*—she got attached to him somehow, her feelings wouldn't stop her from completing the mission. Nothing would stop her. She owed it to Tank. To every Earther on the planet.

Her stomach growled. Whatever he was cooking smelled great. Could it really be eggs? Only one way to find out.

She kicked off the blanket and sat up. The room was warm; even the tiled floor was surprisingly warm under her bare feet, as if the tiles themselves were heated. Maybe they were. Even though Gray's quarters were minimalistic, he probably had the nicest ones on the whole ship. After all, he was the most important passenger. And she'd spent the night with him, just like Tank had planned. Now she'd go out there and eat breakfast with him as if waking up in his bed was the most natural thing in the world.

She padded barefoot to the small alcove next to the shower and looked in the mirror that hung on the wall. Her face didn't look all that bad, considering. With a light touch on the side of the metal mirror, the front snapped open to reveal the recessed med cabinet. She found a toothwash caplet and popped it into her mouth. The fizzing mint made her mouth water, but her teeth were clean when it was gone. After a quick finger-combing of her hair, she walked into the other room.

There he was, standing at the small alien stove in a loose pair of pants and a long-sleeved shirt, both black. A bowl filled with an odd purple rice-like substance was steaming on the table, next to a couple of small bowls, glasses of water, and utensils that looked remarkably like normal Earth forks. Quite the homey little scene.

"Good morning," she said.

He turned and smiled at her. One of those smiles that lit up his whole face. One of those smiles that almost made her feel guilty for deceiving him.

Not that he'd been entirely honest with her. He'd evaded her questions, avoided telling her anything solid about his mission. And he'd never mentioned that he was related to the Premier Leader.

His gaze swept her from head to foot and back again. "Good morning. Are you hungry?"

She nodded. "Ravenous."

His smile grew. "So am I."

He came to her and took her in his arms. Before she could even draw a breath, he kissed her. A long, wet, deep kiss. His hands roamed over her back; his tongue swept her mouth with gentle insistence.

Her body swayed into his like a vine clinging to a tree. Christ, she was putty in his hands. Why wasn't she prepared for this? This shower of heat? Hell, nothing could have prepared her. His hair slipped through her fingers, silky soft, before she even realized she'd lifted her hand. Desire rushed through her veins as he stroked her hair, then cupped the back of her head, holding her still, making sure she couldn't move away. His chest pressed against hers. Could he hear her heart hammering? Could he feel it?

He broke the kiss and rested his forehead against hers, his breath hot and moist on her face. "Mmm. Minty."

She couldn't think of anything to say. She could barely think at all. And she didn't want to. She just wanted to feel his body pressed against hers, his breath tickling her nose, his arms wrapped around her, strong and secure.

He kissed her again.

His lips made her dizzy. Or maybe it was the lack of oxygen. She could learn to live without oxygen. Kisses like this were worth a few suffocated brain cells.

One of his hands curved under her ass, lifting her until she had to stand on her toes, until her belly pressed against his cock. His already hard cock. An answering heat rose in her own sex. Her *nest*. God, in another minute she'd drag him down to the floor.

But first she needed to breathe.

She put her hands on his chest and pushed, just a little.

Those strong arms released her. Slowly. Reluctantly. His eyes were glowing, heavy-lidded. Bedroom eyes. And a bedroom was less than ten feet away.

She leaned closer, not *really* wanting to let him go…all but begging him to take her. Shameless. Utterly shameless.

And he'd liked the shy act last night. She shouldn't appear too willing now.

"The food will burn." Good, that had just the right note of half-heartedness.

"I'll make more." He sounded frustrated. Regretful. Was he going to press her? God, she hoped he did.

But no—he took her shoulders and gently pushed her away.

After a lingering kiss on her forehead, he stepped back and turned to the stove again.

She groped for the table, seeking support, and sank into a chair.

She should probably offer to help cook, but her knees wouldn't hold her. And why not let him feed her? At least eating in his quarters guaranteed that she wouldn't have to face the crew, if any of them were awake. After a night of wild revelry, they'd probably sleep all day.

"What time is it?"

He glanced at the identikit card strapped to his wrist. "Oh-nine-oh." With a quick motion, he deftly flipped the eggs in the pan. "We have time to tour the city before my meeting this afternoon. I'd like you to accompany me...if you will it."

Oh, she willed it all right. She needed all the time with him she could stand. She still had no idea how she was going to keep him from getting this new constitution approved. If she stuck close to him, she'd find a way. "I'd like that."

Gray brought a pan to the table and set it down. Fried eggs after all. He scooped some of the purple rice into her bowl, then topped it with two of the eggs and moved to add a third.

She held up a hand. "Whoa."

He stopped. "What does that mean?"

The least she could do was tutor him. He'd played right into her hands with that silly job offer. The man was too nice for his own good. "It's an old word that people used to say to horses, back in the days before gas-cars were invented. It means stop."

"Hmm. Is it in common use?"

She shrugged. "I wouldn't call it common, but I still hear it every now and then."

He handed her bowl to her, then started to dish out food for himself. She dug in before he even sat down. The rice tasted a little nutty, with an almost tangy aftertaste, but it went well with the blandness of the eggs.

"What kind of rice is this?"

He sat down and stirred the egg yolk with his fork, mixing it into the rice. "It's not really a rice. It's *quaanti* grain."

He looked expectant, like he wanted her to respond.

"It's good."

"I hated it as a child. Only in recent years have I come to appreciate the taste."

"Oh." For the life of her, she couldn't think of a better response. She'd fucked him twice, but she didn't really know him. Not even her research—facts and figures, physical details—had prepared her for the reality of sitting at this table with him, eating breakfast, trying to make conversation. She'd read all about him, but in person he seemed nothing like the facts she'd learned. He seemed…sensitive. Nice. Sexy as hell. And even though he might fool her into liking him—into liking sex with him—she wasn't about to get attached. She had a job to do.

They ate in silence. It didn't take her long to get full. She rested the fork in her bowl and watched while he scraped out the last bites from his.

He pushed his empty bowl away and looked at her curiously. "You're not hungry?"

"Not anymore. I'm not a big breakfast eater." She should compliment him. "The food was great, though."

He reached across the table and took her bowl, using her fork to eat from it until the last bite was gone. He had a hell of an appetite for a skinny guy. Well, not really skinny...just lean. He was all lean muscle. Lean muscle with agile fingers. And a devilish tongue.

"We should stop at your home," he said suddenly.

Uh-oh. "Why?"

He looked amused, a small smile quirking his lips. "I assumed you'd prefer to wear your own clothing to the meeting this afternoon. Although I won't object if you wish to continue in my shirt."

Clothes. Damn. She had nothing but her hooker clothes. And a lousy ten credits on her ID card. Not even enough for a pair of socks.

But first she had to come up with an excuse for not taking him to her home. One that would make him let her stay with him around the clock. Hell, the truth would do that nicely. "I'm homeless."

He set his glass down with a loud bang. "Homeless?"

She nodded. "The place I lived in...it burned down."

"When?"

Yesterday? No, too coincidental. Too much had happened yesterday. But if she made it too far in the past, he wouldn't believe that she hadn't found another place to stay by now. "Two days ago."

He frowned. "I'm sorry."

Pity had never done anyone any good. She shrugged. "It wasn't your fault."

His frown cleared. "You do have a home. You live here. With me."

He said it like he owned her. Oh, how she wanted to argue with his arrogance. But she couldn't afford to be stupid. She needed to stay with him. It was critical to finding a way to stop his plans for Earth. His plans to formalize the Prendarian oppression of Earth.

"For a time," she said, repeating the phrase he'd used last night. Good, she'd almost sounded reluctant. Like she didn't want to take advantage of him.

He finished the last of his water and stood, moving to the small cabinet under the stove. He pulled out a drawer, fumbled around in it for a moment, and came back with a small envelope, thin and maybe two inches square. With a flick of his fingers, the packet slid across the table to her.

The writing on it was Prendarian, but she didn't know the word. "What's this?"

His eyebrows rose. "It's a female contraceptive. Pour it into what's left of your water."

Did he think hookers didn't take care of birth control themselves? "It's not necessary."

"Drink it anyway. Best to be doubly cautious."

He looked like he'd sit there as long as it took for her to do his bidding. Maybe he didn't quite trust her yet. Maybe other women had tried to get pregnant to have a hold over him. Or to extort money from him.

She ripped open the packet and tilted it over her water glass. She'd expected powder, but a thick liquid slid from the package in a solid, gelatinous glob. Yuck. It spread through the water like a chemical reaction, turning everything a light blue.

She took a small, very cautious sip. At least it didn't taste bad. Kind of spicy, like chicory.

He watched her quietly. Seriously.

"No contraceptive drink for you?"

"I take one daily. But the female ones are more effective."

He took one daily? No doubt he needed to—he probably had a woman every night of the week. She couldn't think of anything to say. Oh well. She sipped her spicy contraceptive water.

"Do you have any possessions at all?" he asked. "Things you'll need while you're with me?"

He looked so sincere. More like a Boy Scout than a collaborator.

"No. I have no possessions at all."

His mouth fell open for just an instant. "You have nothing?"

"Nothing but the clothes on my back. Or rather, the clothes on the floor of your bedroom."

He didn't crack a smile. "We'll go shopping, then."

She drained the last of the birth control potion. "Every man's nightmare."

"Why do you say that?"

"Most men don't like... Oh, never mind."

No point in explaining humor to a Prendarian. And Gray might not be a Prendarian by blood, but he was close enough.

Hell, he was worse than a Prendarian. He was a traitor. Here to do the bidding of the most powerful Prendarian of them all.

And only Daria could stop him.

Chapter Five

Gray walked down the corridor, Daria at his side. A cool breeze blew through the dock, a hint of salt in the air. Moist air. Had he felt similar breezes as a child? He must have.

The breeze grew stronger. The portal, the main exit from the docking chamber, must be around the next turn. Already he heard strange bird calls, hawking and lilting. Oddly familiar, though he didn't remember the animals very well.

After more than thirty Earth years, he was finally back home.

Home.

Or was it?

If this was home, what was Prendara? Prendara, the only planet he recalled in detail. Yet even in Rigah's home, he'd been one of only two Earthers. A stranger on a strange planet.

As he was on Earth.

Perhaps neither world was his home.

Gods, he'd never felt so conflicted.

The last turn was only twenty steps away. Gray nearly held his breath. He slowed his pace, dropping behind Daria.

She still wore his gold shirt and her stretchy little skirt, with those spiky shoes accentuating her legs. She'd refused to borrow clothes from one of the women on board. A streak of pride ran through her core, that was plain. She looked rather ridiculous, in his huge shirt and her tiny, clinging skirt. But he little minded. No matter how conflicted he felt about being on Earth, the sight of her long, luscious legs was one thing he could enjoy with no conflict.

Perhaps they should return to his quarters so he could explore those legs in detail. In glorious detail. He could see the fine tracing of veins on the backs of her knees. The skin there looked enticingly soft. If he followed those lines with his tongue, would she moan with pleasure? Or squeal with ticklish laughter?

He reached out and took Daria's hand, stopping her just a few steps from the fateful last bend in the corridor.

She didn't speak, just stood with him. He liked that about her—her calm patience, her ability to accept whatever the moment brought her. Too many people railed against circumstances. There were still people fighting the Prendarian presence on Earth, though the war had ended thirty years ago.

He would put an end to the scattered fighting, to the endless vying for political power. He would unite Earth under one government.

And Daria would profit from witnessing the negotiations. She'd see that Prendarians were not evil people; they were simply people, to be judged on individual merits.

He squeezed her hand. "I'm glad you're here with me."

She smiled up at him. "So am I."

She stood patiently, holding his hand, waiting. Her gentle clasp relaxed him. He would have thanked the gods for bringing her to him, but he couldn't be thankful for violence. Whenever he pictured her struggling with those men, men who would have taken pleasure from her by force... The memory alone made his stomach clench, his blood run with fire. The words did not exist to define his rage. He needed no words. He only knew that he didn't want to let her out of his sight. She needed protecting, this brown-eyed, blushing woman.

Ah, she was blushing right now. Just a little, just enough of a pink tinge to charm him. Perhaps he stared at her too intently.

She tilted her head and gave him a quizzical look. "What's wrong, Gray?"

Her quiet use of his name brought the truth from him. "I suppose I'm a little nervous. I haven't seen Earth since I was six years old."

She squeezed his hand. "Sure you have. You saw the space dock last night. It's part of Earth."

Such a practical response made him smile. "True."

"Are we going to stand here all day?"

"Would you mind if we did?" His voice sounded rueful. At least he hoped it did. He didn't want to sound as pathetic as he felt.

"It's just a city," she said. "Like any other."

"It's just a planet," he countered. "Unlike any other."

She tugged his hand gently. "Come on, space cowboy. The planet isn't getting any younger. And if we stand here much longer, I'll have to wear these clothes to your big meeting this afternoon."

He let her lead him around the bend. A gust of air hit his face, and he closed his eyes against the sensation. But the wind held no sand, not like such a breeze would on Prendara. No dust filled his nostrils—just the musty scent of fish. Salt. The sea.

They stepped outside the portal into a bright, crisp day. He stood blinking in the sudden sunshine, trying to see everything at once through his stinging eyes.

The sky was unbelievably blue, more brilliant than he'd ever have imagined. Puffy clouds, gray and white, scudded quickly across the sky, their edges rimmed with the bright silver glow of a hidden sun. A wide street lay before them, with vehicles of every description racing along it. A hovercraft, tens of old gasoline-engine cars in every color, even a conveyance. He'd never seen so many vehicles in one mass.

And alongside the road, people scurried, strolled, simply walked, all hurrying to get somewhere. So many people. A woman carrying a large rectangular bag over one shoulder brushed against him as she passed. He stared at her retreating back, watching as she hurried across the busy road and disappeared behind a building on the other side.

The buildings. So huge...enormous rectangular structures that rose to the sky. So different from the low, rounded buildings of Prendara. So...alien.

A young man approached, a crewman from the ship. His wrinkled uniform had a large stain on the sleeve. His eyes were bleary, his hair wildly disarrayed. Probably not only from the wind. He paused and gave Gray a respectful nod. "Greetings, *Sarjah.*"

Before Gray could speak, the man's gaze dropped to Daria's bare legs. Gray stepped closer to her and slipped an arm around her waist. That brought the man's attention back to him. "Good morning, crewman."

With a nod and one last lustful glance at Daria's legs, the young man walked through the dock's portal, his boots thumping on the wooden planking.

Daria looked up at him. "*Sarjah?*"

"You need not call me that."

She rolled her eyes. "I wasn't *calling* you. I was asking what that word means."

She'd learn the meaning eventually. But not now. "It's a title of respect. A common title." In truth, the word was reserved for an elite echelon. An echelon he had attained not through his own merits, but because of his relationship to the Premier Leader.

But Daria knew nothing of that relationship. Not yet.

He took her hand again. "Do you have a preference in stores?"

"Not really. Let's just head downtown."

"Down town?" He knew the words, but couldn't grasp the meaning.

"It's just another word for the main business district." She pointed down a wide street. "That way, just a few blocks."

When he took a step, she pulled him back. Her teeth were nibbling at her lip. "I may…I need an advance."

What did that mean? "An advance?"

Her chin lifted just a tiny bit. "An advance on my salary."

Ah. He should have suspected. And though he'd happily pay for all of her clothes, for anything she needed, no doubt her pride would cause her to balk at receiving gifts. "Fine. That looks like a credit kiosk across the street."

"You can also call it a bank." Her tone seemed caustic. "If you want to sound like a native instead of a damned Pr—"

She stopped and dropped his hand.

He wouldn't press her to continue. He didn't want to hear more of her prejudice. What kind of life had she led, to feel such strong negativity toward Prendarians? There had been atrocities committed on both sides during the invasion, but that had been decades ago. Before Daria's birth. Why did she cling to the horrors of the past?

She led him across the busy intersection to the kiosk. The machine was as modern as any he'd ever seen on Prendara, with a full screen and holographic capabilities.

When she pulled a small card out of the back of her skirt, he held out a hand. "Give me your identikit. I'll transfer a week's salary to you."

She seemed reluctant to give him the card, slowly moving it toward his outstretched hand—as if hoping she might think of an excuse to keep it if she delayed long enough. As if wishing to keep her data private. At last the card reached his palm.

"You should just call it an ID. No one uses the word *identikit* anymore." Her voice was tinged with resentment.

He nodded. "Thank you."

She frowned. "For what?"

"For correcting me." *And for trusting me with your ID.* He slid her card into the machine, then pulled his own from his wristband and added it. He tried to block Daria's view of the screen. She'd learn the truth of his status soon enough.

In an instant, their respective information displayed side-by-side. He quickly tapped the Secrecy button that appeared above his data. The bulk of his statistics blanked out, leaving only his identity number and name.

He scanned Daria's information with a quick glance.

Identity—Earther 010 723 439 959

Colloquial Name—Daria Viktorovna Cohen

Available Credits—10

Criminal Confinements—0

Affirmed Criminal Affiliations—0

Suspected Criminal Affiliations—0

Residence—San Francisco City, California State

Birth—12 July 2011 Western Earth Calendar

...*more below*...

The information spilled off the bottom of the screen before her sanctioned occupation was displayed. Much as he wanted to know what she was supposed to be doing to earn her credits, he couldn't shift the data on the screen to see more. Not with her watching him. This one display had probably given him more information than she would have willingly divulged. He should respect her privacy.

Only ten credits to her name. No wonder she was selling her body. Perhaps her sanctioned occupation paid too little. There should be a way to ensure that women like her had enough means.

When he glanced at her, she seemed annoyed, a small furrow between her brows. Daring him to say something? Something about her lack of funds?

Perhaps he could deflect her anger with a mundane comment. "Viktorovna?" he said, hoping the pronunciation was close. "Is this a common name?"

"Not anymore."

Again she used a hard, cold voice, as she often did when he asked a personal question. "What does this name signify?"

"What does it *mean*," she corrected. "It's a variation of my father's name. Viktor. It means *I will win*."

The tilt of her chin seemed oddly belligerent. Interesting. "So your parents wished you to fight?"

"No."

"Then why—"

"My parents were Russian. In old Russia, children were given a middle name based on their father's first name."

He knew nothing of Russia or of Earth naming traditions. But she seemed annoyed to have told him so much; he wouldn't ask for more details. "Will a week's salary be enough?"

She nodded.

They hadn't agreed upon payment for her services. Not that money was a concern to him. How much would she need to find a home, buy necessities? He would give her enough to live for years without resorting to prostitution, but he need not transfer that much to her at once. Just enough to grant her the means to buy whatever she wished in the next few days. The means to find her own quarters, if she chose not to stay in his. It should be her will to stay with him, not a necessity.

He turned back to the kiosk and transferred ten thousand credits to her card.

With such a substantial sum at issue, the machine insisted that he confirm the transaction. Twice. And on the second confirmation, he had to press his hand against the verification screen so that his bio-signature could be scanned.

Daria peered around his side, then gasped and grabbed his arm. "Ten thousand credits? For one week?"

He couldn't resist the opportunity to tease her. "Is it not enough?"

Those full lips scowled at him. "It's what most people earn in two months. And you know it."

"You're fortunate, then, to have a generous employer."

He meant to tease, but her eyes grew fiery. "What are you trying to buy from me, Gray?"

He frowned. "Nothing. You may consider this a free gift, if you will."

She was shaking her head before he finished. "No gifts. I'm supposed to be working for you."

"As you are. You've been correcting my English almost every moment." And she'd warmed his bed quite nicely. But he wasn't paying her for that.

Her eyes narrowed. "I'm not worth ten thousand credits a week, and you damn well know it."

She was worth far more than ten thousand credits. "Daria..." Gods, what could he say? He fumbled for words. Honest words. "I'm not certain why you are so angry."

"I told you last night, I won't be your charity case."

Sanwar, he'd offended her pride. "Daria, please take the credits. They mean little to me. But you—"

You mean a great deal to me. The thought burst into his brain and seized him, staggered him, paralyzed his tongue. She truly meant a great deal to him. After only one night. He felt dizzy. Disoriented. Everything faded—the sunshine, the sky, the noise of hawking birds and traffic on the street—everything faded until her face, her *scowling* face, was the focus of his entire...his entire *world.*

No. No, this could not be.

"You'll be helping me more than you know," he said at last. "These meetings...they'll be conducted entirely in English. It's critical that I speak well. That I understand every nuance of what's said by others."

She scowled at him still.

He touched her elbow gently, caressing her through the fabric of his shirt. "I want you to be free to buy whatever you will." *To leave me, if you will it.* No, he wouldn't give her that thought. Just the idea made his fingers tighten a little on her arm, as if she had already pulled away. "Daria, accept the credits. Please."

Her frown slowly faded. At last she gave a grudging nod. "As you will."

***

Ten thousand credits.

Unbelievable.

Unbelievable to *her,* at any rate. The ID card of Daria Viktorovna Cohen had never held anywhere near that much money. She'd never even *known* anyone with that kind of money. And Gray had handed it over like spare change. Like he had plenty more where that came from.

Shit, he must be richer than any of them had ever dreamed. And that little joke he'd made—*Is it not enough?*—oh, very funny, trying to impress her with his wealth.

He'd impressed her, all right. He'd impressed her by showing her a whole new reason to hate him. Being a collaborator must pay better than any of the shit jobs she and her friends had been given by their Prendarian masters.

And all you had to do to get those big bucks was betray your race.

She'd hate him if she wasn't having so much fun spending his money. Spending his money and dragging him into swanky department stores like this one.

She followed a skinny, smiling, impeccably-groomed sales clerk down a wide pastel hallway with huge private dressing rooms on the right-hand side. The woman hadn't even blinked at the weird clothes Daria was wearing. Hell, she must know Daria was about to spend a fortune—she'd seen Gray waiting with a boatload of shoes Daria had bought earlier, and now the woman's arms were full of clothes, clothes she'd taken from Daria and insisted on carrying.

The clerk stopped at a doorway halfway down the hall and stood back, ushering Daria inside.

The room was huge, with a sofa, an upholstered high-back chair, and an elegant, Victorian-looking garment rack. Large mirrors hung on all four walls, strategically placed to give a 360-degree view, reflecting the deep golden brown walls.

The clerk hung the armload of clothes she'd been carrying on the garment rack; enough clothes to fill a whole closet. Daria had never owned so many clothes at one time.

"I'll check with you in a few minutes," the woman said, smiling through her immaculately lipsticked-and-penciled lips.

Daria pulled off her shirt and skirt, then turned to the rack. Even the bras were on hangers. Gorgeous bras, made from lace and a stretchy, satiny material, supportive but sexy as hell. More beautiful than any bra she'd ever seen. She slid the beige one on and hooked it. Beautiful and comfortable.

She grabbed the first garment on the rack—a rather staid business suit, charcoal gray with a regulation-length pinstriped skirt and matching one-button blazer. Exactly the kind of suit that the assistant to a boring diplomat would wear.

There should be an ivory silk blouse here somewhere—there it was, in the back, on a specially-padded hanger that protected the delicate fabric. She slipped the blouse on and buttoned it up.

A pity to hide the bra, but the shirt looked great, too. She'd never owned anything this expensive.

And she'd never been in a store this exclusive. Hell, it wasn't even all that exclusive, not like some of the trendy little custom boutiques. Even so, these clothes were pure luxury...and she wanted to revel in luxury for just once in her life. To live the way the wealthy lived, the people who didn't have to spend every dime just surviving. People who could drop ten thousand credits like it was nothing.

People like Gray. This was his money anyway. Might as well blow it on clothes.

Oh, she'd save a little, have a bit of a nest egg, but not much. She might end up in prison when this was all over. Why not live for today?

Live for today. With no home and not a friend in the world, that might as well be her new motto.

When she looked in the mirror, she gave a start. Was that really her? The suit looked great. Very professional. She wanted to look like a real assistant, not a fuck-buddy with a sham title. The more she dressed the part of a serious assistant, the more likely people would be to trust her. And she'd use their trust against them. That was the name of the game.

Gray knew the game, too. He'd get the Earthers to trust him, get them to sign this sham of a constitution, but the Prendarians would still be in control...even more entrenched than they were now, their presence sanctioned by the signatures of Earthers. Earthers that Gray misled. She had to stop him somehow. And dressing well wouldn't hurt.

She went through the clothes one by one, trying each garment on and making snap judgments about whether or not to keep it. After half an hour, Daria had a huge pile of keepers and only two dresses that didn't work.

At least all of the skirts were keepers. Gray seemed to like her legs; showing them off would probably keep him happy. She'd have to remember to pick up a razor. Hell, with ten thousand credits, she could afford one of those new sonalaser hair removal places. Then she wouldn't have to shave for half a year. God only knew where she'd be in half a year...maybe she'd have the smoothest legs in prison.

She checked out the last outfit in the mirror. Another skirt, and this one just might drive Gray crazy. The sky-blue silk was gauzy and almost transparent, the hem fluted and radically asymmetrical—up to her thigh on one side and just below the knee on the other.

But no matter what Gray liked, she needed to pick up some jeans.

She opened the door and found the sales clerk at the end of the hallway with the same careful smile on her lips.

"May I help you?" the woman asked.

"I'll take everything but the two dresses on the left. And if you could bring me three or four pair of jeans to try on, that would be great."

The woman came in and took the two rejects. "Of course. I'll be right back."

Daria turned to the rack. What else would she need? She pushed through the clothes to check. Jacket, casual dress, coat, casual shirt, business suit, casual pants, a handful of skirts, another dress, silk shirts... Yes, all she needed was a couple pair of jeans. And maybe a few T-shirts. She'd have to ask Gray about the material of the shirt she'd borrowed. The cloth felt soft and silky, but it hadn't wrinkled even though she'd slept in it. Great stuff. Sometimes the aliens did things right...but that didn't mean she wanted them on her planet.

A light knock sounded through the door. The clerk with her jeans.

"Come in."

Gray walked in, a few pair of jeans over his arm.

Her mouth opened in surprise. "What are you doing here?"

He closed the door and put the pants down on the chair. "I persuaded the clerk to let me bring you these...pants."

She almost smiled at his hesitation. "They're called *jeans*. And they're more comfortable than they look. What are you doing here?" God, she was repeating herself. Must be the shock of having him invade her privacy like this.

"You've been in here for a long time. I wanted to see you."

As if he'd missed her. She bit her tongue to keep from saying anything sarcastic.

His gaze scanned her from head to toe, then seemed to fix on her legs. "I like that skirt."

She grinned. "I thought you would."

His gaze roved up and down her legs...elevator eyes. Finally he focused on her face. "I want to sleep with you," he said bluntly. Bluntly and kind of loudly.

"Gray!" she whispered. "There are people down the hall."

"Yes, there are." He took a step closer, then another, and put his hands on her waist. His gaze dropped to her shirt—her breasts—then came back to her face. He smiled a little. "And if they knew what we're doing in here, they'd be envious."

He took her in his arms then, his hands stroking down her back through the thin fabric of her clothes. She felt his cock against her belly, already hard. Damn, he was ready just from looking at her. Ready to fuck her in the dressing room of the nicest store she'd ever been in.

Just like he'd do with a whore.

She tried to push him away, but he lifted her off her feet a little. Swept off balance, she had to cling to his shoulders to steady herself. He kissed her, kissed her with his tongue, making smooth little thrusts into her mouth.

Oh, hell. Why fight it? She wanted him to get hooked on her. She pressed closer and kissed him back.

After long moments of slurping, wet, open-mouthed kissing, he freed her lips and slowly set her back down on her feet. She panted for breath. What had she been saying? After a kiss like that she could barely remember her name, let alone why she'd been objecting.

A cough came from down the hall. Oh, right. "Someone will hear us."

"Then we'll have to be quiet," he whispered back. His smile was all sinful challenge. The kind of smile that said, *I dare you.* "Can you be quiet, Daria? Can you stop yourself from crying out when you come?"

She gasped. The shock of hearing him say it—so blatantly—made her flush with heat. She loved when he talked like this...when he talked dirty in that smooth cultured voice, with just a hint of a lilting accent.

Just a hint of a *Prendarian* accent.

Hard to care about that now, with one of his hands on her breast and the other on her ass.

His fingers feathered over her breast. "What are you wearing under this shirt?"

What a time to ask for an English lesson. "The word is *bra*."

"Show me."

His hands went to the bottom of her shirt, pulling it up a few inches. She put her hands over his, stopping him. One last try. "But your meeting...it starts in a couple of hours."

He bit her neck, and her nerve endings fired like sparklers. She squirmed against him.

"We have time," he murmured. "You'll even have time to shower beforehand."

She knew where that would lead. "If we get in that shower together, we'll never make the meeting."

He smoothed her hair back with one hand. His eyes were vivid, glowing like amber lit by fire. "Oh, I won't shower. I want to go to that meeting with your scent on my hands." He dropped his head, kissing her with open-mouthed warmth. "With the taste of your nest in my mouth."

Exactly the right words to melt her resistance, to flood her body with need. She swayed a little, leaning into him, clutching at his shoulders. He bit her neck again.

"I want to feel you beneath me again," he murmured, his lips moving against her neck. "I want to feel you come around my cock."

She could almost come just from hearing him talk like this. "But..." God, she could barely think when he licked her neck like this. "Let's go back to the ship."

"No. Here." He rubbed his mouth on her neck, spreading warmth and wetness. "Now."

Oh, why the hell not? She reached up, tangled her fingers in his hair, and pulled his head down for another kiss. His hand slipped under the hem of her skirt and teased its way between her legs. Clever fingers found her clit and stroked, generating heat and friction. She moaned.

"Shh," he whispered, a long, teasing exhalation against her neck. "You don't want anyone to hear you. Can you be quiet?"

"Yes, yes."

His fingers stilled. "If you can't be quiet, I'll stop."

"No!"

He chuckled. Those wicked fingers curled against her, again and again, lightly scratching her clit through her underwear. "Are you certain? Can you stop yourself from making those hungry little noises when I touch your cunt?"

A finger slipped under her panties, rubbing fire over her aching sex. With every stroke, she whimpered.

He groaned. "You can't. Because you want me."

"Yes," she whispered.

"Tell me."

"I want you."

He bit her neck again, hard enough to leave a bruise. She'd have to buy a scarf to hide it. She tilted her head, inviting him to bite her some more. He licked instead.

"Tell me exactly what you want," he urged, pressing a long finger deep inside…filling her, but not enough. She gasped when he withdrew. "Give me the words."

Maybe talking dirty would get *him* hot, too. She buried her face against his chest, but still felt the fire of a blush in her cheeks. "I want you to fuck me," she whispered.

He pressed his cock against her stomach, hard, grinding a little in rhythm with his tormenting hand. When he released her, she could barely stand. Her sex felt achy, swollen. Ready.

He drew her to the couch, but didn't sit down. With a quick lift of his hands, her translucent shirt came off and fluttered to the floor like a sexy white flag. The white flag of surrender.

His fingers traced over the lace edges of the bra, his gaze riveted to her breasts as if he'd never seen them before. Maybe it was the bra he liked. "You *will* buy this."

Hard to argue with his dictatorial tone when he looked at her like a starving man at an all-you-can-eat buffet. "Yes."

Hot hands cupped her breasts, his thumbs stroking her nipples faintly through the fabric. Then he bit the slope of her breast above the bra, startling a squeak out of her.

A low, sexy masculine laugh rumbled against her breast. "Such noise. People will hear you."

And he'd love that. Maybe pain would shut her up. She bit her lip, hard.

With both hands, he grabbed the bottom of the bra and wrenched it up, trying to lift it over her breasts. Stretching a bra she didn't even own yet.

"Gray, stop! What are you doing?"

A frustrated groan reverberated against her breast. "How do I remove this wretched garment?"

He'd never seen a bra before? What kind of women… No, she didn't want to think about Prendarian women now, not with his hot mouth against her breasts. "Shh. Let me do it." She reached back and unhooked the bra. His hands skimmed down her arms, sliding it off.

He bent suddenly, wrapped his arms around her thighs, and lifted her. When her feet left the ground, she clutched his shoulders to steady herself. "What—"

Before she could finish, he set her on her feet on top of the couch. She shifted her feet, finding her balance on the cushions. His mouth attacked her breast. Fierce need radiated out from his sucking lips, his licking tongue.

So much for balance; she groped behind her back for support, then leaned against the wall as he fed on her.

His mouth released her with a little popping noise. "Shh, Daria."

God, she'd been moaning. Everyone in the store was going to hear her—and from the way he grinned up at her, he obviously couldn't care less.

He reached up and cupped her cheek. "You're blushing, *dahsh'kara.*"

No kidding—she had every right to that blush. Here she was half naked, dripping wet under a new charmeuse skirt, and about to fuck the richest man she'd ever met...in the dressing room of one of the swankiest stores in town.

"You can't be quiet when I pleasure you," he said, his voice smug.

There's nothing special about you.

Oh, how she wanted to say it. She wanted to deflate his endless arrogance, to punish him for making her feel this way against her will...for making her feel this way about *him.* Even if she had to lie to do it. Because he *was* special, God damn him. No man had ever made her feel this good before.

His hands slid up her thighs, up under her skirt...agile fingers hooked in the waistband of her underpants and drew them down. When the fabric reached her ankles, he tugged on one foot until she lifted it, then the other. With a sexy grin, he put the panties in the pocket of his trousers. "You need not bother to wear these."

The thought of him carrying her soaking wet panties in his pocket... Her knees buckled, and she put more weight against the wall.

His head was at her thighs, his mouth nuzzling the skirt up, his tongue wriggling between her legs...wet, hot...*burrowing.* She wrapped her fingers in his hair, holding him close. When that snaking tongue found her clit, her knees gave out completely. He caught her as she sank to the couch, caught her in his strong arms.

The ceiling rose above her—he'd laid her down on her back. Before she knew it her skirt was up to her waist, his head pillowed on her thigh. He nuzzled against her sex, openmouthed, while his warm hands stroked her legs from calf to thigh and back again.

Every light brush of his lips tortured her clit...the barest of caresses. She pushed against him, trying to get closer to that teasing mouth, but he moved back just enough to keep his kisses light. Gray shook his head, resisting. "Not until you beg."

Damn him. He knew exactly how to make her ache, how to make her clutch his head and try to force him against her. How to make her whimper. Oh, god, how to make her moan. She ground her teeth, but his tongue kept stroking her, kept forcing noises from her throat.

Suddenly his mouth left her; when she reached for him to pull his head back, her hands found only air. She opened her eyes and saw him rise above her, his pants down to his thighs, his cock red, thick and hard.

He came down on her, full length, bracing his weight on his forearms and cupping her head in his hands. His face looked rigid, hungry, as needy as she felt. She wrapped her arms around his back, encouraging him. His hips spread her thighs, and he slowly, slowly pushed in, slowly filled her, until she nearly begged him for it. Her body clenched around his cock.

He stayed motionless, deep inside her, his head thrown back, his teeth gritted. Then he kissed her again, a kiss filled with his tongue, a kiss scented with her sex.

She broke the kiss to breathe. Closing her eyes against the desperation, she pressed her pelvis up, struggling to move against him.

He moved then, setting a slow, steady rhythm. Deep thrusts that had him reaching to her womb, leaving her empty with longing when he withdrew, teasing her clit with the hard brush of his pelvis.

Nothing, *nothing* should feel this good. Every thrust had her throbbing. The heat of his body, the solid press of his chest, the slick skin of his back under her hands. His hips, hard and urgent, plunged between her thighs. And he looked...she opened her eyes and found his gaze already on her face. Oh, he looked fierce, his face flushed, his glittering eyes a reflection of her own burning desire.

"You unman me," he whispered in Prendarian.

Was that really what he'd said? Even on the brink of climax, she had to understand. "What?"

He looked confused and shook his head. "You...you steal my control," he said in English.

No, he had *all* the control. His face dropped to her shoulder, and he pressed kisses against her neck, tickling her skin with heated puffs of breath. His thrusts quickened, driving her higher...faster. His shirt, so soft over that firm chest, stroked her nipples.

She reveled in sensation, let herself simply *feel* him, let herself climb slowly toward the peak. For once she didn't have to strive and struggle. Gray would take her over the edge. She knew it.

His lips found her ear. "Come for me," he whispered. "Give me your release."

The hot words were all she needed. She choked back a moan, her throat tight, and clutched him closer as she strained up against him, strained to get his cock even deeper. His rhythm forced her higher, forced her breath to catch. *Yes, yes!* God, yes. She cried out softly as her body snapped, shaking with the force of a heady, draining orgasm. Waves of pleasure rolled through her and slowly receded, leaving her trembling underneath his heat.

And still he moved, wringing the last drop of passion from her. Then she felt him tense, felt him go still and press deep, deep inside. His last forceful thrust pushed her hips up the couch. He jerked with wrenching spasms, small groans caught in his throat, until at last his gasping weight settled down on her.

She wrapped a leg over his, unwilling to have him leave her too soon. She wanted to revel in the feeling of his damp, lean body: his hips between her legs, his silky, fine hair under her stroking fingers. He felt incredibly good, just resting on top of her.

Frighteningly good.

As if they were lovers in truth.

His breath gradually slowed, but he didn't move away. No, he stayed inside her for long moments, silent and still. Was he going to fall asleep again?

His head stirred, lifted, and she looked up into heavy-lidded golden eyes.

Eyes that looked ready to tease her for being so damned loud. She stiffened.

"You see?" he murmured, planting a gentle kiss on her forehead. "I told you we had enough time."

Chapter Six

The hovercraft turned a corner too fast, and a bag fell over onto Gray's feet.

Daria glanced at him and pulled it back. "Sorry."

She seemed nervous. Did she think he was annoyed? Gray gave her hand a little squeeze of reassurance. "I'm pleased you found a few items worthy of purchase."

She squeezed back, then moved his hand to her smooth, warm thigh. "If I'd bought any more, we'd need two cabs."

He could think of nothing better than having her clutter up his quarters with her clothes. Particularly clothes like the sheer skirt she was wearing. "Two cabs and several people to help carry your bags."

"And I only dragged you into three stores."

"Only three stores?" He looked at the bags on the floor, on the seat. There were eight at least. "I would swear we went to twenty stores."

She smiled. "You have only yourself to blame. I warned you that most men find shopping with a woman nightmarish."

He grinned and stroked her thigh. Had it only been thirty minutes since he'd lain between these beautiful legs? "Fear not. Shopping with you gave me *great pleasure*, Daria."

She blushed, but said nothing—just glanced at the driver, as though worried lest he realize they had pleasured each other.

Were all Earthers so...private about sex? Or was it simply Daria's shyness that made her this way? She'd even covered the passion marks on her neck with a light pink scarf, despite the warm weather.

The hovercraft stopped before he could tease her further. He paid the driver and grabbed as many bags as he could, then stepped out. The cab had taken them to the main entrance to the space dock.

"*Sarjah.*"

Gray turned toward the voice.

Ah, Hento had found him. Gray put down the bags and reached out to shake his Primary's hand.

Hento looked surprised by the gesture.

"Still not used to Earth greetings?" Gray asked.

Hento merely gave him a long-suffering look, perfected over his many years in Gray's service. The man carefully kept his eyes off of Daria, but Gray knew he must be curious about her.

And Hento was one Prendarian that she was sure to admire. Compassionate and innately kind, Hento treated everyone with the utmost respect. Gray draped an arm around her waist and pulled her close. "Daria, this is Hento. My Primary."

Hento offered his hand this time. "Greetings."

Daria shook his hand. "I'm Gray's assistant."

Hento didn't even raise an eyebrow, but he must have been surprised. Gray had at least twenty assistants, all hand-picked by Hento. No doubt his curious Primary would ask about Daria in private. But for now he merely picked up the bags—all of them—and waited for Gray to move.

Gray knew better than to argue with him over lending assistance. Hento would never let him do much for himself. So he took Daria's hand and led her out of the sun, into the sheltered darkness of the space dock.

He looked over his shoulder at Hento. "Have you been waiting a long time for me?"

"No, *Sarjah*. Although I did leave a message for you last night."

A message Gray had ignored. Daria had kept him busy last night. Far too busy to discuss politics. "I knew you would find me today."

"As you will." Hento would never dare to censure him directly. "We must speak before the meeting, *Sarjah*."

Gray nodded. "We'll speak in my quarters."

While Daria bathed. His thoughts would be with her, imagining her washing alone. Remembering the shower they'd shared last night. Despite his earlier words to her, he'd planned to shower with her again. Perhaps later...after the meeting.

The meeting. Would she see him differently when she realized the power he commanded? She'd been annoyed when he'd given her the credits, but afterwards she'd treated him no differently than before.

He'd be careful not to offend her pride again. He little needed her assistance during the meeting, but she would never know that. He'd make certain she felt necessary. Seeing the meetings, seeing Prendarians and Earthers working together, would be good for her. Perhaps she'd be more open-minded.

At last they reached the ship. The loading ramp was guarded by three uniformed men. When they saw Gray they stood tall and dropped their gazes, as respectful as if he was the Premier Leader herself. As if he was more than a normal, mortal man.

Daria gave him a quizzical look as they passed the guards. She must have noticed their unusual obsequiousness.

She'd accepted his wealth...perhaps she could accept his relationship to the Premier Leader as well. In time, she would learn of it from someone. Best to tell her himself.

Perhaps after the meeting.

The ship was silent and still, no one in the corridors. The crew must be sleeping after their wild night. When they reached Gray's quarters, Hento opened the door, then stepped back to allow Gray to pass.

But Daria went through the door first.

Gray smiled at her unconscious breach of Prendarian etiquette. His unflappable Primary gasped.

"We're on Earth," Gray said to him quietly. He left Hento shaking his head and followed Daria into his quarters.

She reached for the bags as soon as Hento came in. "Here, let me take those."

Hento obediently set the bags down, and Daria gathered three of them up and carried them into the next room. Hento raised an eyebrow at Gray, then took the rest of the bags and followed her into the sleeping chamber.

"Oh!"

Her shocked cry drew Gray to the doorway.

Daria had a hand over her chest. "You startled me," she said to Hento. "Just put those down anywhere. I...I need to shower."

Hento put the bags on the bed, then stood tall, head bowed politely. Waiting for her dismissal, no doubt. But Daria just stared at him, clearly at a loss.

Gray could imagine them standing here all day, neither knowing what to say.

He laughed at the thought, and they both looked at him as if he was deranged. "We'll leave the sleeping chamber to you, Daria. Just come into the main room when you're ready."

She smiled a little. "Thank you."

Perhaps it was the smile on her face, or the sight of her legs, or simply the fact that she'd be showering alone...so close to him while he was discussing politics with Hento. Whatever the reason, he couldn't leave without touching her. He crossed the room, took her in his arms, and kissed her.

She resisted, pushing against his chest, turning her head away. "Gray!" she whispered. "Hento—"

"Has left the room by now." He turned her so she could see, then bent his head to hers again.

After a long, leisurely kiss, he released her lips, but kept his arms around her.

She looked annoyed. "Why don't you just put a sign on me?"

He frowned back. "What do you mean?"

Her hands pushed at his biceps, but he didn't release her. "Are you going to tell *everyone* that we're sleeping together?"

Sleeping together. No matter how often he heard it, how often he used it, the phrase would never make sense. *Sleeping* was far too passive a word for the pleasures they shared.

He almost shrugged, but restrained himself. A casual dismissal would probably anger her further. "Why should I hide this fact? We *are* sleeping together."

"But everyone will think you're paying me to sleep with you. I'm supposed to be your assistant. No one will take me seriously if they think I'm just a—"

Prostitute. The word might as well have been said.

He stroked her back lightly. "A Prendarian would never think that I pay you for pleasure. In truth—"

He stopped an instant before revealing too much. Before revealing that every Prendarian in the galaxy would grant her *more* respect for sharing his quarters. Telling her this would sound like conceit.

Her chin tilted with endearing belligerence. "You might as well finish that sentence."

What could he say to reassure her? "In truth, Daria, you are too sensitive about this matter." She stiffened, but he didn't let her pull away. "You are one of my assistants, and we share a bed. No one will find such a thing worthy of comment."

She bit her lip. "Earthers will."

No doubt hundreds of Earth men had paid her for sex. Why did she care if others believed he was among their number? But the thought was too harsh to say aloud. If she wished to be seen as merely his assistant, he would grant her that favor.

"As you will," he said at last. "Only Hento will know that we sleep together." Although many others would assume that they did. He need not share this fact with her.

She relaxed in his arms then, and her tiny smile seemed like a great gift. "Thank you."

He kissed her forehead gently. "I must speak with Hento now. Enjoy your lonely shower."

He left her digging through her bags and went into the next room, sliding the door closed to leave her in privacy.

Hento was sitting at the table, hands folded in his lap. His face wore his most carefully bland expression.

He sat across from Hento and waited. Questions were sure to follow that meditative look.

"You have acquired another assistant, *Sarjah?*"

At least Hento's voice was soft enough to prevent Daria from hearing him. Her pride would sting if she knew they were discussing her.

Gray kept his voice low, too. "As you have seen."

"May I know the woman's duties, *Sarjah?*"

"The woman—*Daria*—is helping me improve my English."

Hento raised his eyebrows a fraction. "You are a native Earther, *Sarjah.*"

"Yes, but I don't speak as a native does." Enough of these questions. "She needed an occupation. I needed assistance with my English. That is all."

"I see." From his tone, Hento implied that he saw much more than Gray had stated. "And Daria lives here with you?"

A subtle question. Hento was a master of subtlety, yet an indomitable will lurked behind his placid façade.

"Yes, she lives here. With me."

For a time, she had said. A long time, if he could will it so.

Hento studied his clasped hands in silence for a moment. Without looking up, he spoke. "Is she not a distraction?"

Here was a familiar conversation—Hento chastising him in that gentle, fatherly way. Diplomatically pointing out the problems in Gray's behavior, without ever laying fault in Gray's hands.

"Oh, yes," he agreed blithely. "She's a wonderful distraction. In truth, I can barely recall my own name when she's near me." He spoke in jest, but gods, the words were very near the truth.

Hento glared at him for an instant, then masked his annoyance. "*Sarjah,* you understand the importance of your duty. I would dishonor us both to remind you of something you know so well."

Difficult to find the true meaning behind those careful words. Did Hento believe Gray would be so far distracted as to blunder in his mission? "I can easily manage my duty and one woman. In the past, I've managed my duty and several women at a time."

Hento didn't smile. "You have never shared quarters with a woman before. Such a thing connotes…involvement."

He heard the unspoken question, but he wasn't about to tell Hento how he felt about her. Not before sharing that information with Daria herself. Hento would think him crazy, to feel attachment for a woman he'd recently met. No doubt Daria would, too.

Since he couldn't be truthful, he'd feign indifference. He shrugged. "It seemed a practical thing. She has nowhere else to go."

"Ah. I will find her lodgings, *Sarjah.*"

"No." The denial came out louder than he'd intended.

Hento's eyebrows lifted for a moment, no doubt at Gray's harsh tone. "Having a woman share one's lodgings can prove inconvenient."

He grinned. "I assure you, sharing quarters with Daria will be very convenient indeed."

Hento's lips thinned, as if he restrained sarcasm. Gray knew the look well. He might as well avert the debate. "She's staying here, Hento." He smiled a little to lighten his vehemence. "I can't think about diplomacy all the time."

Hento gave him a look of pure masculine understanding. "I grant you this." Then he nodded once, briskly. "My duty is clear. To ensure your safety, I will order an inspection of her background."

Gray's hands fisted under the table. Usually he heeded Hento's advice without question, but not this time. He couldn't pry into Daria's background while he kept so many details of his own life private from her. "No."

"*Sarjah,* it would be unwise—"

"No," he said again, louder. "I've seen her ID records." The first screen, at least. "I know everything I need to know about her."

"*Sarjah,* you well know that information may be obtained beyond the identikit records. Best for us to learn all we can about her."

Oh, gods. Hento would look into Daria's background—or worse, have his staff look into it. They'd all learn that she had some low-level occupation, that she supplemented her meager income with prostitution.

With *unlicensed* prostitution.

And though Gray did not hold this against her, Daria would be shamed before his entire staff. Worse than shamed—if they discovered her secret, he'd have to find some way to shield her from confinement for her illegal lack of licensing. His staff would turn her in as a matter of duty. They would feel no compassion for her. They would never wonder what might have driven her to break the law.

Better to keep her secret safe, even from Hento. "There is no cause to investigate beyond her identikit records."

Hento looked unconvinced.

"My instincts guide me in every negotiation, Hento. I rarely question the inner voice. And my instincts tell me that Daria is as trustworthy as any of my staff."

Hento gave him a long, steady look. An odd look, as if he saw more beyond Gray's words. What was there to see? He trusted her. A simple thing.

Hento spoke at last. "I am happy you feel this way, *Sarjah*. But trust is not in my nature. And my foremost duty is to guard you. I have sworn this to the Premier Leader herself."

Sanwar. Gray knew from long experience where this was leading. Hento would stop at nothing to ensure his safety. He'd order an investigation of Daria whether Gray willed it or not. The only way to prevent it was to forbid his loyal retainer from doing his duty.

"Hento, you will *not* have the staff inspect her background. You will *not* assign a sentry to observe her actions. You will grant her the same dignity and respect which you grant to me. Is that plain?"

Hento put one hand behind his neck and pulled hard, a massaging gesture he used when he was seriously annoyed. "As you will, *Sarjah,*" he said at last. "I would not dishonor you by daring to question your judgment."

Despite the conciliatory words, Hento sounded completely disgruntled. Being ordered not to ensure the *Sarjah's* safety challenged the man's cautious nature. Gray smiled at his long-suffering Primary. "Questioning my judgment is your job, Hento. And you perform your duty with admirable skill."

Hento smiled at that. "Perhaps."

"Have no fear, Hento. Daria will never harm me."

Hento's expression grew serious, and his eyes narrowed. "If she does, *Sarjah,* she will answer to me."

After all the years Hento had served him, he knew the man spoke truth. Thank the gods, he had nothing to fear from Daria.

* * *

Daria took deep breaths, trying to calm her rapid heartbeat. Even in broad daylight, walking next to a powerful alien sympathizer and his Prendarian friend, she still got the jitters when she had to come to the Civic Center section of the city.

Once the center of city government, the area now housed all of the major branches of the Prendarian oppression. God only knew why the aliens had chosen San Francisco to be their center of operations on Earth—maybe they liked the rain and fog. A city surrounded by water on three sides must be inconceivable on arid Prendara.

Or maybe they'd picked San Francisco because it hadn't been devastated by the wars like other Earth cities. Washington and New York had been wiped out in the alien invasion; Los Angeles, London, Paris, Beijing and a dozen others were destroyed in the last Earther war, the Third World War. Maybe they'd chosen San Francisco by default. Less need for rebuilding meant more time could be spent enslaving and oppressing the native Earth population.

The Prendarians had prettied up the area, with fountains and row after row of flowering cherry trees. They'd even put in tiny little hills covered with tulips to give the flat grounds some interest. When she'd been a kid, nothing but grass and cement had surrounded these large, stately buildings.

Gray and Hento walked briskly, easily, as if they owned the place. Daria tried not to cringe as they walked past a group of uniforms. Three Prendarians and two Earthers. More and more Earthers were putting on that uniform every day.

She kept her gaze down as they passed the huge Criminal Processing Center. Were Don and Trisha somewhere inside, or had they already been moved to Confinement?

Confinement. A nice euphemism for prison. If Gray got this constitution implemented, more Earthers might end up there. Every time the aliens changed the laws, things got worse.

She should be excited, not nervous. Gray already trusted her enough to take her along to his first meeting with the constitution delegates. Tank would have been so pleased. He'd always worried about her, had never liked putting her in the field where she'd be at risk. God only knew where he was now. Her mentor...her father, really, though not by blood. She could never repay him for everything he'd given her, but she'd do him proud on this last mission.

And things couldn't be going better. Gray was taking her right into the meeting. She'd meet the Earth delegates, and she'd find an ally. She desperately needed an ally.

Gray and Hento spoke to each other quietly as they walked up the wide, low stairs of a beautiful old Romanesque building.

Letters blasted into the marble over the staircase proclaimed this the War Memorial Opera House. The former home of the city's opera. God only knew what use the Prendarians had found for it. And God only knew which war it had been built to memorialize.

The lobby was cavernous, with ceilings easily thirty feet high. Elaborate vertical wooden beams on the walls heightened the effect, and a huge, detailed plaster relief covered the ceiling, depicting some ancient Roman or Greek scene. Lots of people in robes up there.

The men fell silent as they approached the security checkpoint in the lobby. Damn, had she missed something confidential? Something they didn't want the guards to overhear? She'd better keep her mind from wandering. She needed to come up with a way to stop this constitution, and daydreaming wouldn't help.

She followed Gray and Hento through the bank of weapon detectors. The guards gave Gray the red-carpet treatment, murmuring polite greetings with downcast eyes as they stood at attention. Daria could barely stand to look at them. Just being around Prendarians in uniform made her want to run—an impulse she'd learned in childhood that had served her well over the years. Avoiding Prendarians would never do her harm.

But she was with Gray now. If Prendarians looked at her, they'd see the trusted assistant and close acquaintance of their precious *Sarjah*. Part of his inner circle. She had a cover no one would dare to question. No reason to feel intimidated by a few security guards.

Easier said than done. The guards were stone-faced and silent. Nerve-wracking. She kept her gaze on Gray instead. He looked sharp in that modern, collarless suit. He could almost pass for a regular Earther, except his clothes screamed *outrageously expensive.* Quite a contrast to his usual minimalist look.

After the weapons detectors, a second set of guards waited. "Just a formality, *Sarjah,*" a female guard assured Gray. He stripped his ID card from his wrist and passed it to the woman with a smile.

A uniformed guard—an Earther with slightly Asian features—held out his hand to Daria. With shaking fingers, she found her ID in her small purse and handed it over. She held her breath while the man slid it through a scanner. After no more than an instant, he gave it back with a brief smile and a nod.

When they made it into the elevator—just her, Gray, and Hento—she breathed more easily. Getting away from all of those uniforms felt like escape.

Hento inserted a card in a slot in the elevator access panel, and the light for the top floor lit up. After the door closed, he turned to Gray. "*Sarjah,* you must take the dissension within the Earth faction seriously. If they fight amongst themselves, uniting them to vote as one entity may prove more difficult than you imagine."

She certainly hoped so. But she wouldn't count on it. The Prendarians had thrown a lot of reformist bones to the Earthers over the years, and the Earthers fell for them every time. Still, if they were fighting among themselves, maybe she could find one or two who'd be willing to help her disrupt the meetings or something. A delegate could spread rumors, foster fear and uncertainty about the constitution. Anything to keep it from being passed.

Gray smiled, that arrogant, cocky smile that said *I own the world.* "Hento, you know I enjoy the illusion that negotiations will be simple and easy. Must you put a stop to my enthusiasm?"

"My sorrow, *Sarjah.*"

Gray turned to her. "Daria, what is the natural way to say that?"

She gave a start. Was he really asking her to correct his Primary? This dignified man hardly looked like the type to welcome a correction. "You'd say, *I'm sorry.*"

"Even though I bear no fault for the dissension?" Hento asked. He didn't sound annoyed at all.

"Yes. We Earthers are always ready, willing, and able to apologize for things that aren't our fault."

No laughter, no smiles. Neither man appeared to grasp her sarcasm.

Hento gave her a brief nod, one of those little alien gestures. "Thank you for explaining, Daria."

In all her life, a Prendarian had never thanked her for anything. Hell, none had ever even spoken to her politely. Yet here was Hento, surely a powerful man, giving her a measure of respect. Amazing what screwing a collaborator could do.

"You're welcome." The words sounded strange. She'd never said them to a Prendarian, either.

The elevator stopped and the doors opened. A lovely Prendarian woman, tall, pale and blonde, stood just outside the elevator. With her hair swept back in an elegant bun, her expression and bearing so regal, she made that form-fitting navy blue uniform look refined.

Her gaze fixed on Gray with barely a glace at Hento, and no acknowledgement of Daria at all. Just as well. The fewer people who noticed her, the better. Tank always said that invisibility was an asset.

"Greetings, *Sarjah*." The woman's voice was as elegant as her appearance. She spread her arm out to the right, parallel with the floor. "Your preparation room lies this way. You can enter the delegation chamber from there."

Gray headed down the hall, and the woman and Hento followed, leaving Daria to bring up the rear.

"How many delegates are here?" Gray asked.

"Two hundred eighty-four," the woman replied.

"So few? I wanted at least three hundred."

They came to another hallway, and the woman pointed left. Gray took the lead again.

"There are enough, *Sarjah*," Hento said.

"No, there aren't," Gray replied. "Three hundred would give this meeting more stature. The perception of adding just a few to make a round number... Well, no matter now."

"My apologies, *Sarjah*," the woman said. "I should have doubled the number of invitations to ensure enough would attend."

Gray waved a hand dismissively and paused to give the woman a smile. "A trivial thing. I do not hold you at fault, Reema."

Reema. Even her name was regal. And the look she and Gray exchanged...not a heated look, but still—*something* passed between them. Something that made Daria's stomach knot up.

God, if she was going to get jealous of every woman Gray smiled at, she was in deep trouble. She had no reason to be jealous over him at all.

When they reached the end of the hall, Reema held a door open. A wave of sound came from the room beyond—voices chattering excitedly, mostly in English, a few in Prendarian. Daria couldn't make out any words over the general roar.

Gray looked back at her and gave her a smile, a confident smile. At least he hadn't completely forgotten her existence. He looked more excited than she'd ever seen him. A collaborator in his element.

She managed to flash a sickly smile at him.

He winked, so he must not have noticed anything wrong with her expression. Then he turned and headed into the room.

A hush descended suddenly...total and absolute quiet.

With Gray, Hento, and Reema all in the doorway, she could barely get a glimpse inside. She saw a few heads, mostly blonde, but nothing more.

"Greetings," Gray said loudly. Clearly addressing a crowd. "We are fortunate to be here today to fulfill our duty."

A low rumble came from the crowd—"Greetings, *Sarjah*," repeated many times. At last Hento and Reema moved, and Daria squeezed into the room.

God, the room was full of dozens of people. A whole roomful of uniforms. All Prendarians—except for Gray. And her. She shrunk back into a corner. A few people glanced at her, but they looked curious, not hostile. She hoped.

Only a handful of them could get close to Gray, but they all pressed in. One held a hand to Gray's ear, attaching a small device that Daria could barely see.

Gray reached for his ear, twisting something behind it. "Yes, I can hear you," he said, to no one in particular. Then he laughed. "Cease. You must remember, I can only understand one of you at a time."

Someone must be speaking into his ear. Several people, from what he said. Oh, of course. They'd be feeding him information during the meeting—information to help him get the delegates to toe the line.

"Have no fear, *Sarjah*," Hento said. "Reema and I will maintain order over your eager assistants."

Gray put a hand on Hento's shoulder. "Excellent."

Good lord, were *all* of these people Gray's assistants? There must be nearly thirty of them. Why had he bothered to hire her? He didn't need her at all.

Not at all.

And even worse, if he was leaving Hento and Reema here, he certainly wouldn't be taking Daria to the meeting. Damn. She needed to get closer to those Earth delegates.

Gray turned and scanned the crowd. "Reema," he called.

The small group around Gray parted, allowing Reema to move to his side. "Yes, *Sarjah?*"

"How long until the meeting?"

She looked at her ID band. "Twenty Earth minutes, *Sarjah*."

"Perfect. I'll go in and greet the delegates individually before I call the meeting to order."

Reema pointed to a set of double doors at the far side of the room. Blast-proofing metal covered the entire wall, including the doors. They weren't taking any chances. "The delegation awaits you beyond those doors, *Sarjah*."

Gray nodded.

A young man carrying a shimmering vest worked his way through the crowd and tapped Hento on the shoulder.

Hento turned. "Ah, thank you." Then he held the vest out to Gray. "*Sarjah*, I have a shielding vest for you."

Gray shook his head. "No, Hento. I will not wear armor to a diplomatic meeting."

What? Why would he take such a risk? The crowd fell silent again. Everyone must be listening as avidly as she was.

Hento gaped for an instant, clearly shocked. "You must, *Sarjah*. The dissension within the Earth faction makes the situation most unstable. Any of the Earth delegates might do harm to your person."

"With a weapon? Do you imply that the security detail is incompetent?"

Hento bowed his head, more deferential than Daria had ever seen him. "Extra precautions are always wise, *Sarjah*. This you well know."

Before Gray could speak, the young man who'd carried the vest spoke. "*Sarjah*, I beg you to wear the armor," he said vehemently. "You dare not trust any Earther."

Damn the man. How trustworthy would the Prendarians be if Earth had invaded *their* world? Bitter experience had taught her not to trust *his* kind, that was for sure. And even though she'd just been insulted—the only *real* Earther in the whole damned room—no one even looked at her. She might as well not exist.

Her jaw ached. Damn, she'd been grinding her teeth.

Gray gripped the young man's bicep with one hand. "We must learn to trust them," he said, his voice quiet but clear in the silent room. "If we cannot, then our mission has already failed."

The man bowed his head. "As you will, *Sarjah.* Go with the gods."

"Go with the gods," other voices echoed.

He could go with the gods or with the devil, as long as he brought her along.

Gray turned to Hento, grasped his hand and shook it. "Fear not. All will be well."

Hento said nothing, merely looked grave. He moved back, blocking Daria's view, so Gray could step past.

As if they shared one mind, the fawning crowd parted to give Gray a pathway to the door Reema had pointed out. He started down the human corridor.

Damn, he was leaving her behind. With all these Prendarians for company…and no hope of even seeing the Earth delegates, let alone speaking to them.

But before he took another step, he turned and searched the faces in the room. When his gaze met hers, he smiled. "Daria, come with me."

Yes!

She managed not to shout the word, but she couldn't restrain her grin.

Several Prendarians gasped. No doubt everyone felt the same shock she did. But she stepped out of her corner and moved to Gray's side with her head high, as if his order was the most natural thing in the world.

He led the way down the long corridor of Prendarian uniforms, and she trailed behind him with her head bowed, trying to hide her gloating smile. He might not need her, but he was taking her with him anyway.

After he'd singled her out like this, they probably all thought she was sleeping with him. She didn't even blush. Who the hell cared? She'd find an ally behind those blast-shielded doors, and that was all that mattered.

When they reached the doors, he stopped for a moment and gave her a cocky smile. Then he took a deep breath and pushed open both doors, as if making a dramatic entrance. Why shouldn't he? With his unshakable confidence, he probably thought this was going to be a party. *His* party.

She followed him through the doors and found herself at the top of a small flight of stairs that led down to the sloping floor of a huge room. A huge room filled with people…hundreds of people. How many had Reema said were here? Two hundred eighty-four? That made her odds of finding an ally pretty good.

The furniture was nothing but long, curving tables that formed huge half-circles along the sloping floor. Evenly-spaced chairs lined each table, all facing a small stage. No need to guess where Gray would be sitting. The stage was the only place for a man like him.

The delegates were scattered among the narrow rows of tables and chairs, but the two camps were clearly separated— Prendarians milled around one side of the room, while the Earthers stood in small clusters on the other. Great, the Earthers were already divided along racial lines. They couldn't even unite to fight a common enemy. No wonder the Prendarians had won the war in just a few months.

The Prendarian contingent had gathered closest to the door, and they fell silent when they caught sight of Gray. The silence swept through the room in waves, although a few indistinct grumbles came from some of the Earth contingent. Good.

Daria looked around. Damn, everyone was staring at her. No, they must be staring at Gray. She just happened to be standing close to him.

Gray went down the stairs with Daria following. He worked his way to the right, greeting the first person he came to with a handshake.

"Greetings, Marta."

Marta, a tall woman, looked startled by having her hand clasped. "Greetings, *Sarjah*."

Gray turned to the next Prendarian, leaving Marta to give Daria a long, measuring look. A look Daria had seen on many Prendarian faces.

This woman didn't trust her. Not one bit.

Oh well. Daria didn't need her trust.

Gray hadn't bothered to introduce her. "I'm one of Gray's assistants," she said to Marta.

Marta said nothing, as if Daria wasn't worth speaking to. Her gaze went back to Gray. Daria could see the doubt in the woman's eyes.

Doubt about Gray.

Gray had already moved past several other Prendarians. They merely gave her curious glances as she walked past them to catch up with him.

"I'm pleased to meet you, Shondo," he said to a dignified, older man.

Shondo gave a brisk nod. "*Sarjah.*"

And then Daria got another slow, assessing look, which passed back to Gray.

Damn. They were all suspicious now. Suspicious because he'd brought *her* with him. An Earther.

And none of them trusted Earthers. Gray didn't count—he was a collaborator, an Earther raised on Prendara, a relative of the Premier Leader. But even that elevated stature couldn't quite hold up when he had an Earther like her in tow.

Maybe Gray thought his importance could withstand the suspicion. Or maybe he hadn't thought about the consequences when he'd brought her along with him.

And why the hell did she care? If her presence made them suspicious of Gray, that worked in her favor.

She didn't bother introducing herself to... *Shondo,* she saw on his small, elegant nametag. What could she say? "I'm his fuck buddy?" They were all thinking it, no matter what she said.

She had to walk by three other assessing Prendarian faces before she stood next to Gray again. "Greetings, Grelden," Gray said.

Grelden merely smiled at Daria as she passed. Maybe he was better at hiding his doubts than the others.

It took at least ten minutes of hand-shaking before Gray finally made his way to an Earther.

Daria didn't recognize the first man in line.

"I'm pleased to meet you, Brian," Gray said. "May I call you Brian?"

"Of course, *Sarjah.*"

"Oh, you must call me Gray."

None of the Prendarians had been offered that informality. Their culture seemed rigidly stratified, so maybe Gray knew that none of them would dream of calling him by his name, even if he invited them to do it.

But Brian, the gullible Earther, was positively charmed. A brilliant smile lit his round face as she passed him. At least he didn't appear to hold her in mistrust. But he didn't look like he'd be willing to help her overturn this constitution, either. Far from it.

She tuned out Gray's voice, focusing only on the delegates' faces, looking for any sign of tension or dislike.

What about this man? No, he seemed too impressed with Gray. Too fawning.

The next one looked too trusting.

This woman was too accommodating.

Another fawning man, beaming at Gray and bowing repeatedly as if he'd just met some kind of messiah.

Oh, this woman looked like a possibility—*Janice Anglish*, her nametag read. Daria committed that name to memory. If she got desperate, she'd hint around, see if the woman was likely to help her.

Gray turned to the left, greeted a man, and walked past him to the next one.

Daria gazed at the man's face, barely three feet away, and her breath caught. A familiar face. A familiar *Earther* face. Thank God.

The man was looking at Gray's back. When he focused on her, his expression didn't change. Not a flicker of an eyelid, not a blink of surprise. But his gaze moved from her to Gray, then back to her. And he smiled...a slow, cagey smile. If a fox could smile, it would look just like that.

His nametag read *Henry Reed Jamison,* but she knew him as a different name.

Spider.

One of Tank's best friends.

Thank God.

Chapter Seven

For the second time in her life—twice in the same crazy day—Daria climbed into a hovercraft. She held both sides of the door for balance, even though the vehicle only rocked a couple of inches when she stepped aboard. Probably less movement than a gas-car made. But this damned alien thing just felt so...so *unstable.* No wheels, no visible means of defying gravity, yet it hovered a few feet off the ground even when the engine wasn't humming.

She settled in the back on a cushion that felt more like a couch than a car seat. At least the hovercraft was roomier than she'd have imagined from the sleek exterior. One of the benefits of riding in a more expensive model than the utilitarian cab she'd been in earlier today, no doubt.

She didn't even know where Gray had managed to get this hovercraft. They'd taken a cab to the meeting. People must bend over backwards for you when you had as much money and power as Gray.

He got in and sat next to her, grinning as he slid an arm around her shoulders. He looked so damned happy.

She smiled back at him—a genuine smile. She felt pretty good herself. Now that she'd seen Spider, the mission was a guaranteed success. Tank and Spider went way back. What a shock to see someone like him among Gray's delegates. Reema must not have screened the candidates very well, if someone like Spider could slip through the cracks.

He was probably working an inside angle to derail this constitution. She'd find a way to talk to him tomorrow...see if she could do anything to help.

Hento stuck his head in the open doorway and looked at Gray quizzically. "You don't wish to pilot the craft, *Sarjah?*"

Gray pulled her a few inches closer. "I leave the craft in your capable hands, Hento." Then he put his lips to Daria's ear. "I plan to keep my own hands busy."

She felt her cheeks heat, even though Hento couldn't have heard.

A wet lick on her earlobe made her squirm and tilt her head away from him. "Stop that," she hissed.

Gray nuzzled her neck. She pulled away, or tried to—his arm held her tight against his side. But he relented on the kissing, turning his head forward.

Hento settled in the front, and Reema climbed in beside him. Apparently Reema lived on Gray's spaceship, too. How convenient. She'd probably spent most of the trip to Earth in Gray's bed. Well, Daria would be there tonight. She edged a little closer to him.

The motor purred to life. Did Hento really knew how to fly this machine? It didn't seem like the usual kind of thing for a diplomat to do. All the cab drivers had to take special classes. She'd heard it was twice as complicated as flying an airplane.

The craft moved upwards in a long, smooth glide. She let out a deep, slow breath.

Gray squeezed her shoulders. "Nervous?"

As if she'd admit it. "Not at all."

He chuckled, then leaned forward a bit. "Now that we're alone, Hento, tell me your thoughts on the meeting."

It took Hento a moment to reply. "The dissension within the Earth contingent appears strong, *Sarjah*. They argue vehemently amongst themselves."

Yes, they did. Arguments about things that happened decades ago.

"If they remain divided," Hento continued, "they may never agree to your plan for apportioning the representatives. The equitable division of voting power is the root of the constitution."

Gray took his arm from her shoulders and slid forward on the seat so he could speak more easily to Hento. "Yes, but they will come to see the necessity of apportioning the representatives according to economic strength. It's served us well on Prendara."

"I admire your optimism, *Sarjah*. Yet the Earth delegates appear reluctant to agree that economics are important. Rather, they cling to their racial differences."

She couldn't argue with that. The Earth delegates were clearly divided along racial lines. The Prendarian occupation had seen an end to the boundaries of countries, and now only race was left to argue about. They couldn't see past their differences to unite against the Prendarians.

"All the more reason for them to accept the constitution," Gray said. "It alleviates the racial boundaries."

As if Gray had the solution to thousands of years of racism. Was there no end to the man's confidence? Probably not.

"The Prendarian delegates seemed..." Hento paused. "They appear less unified than we expected, *Sarjah*."

Gray straightened. "Why do you say that?"

"There were subtle gestures..." Hento trailed off.

So they'd been *watching* the meeting, too. She should have known they'd be watching as well as listening. All those assistants had to have something to do. No doubt Hento had noticed the way the Prendarian delegates looked at Daria—with suspicion. Suspicion they'd transferred to Gray.

Reema turned and spoke over her shoulder. "They appeared to be slightly nervous, *Sarjah*. Perhaps because many of them were meeting you for the first time."

Or because he'd brought Daria with him. His right-hand aide, the only one he brought into the meeting—an Earther born and bred.

"I wanted the Earthers to trust me today," Gray said. "My goal was to ease their acceptance of me as arbitrator. But I'll be certain not to neglect the Prendarian delegates."

"That would be wise, *Sarjah*." Hento's voice trailed off, as if he'd like to say more. An unspoken *but* lurked at the end of his words.

"Speak freely, Hento," Gray encouraged.

"As you will," the man replied. "*Sarjah,* you must not assume that the Prendarian delegates will vote for this constitution. They are used to having complete dominion on this world."

"They wouldn't dare vote against the constitution," Gray said. "They know that my—" He stopped and cleared his throat. "They know that the Premier Leader would be most displeased if anyone defied her orders to integrate the government."

Integrate the government. Did he really believe that? She didn't know much about politics, but it seemed like the Prendarians just wanted the Earthers to sanction their power. To give the Prendarian government their blessing. To willingly participate in their own oppression. That's what everyone she knew thought. Tank, Don, Trisha…everyone.

She nearly missed Hento's response.

"You must not count on their loyalty to the Premier Leader, *Sarjah*."

"I don't. I want them to approve the constitution because *I* have convinced them that integration is best for all."

"I am certain you will succeed," Hento said soothingly.

"With your guidance, I'm sure I shall."

Gray sounded a little anxious. Not as confident as he appeared on the surface. Even arrogant men like him must have private doubts.

"May I offer a comment, *Sarjah?*" Reema asked in her dulcet voice.

Gray smiled, even though she wasn't looking at him. "You would find a way to tell me, regardless of my wishes," he said, a playful note in his voice. "Best to state your opinion plainly."

Did they have to openly tease each other this way? Right in front of her? *She* was the one living in Gray's quarters. Not Reema. She laid her hand on his thigh. He covered it with his own hand and squeezed.

Reema turned sideways in her seat, looking back to give him a soft smile. As if she didn't see Daria's hand on his leg. "The Prendarian delegates seemed to object most strongly when you insisted on a living wage for all, regardless of their sanctioned occupation."

Daria had been surprised by that, too. Surprised and angry. The wages were the least of the problems with the sanctioned occupation system. Locking young children into a career without giving them any choice...the whole system was cruel. Yet all of the delegates had nodded when Gray suggested continuing the program. The only thing they all agreed on. They'd argued about guaranteeing a minimum wage, but that was the only argument about the program.

Gray turned to Daria and gave her a long, measuring look, as if he somehow sensed her annoyance. Impossible. His eyes were just an unusual color—the kind of eyes that made a person think he could read minds.

"I will not budge on that issue, Reema. Regardless of assigned occupation, everyone needs to receive enough credits to live. We must find a way to make the living wage agreeable to the delegates."

"As you will," Reema murmured, turning forward again.

Gray kept his gaze on Daria. Why was he looking at her like this? Like she had some vested interest in this conversation? He couldn't possibly know her thoughts on the subject. And he never would.

She looked away from his intense gaze and saw the neat rows of lights marking the space dock out the window. They'd be home in a few minutes.

No, not home. Just a temporary living space until she moved on.

"You will have an opportunity to begin your persuasion this evening, *Sarjah*," Hento said. "I'm certain you recall that we are expected to dine with two of the Prendarian delegates and their mates in one hour."

"So soon?" Gray's hand found her knee and eased up under her skirt.

How far would that stroking hand go? Up to her thigh...and no further. His thumb drew tantalizing patterns on her inner thigh, just a few inches from her clit. Damn, he knew how to make her hot. She squeezed her legs together.

She could feel Gray's gaze, but refused to look at him. If she did, he'd use those sexy eyes to put the whammy on her. Those eyes would make her part her legs and let him feel her up right here in the backseat of the hovercraft, like a couple of horny adolescents.

He took her hand and put it in his lap...holding it right on top of his hard cock. Hard for *her*. She might not be as pretty as Reema, she definitely wasn't as dignified, but *she* was the woman Gray wanted to thrust this big cock into. She couldn't resist. Her fingers stroked him, teased him, tested his length.

Hot lips nuzzled at the side of her head, pushing her hair out of the way. His panting breaths in her sensitive ear raised goose bumps all the way down her neck. "Trying to make me moan?" he whispered.

A wicked sense of daring possessed her. She'd never made out in a car before. All Hento—or Reema—had to do was turn, and they'd see... God, the thought made her hot. She nodded.

"I wager you'll moan first." His whisper made her shiver, but she kept her hand on his cock, squeezing and stroking by turns. Daria Cohen never lost a bet.

His hand moved to her thigh again, sliding up under her skirt, spreading a trail of fire. Where her thighs met, his fingers made teasing little circles. Fair was fair. She shifted her legs apart, just a little, just enough to let his fingers reach her aching sex.

He pressed against her, rubbing heat through her panties. Her hips nearly flew off the seat. God, she was wet. And she wanted nothing more than to have him push her underwear out of the way and thrust a finger deep inside.

He nipped her earlobe. "Remember this afternoon at the store?"

As if she'd ever forget the closest she'd been to having sex in public. She nodded.

His tongue traced her inner ear, making her press down into the seat. "I still have your undergarment in my pocket."

Oh, God. She gripped his cock hard…and gave a little whimper. Damn.

Gray pulled those tormenting fingers back down to her thigh. She squeezed her legs together, trapping his hand.

"Postpone the meal, Hento." Gray sounded hoarse. "I shall require…ninety minutes before we dine."

"As you will, *Sarjah*." Hento's voice had never sounded so dry. "I shall tell them you are… *volshano*."

Gray burst out laughing. "No, don't tell them that. Just fabricate an excuse, Hento. A decorous excuse."

She spoke a lot of Prendarian, but that was another new word for her. She had to know. "*Volshano?* What does that mean?"

The men laughed.

Reema turned to her with a wide smile, and Daria yanked her hand off of Gray's cock. His fingers tightened on her thigh, daring her to try to pull them away. She didn't. Tugging at his hand would only draw more attention to it.

"It means you have a desperate need," Reema said. Her tone seemed oddly kind. "A desperate need for sexual pleasure."

Oh, my God. Hento had suggested telling the delegates that Gray was late because he needed to get *laid?* Her face burned. Oh well, at least now Reema knew that Gray wouldn't be seeking her out tonight, if she'd been in any doubt.

Reema murmured something to Hento, something Daria couldn't quite hear. Gray's teasing thumb seemed to suck up all her attention.

"Fear not, Reema," Hento said quietly. "I shall appease your hunger *before* we dine."

God, did these people just run out and fuck whoever happened to be handy? Gray was busy with her, so Reema would go off with the next best thing?

Reema laughed softly. "Assuredly you shall, *dahsh'kara.*"

Daria opened her mouth, then closed it. She didn't have the nerve to ask for a definition of *dahsh'kara.* She already regretted asking what *volshano* meant.

The hovercraft slowed and came to a stop. While Reema stepped out, Gray turned to Daria and smiled. One of those slow, sexy smiles.

"Ninety minutes," he murmured. "Ninety *short* minutes. Best we hurry."

He jumped out of the hovercraft, then reached for her waist and helped her down. When her feet were on solid ground, he took her hand and hurried down the dock with her in tow, not even waiting for Hento and Reema.

He seemed *volshano* for sure.

And after all that petting in the hovercraft, so was she.

* * *

The security envoy gaped openly as Gray and Daria rushed up the loading ramp, hands clasped. Gray all but pulled her along. Need spurred him on—the need to feel her beneath him, the need to hear her cry out in pleasure and shudder in his arms.

The need to prove she would treat him no differently than before.

She hadn't balked, hadn't looked at him in awe, hadn't behaved as though he was anything but a mortal man. Not when his assistants fussed over him, not while he greeted each delegate, not even during the meeting.

She fit into his sphere as perfectly as if she'd been born to it. She'd been grave, serious, polite—and unspeakably lovely.

He'd directed the meeting for long hours, persuading and cajoling and arguing over every clause of the document that would re-shape Earth, with her tempting body right beside him. He knew she wore a beautiful bra under her staid jacket, that her thighs were generous and strong under the barrier of her skirt. He imagined it every moment. So tempting that he'd wanted to forget the meeting and pull her from the room, drag her past all two hundred and eighty-four delegates, and pleasure her until they fell asleep from exhaustion.

The urge came upon him during the first half hour of the meeting. His root had been stiff as a pike through the remainder.

Now he had her alone at last, and only ninety minutes in which to indulge their pleasure.

He didn't pause until they were at the door to his quarters. He slapped his free hand against the lock and waited a virtual age for the door to slide open.

Once inside, he pulled her into the sleeping chamber, into his arms, before the door had even closed. His mouth met hers, tongue seeking. Her body pressed against him, rubbing his cock, fueling his ache.

He fumbled with her jacket, pulling it off her shoulders without releasing her lips. She took her arms from around him and shrugged the fabric off. Then her hands were between them, pushing him away.

Pushing him away? No, merely peeling off his jacket.

Yes. Yes, he wanted her naked, against his bare flesh.

His fingers seemed thick and unsteady, struggling to free the buttons on her silky shirt, but finally he could pull the garment open to see those pert breasts, hidden in this bra thing she wore. A lovely, enticing garment, but it covered her completely. He turned her around and fumbled with the little hooks. When the bra was loose, he stripped it down her arms, reached around her from behind and cupped her breasts.

Oh, yes. So warm, soft and yielding. His fingers stroked her nipples, so thick and irresistible. But too much clothing separated his cock from her rubbing, stroking ass.

When he took his hands from her breasts, she whimpered.

"Shh," he soothed against her neck while his fingers skimmed the waistband of her skirt. *Sanwar,* where was the fastener?

She brushed his hands aside. He heard a zipper sliding, then felt the material fall to the floor. He tugged off his own pants, stepped out of his shoes, started to open his shirt. Her hands tangled with his; she stripped his shirt off. Then they were naked, in each other's arms, moaning into each other's mouths.

If only he could speak, could find the words, could tell her what she meant to him. But he couldn't stop kissing her.

Words would wait. For now his body would tell her.

He bent and sucked her breast deep into his mouth.

Mine.

She grasped at his head, pulling him closer. Her panting breaths made her belly pulse against his cock.

He dropped to his knees and looked up at her face. So lovely...her eyes burned with desire. Desire for *him.* Yes, she wanted him. Not his wealth, not his power. She wanted him as a man.

His hands slid around her smooth thighs, holding her still. Then he nuzzled against her sex, felt the silky hair of her nest against his face. With a little gasp, she clutched at his shoulders.

Mine.

His lips burrowed even further, his tongue pressed between her legs, until she quivered under his palms. Further, further... Finally he tasted the musky tang of her pussy, felt the hard little nub of her clit.

Mine.

He worked her bud with his tongue, stroking firm and hard. A strangled cry left her throat, an urgent, needy call for more. Her fingers tangled in his hair, holding his mouth against her sweet nest.

My...my mate.

Oh, yes. His mate. His partner.

He groaned, and her body sagged against him. He gripped her thighs, supporting her weight, but she went to her knees and wrapped her arms around him. "I can't...can't stand anymore," she said, panting.

"Yes," was all he said. All he *could* say, with his body aching for her, aching to complete the mating his mind had finally acknowledged.

The bed seemed too distant—at least five steps away. He needed her now. With trembling hands, he urged her onto her back, right here on the floor.

She reached up to him, as welcoming as ever, and he settled into her warm embrace.

Words came to him then. The words that began the partnering ceremony he'd witnessed countless times. "I take you," he said urgently, in Prendarian. *I take you as my partner. As my life's companion...*

Hot, slender hands slid around his back and pulled him closer. "Yes," she answered in the same language. "Take me."

He pressed slowly into her soft, welcoming warmth, the warmth he'd sought for ages. They moaned together—as if she felt the same craving he did. She must.

He rode her with steady, deep thrusts, driving himself higher...taking her with him. If only this first mating could last forever.

She was his. *His.* He bit her neck, marking her...and she cried out. Ah, he'd hurt her. He licked her neck, soothing her, never ceasing his relentless rhythm.

She clutched at his shoulders as he moved, her hips lifting to meet his, her breath hot and moist in his ear. Nothing, no one, moved him the way this woman did. Moved him to mindless, frantic desire, desire wrought with aching tenderness and fierce possession. He could barely breathe, panting and gasping, striving to satisfy her...to satisfy them both.

"Your legs," he urged. "Put your legs over..."

Those smooth limbs wrapped around his, holding him tight.

"Yes," he said, groaning.

"Harder," she answered.

He thrust harder, gave her the firm stroke of his cock against her tender bud, tilting his pelvis to give her still more pleasure. She whimpered and moaned, soft little feminine noises that nearly unmanned him. He tried focus on something...anything...anything but the soft welcome of her body under his, the wet heat of her cunt gripping his cock. Pointless. With every thrust, she lifted against him, trying to drive him deeper...harder. As if she needed his release as desperately as he needed hers.

Gods, he'd climax in a moment. But not before her. *Sanwar,* not before her.

He bent his head and bit her earlobe. "Now, Daria. Come now."

"Oh..."

He nipped her earlobe again. "Now."

The fierce bite of her fingernails stung his shoulders. She seemed to freeze, seemed to hold her breath for just an instant, and then little gasping cries left her throat as she shuddered beneath him. The contractions of her body gripped him with tight, insistent pulses, milking him with feminine muscles.

He let go, let go of his control, driving into her in a frenzy, over and over again, plunging deep and fast, until he climaxed at last, pouring all of his yearning desire into the heat of her soft, giving body.

Then he collapsed, panting, resting atop her. He managed to keep most of his weight on his forearms, trying not to crush her. Never—not even in his most private dreams—had he imagined such pleasure existed. The pleasure of mating with his partner.

He didn't want to pull away, didn't want to admit that this first mating was over. But they would have more matings. Many more.

And another *first* mating, after they officially partnered.

He smiled. She'd think him insane, to speak of partnering so soon. He must restrain himself a while longer.

Her fingers idly stroked his hair. "You need to get ready to leave."

"As do you."

"I do?"

Speaking quietly with his mate, their bodies still joined—even small things like this seemed wondrous. Without lifting his head, he spoke. "Do you not wish to accompany me?"

"I thought…I assumed you wouldn't want me to come with you."

He chuckled and nuzzled the tender skin where her neck sloped into her shoulder. "I always want you to *come* with me."

Her laugh sounded tired—a brief exhalation of breath. "I must be an excellent tutor. You're already making silly puns."

"Puns?"

"Jokes. Jokes based on the different meanings of similar words."

He lifted his head and looked down into her face. Her lush mouth was definitely too wide for that narrow chin, and her nose was merely uniform. His rational mind could see this. But somehow all of her un-beautiful features coalesced into the most beautiful face he'd ever seen. And her eyes, such a deep brown, were truly lovely.

He framed her face in one hand. "You're beautiful."

Her cheeks flooded with color. "Don't say that."

Did she doubt him? "Withholding these words will not change their truth."

She frowned and stirred a little. "We need to shower."

He kissed her frowning mouth lightly. "We have an hour left. Sixty whole minutes."

"Gray, please." She sounded quite annoyed.

"Sixty minutes is not enough time?" He kissed her nose. "In truth, we could sleep together once more before we need to leave. Even though I'm no longer as *volshano* as I was."

Her brows furrowed. She didn't look *volshano* at all. "I don't want to go to dinner reeking of sex. It's bad enough that Hento and Reema know we just got laid."

"Got laid?"

"Had sex."

At least that expression made a bit of sense. One did lie down for pleasure—usually.

She pushed a little at his shoulders. He must be getting heavy. He rolled off and watched her stand up, then stretch. His gaze moved up her legs. Mmm. She'd have him *volshano* again in a minute. Was there no end to his desire for this woman?

He stood and took her hand. "Lie down with me for a moment. Please?"

She nodded, and they stretched out next to each other on the bed pallet, on top of the thermo blanket. Her face still looked closed. He put a gentle hand on her waist. "Daria, what troubles you?"

"Nothing."

"Hento and Reema will understand. No doubt they are still sleeping together themselves."

"No doubt. Do all Prendarians jump anyone that moves?"

Gods, her expressions amused him. He smiled, even though she was frowning. "Hento and Reema are partners, Daria."

Her eyes rolled, an exasperated, endearing gesture. "I figured that out. Doesn't it bother you?"

A strange question. "Why should it bother me? I am happy for them."

She shrugged. "I guess things are different on Prendara. On Earth, we tend to get jealous when our…partners sleep with other people."

Why would she think… "Hento and Reema are partners."

"You said that already."

Ah, he'd heard Earth customs were different in this matter, that partners often proved faithless. "On Prendara, partners do not sleep with others. Never."

Her mouth fell open. "You're kidding."

He nearly laughed at the shock on her face. "No, I'm not. When a couple decides to become partners, the arrangement is a formal one. With a partnering ceremony. And they are...monogamous from that date onwards." *As you and I will be, dahsh'kara. From this date onwards.*

She looked flustered. "Oh. Well, then...I guess it doesn't bother you. I mean, I guess you're over her."

Over who? Over Reema? That made no sense. "What do you mean?"

"Nothing. It doesn't matter."

Her face looked set, resolute. He knew that stubborn tilt to her chin. She would say no more.

He ran one finger over that obstinate jaw. "You are teaching me well. I now know many words for the sex act."

She smiled. "Let's see...sleeping together...getting laid... What others?"

"Fucking," he supplied, hoping to see her blush.

She did. "You can't use that word in public, you know. Only with very close friends."

"Like you, *dahsh'kara.*"

Her smile wavered for an instant. "Or Hento. It's usually okay to say crude words around men."

Perhaps she'd tell him more. More to make her skin redden. "Are there other words?"

"Screwing."

"*Screwing?*" Another one that made no sense.

"Yes, screwing. But that's crude, too. Oh, and making lo—" She stopped abruptly.

Interesting. "Making what?"

She shook her head. "Never mind."

"You will tell me."

"No, I won't."

A quick roll, and he pinned her to the bed with his leg. He reached out and tickled her side; she shrieked with laughter.

"Stop!"

He stopped, but held his hand over her stomach threateningly. "Tell me."

She was still gasping. "I'll tell you if...if you tell me what *dahsh'kara* means."

He teased his fingers through her hair, drawing a long section forward to lie across her lovely breasts. "As you will. But I still intend to see you climax five times in one bedding."

Her fiery blush made him laugh.

"Quit trying to distract me," she said. "*Dahsh'kara?*"

"*Dahsh'kara,*" he repeated, correcting her pronunciation. "It means..." What *did* it mean in English? He took a moment to translate. "It means candy...the candy my heart craves."

Her eyes went wide. "Oh."

"Is there an English phrase for this?"

Those eyes looked moist now. She nodded. "Sweetheart."

Oh, yes. The perfect endearment for his mate. "Sweetheart." He kissed her lightly.

She shook her head. "You don't have to call me that."

"I know." He kissed her again. "Sweetheart."

"Please, don't." She sounded very close to tears.

Too soon. Too soon for this.

No doubt her shyness made her cautious. She needed more time. This he could grant her. They would spend the rest of their lives as partners.

"As you will, Daria." He drew away and settled beside her. "Now tell me the other phrase. Making…"

She bit her lower lip. Was it such a terrible thing to say?

"Making love."

His breath seemed to stop.

"But that's not appropriate for us," she rushed on. "We sleep together. We…we fuck, but we don't…we don't make love."

"I must disagree, Daria." *Sweetheart.* "Making love…this is *exactly* what we do."

She shook her head. "No," she said, as vehement as he'd ever heard her. "We don't."

Liar. He knew she lied. The fright in her eyes made his chest burn with tenderness. "Daria, I do lo—"

Her fingers pressed against his lips, stopping him. "Stop. Don't…"

He kissed her palm, and she took her hand away.

"We have nothing in common." Her voice sounded higher than usual. Desperate. "You're wealthy, powerful…before I met you, I had ten credits and no place to live."

Foolish woman. Why did she fight her feelings? "That does not mean we have nothing in common."

"You don't know me at all."

"I know you very well indeed." He brushed the backs of his fingers against her cheek. "I know how to bring a blush to your lovely face. I know you're strong and brave…brave enough to fight two criminals by yourself. I know your fierce pride makes you long to return credits that you desperately need."

He cupped her bare breast, drew his thumb over the nipple, and felt her shiver. "I know what makes you cry out with pleasure."

But he wanted more than passion from her. He wanted her love. Her trust. He gazed into her eyes. "And I would know why you dislike the darkness, so I could ease your fears."

She didn't speak, but her eyes were huge.

"You see?" he prodded. "I know much about you."

"Maybe...maybe I don't really know you."

"Then I'll tell you who I am." And he knew where to begin. He took a deep breath. "My aunt...my Prendarian aunt..."

She said nothing, didn't nod or look a question at him. She merely waited, her expression serious and unblinking.

"My aunt is the Premier Leader."

No reaction. No shock. As if she'd known all along.

Could she possibly have known? Few people on Earth had ever heard of his existence. Who could have told her? She hadn't been alone with any of the delegates, or with Hento.

"Oh," she said at last.

Perhaps she was too startled to react. At least she didn't appear to think of him any differently.

"No wonder this constitution means so much to you." Her voice seemed calm.

"My aunt would see the government on Earth integrated, as on Prendara. But the constitution means even more to me than it does to her."

"Why?"

Hard to explain something he had never discussed with another living being. Yet he wanted her to understand. To *know* him, as a partner should.

Best to start at the beginning. "I was taken from Earth as a child. When we arrived on Prendara, my uncle and I were kept as slaves for several years." Several horrible years. Without his uncle, he'd never have survived.

"Then my uncle partnered with my aunt, and I went to live with her." *The best thing that ever happened to me…until I met you.* He touched her shoulder gently, just to have a connection to her. "My aunt saw me trained in diplomacy. When I was old enough, she gave me a diplomatic position. As a negotiator."

Daria nodded, encouraging him.

He stroked down her arm and held her hand gently. "I had some success in my missions. She elevated me to a position of more stature. Again and again. I learned much. I did improve. But I always wondered…"

No. He couldn't say it aloud.

Daria didn't say anything, just looked at him steadily with her usual patience. Didn't she wish to know his thoughts? Perhaps her shyness made her reluctant to press him.

He took a deep breath. "I've always wondered if I succeeded on my own merit, or because of her influence."

"Her influence? Would she threaten people if they didn't see things your way?"

"Threaten? No. She would have no need to do so. The mere fact that I'm her nephew—"

"Oh," she interrupted. "I see."

"But here on Earth, even though she has dominion, she is not present. Her influence is remote. She cannot control what happens here. People will judge me on my own merits. If I succeed, it will be because of my own strengths."

"And if anything goes wrong with the constitution, you'll think it's your fault."

"It *would* be my fault."

She shook her head. "You don't control what others do, Gray. If they vote against the constitution—"

"But I am expected to influence them. To persuade them to vote in favor. If I fail, then I was never anything more than a...a... I don't know the English word. A *therkan*."

"A fraud," she supplied. "You know, you're demanding a lot of yourself. One...one failure doesn't mean that all of your past successes were frauds."

She didn't really understand. "On Prendara, everyone recognizes me. Everyone. Wherever I go, I am the nephew of the Premier Leader."

"But you can be yourself here?"

"Yes, but that is not my meaning. On Prendara, I had no opportunity to succeed on my own. Whether I willed it or not, my relationship to the Premier Leader influenced every meeting I conducted. Every treaty I negotiated. Every woman I—"

No, he wouldn't tell her that.

Her lips quirked in a wry smile. "Yes, I'm sure a good-looking man like you can only pick up women because you're related to the Premier Leader."

He laughed. "*Pick up* women? Truly, your expressions are bizarre."

She shrugged a little. "I can't explain that one. But seriously, Gray, you can't believe that's the only reason women would sleep with you."

"Perhaps not the only reason. But many women seek political favors in bed."

"Well, at least some things are the same all over the universe." She put a gentle hand on his chest. "But here...being her nephew might actually work against you."

"What do you mean?"

She glanced away for a moment. "Not everyone on Earth is impressed by your aunt."

"True. There are those who will fight me because they resent her power." He'd relish the challenge. "My victory will be all the sweeter."

"So you want to see this constitution ratified just to prove a point to yourself." Her voice sounded oddly flat.

"That isn't the only reason. I truly believe this is the best plan for Earth. And surely you would like to see the power distributed more fairly."

"I guess that would be better than nothing."

He frowned. "I don't understand."

She shook her head. "It doesn't matter. And we'd better get up, or we'll be late."

They'd passed nearly an hour in conversation. With nothing resolved but the fact that he must exercise patience with her. *Sanwar.*

Perhaps this was just as well. Daria would be with him, living with him, spending her days with him. And her nights. He could grant her patience.

The constitution should be his primary concern. And though it wasn't—not any longer—he would still succeed.

In *both* of his primary concerns.

Chapter Eight

For the second morning in a row, Daria sat at the table while Gray stood at the stove, cooking her breakfast. The man certainly knew the way to a woman's heart.

He smothered a gigantic yawn with one hand.

She couldn't resist. "That'll teach you to keep me up half the night."

He turned and smiled at her, an odd spatula-like implement in his hand. "Me? I distinctly recall you begging me to—"

"Begging you to let me sleep."

He flipped something in the pan. "That is *not* what you begged me for, Daria," he said over his shoulder. "Perhaps later I shall remind you."

"Do you promise?" God, what was wrong with her? Teasing him as if they were...*partners,* as he'd called it.

His smile was unspeakably wicked. "I promise." He faced the stove again and shook the pan with practiced skill.

"Can I help?"

"I thank you, but no. You need your rest."

"You were awake as long as I was." And he had a meeting to preside over this morning, too.

"Yes, but you expended more energy than I."

But *he'd* been on top. Most of the time. She'd probably regret asking, but she had to know. "What do you mean?"

He grinned. "You are the one who climaxed three times. Not I."

She'd begged for that third one...and he'd resisted for half an hour, tormenting her ruthlessly, until she'd almost cried from frustrated need. "I'm working up to five."

His laughter nearly brought tears to her eyes. God, she was a fool. Why had she ever thought she could sleep with a man and not get attached to him? Especially a man like Gray.

"I am happy to exert myself toward your efforts." He carried the pan to the table and lifted an oblong slice of sizzling...something to her plate.

"What is this?"

"*Tenfar.* A kind of plant food."

She cut a piece off with her fork and took a cautious bite. The texture was firm, the flavor mild. A little like salmon, actually. "I like it."

He sat across from her. "I am pleased."

She took another bite. "Where did you learn to cook?"

He looked up from serving himself, his eyebrows raised in surprise. "Is this not a common skill?"

She shrugged. "Most everyone can heat up prepared foods, but not many can cook from individual ingredients." And especially not people as rich as Gray. He'd probably had servants waiting on him right and left for most of his life.

"Hmm." He took a bite himself. "On Prendara, cooking is considered a necessary skill. And it's expedient. In the morning, I prefer not to take my meals with the ship's crew."

Thank God for that. She couldn't face another room full of Prendarians, all looking at her in blatant speculation.

"I can't imagine the Premier Leader cooking a meal."

He swallowed before answering. "In truth, I doubt my aunt can cook with any expertise. Other activities consume much of her time."

Must take a lot of time, planning ways to make sure Earth stayed in Prendarian hands. "I imagine so."

"Were you bored at dinner last night?" he asked.

"Not at all."

The conversation had mostly been casual, the Prendarians polite. No one had asked any uncomfortable questions about her background. They'd been...nice. Nicer than any Prendarians she'd ever met. Prendarians she could actually like—if only they weren't Prendarians.

Hell, they'd probably only been nice to her because she'd been with Gray. Despite the private doubts he'd confessed to her, he obviously wielded considerable power in his own right. The Prendarians had been all too willing to listen to his opinions.

"You charmed everyone, you know." He looked pleased.

She nearly choked. Charmed all those Prendarians? Not likely. "I barely said a word."

"You listened. They were flattered." He gave a little laugh. "Politicians are more accustomed to having people interrupt them."

She'd been too nervous to talk to them. "I didn't have much to say."

"But what you did say held merit. Even Hento declared you a woman of great sense."

Yeah, that had been a shocker. "He only said that to irritate Reema."

"No, Hento never gives false compliments. And Reema agreed with him."

Reema *had* agreed. She'd even sounded sincere. "She just wanted to be polite."

They ate in silence for a few minutes. Then Gray spoke. "You seemed uncomfortable when we discussed the constitution."

No wonder he was such a successful negotiator. He could read people like books.

"I just couldn't think of anything to say. I don't follow politics." But since he'd given her an opening, she'd ask the question she'd been dying to ask. "Why are you so committed to this living wage plan of yours?" It didn't seem like a smart move, risking the whole constitution just to give Earthers a raise.

He froze with his fork halfway to his mouth. "Because everyone should earn enough wages to purchase common necessities. No one should be desperate for credits for food, shelter, or clothing."

But that didn't tell her why it mattered to *him*. If he cut that amendment, the constitution would pass with ease. She'd never point that out to him, but he had to know it already. Last night in the hovercraft, Reema and Hento had both told him as much. "Why not make those things available to people who are too poor to buy them?"

His smile seemed gentle. "Better to give them a means to pay. A proud person would not wish to be...a charity case."

A proud person like her. "One of the Prendarians—Biitna—said your plan would strain the economy too much."

He shrugged. "Not unduly. People need occupations. They also need to be paid enough to survive."

When had he stopped eating? His fork lay on the table, and his serious gaze was wholly focused on her. "I should think you, of all people, would understand why this is a vital provision to me."

He looked at her so calmly, as if he hadn't just admitted that he was risking everything, risking the whole constitution, because of her. Because of misguided feelings for her. She wanted to duck her head and hide. Damn it, why the hell was she feeling guilty? She didn't want the constitution to pass, and Gray was helping her succeed.

"What is your sanctioned occupation, Daria?"

Lie. No, she'd lied to him enough already. "I'm a software programmer."

He frowned. "Such an occupation should pay adequate wages."

She shrugged. "It paid better ten years ago. A lot of the old computer systems have been replaced with alien technology."

"Even so, you should be earning enough that—" He stopped abruptly.

"What?" Damn, she shouldn't have asked. Now he'd probe, and force her to lie.

He took a drink of water—probably to think of a more diplomatic thing to say—then set the glass down and gazed at her steadily, his expression neutral. "You should be earning enough that you do not need income from additional sources."

Uh-oh. She'd blown her cover. Was that suspicion in his voice? In his eyes? "I don't like programming."

His brows drew together in a frown, almost a scowl. "You prefer prostitution?"

He sounded sarcastic. Viciously sarcastic. But at least he still believed she was a whore. She couldn't think of a damned thing to say. Might as well use the fork in her hand to distract herself. She looked down at her plate and diligently ate another bite, avoiding his all-too-perceptive eyes.

"I'm sorry," he said gently.

That brought her gaze back up. "For what?"

"For speaking harshly. I do not think any less of you because you were forced to...increase your income."

God. An honorable man like him, apologizing to a woman he thought was a whore. And even though he thought she was a whore, he still cared about her. Just last night, he'd said... He'd *almost* said...

Could a man like this *really* love her?

No. Not if he knew the truth.

He might not hate her for being a whore, but he'd certainly hate her for being in the resistance. And even though he had a few good qualities, he was still a collaborator. He still wanted to cement the Prendarian presence on Earth. If this constitution passed—the constitution that meant so much to him—the aliens would be here forever.

She couldn't let that happen. Even so, he didn't deserve to be used the way she was using him...and he didn't deserve to feel guilty for snapping at her. No, all the guilt belonged on her shoulders. "You have nothing to apologize for, Gray."

"Thank you."

He returned to eating, and so did she. If he wanted to talk, he could bring up the next topic. She wasn't about to set another trap like that last one. As soon as she finished eating, she'd run into the shower. And hope he didn't follow her.

If he did, she'd hope his mind wasn't on talking.

"Daria."

Uh-oh. She looked up, trying to keep her face relaxed. Unworried. "Yes?"

"If you have opinions about the living wage plan, I would like to know them."

It sucks. The whole constitution sucks. Take your Prendarian friends and go home. She tried to give a careless shrug. "Like I said, I don't know much about politics." Shit, that sounded defensive.

"But you know what matters to you personally. And what matters to you is probably of concern to many others."

She fumbled for words. "I can't think of anything. Really." Great, now she sounded like an idiot. Even whores had opinions. He must think her the most shallow woman on the planet.

"I'm surprised that you don't appear to support the living wage. I thought you would be pleased by the plan."

Oh, he was good at probing. And if he really wanted to know, she'd tell him. Give him some real information to think about. "Well, there's one problem with your living wage plan. It assumes that the sanctioned occupation system is going to continue."

He nodded. "Of course it will. The system guarantees employment for every person. Without it, people would have to struggle to find occupations. The plan has been in place for decades, and all agree that it works well."

All agree. Like he'd taken a planet-wide survey. "That's easy to say when you're not a victim of it."

He frowned. "A victim? The system provides an occupation based on individual talents. It costs much to administer. More than any other program. But it's worth the expense."

"An expensive failure."

He put down his fork and leaned forward, resting his elbows on either side of his plate. "Speak plainly. You make little sense."

Arrogant jerk. "If I make no sense, I'll just shut up."

He said nothing. Well, now she knew better than to try to explain anything to him. She took a bite of her cooling food.

"Daria." His voice was quiet, his eyes concerned. "I would like to understand your opinion. Please tell me your true thoughts about the program."

She dropped her fork to the table. "Fine. I think the whole program stinks."

He looked completely shocked. "You do?"

"Yes, I do. I hate it."

"Why?"

He sounded bewildered. As if he couldn't imagine anyone having a different opinion than his own. "Because it's cruel. When I was four years old, a bunch of aliens gave me a test and decided that I was destined to be a programmer. I never had any choice."

"What would you have chosen instead?"

She gestured impatiently with her hand. "God, I don't know. I never got to find out what other jobs existed."

"You received schooling. It's another benefit of the program. Many years of—"

"Yeah, I got schooling all right. Just enough schooling to do my *sanctioned occupation.* I wasn't taught anything but the basics of other subjects. And all because some damned alien looked at a test score from when I was practically a baby and labeled me a programmer."

Her breath came fast, her throat felt tight. She swallowed a hard lump and fell silent. Damn, she'd said way too much. Revealed too much.

His face seemed grave. Serious. Finally he gave a short nod. "The system will be modified. Children will be periodically reviewed to ensure that they still have an aptitude—and a desire—for their sanctioned occupation. We will give them...a choice." He paused. "Tell me your thoughts. Will this resolve the problem?"

He couldn't be serious. "Just like that? You'll change the whole system, just because it pisses me off?"

"Yes. If you are...pissed off, no doubt many others are as well. I didn't realize the system was flawed."

She shook her head, dazed. "But...how can you do this?"

He finished the last bite of his food. "I'll contact Hento. One of my assistants will write a new provision for the constitution before the meeting today."

"What if...what if the delegates don't like the change? They all seemed really happy to continue the program as is. It's the living wage they objected to." Why the hell was she bringing this up? If they objected, they'd be less likely to approve the constitution. That was exactly what she wanted.

But it didn't feel like what she wanted. Shit.

Gray raised an eyebrow, a supercilious look he might have learned from the Premier Leader herself. "If they disagree, I will persuade them to agree."

Must be nice to have that kind of confidence. But still...he'd listened to her. She'd told him her concerns, and he jumped to take action to fix things. For her. Even though these changes might sink the constitution.

God, he must really love her.

No. No, he must really *think* he loved her.

"Does anything else trouble you, Daria?"

Only the fact that you're trying to solidify the Prendarian control of Earth. Well, that was one thing she could never tell him. One thing he could never fix for her. She'd fix that herself, with Spider's help. "No. Honestly."

Gray stood, came to her side, and dropped a brief kiss on top of her head. "I must contact Hento now about the amendment."

She nodded without looking away from her plate. One glance at her eyes would show him she was on the verge of tears.

His thumb stroked over her cheekbone in a gentle caress. "Thank you for sharing your thoughts with me."

She didn't watch him leave. After a moment, she heard his voice from the other room, speaking to Hento over the command center. Giving him orders. Orders that could mean the death of the constitution that meant so much to him. And even if the changes to the sanctioned occupation plan didn't sink him, Spider would.

She should be happy.

Her chair scraped against the floor when she pushed back from the table. Maybe she could sneak into the shower while Gray spoke to Hento.

The shower would cover the noise of a good cry.

* * *

When a Prendarian woman stood, her face angry, Daria held her breath. More opposition. This must be the fiftieth delegate to complain, and they'd only been debating the new provision for an hour. Even the few Earthers who'd spoken up seemed doubtful.

From the edge of her vision, she saw Gray's fist clench behind the narrow podium.

The woman scowled openly at Gray. "I add my voice to the dissent. We have no cause to tamper with a system that has served us well for three decades."

"I understand your concerns, Janta," he began.

Amazing, the way he could remember all those names. He hadn't forgotten a single one.

Gray leaned forward and gripped the edge of his podium. So earnest. "But any system can be improved. The modification is small, but will dramatically improve the productivity of those with sanctioned occupations. And it will not unduly strain the treasury."

Nice job, putting his response in terms of productivity. Terms that Prendarians could appreciate.

"But the new wage provision *will* strain the treasury," the woman insisted. "Earth must become self-sustaining. We can't rely on Prendarian support forever."

"The base wages will create only a nominal increase," Gray replied.

Daria tuned him out. She'd heard it all before. Seemed like Gray had been repeating the same arguments all morning, just using different words. Different words, a different tone of voice, whatever he thought would be persuasive. Throughout the long morning, he'd been quick on the draw, ready with just the right thing to say. Witty or insightful or blunt by turns, modifying his approach for each delegate. No doubt about it, Gray was good at his job. A masterful negotiator, regardless of any family connections he happened to have.

When he banged a small gavel on the podium, Daria jumped. Damn, her mind had completely wandered. Gray must have called for intermission. The delegates stood, many of them stretching, murmuring amongst themselves, clearly sharing their objections.

Gray didn't turn toward her, just stared out over the milling sea of delegates with a thoughtful smile on his face. The smile looked fake. He must be worried. After an hour of haranguing and arguing, even his considerable self-confidence must be shaken.

And no wonder. All of the delegates seemed pissed off. He'd be lucky to get fifty votes. It looked like her mission might succeed after all. Despite her confusion, her inexperience, she'd pulled it off.

Tank would be so happy.

And if the constitution didn't fail because of the new amendments, Spider would have some kind of backup plan. Some way to make sure the aliens didn't get their power sanctioned by Earthers.

One way or another, Gray's constitution was toast.

And without the constitution, the aliens would go back to...

The Prendarians would go back to...

Hell, they'd go back to being the only ones in power. Just like before.

The Earthers would have nothing. Nothing but sanctioned occupations, nothing but cheap bones thrown to them by their Prendarian rulers. New freedom fighters would come along, Earthers who resented the aliens. They'd keep the resistance alive, keep fighting for the cause.

More fighting. More petty sabotage, feebly throwing tiny pebbles at Goliath.

God, just the thought made her weary.

Maybe... Maybe Gray was right after all. Maybe they could find a way to work with the Prendarians.

No. You couldn't work with people you didn't trust.

Gray put a hand to his ear. One of his assistants must be speaking. Hento, perhaps.

She trusted Hento. Maybe even Reema. They weren't monsters. They didn't treat her like a lower form of life. No, Hento and Reema were good people. Honest people. People who sincerely wanted Earthers to have a voice in their own government.

Gray came to her side and sat down in the empty chair next to her. Though he smiled, the small worry lines between his brows were deep. He wanted this constitution so much. And he argued for this new provision, simply because it was important to her.

No, not only for her. He fought for the provision—for the constitution—because he thought it was the best thing for everyone. Because he believed in it.

And she believed in him.

Without even trying, he'd convinced her to believe in him. To believe in his vision. Where was the amoral collaborator, the traitor, the *target* she'd hated from day one? She'd been wrong about him. Wrong about everything. If the constitution failed, she'd never forgive herself.

Damn it, Gray had turned her world upside down.

She wanted to take his hand, to reassure him. But she couldn't, not with so many of the delegates glaring up at the podium. Gray watched them, looking like his usual calm self, but a muscle tightened in his jaw.

She leaned closer to him. "Gray, you have to back off. They won't agree to either of your new provisions."

His mouth curved in that cocky smile. "Yes, they will. They are merely surprised by the changes."

If only she could believe him. God help her, she wanted him to succeed. She wanted this constitution to pass. And not just because she was crazy about him.

Whoa. She really was crazy about him. A collaborator. No, not a collaborator. A man who stood up for what he believed in. Who put his own career on the line to see the right thing done. A man who'd give ten thousand credits to a whore, just because she needed them.

There had to be a way for her to help him, for a change.

She shifted in her seat to speak close to his ear. "Maybe you can take the new provisions out, just to get the initial constitution passed. Then add them in later."

He took her hand. "The battle is far from over, Daria. I have until tomorrow to convince the delegates to vote in favor."

"Tomorrow?"

He nodded. "Tomorrow afternoon. The sooner we vote, the better. I will not have the delegates believe that they can squabble about the constitution endlessly. Earth needs an integrated government now."

Shit. She had to get to Spider today. Find a way to stop whatever the hell he had planned. If the vote was tomorrow, Spider would act soon.

Gray put his hand to his ear for a second. "Hento is calling for me, Daria. I must leave to speak with him. Will you join me?"

Yeah, he probably needed to speak to Hento big time. Get some more ammunition for his arguments with the delegates. But this gave her the perfect chance to talk to Spider. Maybe she could at least find out what he was up to and warn Gray.

"I'll stay here."

"As you will."

He leaned closer, as if to kiss her. In front of all these people? She pulled away quickly.

He chuckled. "You shall repay me for that missed opportunity later, sweet—"

No wonder he cut the endearment short, after the way she'd freaked out on him last night. She smiled as if nothing was wrong. "As you will," she echoed.

She watched him move through the crowd, stopping to say a few words here, to shake a few hands there. When he finally escaped through the blast-shielded doors to his preparation room, she turned her gaze to the crowd of delegates.

One thing about the Prendarians—since most of them were fair-haired, skipping over them was easy. She found Spider quickly. He was standing with only one other delegate, a small gray-haired woman. Maybe she could separate them. Get Spider alone.

She stepped off the stage and made her way slowly up to the tier Spider was on. No, not Spider—Henry. She had to think of him as Henry now.

His gaze caught hers when she was still more than twenty feet away. He turned back to the woman, said a few words, and shook her hand. Then he turned and walked toward Daria.

Good, he wanted to speak to her, too. This should be easy.

He nodded at her. "Come with me."

"All right."

He led her down a few tiers and off to the right, into a small anteroom. The room was small and empty, just a few comfortable chairs and a small side table set with clean glasses and an elegant, old-fashioned pitcher of water.

She sat in one of the chairs. Henry shut the door, then sat next to her and smiled. "Well, well. What's a nice girl like you doing in a place like this?"

Be cagey. She could almost hear Tank's voice. Tank. Would he ever forgive her if he found out she'd changed sides? No time to worry about that now. Guilt could come later. "The same thing you are, I imagine."

He raised his eyebrows. "I doubt that. I'm a respected delegate, and you…"

Don't answer, Tank would say. *Let him keep talking.* "I'm…what?"

"You're fucking William Gray."

Hmm. Maybe Tank hadn't told Henry about the kidnapping mission. *Don't give him information he doesn't already have.* "So?"

"So maybe you're playing a better game than I ever gave you credit for."

Now turn it back on him. "Look who's talking. This is quite a game *you* have going, Henry."

"I'm surprised to see you. I thought everyone in your group was identified."

He hadn't taken her lead. Damn. "Everyone but me, I guess. It's good to see you again. I thought all of my friends were in prison."

"Only the ones who are guilty of something, I suppose."

He knew this game a lot better than she did, damn it. He wouldn't tell her a thing until she tipped her own hand. Convinced him she was on his side. She gave him a bright smile. "Look, Henry, I'm sure we have the same goal here. Let's work together."

He didn't smile back. "How do I know we have the same goal? Last I heard, you were living with a bunch of terrorists. Now you show up on the arm of William Gray."

"And last I knew, you were best friends with a terrorist ringleader."

"But look at us now. I'm a respected politician, reshaping the future of Earth. And you—why, you're fucking a collaborator. Aren't you?"

He didn't give an inch. She'd have to give him a reason that made sense. "Of course I'm sleeping with him. Can you think of a better way to find out what he's up to?"

"I suppose not."

She'd have to draw him in. Pretend to tip her own hand. "Look, Henry, I want to stop this constitution as much as you do."

He gave a barely perceptible nod. "So what's your plan?"

She waved a hand, frustrated. "I don't have a plan. Tank set us up to kidnap Gray. Then everyone got busted but me."

"So your new plan is…what, exactly? To sleep with him? Enjoy his money? Bask in the glow of his power?"

She tried to look casual and shrugged. "Well, yeah. I've been trying to think of a plan, but you know I don't have much experience. Tank was the planner. Without him, I'm lost." Time to make him feel like they were allies. Flatter him. She laid a hand on his forearm. "I know you must have a plan, Henry. I could help you."

His wolfish smile appeared. "What's in it for me?"

Asshole. She took her hand back. "You get my help. Not that you need it. Not with your experience."

He leaned closer suddenly, reached up, and cupped her cheek. Oh, God. She couldn't afford to move away. She closed her eyes. *Please stop. Please.*

"Maybe I don't need your help," he said. "But I'd like something else from you."

She swallowed. No. No, she couldn't do this. Not even for Gray. She pulled back, and his hand dropped. "Stop it. You're like an uncle to me."

He laughed. "An uncle? You certainly know how to hurt a man. I suppose I'm happy you didn't say grandfather. Listen, Daria, I'd be happy to have your help, but I'm not sure I can trust you."

Was he serious? "But...but you've known me for twelve years."

"Yes, but you're fucking a collaborator now. The great William Gray himself. Maybe he sent you here to find out what I'm up to."

Stay calm, Tank would have said. *Use his name.* "I told you, Henry. I'm only sleeping with him to try to find a way to block the passage of this constitution."

"Why should I believe you?"

Confess something small. Pretend to expose yourself. He'll think he can trust you. "That was part of Tank's original plan, you know. Sleep with Gray, get him to trust me, then slip him a drug so we could kidnap him." She took a deep breath. "He doesn't mean a thing to me."

Ah, her best acting job ever.

Henry folded his arms and said nothing.

"You know me, Spider. You know I'd do anything to get these damned aliens off of Earth. I'll even fuck a collaborator if I have to."

He was smiling now. "Why, Daria, I think you've mistaken me for someone else."

She froze. "What?"

"I'm obviously not the man you seem to think I am. Spider? I don't recognize that nickname."

"But…you and Tank…"

His laugh sounded fake. "Me and a terrorist? Why, I've been working to make sure this constitution becomes law. Nothing would please me more. Just ask any of the delegates."

Then why had he toyed with her? "Why?" Her voice came out a whisper.

He reached into the pocket of his suit jacket and pulled out a small square object, then held it out in his palm. The receiver for a holo-recorder. Oh, shit.

The bastard smiled at her. "Because after this constitution is ratified, I plan to be elected Prefect of Earth."

He glanced to the right and nodded. "The recorder's behind that wall. You didn't notice the humming noise when it switched on. The aliens installed it for purposes of their own. Considerate of them, wasn't it?"

"But why…why bother recording this? How can it help?"

"You really are naïve, aren't you? My only real competition for Prefect is William Gray. Your fuck buddy. Although he'll probably dump you as soon as he sees this recording. Perhaps you should reconsider me as a lover. Ah, but then again, my career can't afford the tarnish of having a known terrorist in my bed, either. I'm afraid I must withdraw my offer."

She sat there, stunned. Too stunned to move. To think.

He put the receiver back in his pocket and stood. "I think this little conversation of ours will guarantee me the election, don't you? I must thank you."

She glared at him. Oh, if only looks could kill. "You won't win. Gray will beat you."

He lifted an eyebrow. "So you're loyal to the man after all. Too bad I've already stopped the recording. Too bad for you, that is."

"This recording won't help you, Spider. It's enough to put me in prison, but it won't hurt Gray."

"There you go, being naïve again. As soon as I show this recording around, his reputation will be destroyed. The man brought a terrorist into secure chambers where hundreds of important delegates sat unprotected. My, my. No one will ever trust his judgment again. Not even his powerful aunt will be able to save him." He laughed. "What's the old expression? He won't be able to get elected…dog catcher."

Damn him, the bastard was right. No one would vote for Gray after they saw this recording. No one.

He walked to the door.

Daria lunged for his back. He turned and swung his fist into her chest. Stars burst in her eyes, and a vise clamped down on her lungs. She sank to her knees, gasping.

Henry went to the door and left, as calm as if he'd been chatting quietly with an old friend.

Oh, God. She'd destroyed Gray after all—without even wanting to.

* * *

Gray rushed to his quarters with Daria in tow again. She'd been clearly distressed all afternoon. Worried about the constitution. Worried about *him*. A novel thing, to have a partner worry about him.

Another wondrous thing.

He could easily become used to these daily wonders. Although he disliked seeing Daria troubled.

As soon as they were in his quarters, he took her gently into his arms. "Don't worry. The majority of delegates accept the constitution."

She rubbed her cheek against his chest. "A lot of them don't like the new provisions, Gray."

The provisions that modified the sanctioned occupation system. The provisions to resolve issues she had mentioned to him. She must feel responsible for putting the constitution at risk. "The new provisions are fair and moral, Daria. Hento will contact many of the delegates this evening. We will persuade them."

"I hope so." Her voice sounded a bit...distant. "The constitution sets up a Prefect position, doesn't it?"

The only part of the constitution no one had contested. He drew back so he could see her face, but she didn't look up at him. "Yes, it does. The Prefect will preside over the new, unified legislature."

"And you want the job?"

He could read nothing from her downcast eyes. "I do. Very much."

She bit her lip, looking even more anxious than before. "What if you don't get elected?"

He touched her chin, but her gaze stayed low. "Daria...no matter what happens with the constitution, with the election for Prefect, I won't be leaving Earth."

She looked up then. "What?"

"If I don't become Prefect, I'll find something worthwhile to do. But I'll stay here on Earth. In San Francisco. With you."

He pressed a light kiss to her forehead. "And tomorrow, whether the constitution passes or fails, I have a gift for you."

"Gray, no."

"Daria, yes."

She pulled away, but gripped his forearms. "There's something I have to tell you."

Her breath shuddered, and her lip trembled. Gods, she looked near tears.

"Shh." He held her close and rubbed her back with long, soothing strokes. "You can tell me anything," he murmured against the top of her head. "I love you."

She pulled away then. Her tears spilled over, and she wiped at them with shaking hands. "No, you don't. You don't really know me."

Sanwar, would she never speak her feelings to him? Or even allow him to speak his own? "We discussed this last night. I know you well enough. You dishonor me to negate my truth."

"Stop. Just stop it," she said, her voice sharp. "I have something to tell you, damn it."

"As you will. Speak and be done with this."

She took a deep, unsteady breath. "I'm not who you think I am."

"You are not Daria Viktorovna Cohen?" *The woman who goads me to distraction?*

She rolled her eyes. "Yes, of course I am. That's my real name, I mean. But I'm not…I'm not a prostitute."

He should have known. No prostitute could retain Daria's blushing innocence. "Why would you have me believe that of you?"

"Because what I am...what I really am...is so much worse."

Worse? He gripped her arms. "What could possibly be worse?"

Tears flowed freely over her cheeks. "I'm...I'm in the resistance."

He knew the word, but once again, failed to understand her meaning. "The what?"

"The resistance," she repeated.

He shook his head, bewildered. "I don't understand."

"I'm a rebel! I'm fighting against the Prendarian presence on Earth."

Ish ab'tah. He stepped back, away from her. "You... Why?"

Her elbow came up, her arm wiping the tears on her sleeve. "Because I hated the Prendarians so much. Hated them for taking over my world."

The woman made no sense. "Taking over your world? By the gods, they *saved* your world."

She glared at him through wet, reddened eyes. "That's bullshit. Prendarian bullshit fed to us because they won the war."

He gripped her arms. "There *was* no war. Merely an invasion. And do you understand why? Because the Earthers had already destroyed themselves. A petty war over money, over resources, because you couldn't share what some of you had in abundance. The Prendarians saved this world from certain destruction."

She shook her head, her hair swinging with her fierce movements. "That's not true. None of it is true."

"I do not lie. Unlike you."

She glared at him. "You can't understand. A rich man like you...you don't know what it's like to grow up in an orphanage. Educated only so I could serve my alien masters."

"I can't understand? Did you not hear me speak to you last evening? My mother was killed when I was only four. I little remember her. They took me to Prendara when I was six years old and put me to work in the *ab'tah* fields, cutting *quaanti* grain for ten hours a day. I was a slave. A child slaving in the fields on a foreign world. And you *dare* to tell me that I can't understand your troubles?"

She said nothing, but her eyes were angry, her lips frowning.

"Yet despite hardship, I did not become a criminal. I did not plan to...to continue a war that ended long ago. I did not decide to terrorize innocent people."

Her chin lifted. "Go to hell."

"And now you seek excuses. You lied... *Sanwar,* you're a criminal! And you wish for me to excuse your crimes."

"I'm not looking for an excuse. I'm telling you now because..."

Yes, she *was* telling him. Telling him the truth at last. He took a deep, steadying breath. "Why?" He managed to keep his voice even, if not gentle.

"One of the delegates," she said, her voice strained. "Henry Reed Jamison. He wants to be elected Prefect."

"I can withstand a challenge for the position."

"God, is there no end to your arrogance? Will you listen for just one minute? He has a recording of me, Gray. A holo-recording of me admitting...everything."

At last her confession made sense. "And this is why you tell me. Because you have been discovered. Not because you wish to share yourself with me."

She shook his arm. "Listen to me! This is about *you*, damn it, not me. I'm telling you because he's going to use the recording to discredit you. To make you look like an idiot because you trusted me."

He *was* an idiot. To trust a woman on short acquaintance, simply because she blushed at his kisses...and laughed with him...and made him feel like a man instead of a means to a higher station.

Had everything been deceit? "You haven't told me why you allowed me to believe you were a prostitute."

She took a deep, shuddering breath. "My group wanted to stop the constitution. I was supposed to sleep with you and...and help them kidnap you."

No. By the gods, no. "You knew who I was." His voice came out choked, like a groan. "You knew the whole time. That first night..." When she'd been so sweet, so demure. Blushing in his arms like a virgin.

All an act. A deception. A lie.

She nodded. "I knew."

She'd never truly wanted him. Just like all the others. No, worse than the others. He'd been less than a position to her—he'd been a means to obtain a criminal objective. And now she *dared* to rest her little hand on his forearm, looking up at him with pleading, innocent eyes.

Innocent? Hardly. In truth, she was nothing but a liar.

He pulled away from her and gave her his back. "Leave."

"But...Henry said..."

No more lies. No more deceit. If she stayed another moment, he might commit violence against her. "Leave!"

"I want to help, Gray."

As if he could ever trust her again. He walked to the command panel in the wall. "Help yourself. Leave me before I contact the Enforcers."

"Please, don't."

Her voice was soft, beguiling. Even after this betrayal, her voice moved him.

His hand clenched into a fist. If he turned to look at her, he might… "Leave now, and I'll grant you ten minutes before I contact the Enforcers. Stay, and I will see you confined."

The wait seemed endless. He heard nothing but his breath, the pounding of his heart.

"I'm sorry," she said, her voice broken.

And then he heard the door open and close.

He turned. The room stood empty.

She'd left him.

Gray sank to the floor, leaned his elbows on his knees, and put his head in his hands.

Chapter Nine

Daria could barely see through her tears. She stumbled through the corridor, turned left, and found herself in an odd room. A room with five walls, full of oblong tables and low chairs. Damn it, she'd taken a wrong turn. At least the room was empty.

Only ten minutes. Ten minutes to get away.

She turned and headed back the way she'd come. When she tilted around a corner, she ran into a tall figure.

She looked up through blurry eyes. Reema. Oh, no.

"Daria? What troubles you?"

She shook her head and tried to pass, but Reema held her arm in a tight grip. "Come with me. We will speak in my quarters."

The door was only a few feet away, and Reema pulled her inside before she could resist.

"Daria?" Hento's voice. Great, now she'd never escape. "What has occurred?"

"Nothing." Oh, what a stupid thing to say. She was sobbing, nearly hysterical. "Gray…"

Hento grasped her free arm. "Is he injured?"

"No, he…he found out… He found out that I'm not what I seem."

"I don't understand."

"I'm…" Oh hell, she might as well tell them. Gray had probably already called the Enforcers. "I'm in the resistance."

It took them a long moment to absorb that. "Against what do you resist?" Reema asked.

"Against *you*."

"Aaahhh." The long sound came from Hento. "I will go to *Sarjah* Gray."

She heard the door swish open and closed behind her. Now Gray would know where she was. Trapped in his Primary's quarters. The Enforcers would be here in a moment.

"Please." She looked up into Reema's serious, beautiful face. "Please, let me go. He's going to call the Enforcers. I have to run."

"Do you have credits?"

What did that have to do with anything? Yes, she had credits. Thousands of credits, all of them from Gray. She nodded.

Reema crossed the room, opened a small drawer, and came back to Daria's side. "Here." Reema pressed a card into her hand. "This credit card is anonymous. You can use it without being traced."

She looked at the card in her hand, then at Reema. "But… Why are you helping me?"

Reema looked surprised. "Because you need assistance."

She made it sound so simple. "I don't deserve your…assistance."

Reema said nothing, merely went into the other room. Sounds of hard items clanging, like someone rummaging in kitchen cabinets, came from there. Daria followed her, curious.

Reema stood at a dresser-like piece of furniture next to the stove, stuffing a few small containers into a quad-strapped sack. She fastened the bag closed, then walked to Daria and handed it to her.

The bag weighed at least ten pounds. "What's in here?"

"Emergency rations, a thermo blanket, and a portable lamp."

Her eyes teared up again. She rubbed at her leaky eyes, making them sore. "Why are you helping me?" she asked again.

"Because I like you, Daria."

More tears. Damn. "You shouldn't. I'd do anything to get your people off of Earth."

"Anything? Would you kill?"

She slung the bag onto her back. "Well…maybe not *anything*."

"There. Perhaps you aren't as undeserving of assistance as you believe."

"You had sex with Gray." Oh, God. Had she really said that out loud?

Reema's eyes widened. "Why do you believe this?"

She was a fool. A complete fool. What the hell did that matter now? "Never mind. I shouldn't have said that."

Reema tilted her head to the side. "Satisfy my curiosity, please."

"It's just...the way you look at each other, sometimes..." God, she sounded like an idiot. "I'm sorry. It's none of my business."

"Daria. What you believe you see... It is not truth."

For some nonsensical reason, she wanted to believe the woman.

"I am the mate of *Sarjah* Gray's closest friend. The affection between us is based on that truth, and nothing different."

Reema had no reason to lie. Not that it mattered anymore.

Before Daria could reply, she heard the swish of the main door opening. She clenched her fists and turned, ready to face a squad of Enforcers. But only Hento came in, carrying one of her shopping bags.

He handed it to Daria. "A change of clothing," he said, in his usual mild tone.

His face blurred through her tears. "Thank you." She wiped her eyes again, then dried her wet hand on her shirt. "How...how is Gray?"

"Angry."

She looked at the shopping bag in her hand. "But he gave you this?"

"No. *Sarjah* Gray does not know I took the clothing."

Why were these people being so damned kind? Her throat closed.

"Best you leave now, Daria," Hento said. "In truth, he may contact the Enforcers at any time."

She nodded and tried to swallow the lump in her throat. "I know."

She brushed past Reema and headed for the door.

"Go with the gods, Daria," Reema said behind her.

"Go with the gods," Hento echoed.

She turned and gave them a wavering smile. These two Prendarians—people she'd known just a day—had proven themselves truer friends to her than Spider ever had.

"Thank you," she said gruffly. "Thank you both."

* * *

Gray eased the hovercraft to a stop on the right side of the street, as close as he could get to the quiet expanse of water. He sat quietly and stared out the window.

Water…water stretching out as far as he could see under the dim light of a fog-shrouded moon. The *tuaari* lights along the street shimmered on the water's surface, rippling in the light breeze.

So much water. And this was only a small portion of the water that bordered three sides of San Francisco—the part called the Marina. Small floating craft—boats—bobbed on the surface, tied to row after row of old wooden piers.

He climbed out of the hovercraft. Strange tall trees rose from a median in the middle of the street. Palm trees, that's what they were called. A row of small, neat houses lined the opposite side of the street, facing the water.

Maybe he'd pilot the hovercraft to the ocean tonight, after this unpleasant business was finished. He'd planned to take

Daria to the ocean. Now she was gone, leaving nothing but problems behind her. Problems he must resolve as best he could.

The political problems, at least, would be resolved tonight. The problems in his own self... He sighed. How did one resolve betrayal by a loved one? Would the pain ease with time? He had little experience in betrayal...and even less in love.

He walked along the street, studying the houses. Such modest homes. The man must be trying to portray himself as one of the common people. Yet his record showed him a wealthy man, though he owned only a small business. Unexplained wealth—the sign of a criminal operation.

Number 357 was similar to all the other houses—small and neat, with a narrow set of stairs leading to the porch. The windows were large, probably to take advantage of the marina view.

He went up the steps and paused on the porch. How did one signal arrival at an Earth home? On Prendara, a command panel would be embedded in one wall. Nothing here, nothing but a small round button, lit with a dim internal light.

He pressed it and heard a bell inside the house. Excellent.

In confrontation, a calm demeanor is more important than strength, his aunt always said. He would be calm. Ruthlessly calm. He drew himself up to his full height and took slow, relaxing breaths.

The door opened, and the man inside drew back with a little jerk. "Well, this is a surprise," he said with false joviality.

Nervous. The man was nervous. Excellent. Gray already had the upper hand.

Henry Jamison stepped back from the door. "Won't you come in?"

Ah, false politeness. As if he had nothing to fear. Such an opponent was easy to manipulate. Jamison would maintain the illusion of strength at all costs...until he was fully trapped.

Gray would be polite as well. "Thank you."

He stepped inside and found himself in a short hallway. Henry led him into a small room decorated in shades of blue and beige, then settled into a large oversized chair, crossing his legs and spreading his arms over the sides as if to dominate the space. Gray sat on the cushioned sofa facing him.

Henry smiled, looking confident. "Daria told you about our little meeting today, I suppose."

He'd soon lose that insincere smile.

"Of course she did," Gray replied. "She's a loyal assistant."

The smile didn't waver. "I doubt the rest of the world will see things that way. I have a very incriminating holo-recording of her saying rather unsavory things about you."

Unsavory? His stomach tightened, but he resisted the urge to frown. "Things she said at my command."

Henry raised his eyebrows, but fear lurked in the quiver of his chin. "So she was a double agent all along? Well, the girl has more moxie than I gave her credit for."

Gray didn't understand *moxie* or *double agent*, but it mattered little. His point had struck the mark. "The recording you have is worthless. No one will believe that she said those things in honesty."

"You haven't seen the recording yet. But tomorrow, you will. As will many, many others."

Gray kept his voice soft. "You underestimate my political strength. That recording can't hurt me." Only Daria would be hurt. And gods help him, he would still fight to protect her disloyal, betraying self.

Henry shook his head. "Wait until you see it. She admitted the most appalling things. Imagine, one of your loyal assistants, a traitor. The world will be as shocked as I am."

Gray counted slowly, waiting a half-minute before speaking. "I wonder why she felt it safe to express such radical thoughts to you."

"She clearly thought I was a terrorist, too. But hundreds of people know that I'm a big supporter of this constitution. Why on Earth would she believe I have ties to criminal organizations?"

Gray gave him a slow smile. "Because you do have such ties."

"I assure you, my record is spotless."

"Is it?" He leaned forward, meeting Henry's gaze with a steady stare. "Perhaps in the morning, your record will be—spotty. Very spotty indeed."

Henry's eyes widened, the fear in them obvious. "You're threatening to plant false evidence in my record?"

Gray studied the fingers of one hand, pretending disinterest. "Am I?"

Henry slapped the arm of his chair. "Damn, you're good. You have the connections to do it, too. Don't you?"

He nodded.

Jamison's hands clenched. "You wouldn't dare. Those modifications could be traced right back to you."

"Perhaps they could." Gray shifted back in his chair, affecting a relaxed pose. "Or perhaps I have the ability to make them undetectable." In truth, he didn't know for certain. He only knew Jamison held a recording that incriminated Daria. Gray would not leave without the evidence, no matter how much he had to lie to get it.

"If you're caught tampering with my ID, you'll be in a worse position than if the recording is made public. Your career might survive associating with a terrorist, but planting false data in my records would be criminal."

Good, Jamison was trying to reason with him. He knew Gray's threats were sincere. Gray forced a smile, as if he wasn't concerned in the least. "Criminal? No one would dare to see me confined. I have powerful friends, you know. Friends—and relatives—who would realign the sun to protect me." In truth, his aunt would probably confine him herself. But Jamison couldn't know that.

Jamison scowled now, silent.

Time to lay out the man's options, and steer him towards the one Gray preferred. The one that shielded Daria. "You have two choices, Mr. Jamison. Either give me all copies of that recording and survive politically…" He waited until Jamison opened his mouth to speak, then continued. "Or keep your worthless recording and discover just how badly my wrath will burn you."

He could almost see Jamison's mind working, struggling to find an alternative, to think of a plan that would leave him in control. The slight twist to his mouth, the roving eyes, the hint of sweat on his upper lip—all signs of defeat soon to be acknowledged. Gray waited patiently.

"God damn you," Henry practically snarled. "I don't even have a recorder going."

"One should never assume he has the upper hand in a negotiation." Gray stood. "And now you will give me the recording you have of my loyal assistant."

Henry didn't stand. "I don't buy it, you know. She wasn't acting. You didn't know anything about her, did you?"

He'd be damned before he admitted that fact. "She's one of my assistants. I will protect her by any method necessary." *Though she little deserves my protection.*

Henry rose then. "You didn't answer my question, but it hardly matters at this point."

He reached into his pocket and came back with a holo-receiver, which he handed to Gray. Such a small device to cause such trauma in his life. He checked the duplication indicator. Zero. The recording hadn't been copied; Jamison must have planned to keep it on his person at all times.

Excellent. Nothing more to fear from this worm of a man.

Henry spoke again. "You aren't Prefect yet. I hope you understand that I intend to make as much trouble for you as possible in the upcoming election."

Gray gave him an excessively polite nod. "You are welcome to try. But let me assure you of one thing, Mr. Jamison."

He paused deliberately, until Henry raised his eyebrows in question.

"If you say or do anything to bother any member of my staff—anything at all—I will destroy you." He paused again, briefly. "And I'll enjoy doing it. Immensely."

Henry's mouth twisted, as if he'd argue. Then his features relaxed. "Fair enough."

Without another word, Gray walked out of the room.

Henry followed him to the front door. "You may have won this battle, Gray, but you've lost my vote."

A feeble joke. Gray stepped out onto the porch. No need to turn to speak to this man's face. "I don't want your vote. And what's more, I won't need it."

Assuredly, he didn't need this worm's vote. He only needed—

No. No, he didn't need her at all.

* * *

Gray tried not to watch. Tried not to listen. But even with his head turned away, he saw the holographic images in his memory.

"Why, Daria," he heard Jamison's smug voice say. "I think you've mistaken me for someone else."

His hand clenched. At least the worm would cause no more problems. How could Daria have put her faith in such a man?

The recording ended at last. *Enough. No more.* But Hento started the holo-loop over again from the beginning. For the fifth *ab'tah* time in a row.

Gray could recite the dialog along with Daria and Henry. He knew every word, every pause. Perhaps he'd memorized it during the hundred or so times he'd watched it last night.

Hento had invaded the privacy of his quarters this morning, seeking news. Gray had been pleased to tell him the Jamison problem was resolved. But he never should have allowed Hento to view the recording. Especially not here, in his quarters, where he'd be forced to re-live Daria's betrayal again and again.

His judgment was poor indeed. Why try to pretend he didn't still burn from her betrayal? Why pretend that he could watch another man touch her face with rational calm? Why pretend that he didn't long for her still, even knowing her for a liar?

Might as well face the image of his tormentor. He turned.

Oh, excellent—his favorite part. The holographic Daria tossed her head, just enough to send her hair behind one shoulder. "He doesn't mean a thing to me," she said, disdain in her voice.

After hundreds of viewings, the words should no longer pain him. At least his eyes remained dry.

Hento froze the image, then slowly walked around it, as if there was more to be seen from other angles. "I believe she's trying to draw information from him, *Sarjah*."

Impossible. No indications of such a thing were in the recording. He should know—he'd reviewed it far too often, and dreamed of it during the few hours he'd managed to sleep. "You are ever the optimist, Hento."

Hento's brows lifted. "*You* are typically the optimistic one, *Sarjah*."

True. "There is no basis for optimism in this matter. The voice scan was inconclusive."

"The voice scan is calibrated for Prendarian voices. With Earther voices, the results are difficult to gauge. She may be lying to Jamison."

"She's not lying to him." *She lied to me.*

"Perhaps..."

Gray glared at his Primary.

Hento looked away, studying the image again. "Forgive me, *Sarjah*. I must speak. Perhaps you are too engaged to see the matter with your usual clarity."

"What more is there to see? The recording does not lie. The woman is a liar." *And I'm a fool.*

Hento gazed in silence at the floor, clearly gathering his thoughts.

Gray strode to the table, grabbed the holo-emitter, and turned it off. The image of Daria blinked out into nothingness. "I grant you one thing, Hento. The next time I profess to trust a woman, you will investigate her to the boundary of your considerable ability. No matter what I say."

Hento didn't look up, didn't smile. "I trusted her as well, *Sarjah*."

So they were both fools. "At least I'm not alone in misplacing my trust."

"Perhaps our trust was not misplaced. She begins with a plea to camaraderie, followed by flattery. And she deliberately asks Jamison what *he* is planning."

Gray raked his hair back. "Yes. She had no plan of her own. She wanted to help him. She thought he shared her goal, that he wanted to stop the constitution."

"Hmm."

"And she deliberately encouraged me to add an unpopular provision to the constitution. She sought to destroy—" *Me.* "—Everything I've worked for."

Hento sat down at the table and folded his hands in his lap. "Yesterday, *Sarjah,* I heard her speaking to you in the negotiation chamber. She urged you to remove the problematic sections so that the constitution would pass."

Yes, she had. Yesterday—before her meeting with Jamison. He frowned. "Why would she urge me to remove the provisions, only to plot with Jamison a few moments later?"

"Perhaps she sought to help you, *Sarjah*. Perhaps she was trying to draw information from Jamison."

"Information that would help me?"

No, that would be too great a gift from the gods. What was the English phrase? Something like wishing on one's thoughts… If only Daria were here to ask.

He shook his head. "I can't believe it, Hento. When she confessed to me, she admitted…"

She'd admitted that she'd never truly wanted him, that she'd plotted to kidnap him. That she'd lied from the moment of meeting him. But she'd tried to tell him more about Jamison.

And he'd forced her to leave.

"It's best that she's gone. I could never be certain of her again."

Hento nodded. "That is something only you can know, *Sarjah*. Trust requires forgiveness. Perhaps your feelings for her are not strong enough to bear it."

"My feelings? My feelings are nothing to the matter. She's a liar, and even if I can't stop lo—" He took a deep breath and lowered his voice. "Regardless of my feelings, she doesn't wish to be forgiven."

Hento shrugged—a fervent declaration of emotion from his dignified, reserved Primary.

"Speak as you will," Gray encouraged.

"I merely thought, how unfortunate that we have no way of learning if she seeks your forgiveness."

Oh, Hento was crafty, all right. Gray understood his hidden meaning perfectly. "I do know her legal name. We could—" He paused for a calming breath. "If we *wished* to find her, which I *don't*, we could trace her ID. She left with nothing, so she'll have to use credits soon."

Hento pulled at the back of his neck with one hand—his nervous gesture. "In truth, *Sarjah*, I believe she has an anonymous credit card."

No hope of finding her, then. Gray scowled. "Where did she find an anonymous card? And how do you know that she has one?"

Hento pulled at the back of his neck again. "When she left your quarters yesterday, Reema saw her running through the corridors of the ship. She seemed terribly distraught, *Sarjah*. Reema and I were concerned for her welfare."

Sanwar. His loyal Primary of over twenty years, more loyal to the woman who'd betrayed him. What was it about Daria that made everyone wish to protect her? "You helped her escape."

Hento looked down at his clasped hands. "Yes, *Sarjah*. We did provide some assistance."

And that assistance made it impossible to find her. Even if he wished to, which he didn't. But at least she knew that Hento and Reema cared for her. If she needed help, she might contact them. Hento would surely tell him if she…

No. She believed the Enforcers were seeking her. She would not risk asking for further assistance from Hento and Reema.

"Thank you for helping her, my friend."

Hento looked relieved. "You know I admire her, *Sarjah*. She needed assistance. Providing this was no hardship to me and Reema."

"And you didn't know what she was."

"You mean a...what did she say? Something about resistance."

Gray snorted. "A clever euphemism. The word is *terrorist*. Wait—she *told* you?"

Hento nodded. "I confess I sympathize with her plight, *Sarjah*."

He gaped in shock. "Surely you jest. The woman is a criminal."

Hento studied his hands for a moment. "She has been taught to mistrust and fear people from our world, *Sarjah*. Yet she cares for you. Such a conflict must be difficult to resolve."

He turned away and clenched his hands, hard. "Shall we view the recording again? I 'don't mean a thing' to her. She was only sleeping with me 'to find a way to block the passage of this constitution.'"

"The words she spoke to Jamison may not be her truth."

Even if they weren't, even if she'd lied to Jamison, Gray had no way of finding her. He would never know what her motives had been.

Enough. The woman would no longer goad him. "We have a vote in five hours, Hento. Will we prevail?"

Hento sighed. "Only the gods know, *Sarjah*. Most of the Earthers appear to be in favor. The constitution does grant them more control than they have at present, so they appear willing to compromise on most issues. The Prendarian delegates are divided."

Gray sat down across from his friend. "Give me a list of all the undecided delegates. Tell me what you know of their concerns. I will greet them personally before the meeting, and speak to their concerns from the podium."

And even if he failed, at least attempting to persuade them would fill the empty hours before the meeting began.

"As you will. But first, *Sarjah,* I would say one thing."

Hento looked more serious than Gray had ever seen him. "Speak."

"Daria believed that you and Reema were bed companions in the past."

"What? Why would she believe such a thing?"

Hento spread his hands wide. "I do not know, *Sarjah.* But I do know that a woman only feels jealousy if she cares for a man."

"She didn't care for me. She cared only to exploit me." And less honestly than any of the others. "Now let's talk politics, Hento. We have delegates to persuade."

"As you will," Hento murmured.

* * *

Daria pushed the curtain aside a few inches and peered out the narrow window. A thin film on the glass made the view fuzzy, but she could see well enough. Nothing unusual on the street—just the typical traffic. She could see the entrance to the space dock from here. She'd stared at the portal half the night, but no Enforcers had shown up. Maybe they hadn't started searching for her there, although they typically began with a suspect's last known location.

She hadn't left the room since yesterday. *Bunkered down,* Tank would say. She'd run out of the space dock and straight into the nearest hotel, an inexpensive ten-story building designed for space travelers on a budget. Tank would have kicked her ass for staying so close to a place where dozens of people could ID her. But she had nowhere to go, and she'd wanted to get off the street as quickly as possible. At least she'd used her anonymous credit card to check in.

Sometime during the long night, tears had given way to anger. How dare he yell at her? Lecture her? Just because he'd been lucky enough to have a wealthy, powerful aunt. Oh, he'd left that out of his life story. He might have been a slave as a child, but the rest of his life had been lived in luxury.

And he'd kicked her out before she could explain anything. Before she could convince him that she was on his side. Before she could make him strike all those damned extra provisions and get the constitution ratified.

Before she could tell him that she loved him, the arrogant, self-righteous bastard.

Of course, he'd been shocked and hurt. An honorable man like him could never understand why anyone would work outside the law. The law had always been on his side.

But at least he'd given her time to escape.

She looked at the clock on the bedside table. Only thirty-five minutes before the meeting closed and the voting began. Even if the constitution passed, Henry would make sure Gray never became Prefect. And Gray would blame her. Rightly so.

How soon before Spider showed the recording? He wanted the constitution to pass, so he wouldn't show it until sometime after the vote.

And Gray might believe the things she'd said. That she was only sleeping with him to find a way to stop the constitution. That he meant nothing to her.

On the street below her narrow window, a hovercraft sped by. A cab.

If she took a cab, she could get to the meeting in time.

Whoa. In time to do what? To get her ass arrested? A whole platoon of guards waited in that lobby. Guards who'd recognize her. Guards who probably knew that Gray wanted her in prison.

But if she got in...if she could get to Gray...maybe she could explain. Maybe she could help him trap Spider somehow. And if she couldn't get to Gray, maybe she could at least find Hento. Hento would listen. Hento would know how to stop Spider. Shit, Hento probably had a small army just waiting to shake down people like Spider.

She might be able to make it. The Enforcers hadn't shown up at the space dock. Maybe Gray hadn't called them after all.

That was a whole heap of *ifs* and *maybes.*

But Gray loved her—or at least had cared about her—even though he thought she was a prostitute. Only one man in a million would be willing to expose his feelings to a whore.

Gray.

And he deserved to be Prefect.

Even if she couldn't get to Hento or Gray, she could turn herself in. Tell what she knew about Spider...make sure he didn't get elected instead of Gray.

He needed her help, even if he didn't want it. Even if it cost her a lifetime in confinement. After everything he'd done for her, everything he *meant* to her... Losing him felt worse than losing Tank. She had nothing without Gray. No friends, no home, nowhere to go.

No love. No self-respect.

Maybe she could get a little of it back. She could still try to right her own wrongs, face up to her mistakes…and maybe help Gray, too. Even if he never forgave her, even if she'd lost him forever, she could have the satisfaction of knowing she'd tried to help him in the end.

She took a deep breath and turned from the window. Leaning on the dresser, she studied her reflection in the mirror. Only one man had ever called her beautiful.

And today, after a sleepless night, she looked further away from beautiful than ever. Nothing could disguise her puffy, red-rimmed eyes, but she rummaged in her purse for a tube of lipstick and swiped some on, then brushed her hair.

Her jacket still lay on the bed, thrown there last night while she'd indulged in a crying jag. She put it on, slung her purse over her shoulder and headed for the door.

Time to face the music.

Chapter Ten

Most of Civic Center was a pedestrians-only zone. The cab dropped her off three blocks from the old Opera House. She walked down Grove Street with her head held high, eyes straight ahead, as if she belonged here. A group of uniforms nodded politely and smiled as they passed her. Amazing what pretending you belonged somewhere could do.

She turned left on Van Ness. The old opera house loomed next to her—the headquarters for the delegates. Gray's center of operations. The tightest security she'd ever gone through.

She went up the steps at a brisk stride. If this was the end of the line, best to get it over with quickly.

There they were—the first bank of security guards, the ones at the weapons checkpoint. Was that fear in one man's eyes? Maybe not. Maybe he just recognized her. He stood tall and dropped his gaze—they all did. Just like they had yesterday.

She walked through the weapons scanners without hesitating. No alarms sounded. But the guards ahead would scan her ID. If the Enforcers wanted her, her ID would be flagged.

A uniformed Prendarian woman held out a hand for her ID. The same one who'd scanned Gray's ID yesterday. Daria handed her card over without a word, holding her breath as the woman passed the card through a scanner.

From this angle, she couldn't see the scanner screen at all. Would an alarm sound? Or would a silent flag come up on the screen?

It didn't matter. No matter what happened, she wouldn't run. She wouldn't fight. Even if they restrained her until the Enforcers came, she'd stay calm. If she cooperated, maybe they'd let her talk to Gray. Or at least Hento. She'd tell them she had vital information about a threat to *Sarjah* Gray's safety.

The woman handed the card back to her with a smile. "Just a formality."

Oh, thank God. Gray hadn't called the Enforcers after all. He must still... No. She shouldn't read too much into that.

Daria took the card, nodded, and headed for the elevator.

Just a few more steps. One. Two. Three.

"Wait!" a voice called.

She froze. Here it came. They wanted her after all.

"You'll need an escort to the floor the delegates are on," the female guard said. She stepped into the elevator ahead of Daria and slid a keycard into the slot. The light for the top floor went on.

Oh, right. She'd completely forgotten that the delegates were on a locked floor. Thank God this woman trusted her. One of the benefits of having a clean ID—and of being seen with Gray yesterday.

They rode up in silence. When the door opened, she stepped out into the hallway and turned. "Thank you."

The guard looked startled. Did no one ever thank her? "No thanks are warranted," she said in Prendarian. "I...I mean...you are welcome," she stammered in English.

Daria smiled. A Prendarian in uniform, flustered. Flustered by *her*. "Have a good day," she replied as the elevator doors slid closed.

She headed down the hallway, almost sprinting. But outside the doors to Gray's prep room, she stopped to catch her breath. A whole group of hostile Prendarians waited behind this door. And every one of them probably knew why she hadn't arrived with Gray this morning.

Standing out here longer wouldn't help calm her hammering heart. The only way to get to Gray was through this room. She took a deep breath and squared her shoulders.

Her hand shook when she reached for the knob. She grabbed it hard, turned it, and pushed into the room.

No one moved. No one looked. No one noticed her at all. Even the man closest to the door didn't budge, didn't take his nervous eyes from the viewscreen that sat on the table in front of him. The room was full but dead silent. Everyone stared at small viewscreens, frowning, their expressions tense.

She moved closer to the young man's back and looked over his shoulder at Gray's image on the screen. He gestured with his hands while he spoke, his posture and motions urgent. If only she could hear him. They all must be listening through those small ear speakers she'd seen yesterday.

"Daria. Welcome back."

She spun around and saw Hento behind her. "Oh, thank God." She reached out and grasped his forearm. "I have to talk to you. There's a recording—"

He nodded. "Fear not. The recording cannot harm you."

He certainly hadn't wasted any time. Protecting Gray must be his number one job. "What? How?"

"*Sarjah* Gray...retrieved the recording last night."

"He watched it?" What a stupid question. Of course he had. Hento nodded.

"But...he didn't call the Enforcers?"

"I assume not, if the guards below let you pass."

"Why didn't he?" She hadn't meant to say it aloud. Oh well. Maybe Hento would know.

Hento's lips curved. "This you must ask of him."

If she had the courage. "He must be angry."

Hento paused for a moment, thinking in that serious way of his. "Yes, I believe so. But he has also been troubled."

"Will he..." God, she couldn't believe she was asking Hento this. "Will he forgive me, do you think?"

Hento shrugged a little. "I do not know."

At least the man was honest. Her gaze wandered to the image of Gray on the closest screen. She moved a few inches to the left so she could get a clear view. He pounded one hand on the podium as he spoke. "The meeting isn't going well, is it?"

Hento shook his head. "I fear not."

Movement to the left caught her attention—Reema walking toward her. Smiling at her. "Daria," she said softly. "I am pleased to see you. We have been most concerned about you."

She sounded so sincere. Daria felt tears sting her eyes. "Stop it. You're going to make me cry."

Reema drew herself up. "I am sorry. I hoped you would be pleased to see me, not saddened."

"Of course I'm pleased—"

Reema chuckled.

"Oh, you're joking." Daria smiled at her. "I've never heard a Prendarian make a joke before."

Reema touched her shoulder for just a moment. "I'm glad to have surprised you in a pleasant way. But you must go to *Sarjah Gray* now."

That didn't sound like a joke. "I can't possibly go in there. He's speaking. And things aren't going well, according to Hento."

"That is precisely why you must go," Reema replied. "Show him that you wish for his success."

But she couldn't do anything to help him now. With Spider's recording confiscated, he didn't need her help at all. And now that he'd seen that recording, he must be furious with her. He'd get totally pissed off if he saw her. "I should wait. I might distract him."

"No, Daria. You will give him more confidence. Go, now." Reema grasped her elbow and tugged gently, urging her toward the door. Daria took a reluctant step.

Hento made a small palm-out gesture with one hand, as if to signal *stop*. "This is a delicate stage, Reema. She should not interrupt."

Reema lifted her eyebrows. "You question my judgment?"

Hento gave her that little half smile of his. "On very rare occasions."

Reema laid a hand on her husband's arm. "Trust me on this occasion. She will inspire him."

Inspire him? Reema had a lot more faith in her than she did.

Hento took a step back and held his arm out toward the blast-proof doors. "Go, Daria. But if he seems agitated to see you, leave again."

Agitated? He couldn't be more agitated than she was, with her heart thumping in her throat. She nodded, then walked slowly to the shielded doors. One woman gave her a curious glance. All of the other Prendarians in the room were still wrapped up in Gray's speech, eyes glued to their little screens.

She pushed open the door slowly. At least it didn't squeak, didn't squeal. None of the delegates would face this door; they'd all be looking at Gray's podium. Maybe he'd be the only one to see her.

An angry woman's voice reached her from the tiered seating. "Earth has been safely in Prendarian hands for many years. I see no call to risk this world by giving power to those that almost destroyed it."

A low murmur rose from the rest of the room.

Daria kept one hand on the door as it closed behind her, easing it shut to keep noise to a minimum. Her gaze stayed on Gray.

He raised one hand. "Please. Listen to me."

The rumbling gradually quieted.

"This world has seen enough strife. Enough fighting." He looked around the crowd as he spoke. "We must move beyond our disagreements. We must work together. We must—"

His gaze caught hers, even though he stood so far across the room. He looked stunned. And not particularly happy.

She gave him a wobbly smile. He didn't smile back. No, he didn't look happy at all. But his gaze didn't waver.

Even from this distance, she saw him take a deep breath. "We *must* learn to trust each other. To judge each person according to his or her own principles and behavior."

Her own behavior wouldn't stand much scrutiny.

"And we must forgive and move beyond our grievances," he said. "Mistakes have been made on all sides, some of them many years in the past. We cannot hold each other responsible for the mistakes our ancestors made."

He looked away then, looked at someone else in the crowd. "We are all on this planet together," he went on. "None of us have the right to assume total control over its inhabitants. We must learn to share power fairly. And we have all agreed that this constitution ensures a fair and equitable distribution of power."

The vague murmurs around the room seemed positive. As if they agreed.

"The future of Earth is in your hands." He sounded firm, confident. A born leader. "Either approve this constitution, or condemn us all to more divisiveness."

He banged a small gavel on the podium once. "The debate is now closed. The time has come for you to vote. I trust you will act according to your best principles." He banged the gavel a second time, officially closing the meeting. "The certified tally will be recorded in one hour. I thank you all for your service these past days."

She scanned the crowd and saw dozens of people tap the miniature computers in front of them, then stand. Looked like many of the delegates had already decided. All of the chairs being pushed back sounded like a low rumble in the room.

Gray stepped off of the stage and started to climb up the tiers toward her. Many delegates had already stood up and were milling around the aisles, stretching. When a Prendarian delegate spoke to him, Gray stopped. After only a moment, he shook the man's hand and moved on.

Working his way to her.

Another man stopped him, an Earther this time. Gray laid a hand on the man's arm, spoke to him briefly, and started climbing again.

He'd be here in a minute. What could she say? Chances were he'd never forgive her. All that talk about principles and judging each person as an individual—God, he'd been looking right at her when he'd said that. Judging her.

He was staring at her now, moving closer and closer. She gripped the railing in front of her.

He stopped a few feet away. His face looked so serious. Unsmiling. Unblinking.

Unwelcoming.

God, he looked like he hated her. She'd cry in a second.

She backed away a step, toward the door. "I...I shouldn't have come. I'll go." She fumbled behind her for the doorknob, couldn't find it, and turned so she could see.

Before she grasped it, he caught her wrist in one hand. A viselike hand. "No."

He pushed her aside, opened the door, and pulled her into the next room.

Applause came from his Prendarian staff. He stopped short, and she bumped into his back. She tried to pull her arm away, but his grip only tightened.

"Thank you," he said, addressing his team. "I hope our efforts have been sufficient."

Hento came up to him then. Gray bent to speak into his ear. "I cannot stay, Hento. I need privacy."

"I understand."

"I'll contact you shortly. Tell the staff whatever you wish, but give them my sincere gratitude."

"As you will," Hento said with a small bow of his head.

Gray pulled her through the room, and people moved aside silently. She caught shocked stares on several faces before she wised up and kept her gaze to the floor. She wanted to say goodbye to Reema, but Gray strode along like a man on a mission, towing her behind him by that strong grip on her wrist.

Still angry, no doubt.

After what he'd seen on that holo-recording, she couldn't blame him.

The hallway was long and empty. And he still hadn't spoken a word to her. "Are you taking me to the Enforcers?"

He didn't stop until they reached the elevators. Then he glanced down at her. His face looked rigid, obstinate, stern. "I should."

Did he have to bully her? She lifted her chin. "Fine. I'll go with you willingly. You don't have to drag me there."

She pulled at her arm again, and he released her.

"If you run, I will catch you," he warned.

She glared at him. "I won't run. I'm not a coward."

"We shall see."

She swallowed. The worried, rapid beat of her heart called her a liar.

* * *

Gray piloted the hovercraft in silence. Through crowded, busy streets, into the more quiet residential areas of the city, down a narrow street where he stopped the craft at last, after fifteen minutes of total silence.

He could think of nothing to say to her. He wanted to pull her into his arms and kiss her wildly...to simply forget all the pain she'd inflicted. He wanted to yell at her and demand an explanation for the cruel words she'd voiced to Jamison. He wanted to apologize for shouting at her yesterday, for threatening to contact the Enforcers.

He wanted to say everything at once. And so he said nothing.

She said nothing as well, even though she must be wondering why they were here, sitting in a parked hovercraft on this quiet tree-lined street.

They would sit here in silence for hours if he didn't speak. And she had much to answer for. "Why did you come back?"

She didn't look at him. "I thought I could help."

Help with what? How could she possibly help?

"And I wanted to apologize," she went on. "I started out lying to you, that's true. I won't try to make excuses, except to say that I didn't know you then. I thought you were just a collaborator. By the time I realized I didn't want to lie anymore...it was too late."

When she finally looked at him, her eyes seemed troubled. "Can you forgive me?"

Gods, he hoped he could. But first she'd grant him answers to the questions that plagued him. "Why did you go to Jamison?"

"To find out if he was plotting against you."

An easy answer. "And to help him with his plot."

She turned toward him, shifting sideways in her seat. "No. Hento told me that you saw the recording, Gray. But I swear, none of the things I said to Henry were true."

He doesn't mean a thing to me. Would the image never leave his brain? "You are an accomplished liar, then."

She bit her lip. "I guess I deserve that. But I lied to him because I wanted to make him think I was on his side. To get him to trust me, so I could help you. That's all."

Hento's theory. Another easy explanation, perhaps one she'd prepared before coming to him today. But her eyes seemed so sincere. They always had. "And you lied to me for the same reason. To make me believe you were...on my side. So you could use me."

"Only in the beginning. After I got to know you, I fell—" She broke off abruptly. "I changed my mind."

"Why?"

"Because I started to care about you. But there's probably no way I can convince you of that."

Oh, he desperately wanted to be convinced. Even if hearing that she *cared* about him stung. *Caring* was a poor substitute for loving. Assuming it was true at all. Perhaps she lied, even now.

Her eyes seemed liquid. Damp with emotion. He couldn't face her anymore, so he looked at the command console and idly traced the rows of buttons and dials with one finger.

She took such a deep breath, he heard the inhalation. "You'll never trust me again, will you?"

He wanted to, fool that he was. "Will you trust me, Daria?"

She reached toward him, then pulled her hand back and rested it in her lap, as if she was afraid to touch him. "I already do."

How could he believe her? "Words come easily."

Her throat moved as she swallowed. "I...I don't know how I can prove it."

She could begin by telling him personal truths. But he could think of only one secret for her to share. No doubt a trite secret. "Why do you dislike the darkness?"

Her quick indrawn breath sounded like a gasp in the silent hovercraft. "I've never told anyone that."

He looked at her again. A cloud must have moved, because a sudden burst of sunlight glinted through the window, outlining her head with an ethereal glow. She was so beautiful. And so uncertain. Uncertain that she should share even a small secret with him. "I am not *anyone*. I'm the man you claim to *care* about. The man you claim to trust."

"All right." She faced forward again, blinking against the sunlight as she gazed out the front window of the craft. "When I was little, we had blackouts all the time. Sabotage, I think. Every time the lights went out, people would loot and riot."

He didn't know what *loot* meant, but he didn't stop her. The fear in her voice told him enough.

"One night during a blackout, my mom and I locked ourselves in the house. Some men came to the door. Prendarian men. They said they were conducting an inspection for contraband weapons. My mother didn't believe them. She shoved me into a closet and told me not to make any noise. The...the last words she said to me were, 'Shut up, Daria.'"

A tear rolled down her cheek. How cruel was he, to make her relive this pain? "Stop. You don't need to tell me."

"I heard crashing, fighting," she said, as if he hadn't spoken. "I heard my mother scream. But I stayed in the closet. I...I was too scared to go help her."

No wonder she hated Prendarians. At least he hadn't witnessed his own mother's death. He reached out and touched her arm briefly. "She wanted to protect you. She wanted you to stay safe."

"Oh, I stayed safe all right." Her voice was thick with tears. "I stayed in that closet while they tore the house apart. I heard them. Then I heard a siren go by, and everything got quiet. It must have scared them off."

Her chest was heaving with deep breaths. "I waited for hours. Well...I don't really know how long. It seemed like hours. Hiding in the closet like a coward."

"Daria," he said sharply. "You were only a child."

She rubbed at her cheeks, but tears kept flowing. "When I finally opened the closet door, the room was pitch black. I couldn't see a thing. There was so much rubble on the floor—busted furniture, I guess—that I kept tripping. Finally I stayed down and crawled around in the dark, screaming for my mom. I got something sticky on my hands..." Her voice faded to a whisper. "I didn't know it was blood until later. All I know is that I crawled right into my mother's body."

He slid across the seat and took her in his arms. She pressed her head against his chest, wiping her cheeks on his shirt.

"I'm sorry."

A sniffle answered him. "I don't want you to forgive me just because you feel sorry for me."

Still his proud Daria. He stroked her hair behind her ear, hoping to look into her eyes, but her face was hidden against his chest. "I've been planning to forgive you since this morning."

She looked up at him then. Her beautiful eyes were rimmed with red. "Really?"

He nodded. "Yes, I—"

Movement outside the craft caught his attention. A couple walked past in the dappled sunshine, staring curiously at him and Daria. In a neighborhood this exclusive, people sitting in a hovercraft drew attention. And he wanted to be alone with her.

He opened the door. "Come with me."

She climbed down and closed the door. He didn't take her hand, didn't touch her, merely walked up the stone-paved entryway to a house shrouded by trees. He took a keycard from his pocket and slid it into the command panel next to the door. The lock clicked open.

He pushed the door wide open and stepped back for Daria to walk in first. The lights turned on automatically.

She said nothing, merely wandered across the huge open, empty space of the main chamber, her feet soundless on the thick carpeting. She went straight to the enormous windows—just as he had yesterday, when he'd first seen the house.

"My God," she breathed.

He came up behind her. The view was truly spectacular—the gray-green water of the ocean spread out below as far as he could see. With a dull roar, a wave crashed against the cliff the house sat on, sending droplets of water spraying up right in front of the window. If he craned his neck to the side, he could see the top of a bridge that marked the entrance from the ocean to San Francisco Bay.

She looked around the empty room. "Does anyone live here?"

"Not at present." He took her hand and put the keycard in her palm, then wrapped her fingers over it. "This is the gift I spoke of yesterday."

Her mouth dropped open. "You can't give me this house."

He smiled at her shock. "I'm giving you the key. The house, I hope we can share."

Her eyes grew wet, shiny. She blinked rapidly. "You want to live with me?"

"I do. Very much."

She threw herself against him. He staggered, but caught his balance before he fell. His arms came around her, clutching her warmth closer, and his mouth found her forehead. Touching his lips to any part of her skin felt sublime. When she rubbed her stomach against him, his cock stirred.

"I love you, Gray." The words were muffled against his chest, but still impossibly sweet to hear.

He could never hear them enough. "What?"

"I love you," she said again, more clearly.

He pulled back just enough to see her face. Why hadn't he noticed how beautiful she was right from the beginning? He could happily drown in those huge brown eyes. For the rest of his life. "Marry me."

She dropped her gaze and bit her lower lip.

Sanwar. Why did she resist? "I want everything, Daria. I want all of you."

She took his hand and pressed it to her chest, where the steady thump of her heart beat under his palm. "This is all yours," she said, her eyes solemn.

He wouldn't pressure her for commitment. Not yet, not with his cock rising and urgent, pressing against her belly. He moved his hand and cupped her breast. "And this?"

Her husky laugh hit him right in the gut. As usual. "All yours."

He reached low...low enough to slip his hand under her skirt and cup her nest...her pussy...her cunt.

"Yours," she whispered.

His fingers stroked her through her thin undergarment, and she swayed against him. She felt so hot in his hand, in his arms. "Tell me again."

"All yours."

He smiled. "Not that."

"What... Oh! Oh, I can't think when your hand's between my legs."

He wriggled his fingers more firmly. "Tell me how you feel about me."

She gasped. "I love you."

He kissed her then, his mouth urgent, his tongue questing, mating with hers. Somehow they ended up on the plush carpeting, kissing, groping, pulling at clothing. They struggled to get each other's clothes off, to get to skin. Her jacket came off easily. She stripped off his shirt and nuzzled at his chest. Her hot mouth felt so good...he lay back and let her kiss and nip his flesh.

But he needed to touch her again. He grabbed at her own shirt, tugging the fabric loose from her skirt. The buttons somehow opened beneath his clumsy fingers, but her bra blocked his view. Gray pulled the thing down, desperate to get at her breasts. Ah, there. He pushed her onto her back and bent over her, sucking one nipple fervently while she held his head against her hot flesh and moaned, her pleasure sounds deep and needy.

He lifted his head, panting. "Tell me again."

Her eyes were glazed, heavy-lidded; her fingers tangled in his hair. "I love you," she whispered. "With all my heart."

Irresistible, those lush, wide lips. He kissed her. "As I love you. And now I will *make love* with you."

"Yes."

Before he could move, she tugged at his pants, pulling them open and down to his knees. Her hand grasped his cock and pumped. He groaned and rolled to his back, letting her stroke and tease him. Oh, how he'd missed the feeling of her warm hands on his body.

Her hair tickled his skin when she slid lower and pulled his pants all the way off. Then she took his cock into her hot hand and planted sucking little kisses on his chest. "You have a great chest," she murmured. "I really meant that. Even on that very first night."

With her hand wrapped around his cock, he could barely understand her. And then he felt silky hair against his stomach...and the wet heat of her mouth sucked his cock inside.

He tangled his hands in her hair, felt her head move as she suckled him. Her motions were hesitant, inexpert...but enthusiastic. As if she wanted to pleasure him, but didn't quite know how. Gods, she pleasured him like no other woman could. Her hot mouth would force him to climax in a moment.

"Enough." He took her shoulders and pulled her up over his body. She came willingly...but paused, kneeling over him, to strip off her shirt and bra. Her smile was warm and tempting...and open, so very open. As if she trusted him completely. As if she wanted him with every fiber of her being. The way he wanted her.

He couldn't wait to get inside her. He fumbled with her skirt, pulling the fabric up, and she shimmied out of her undergarment. With her hands planted on his chest, she shifted and wriggled her hips, struggling to settle on his cock, until he nearly screamed with frustration. In another second he'd roll her to her back and ride her.

After endless moments of squirming, she finally reached down and grasped his cock, holding him still while she sank down, taking him inside. Such heat, glorious heat. He groaned...she whimpered.

Her hands pressed against his chest as she thrust, and he grabbed her hips, helping her go faster, harder. Her hair swung back and forth with their mating rhythm.

"Come for me, Daria."

She moved eagerly, making hungry, desperate little noises deep in her throat that drove him higher. Her face looked taut, strained with desire. So beautiful in her need...her need for *him*. Only him. She bit her lip, riding him steadily, urgently, her rhythm fast and fierce. *Sanwar,* he couldn't wait much longer.

"Hurry," he pleaded.

A little whimper left her. He slid a hand between their bodies, forcing his way down until he reached her nest, pressing his fingers as close to her clit as he could, giving her the hard strokes he knew she liked.

Her eyes went wide, then closed tight. "Oh...Gray...oh..."

Her incoherent little sounds almost made him smile. Gods, he'd never felt anything as wonderful as this. "Fuck me, Daria. Make me come."

She cried out then, her body jerking with quick little contractions of release that forced her pelvis down hard on his, forced his cock deep inside, until he felt the blunt, welcoming edge of her womb. Her mouth opened as she spasmed, but her expression stayed trusting...so trusting, so *loving*...and awestruck, as if she couldn't believe the pleasure she felt. The pleasure *he* felt, as her wrenching orgasm squeezed his cock hard. He grasped her hips, kept her moving, until he burst inside her with blessed spasms of his own.

They were mated. Partnered. Whether she acknowledged this or not, truth would be truth.

She collapsed on top of him, her breath hot against his neck. He felt her hair draped across his shoulder, tickling him as each harsh breath stirred the fine strands. Her heart thumped rapidly against his chest.

Gods, she robbed him of all control. One day he'd restrain himself—somehow—and give her the five orgasms he'd promised her the night they'd met.

"Tell me again." Lack of breath kept his voice soft.

Her own breath huffed against his neck. "Such a demanding man," she murmured. She propped her chin on one hand and looked down at him. "I love you."

Her face was a little too close for him to focus on. He turned to his side, taking her over with him. His cock left her body, and the rush of cool air on his wet skin made him shiver. He'd be inside her warmth again soon. Very soon. He cupped her perfect little breast, and the areola contracted. Mmm. Very soon, indeed.

She settled her head on his arm. "I do love you, Gray."

He left her breast and stroked her hair back over her shoulder. "Even though I'm arrogant?"

He meant to tease, but her glow faded and her expression grew troubled. "I'm sorry. I never should have said that."

"You can always speak truth to me, Daria."

"Well, it may be true...but it's one of your charms."

She must truly love him, to consider arrogance charming. "Tell me more of these charms I possess."

"Oh, now you're demanding compliments."

He loved hearing that playful, teasing note in her voice. "Yes. And you will oblige me, woman."

She grinned. "If you insist. Let's see... Hmm... I should be able to think of *something*."

He tickled her side. She giggled and grasped his hand. "All right, all right! You're smart. And funny, in your own quirky way. You're determined, and generous, and idealistic. And you care about doing the right thing."

Nothing about his wealth, his power, his fame. To Daria, those were probably detriments. "These are not remarkable qualities."

"When they're all wrapped in *you,* they are."

He laughed. "As you will. Please continue to list my remarkable qualities."

Her smile warmed him. "You have a sexy accent. And you're very...reliable."

He restrained his laughter this time. "*Reliable?* By the gods, Daria, you certainly know how to flatter a man."

She looked adorably flustered, blushing and struggling for words. "Well, I haven't met all that many reliable men. Trust me, it's a real turn on."

"A real turn on? What does that mean?"

"It means you make me *volshano*."

A turn on. He'd remember that phrase. He kissed her. "That's another feeling we share, *dahsh'kara*."

She suddenly looked troubled. "Gray..."

"Speak truth," he encouraged.

"I just wanted to say that I'm sorry. For lying to you, and for that mess with Henry. Honestly, I thought I could help you. Find out what he was planning...find a way to stop him..."

He pulled her close and pressed a kiss to her forehead. "I know. In future days, you will tell me when you wish to help."

"You forgive me?"

She sounded forlorn, as if she truly didn't know. "As I said, I decided to forgive you this morning. I could see that you were trying to manipulate Jamison." He'd never reveal that Hento had pointed out her machinations. No reason to tell her how deeply the recording had wounded him.

"But how did you know you'd have the chance to forgive me? How did you know I'd come back?"

As if he would leave such a thing to chance. "I planned to find you, Daria. I had an alert attached to your ID today, right before the meeting began." When her anonymous credit ran out, he'd have found her.

She sat up straight, which took her out of his arms. "But the guards let me in. One of them even brought me to the top floor."

He nodded. "The alert was to bring you to me, sweetheart. Not to confine you."

"Oh." She settled back in his arms. "No wonder they were all so respectful."

"And now may I ask *you* a question?"

She looked fearful, but nodded. "Ask me anything, and I'll tell you the truth. Always."

What did she think he planned to ask? No matter; her assurance of truth was all that mattered. "You never need to fear speaking truth to me." He curved one hand around her neck. "I may not always enjoy your truth, but I will honor you for sharing it with me."

She nodded. "Ask me anything," she repeated.

"How many men have you slept with, Daria?"

She blushed a little. "Including you?"

He nodded.

Her eyes gazed upwards as if she counted to a great number, hesitated, then met his. "Four."

On Prendara, a woman would have at least four men in her first month of sexual activity. No wonder she still blushed.

"I'm pleased," he admitted. "Pleased to learn that all but four of the men on this world are blind."

She pushed at his shoulder in a playful gesture. "I think *you're* the blind one." Then she frowned. "You've probably been with dozens of women."

Dozens? No need to tell her the answer was closer to hundreds. He stroked her cheek with the backs of his fingers. "Do you not remember? On Prendara, partners are monogamous. And even though I live on Earth now, that culture is still my culture. I will sleep with only you from this date onward."

"If you say so." Her voice sounded cautious.

"I swear it."

She didn't look convinced.

"You doubt my fidelity? Is this the reason why you won't formally partner with me?"

She bit her lip in that endearingly hesitant way of hers. "No. I'm just... I'm afraid you'll regret it."

"Never."

She rested one hand on his chest. "You don't know that. Just look at what happened with Henry. I might be bad for your career."

She'd bring him far more joy than trouble. She already had. "I will deal with any worms like Jamison quite efficiently, you may be certain. As for you and I—we will be stronger together. You will help my career, Daria, by making me happy. By helping me see differing opinions...and by educating me when I don't understand your concerns."

Her fingers idly stroked the hair on his chest. "Speaking of your career...shouldn't you find out if the constitution passed?"

He tipped her chin up and kissed her. "I'm more interested in convincing you to partner with me."

"Come on, Gray. Hento must be chomping at the bit for you to contact him."

He laughed. "Chomping at the bit? Your expressions will always entertain me, *dahsh'kara*."

For the rest of our lives. Whether you formally partner with me or not.

Ah, but she would agree someday. Someday soon. When faced with a difficult opponent, he never accepted no as an answer.

EPILOGUE

The huge spaceship came in with a roar and a blast of air so fierce that the pre-fab walls of the space dock rattled. Daria covered her ears with both hands, squeezing her eyes shut against the wind. Her hair whipped around her face, stinging her chin with a harsh slap.

When the engines stopped, she let go of her ears and pushed her hair back with shaking fingers. Useless. Why hadn't she brought a hair brush? She must look like a mess.

At least the slow dying whine of the cooling engines didn't hurt her ears.

Gray took her hand, and she looked up into his smiling face. Even after all these months, her knees went weak whenever he smiled at her.

The excited, boyish glow in his eyes made her smile back. She loved being happy just because Gray felt happy.

She loved *Gray*, pure and simple. And he seemed to love her. What a miracle.

"I can't wait for you to meet them," he said, probably for the fourth time today.

She squeezed his hand. "I can't wait for you to see them again. I know how much you've missed them."

The sound of clanging metal came from one of the corridors of the space dock—the ship's loading ramp being lowered. God, they'd be here any minute.

He pressed a kiss to her forehead. "Don't worry, sweetheart."

"I'm not worried."

He smiled tenderly. One thumb stroked the corner of her mouth. "You're biting your lip. You always do that when you're worried."

Damn, he could read her like a book.

"Here." He framed her face with both hands. "Let me give you something else to do with your lips."

He kissed her, and she smiled against his mouth. "Your English is nearly fluent now. But I'm glad you haven't lost that sexy accent."

A light breeze blew through the corridor, stirring his hair. "And you're speaking Prendarian very well yourself. My aunt will be pleased you made the effort."

"I'm so nervous, I'll probably forget every word."

He absently rubbed her finger—the third finger of her left hand. A habit he'd adopted after learning that most Earthers wore wedding rings on that finger. "They'll love you, Daria. Simply because I love you."

Typical Gray, assuming that everyone would just fall in with his plans. "You don't know that. They could hate me just as easily."

"They won't. But even if they do, I'll still love you."

Footsteps sounded from far down the corridor. Oh, God.

"Billy?" A woman's voice.

They came around the corner then—a tall Prendarian woman in uniform and an even taller man with graying hair. Gray's uncle and the Premier Leader. She saw Gray, gave a little cry, and ran toward him.

Gray dropped Daria's hand and ran the last few steps to meet his aunt. They hugged each other fiercely, murmuring greetings in rapid Prendarian. When they parted at last, the men hugged.

Maybe she could sneak off in all the commotion. Tempting, but the embarrassment wasn't worth it. She still had her pride. Hell, she was every bit as worthy as the Premier Leader. Having wealth and power didn't make Rigah a better person than anyone else. It just made her more powerful. The most powerful woman in the galaxy.

No wonder her knees felt shaky. Even worse, these people were the closest thing Gray had to parents. And she was an upstart rebel who lived with their precious nephew. They'd probably wonder what the hell he saw in her.

She still wondered herself. Sometimes.

"Prefect of Earth," Rigah said in Prendarian. She took a step back from Gray and made an odd alien gesture, thumping one fist against her chest. "My nephew, Prefect of Earth. I could not be more proud if you were my own offspring."

Gray bowed his head. "My thanks to you, *Senhab* Rigah."

Senhab? Damn, she'd never asked Gray what she should call this woman. Was *Senhab* only for family members?

They turned to her then, as a group. Rigah and Jason looked at her curiously. Judging her. At least Jason's eyes were warm, the same warm amber brown as Gray's eyes. Rigah's eyes were a cool, assessing silvery color.

Gray came to her side and slipped one arm around her waist. "This is Daria," he said, in English. "Daria, my Uncle Jason and Aunt Rigah."

"I am pleased to meet you," Rigah said stiffly, as if she wasn't pleased at all. Or as if she'd rehearsed the words.

Daria's palms felt sweaty, but she couldn't wipe them on her skirt and show it. "Welcome to Earth."

"Billy tells us you're going to be partners," Jason said in English. "Welcome to our family."

"Oh, but we're not going to—I mean, I haven't agreed to—"

"Daria doesn't wish to marry me," Gray supplied. Then he repeated the words in Prendarian. The wretch.

She nudged him with one elbow. "Thanks a lot," she hissed.

Rigah gave her a sharp stare, raising one eyebrow. "You dare to refuse my nephew?" she asked, in Prendarian. She must practice bullying on a daily basis. That icy tone would make a battalion of soldiers tremble.

She'd sooner die than let this woman see how much that supercilious attitude intimidated her. At least she knew enough Prendarian to answer in the same language. She raised her chin. "I have my reasons."

"Relax, Aunt Rigah." Gray stepped into the breach, also speaking Prendarian. "Daria's afraid that partnering with her will damage my career."

Oh, great, now she'd want to know—

"Why?" Rigah asked.

What could she say? Never the truth.

"She used to be part of a rebellious faction," Gray said. "She once plotted to kidnap me."

Daria gasped. "Gray!"

Rigah waved one hand dismissively. "A trivial matter. Why, Jason once plotted to murder me."

Jason rolled his eyes. "I did *not* plot to murder you." He took Daria's hand and shook it, grinning at her. "She tells everyone that story," he said in English. Then he held her hand between both of his and winked. "She doesn't really speak any English at all, so it can be a secret language of our own. Use English anytime you want to flirt with me."

No wonder Gray was so charming—he must have inherited a family gene for it. He chuckled behind her. A quick glance at Rigah met with a fierce glare.

"She's mad because she can't understand me," Jason said, again in English. "And because I'm holding your hand for so long. She gets insanely jealous. Don't worry, though, she won't hurt you. I know how to control her."

Daria laughed, as he no doubt intended.

"Welcome to the family," he said again, in Prendarian this time.

"But... I haven't agreed..."

"You will," Jason said, releasing her hand at last.

"You will," Gray echoed.

Rigah smiled at her then. Much, much better than the glare. "Best to accept their plans, Daria. They are exceptionally stubborn men." Reaching out, she laid her hand on Daria's shoulder. Her flesh felt cool, but her silvery eyes seemed sincere. "Billy tells me you have no relatives. If you choose to partner with him, I would be pleased to welcome you into our family."

Family. If she married Gray, she'd have a family. Maybe even children.

Gray gently pushed his aunt aside and took both of Daria's hands in his. "Everyone's touching you but me."

He rubbed her ring finger again, smiling down at her tenderly—as if they were alone. "Marry me, Daria. Marry me while my aunt and uncle are here to see the ceremony."

At least Rigah didn't understand him, since he'd spoken in English. Still, she felt a blush heat her cheeks.

She gripped his strong, warm hands. The expression in his eyes looked so compelling. So loving. He'd keep asking until she said yes. Or until she dented his pride with her constant refusals.

For the life of her, she couldn't think of a single reason to keep refusing. "You're sure?"

"I'm sure."

She took a deep breath. "Well, then... As you will."

A brilliant smile lit his face. He wrapped both arms around her, lifting her off of her feet for a deep, thrilling kiss. Right in front of his uncle and the Premier Leader.

The crazy, wonderful, uninhibited man.

She kissed him right back.

When he released her at last, she saw that Jason and Rigah had turned away slightly, giving them some privacy after all.

Gray gave her another kiss, then nuzzled her hair out of the way so he could press his lips to her ear. "I know what to give you for a marriage gift, Daria."

"A wedding present," she corrected automatically. She knew better than to tell him not to buy her anything. The more she protested, the more he spoiled her. "What do you want to give me?"

His breath rushed over her ear, hot and moist. "You've already had five," he murmured. "For a wedding present, I'll give you six."

Her face felt positively fiery, but she met his gaze anyway. "As you will."

Doreen DeSalvo

A lifelong daydreamer, Doreen DeSalvo sold her first short story at the age of eight. Her payment was a candy bar. Over thirty years later, her passion for writing—and chocolate—remain. Her work has received the National Association of Independent Publishers' *Fallot Literary Award* and the Doubleday Venus Book Club's *Best Book of the Year* award. She currently lives in a Victorian house in San Francisco with her husband of over 20 years, and considers herself fortunate to be writing stories that always have happy endings.

NOW AVAILABLE In Print

ROMANCE AT THE EDGE: In Other Worlds
MaryJanice Davidson, Angela Knight and Camille Anthony

CHARMING THE SNAKE
MaryJanice Davidson, Camille Anthony and Melissa Schroeder

WHY ME?
Treva Harte

COMING SOON in Print

HARD CANDY
Angela Knight, Morgan Hawke and Sheri Gilmore

FOR THE LOVE OF…
Kally Jo Surbeck

Publisher's Note: All titles published in print by Loose Id™ have been previously released in e-book format.

Printed in the United States
38408LVS00006B/76-510